91215

19 MAY 2016

D1141116

30131 05365539 2

LONDON BOROUGH OF BARNET

The Miner's Daughter

By Jennie Felton

The Families of Fairley Terrace Sagas
All The Dark Secrets
The Birthday Surprise (short story featured in the
anthology A Mother's Joy)
The Miner's Daughter

JENNIE FELTON

The Miner's Daughter

headline

First published in Great Britain in 2015
by HEADLINE PUBLISHING GROUP

1

Cataloguing in Publication Data is available from the British Library

ISBN 978 1 4722 1006 7

Typeset in Calisto by Avon DataSet Ltd, Bidford-on-Avon, Warwickshire

Printed and bound in Great Britain by Clays Ltd, St Ives plc

Headline's policy is to use papers that are natural, renewable and recyclable
products and made from wood grown in well-managed forests and other
controlled sources. The logging and manufacturing processes are expected
to conform to the environmental regulations of the country of origin.

HEADLINE PUBLISHING GROUP
An Hachette UK Company
Carmelite House
50 Victoria Embankment
London EC4Y 0DZ

www.headline.co.uk
www.hachette.co.uk

For my dear daughters, Terri and Suzanne (Suzie).
With all my love.

Acknowledgements

I always find there's nothing more off-putting than a long list of acknowledgements. Who wants to plough through a lot of names that mean nothing whatsoever to them? But of course there are wonderful people who deserve a mention, and without whom I'd be lost.

First and foremost I'd like to thank my wonderful editor Kate Byrne. Then there are all those who beaver away behind the scenes to produce the book and get it on the shelves. And I'd also like to make a special mention of my brilliant copy editor Jane Selley who puts odd bits and bobs to rights without ever trying to rewrite the fruits of my labours.

Huge thanks too to my agent Sheila Crowley and Rebecca Ritchie who is always there for me.

And last but not least my lovely daughters, to whom I have dedicated this book, their husbands, Andy and Dominic, and my four wonderful grandchildren, Tabitha, Barney, Daniel and Amelia. There you are, Barney – you got a mention this time! And of course the good friends who keep me going, even though they don't always succeed in keeping me on the rails. I love you all.

Coal dust and cornfields
Poppy-strewn grain
Sunlit paths that I walked
But will not see again.

Hooters and houses
Fire on the batch
Woodsmoke and cooch smoke
Doors left on the latch . . .

Cows in a cluster
In fields and by stream
All of these things now
No more than a dream.

A kiss in the shadows
The touch of a hand
Shifting and fleeting
As footprints in sand.

The lights of the city
Were calling to me
I ran from your arms
But now I can see

All I want, dearest love
All I wish for is there
Your lips on my lips
And the breeze in my hair.

I long to be with you
And once more to roam
The hills and the pathways
The fields of my home.

'Coal Dust and Cornfields'

Chapter One

When as a child I laughed and wept
Time crept.

1897

The little girl sat curled up beneath the huge umbrella-like leaves of the rhubarb plant, crying. Her head was buried between her knees, her tears soaking the cotton cambric of her pinafore, her slight shoulders shaking in time with her sobs.

Lucy Day didn't often cry, though there were plenty of times when she wanted to, and when she did, she made sure it was somewhere where no one could see or hear her. Though she was only seven years old, she had her pride. Only babies cried, and she wasn't a baby any more. She hadn't been for a long time now; the last time she had allowed anyone to see her tears was when her father – her real father, not that monster she was now supposed to call Papa – had died in a terrible accident at the pit where he had been a collier.

Lucy had never known exactly what had happened; she'd been spared the gory details. Everyone had thought she was too young to be told that the rope bearing the hudge that took the miners into the bowels of the earth had been severed and it had

1

gone crashing down, taking twelve men and boys, her own father, John, amongst them, to their deaths. All she had known was that her daddy was never coming home. She'd cried when Annie, her mother, had told her and her older sister Kitty, cradling them both in her arms, but mostly she had cried because Mammy was crying too, tears streaming down her face. Lucy had never seen Mammy cry before, so her own tears were mostly of fright. She hadn't really believed then that Daddy was gone forever, and when it was time for him to come home from work she had crept out of the little house in Fairley Terrace that felt heavy and oppressive with all the sorrow trapped inside it by closed doors and tightly drawn curtains, made her way along the track that ran along the back of the Ten Houses, as Fairley Terrace was always known locally, and waited at the corner, as she always did, for the gaggle of miners and carting boys making their way home. The moment they came into sight she would run along the lane, which was bordered by cornfields, in the direction of the main road. John would scoop her up and sit her on his shoulders, still black with coal dust as he was, so that Mammy would scold them both when they got home. She'd make Lucy hop into the tin bath in front of the fire before John got in himself and turned the water black and scummy, and lay out clean drawers and pinafore for her to put on. Every fine day in summer it was the same, and on bright cold days in winter too, though John would only ruffle her hair and take her by the hand then, mindful that whereas a pinafore could go into the wash tub, a woollen coat could not.

But that day in early June two years earlier, Lucy had waited in vain; Daddy and the others had not come, and as she grew more and more anxious, there seemed to be a nightmarish feel about the bright sunshine, the long, sharp shadows and the unnatural quiet. She'd begun to panic, her child's mind still not grasping the enormity of what had happened, but knowing that something was terribly wrong. She'd ventured then further than she'd ever gone alone before, to the end of the track, so that she could see the length of the main road stretching away between the hedges in the direction of the little town of High Compton, but there was still no sign of Daddy and the others, only Farmer Barton's herd of cows, away in the distance, being driven in for milking. And still she couldn't believe that Daddy would never again come walking up that road. She bunched up her petticoats and sat down on the grass verge, trying not to cry, and how long she'd have stayed there, half hidden in the tall white cow parsley, she'd never know – all night, perhaps, if needs be.

It was Dolly Oglethorpe, their next-door neighbour, who found her there, quite by accident. Annie Day was so distraught, she hadn't even noticed her younger daughter was missing.

Dolly, who was a good soul, had been into town to collect a bottle of medicine Dr Blackmore had prescribed for Queenie Rogers from number 2, whose son Frank had been amongst those killed, and she was startled to see the little girl sitting on the bank.

'Lucy Day! Whatever do you think you're doing?' she exclaimed.

Lucy's lip wobbled and she looked up at Dolly with anguished eyes.

'I'm waiting for Daddy. But he's ever so late.'

'Oh dear, dear, dear.' Dolly scarcely knew what to say. Truth to tell, she felt overwhelmed herself by the terrible events of the day, though, thank God, none of hers had been on the hudge.

'You can't stay here,' she said. 'Your mam would have a fit if she knew you were up here on the main road all by yourself. Come on, my love, you've got to go home.'

3

'But Daddy . . .' Lucy was desperate to be told that everything was going to turn out right. But Dolly could offer her no comfort.

'Your dad won't be coming tonight, my love. And your mam needs you home and safe. Come on now.'

Obediently Lucy got up, brushing the grass seeds off the seat of her drawers and taking the hand that Dolly offered her.

'Tomorrow?' she whispered pleadingly.

'No, my love. Not tomorrow either.'

It was then that Lucy knew that what Mam had said was true. Daddy wasn't coming home. Not today. Not tomorrow. Not ever. A great sob rose in her throat and the tears rolled down her cheeks.

'I want him!' she cried brokenly. 'I want my daddy!'

Wrenching her hand away from Dolly's, she began to run, too fast for Dolly to be able to catch her, down the lane, back around the corner of the rank, heading for the only refuge she knew, the house that had been her home, along with Daddy and Mammy and Kitty, from the day she was born.

Except that Daddy wouldn't be there. And still she didn't really know why.

Now, two years later, hidden beneath the rhubarb leaves, Lucy stuffed her fists into the sockets of her eyes and cried for him again.

'Daddy! Daddy! Please, Daddy, where are you? I want you, Daddy . . .'

It would do no good. She knew that. But oh! she wanted him so. Wanted him to hold her hand in his big rough one, blue-veined from coal dust. Wanted him to hoist her up on to his shoulders again, though she thought she might have grown too big now for him to do that. Wanted him to dry her tears and make her laugh the way he used to. Wanted him to make things right.

4

Nothing was the same as it used to be, nothing. Everything now was just awful – the house they'd moved to when Mammy got married again, far from the friendly rank of the Ten Houses where she'd known everyone and everyone had known her; the life so different to the carefree one she'd imagined would go on forever. Even Mammy was different, never singing as she went about her chores as she used to, but sad and snappy. And worst of all . . . *him*, the man she was supposed to call Papa. Lucy's eyes squeezed tight shut but the tears still escaped, running in hot rivers down her cheeks. Oh, she hated him – she hated him! He was horrible, horrible. And she'd never forgive him for what he'd done today, never, never, no, not as long as she lived . . .

The rhubarb leaves rustled suddenly, parting around her head so that sunlight filtered through, and Lucy's eyes flew open as she instinctively tucked back more tightly into her hiding place. But the boots that were in her line of vision were too small – and too dirty – to belong to *him*, the legs growing out of them bare and suntanned. The leaves parted further, so wide that one of the stalks of rhubarb snapped clean off, and Lucy lifted her head to see the freckled face of a boy looking down at her.

'What's up with you, Lucy?'

Joe. It was Joe, *his* son – well, not really his own son, Mammy had explained, but the son of his first wife, the wife who had died. It was all a bit complicated for Lucy to make sense of. She only knew that Joe called him Papa as she and Kitty were supposed to, that he lived with them, and that he was nice – well, as nice as a nine-year-old boy could be. He wasn't her friend exactly – she hadn't known him long enough for that, had never so much as set eyes on him before she and Mammy and Kitty had moved into the house where he and that horrible man lived. But *he* didn't seem to like Joe any more than he liked

Lucy. *He* spoke to Joe in just the same overbearing, disapproving way, and sometimes when he was chastising them Joe would catch her eye and grin ruefully, or wrinkle up his nose at her. Once *he* – Papa – had caught him doing it and cuffed him sharply around the ear, calling him 'disrespectful' and sending him to his room.

All in all, Lucy liked Joe; he was the only good thing in this horrible place, and the last thing she wanted now was for him to see her crying.

She dashed her hands across her face, wiping away the tears, but it was too late, and in any case, the soft hiccuping sobs that were still pulsing in her throat would have given her away.

'What's the matter?' Joe asked again, peering down at her.

For a minute Lucy couldn't bring herself to answer. She knew if she did she would only begin crying again properly; she wouldn't be able to stop herself. But Joe wasn't going to give up. He squatted down beside her, wriggling as far as he could into her hiding place and snapping a few more stalks of rhubarb as he did so, so that the leaves now slanted at a crazy angle like an umbrella that had blown inside out and been righted again but with its ribs broken.

Lucy scooted on her bottom out from what remained of the canopy, frightened now at the thought of the consequences of ruining the crown of rhubarb.

'Stop it, Joe, or we'll be for it!'

'It'll grow again,' Joe said nonchalantly, and as if to show he didn't care, he snapped off yet another stick of rhubarb and tossed it on to the strip of garden on the other side of the path where the broad beans sprouted in neat rows some two feet tall.

'What were you crying about anyway?' he asked, turning back to Lucy.

Still she hesitated, but suddenly she could contain it no longer. Her lip wobbled uncontrollably.

'Victoria,' she said, barely able to speak her precious doll's name. 'He took Victoria away. And she's broken! She's broken!'

And once again the tears ran down her cheeks in a scalding flood.

It would never have happened if she hadn't defied him and taken Victoria to chapel with her this morning. She'd thought he would be none the wiser; he always left for the service half an hour earlier than they did and stayed on later, talking with the minister and the other important members of the congregation and only arriving home in time for the joint of roast meat they always had at twelve thirty sharp on Sundays. Lucy hated having to go to chapel; they'd never used to go when they'd lived in the Ten Houses, and it was so tedious she could never sit still unless she took something to play with. Usually it was something small that she could hide in the pocket of her pinafore, just as Joe secreted a prize conker or a lead soldier in the pocket of his trousers – Kitty, of course, never did anything of the sort; she was far too pious. And if she had, and been caught, then in all likelihood she would have escaped with a mild rebuke.

Lucy had known she'd really be for it if *he* found out she had Victoria hidden beneath the folds of her cape – he said it was disrespectful to take a doll into the House of God. But this morning she simply couldn't bear to leave her at home. Mammy had made a new dress for her from a scrap of white silk and decorated it with lace and a tiny pink rosebud, and Lucy just couldn't stop looking at it and touching the soft smooth fabric that felt like the height of luxury and made Victoria look like a fairy-tale princess.

7

She was so, so beautiful, with her glossy brown hair and her go-to-sleep eyes, which were blue as cornflowers when they were open, and the long dark lashes that brushed her porcelain cheeks when they were closed. Her head swivelled on her neck and her arms and legs could be moved too – they were attached by a length of elastic that stretched through her smooth pink body. Never in all her life could Lucy have imagined owning such a doll, but she had been given to her by Lady Elizabeth Fairley, sister of Sir Montague, who owned Shepton Fields, the pit where Daddy had worked until the day of the terrible accident, when she had visited to offer her condolences in the days that followed the tragedy. Victoria had come all the way from France, Lady Elizabeth had said, and Lucy had fallen in love with her the moment she set eyes on her. She took Victoria everywhere with her, carefully wrapped in a shawl that had been first Kitty's when she was a baby, and then hers, to ensure the doll didn't get dirty or damaged in any way, and at night she put her to bed in the top drawer of the tallboy in her bedroom, covered with a folded petticoat and with a pile of clean undergarments under her head for a pillow. She always left the drawer open, of course; Victoria wouldn't like to be shut in.

Lucy talked to Victoria constantly. It was like having her own special friend, which became even more important to her after Mammy married *him*. Lucy had been very lonely since they'd left the Ten Houses and moved to his house, which stood on a steep rise on the road linking High Compton to the neighbouring town of Hillsbridge. It wasn't entirely isolated, in fact it had a mirror-image twin sharing the adjoining wall, but there was a high, thick laurel hedge between the two houses at the front, and because they had been built into the hillside, steps led down from the long back gardens into small walled yards separated by a single-storey extension that housed the

WC, as *he* called it, and the copper that was used for heating water. In any case, the people who lived in the other house were old, and, Lucy thought, a bit peculiar, though she knew next to nothing about them except that they were called Latcham and Mammy said she didn't believe Mrs Latcham ever washed her sheets properly, just hung them out on the line on a Monday when it was fine and dry, to air. Oh, and Mrs Latcham was very deaf. When Lucy was playing in the back yard she could sometimes hear Mr Latcham shouting very loudly at his wife, not angry shouting, but shouting all the same, and Mrs Latcham shouting back: 'What d'you say, George? What d'you say?'

'Is she all there?' Mammy had asked *him* soon after they had moved in, and he had replied, 'Yes, of course. She's just hard of hearing. And I wish you wouldn't use that expression.'

But hard of hearing or not all there – which in local parlance meant lacking in mental faculties – Mrs Latcham wasn't at all like the neighbours Lucy had known when they'd lived in the Ten Houses. There, back doors had always been open, the menfolk worked their gardens or sat on benches outside in the evenings or on Sundays, the women popped into one another's houses, the children played in the alleyway that ran between the dwellings and the blocks of privies, wash houses and bake ovens on the far side. Everyone knew everyone else and looked out for them, even the less popular ones like Hester Dallimore, known for a gossip, and old Mark Gardiner, who was too sick with silicosis, the miners' disease, to work any more and who could scarcely walk across the alleyway to the privy without stopping to get his breath or hawking up globules of phlegm, which he spat on to the cobbles.

Lucy missed them all, but most of all she missed Edie Cooper, who was the same age as her and lived at number 1.

From the time they were toddlers, she and Edie had played together. They'd had an old pair of trucks to serve for a dolls' pram; they'd made a pretend house behind the bean sticks; they'd spent hours unearthing bits of old broken china or glass that had been buried in their gardens; they'd drawn grids on the cobbles with a chalky stone to play hopscotch. They'd started school together, walking in on their first day holding hands tightly, and their mothers had taken it in turns to collect them at going-home time.

Lucy was much closer to Edie than she was to her own sister, Kitty, and she missed her dreadfully. Kitty was no fun at all. She was prim and never wanted to be bothered with Lucy, and when she did deign to play with her, she had to take charge, bossing Lucy about and telling her which role she had to take, which was always inferior to her own. So Lucy drew more and more into herself, and Victoria, her precious, beautiful doll, became her companion and her confidante.

But now *he* had confiscated Victoria, and, even worse, she was broken. And all because Lucy had defied him and taken the doll to church.

Why had she done it? Why? How could she have thought for a moment that she'd get away with it? Nothing escaped *his* eagle eye. But this morning he'd left even earlier than usual – Reverend Boody, the minister, was away on holiday, and *he* – Algernon Pierce, Papa – was taking the service. Flushed with daring, Lucy had tucked Victoria under her cape, so not even Mammy had noticed until they were seated in their usual pew. When she had, she'd scolded Lucy.

'Whatever are you thinking of? You know Papa doesn't allow dolls in church!'

'There were dolls in the crib scene at Christmas,' Lucy had pointed out.

10

'That's quite different,' Mammy had whispered sharply, and Kitty had smirked and rolled her eyes, smug in the knowledge that she, at least, knew how to behave in the House of God.

Lucy had kept Victoria well out of sight for the first part of the service. But the sermon went on interminably, because when he was preaching, Algernon liked to make the most of it, and even Kitty had become bored and her attention had wandered to Victoria, tucked within the folds of Lucy's pinafore.

Kitty had been given a doll, too, by Lady Elizabeth, but she never took much interest in her, which was why it was for Victoria that Annie had made the new dress, and truth to tell Kitty was a little jealous. It wasn't so much that she wanted to be able to change her own doll's clothes; it was the fact that Annie had done something for Lucy, and not for her, that irked her.

'That's a stupid dress,' she whispered now, poking the doll with her finger.

'It's not stupid! It's pretty!' Lucy was unable to keep her voice as low as her sister's; the lady sitting in the pew in front of them turned and glared at her, pursing her lips.

Kitty, of course, was staring straight ahead with a butter-wouldn't-melt expression; it was Lucy who was attracting the admonition.

After a minute or so, Kitty began fingering the new dress, glancing at it surreptitiously beneath her lashes, and then raising the silk skirt to expose the matching drawers that Mammy had made and tugging at them. Possessively, Lucy dragged the doll away, tucking her under her cape, and Kitty's hand followed, grasping Victoria by her jointed leg and pulling.

'Stop it!' Lucy hissed, and again the woman in front of them half turned accusingly.

But Kitty was having too much fun, teasing Lucy and yet not being blamed for it. She grasped Victoria firmly around her waist, tugging again, so the sisters were tussling silently over the forbidden doll.

And then it happened. Just as Algernon paused for effect at a crucial point in his sermon, Lucy lost her hold on Victoria and the doll clattered down on to the tiled floor.

Lucy squealed in dismay, she couldn't help it, and scrambled down to rescue Victoria. Annie made a vain attempt to stop her, and Lucy, wriggling out of reach, fell over, only succeeding in pushing Victoria clean under the pew so that she ended up between the feet of the woman in front of them. Indignant, the woman picked up Victoria but did not return her, laying her instead on the pew beside her before glaring once again at Lucy and then presenting her with her stiff back.

Mammy shook her head at Lucy, sighing; Joe, on the far side of Kitty, was stifling laughter, and Kitty, of course, still sat demurely, her eyes fixed on *him* – Papa – who looked as if he might be going to suffer an apoplectic fit. After a moment, however, he recovered himself and once again his droning voice echoed around the body of the chapel and up to the far reaches of the gallery above, where yet more of the congregation sat on hard wooden benches tiered upwards. But Lucy heard not a word he said. She sat, stiller than she had ever sat through one of Algernon's sermons, mortified and trembling, but never taking her eyes off Victoria, whose bare feet were the only bit of her that she could see.

She was for it, she knew. Being responsible for such a commotion when *he* was in full flow was unforgivable in itself; that her doll should be the cause of it only made things a thousand times worse, and from his elevated position in the pulpit, Algernon would have had a clear view of what was going on, could perhaps even now see Victoria lying on the wooden seat beside the woman.

It wasn't until the service was over and the organ playing soft reverent music while the congregation filed out that the woman turned round, holding out Victoria in a gloved hand, not to Lucy but to Annie.

'I do think you might keep your children under control during service. All this chatter and fidgeting is entirely inappropriate and most disconcerting.' Her tone was taut with disapproval and she thrust Victoria into Annie's hands. 'I hope such a thing won't occur again.'

'You can be certain it won't,' Annie said fervently, and Lucy could hear a small tremble in her mother's voice. Annie was clearly both embarrassed and upset. 'I am so sorry, really I am.'

'Yes. Well.' With another glare at Lucy, the woman swept out of the pew, leaving only a whiff of lavender perfume and mothballs behind her.

'Oh Lucy, you've really done it this time!' Annie shook her head despairingly. 'Don't you know who that was? Miss Broadribb, the sister of the schoolmaster at the big school. She runs the Temperance League and goodness knows what else. She's ever so important.'

Lucy didn't know what the Temperance League was, she didn't know Miss Broadribb or her brother, the schoolmaster, though she supposed she would in a year or two when she moved up from little school. But she did know she was in disgrace and that she had upset Mammy. And she desperately wanted Victoria back in her arms, wanted to cuddle her and bury her chin in her dark cottony hair for comfort.

'Can I have her? Please, Mammy?' She tugged at Annie's sleeve, but Annie shook her head.

'I think I had better keep hold of her for now,' she said, and Lucy guessed the reason. They still had to run the gauntlet;

Algernon always stood by the chapel door, bidding farewell to the congregation as they left.

She could see him there now, nodding gravely, smiling occasionally, that plastered-on smile that moved his fleshy lips but never reached his small, beady eyes, as he dispensed pious words to the departing flock.

'The Lord be with you, Mrs Clarke . . . Good morning, Mr Treasure . . . The Lord be with you . . .' Laying a hand on a small boy's head: 'Good to see you here, Tommy.' Turning solicitously to a shrunken little woman: 'Are you quite recovered now from your pneumonia, Mrs Brown? I'm glad to hear it. The Lord has indeed been merciful . . .'

That pasted-on smile did not even slip as his own family approached; Algernon was much too conscious of the image he presented to the world. But he lowered his voice as he spoke to Annie, and there was no mistaking the barely controlled fury in his tone.

'A most unedifying performance, Mrs Pierce.'

Then, for a long moment, those beady eyes were fixed on hers, and Lucy quailed.

'We need to talk, young lady. The moment I get home.'

And then they were past him, moving on to the broad sunlit path between neatly barbered lawns and rose beds, and he had turned his attention and his horrible false smile to the couple behind them.

She received another scolding from Annie, of course, as soon as they were out of earshot, and though she thought it dreadfully unfair that Kitty should escape scot-free when it was she who had started the trouble, Lucy said nothing. Annie probably wouldn't believe her, and Kitty might well give her a sly pinch if Lucy told on her.

Annie didn't return Victoria to her until they reached the

house she now had to call home, and then it was with the warning that she'd better leave Victoria upstairs, out of sight, for today at least.

'We don't want any reminders of what happened in chapel,' she said, and Lucy obediently did as she was told, laying Victoria in the drawer and tucking the old shawl around her.

'You need a little rest, Victoria,' she said solemnly. 'Go to sleep now, and be a good girl.'

Kitty had followed her upstairs; they both had to change out of their Sunday best into their everyday dresses and pinafores.

'It was all your fault,' Lucy couldn't resist saying to her sister.

'Wasn't! You shouldn't have taken your stupid doll to chapel anyway. You know you're not allowed.'

'She is not stupid! And nobody would have been any the wiser if you hadn't—'

'Well, it serves you right. And she is stupid.'

'It's your Margaret who's stupid. And ugly. Victoria is so much prettier than her.'

'She's not! Not even with that silly dress Mammy made.'

'Are you two quarrelling again?' Their raised voices had carried downstairs; now Annie was in the hallway, shouting up to them. 'Stop it, both of you, before Papa comes home.'

They stopped, though still glowering at each other, changed their clothes and went back downstairs.

'Now go and read quietly,' Annie warned them. 'I've got dinner to cook. On second thoughts,' she added, 'you can shell the peas for me. They're in a bowl by the back door, and you know where the colander is.'

Lucy didn't mind that. She quite liked shelling peas; there was something satisfying in squeezing the pods between her fingers to make them pop. And reading books on a Sunday was no fun – the only ones they were allowed were books of prayers or children's versions of the Bible stories, and they were boring. But then everything about Sundays was boring; there were so many things they weren't allowed to do. They weren't allowed outdoors to play, and proper games were banned even inside the house. No dominoes, no cards, such as Snap or Old Maid, no jack-in-the-box. The rules were endless. Annie wasn't allowed to do any housework either, apart from cooking the Sunday roast, the smell of which was already filling the kitchen. Once, when Lucy had been sick in the night all over her sheets and nightgown, Annie had been going to put them straight in the wash tub, but Algernon had refused to let her do anything more than rinse off the worst of it. 'I won't have washing hanging on the line on a Sunday,' he'd said, and although she didn't agree with him, Annie had concurred, as she always did. She'd have argued with Daddy if he'd done the same thing, Lucy thought – not that he would have, of course – but she never argued with Algernon.

He arrived home today earlier than usual, and came into the kitchen with a face like thunder. Without even stopping to take off the sober black coat he always wore to chapel – though he did remove his hat – he summoned Lucy.

'Now, my lady, I want an explanation of your disgraceful behaviour in church this morning.'

Lucy, who had been setting the table, quailed.

'It wasn't my fault, Papa.'

'Don't talk back to me!' he snapped. 'If not your fault, whose was it, I would like to know?'

Lucy lowered her eyes. There was nothing she could say to make this right.

'You took that doll to church with you after I had expressly told you it was quite inappropriate. How dare you disobey me?'

'I'm sorry, Papa.' The hated name stuck in her throat, but she said it anyway.

'Sorry is not good enough. Do you not know your commandments? Do they not make it clear that thou shalt not bow down before any graven image? And what is a doll but a graven image, might I ask? Where is she?'

'Upstairs, Papa.'

'Go and fetch her. Yes, right this minute.'

Lucy, trembling, shot her mother a terrified glance, but Annie only nodded slightly, looking, if Lucy had only noticed, as frightened as she was. She dragged her feet on the stairs, and Algernon's voice followed her.

'Don't dawdle, girl! I'm waiting!'

As she crossed the landing, she could see Joe through the half-open door of his room. He was lying flat on his stomach on the floor, playing with his lead soldiers. He'd be for it if Algernon caught him, Lucy thought, but she was too preoccupied with her own disgrace to worry about that now.

In her bedroom she pulled the tallboy drawer fully open and lifted Victoria out.

'It's time to wake up, my love,' she said, trying to put a brave face on it.

Back down the stairs she went, cradling the doll in her arms.

Algernon had taken off his coat now; he stood in the centre of the kitchen, back very straight, thumbs tucked into the watch chain that stretched across his not-inconsiderable paunch. As Lucy approached nervously, he unhooked them, holding out a pudgy white hand.

'Give the doll to me.'

Lucy froze, eyes widening with alarm, and clutched Victoria even more tightly to her chest.

'I said give it to me.' Algernon flexed and unflexed his fleshy fingers by way of reinforcing the order.

'Papa . . . please . . .' Lucy begged desperately.

A muscle ticked beneath Algernon's left eye, a sure sign of his growing anger.

'I shall not tell you again,' he warned.

Annie, who had been testing the potatoes simmering on the hob to see if they were done, turned, the fork still in her hand.

'Algernon – please don't take her doll. She won't take her to church again, will you, Lucy? She's learned her lesson.'

'Not well enough, I fear. I will not tolerate disobedience. I will not tolerate idolatry. Lucy must be made to understand that.' Again he turned his cold beady eyes on the little girl. 'You will give the doll to me or suffer the consequences.'

'Lucy, you'd better do as Papa says,' Annie said, anxious and nervous now.

'No! No – I won't!' Afraid but defiant, Lucy made a dash for the door, but it was blocked by Kitty, who had been sitting reading Bible stories, coming in to see what the commotion was about. The sisters almost collided and the obstruction was all Algernon needed to catch Lucy and spin her round.

'The doll, if you please!'

His hand shot out, grabbing Victoria's jointed plaster arm, but still Lucy refused to relinquish her treasure, and the elastic fastening the two arms together through the doll's body gave way with a sharp snap. Though Lucy still clutched Victoria to her chest, *he*, Papa, was left brandishing one bare pink arm. Lucy squealed in horror, so distraught she relaxed her hold on the doll, and Algernon snatched her away. As he did so, Victoria's other arm, no longer attached to its twin, came away and fell to the ground.

'Oh, Algernon! Oh dear, look what you've done now . . .' Her love and concern for her daughter overcoming her fear and respect for her husband, Annie stepped into the fray. She knew what this disaster would mean to Lucy, and she wanted only to comfort her and do what she could to make things right. But Algernon was unrepentant.

'The child has brought this upon herself,' he snapped. 'Perhaps she will learn now that every action has its consequences. When I am certain that lesson has been learned, the doll will be returned to her, and not before.'

With that he swept from the room, taking Victoria with him.

'Oh, my love, he didn't mean for that to happen,' Annie said. She reached out to take Lucy in her arms, but Lucy ducked away, retrieving the doll's one arm from where it had rolled under a chair.

'Yes he did!' she burst out. 'I hate him! I hate him so much!'

Clutching the doll's arm in her small fist, she ran out of the back door and into the yard. The flight of steps slowed her – they were deep for her little legs, and quite steep – but when she reached the top, she began to run again, up the cinder path between the gardens with their rows of peas and beans, cabbages and currant bushes.

The rhubarb patch was about halfway between the house and the back lane, a minor road that had been made to service the rear of the houses and led to nowhere. She dived beneath the canopy of spreading leaves, tucking in as far as she was able, so that only her little booted feet peeped out. It was her special place, far more private than hiding behind the row of bean sticks or the loganberry hedge, and at last the tears she'd been fighting began to run down her face. Hidden there beneath the broad dark leaves, Lucy sobbed, heartbroken; sobbed so hard that her throat ached and her whole body shook.

It was there that Joe found her. He'd heard something of the commotion, heard Algernon come thumping up the stairs and into the room he now shared with Annie, and gone downstairs to find out what was going on. But all was quiet now, though Annie looked distressed as she attended to the dinner, and he knew better than to ask. Kitty was sitting at the half-set table, her Bible storybook open between the knives and forks, and a prim yet almost satisfied look on her face, and of Lucy there was no sign. It had to be Lucy who had been getting the length of Algernon's tongue – Kitty wouldn't have been sitting there looking so pleased with herself if it had been her, and besides, she never was the one in trouble. That was reserved for him and Lucy.

Joe liked Lucy, actually felt quite protective of her. For a girl, she was all right, and it was hard to believe that she and Kitty were sisters. Poor little thing, he thought, and decided to go in search of her. He knew where to look – she thought her favourite hiding place under the rhubarb leaves was her secret, but they didn't hide her quite as well as she thought they did.

Up the garden path he went, and sure enough, there were her feet sticking out from beneath the clump of rhubarb. When he parted the leaves and saw how upset she was, he got down and wriggled in beside her.

'Don't cry, Lucy. It's Papa, isn't it? He's just a big bully. You don't want to take any notice of him.'

'But he took Victoria! He took Victoria – and she's broken!' Lucy wept.

'Oh.' Joe wasn't quite sure what else to say. After the commotion in church this morning, he wasn't a bit surprised Algernon had confiscated the doll – he'd sometimes taken away Joe's treasures, too, as punishment, though more often that came in the form of a few stripes across his buttocks or the palms of his hands from the cane Algernon kept in the cupboard under the stairs for the purpose. Algernon would have given the doll back in the end. But if she was broken . . . Joe knew how much she meant to Lucy.

'She smashed, is she?' he asked eventually.

'No, but her arms came off! Both of them! I've got one, look . . .' Lucy retrieved it from the folds of her pinafore, while fresh tears coursed down her cheeks. 'She can't have no arms! She can't!'

'Let me see.' Joe took the arm from Lucy, squinting as he examined it.

Though he was only nine years old himself, Joe had a keen interest in how things worked. He guessed now that the doll's arms had been held in place by being connected through her body, and the grooves at the top of the tiny arm confirmed it.

'I reckon I could mend her,' he said slowly.

Lucy's eyes, blue as an April sky after a shower of rain, widened with sudden hope. Then her lip wobbled again.

'But he took her away, Joe. I don't know where she is. Oh, she'll be so lonely and frightened, and she must be hurting, too . . .'

Joe was thinking furiously. He had a pretty good idea where Victoria would be – in the big oak blanket chest in Algernon's room. That was where he usually put the things he confiscated.

If he sneaked in, rescued the doll and kept her well out of sight, there was a pretty good chance Algernon would be none the wiser. Lucy had the one arm; the other was most likely in the chest along with Victoria herself. Lucy wouldn't be able to play with her openly, of course, and if he was caught he'd certainly be for it with a vengeance. But Lucy was in such a state, and Joe liked the idea of getting one over on his stepfather, even if it did carry the risk of a sound thrashing.

'Don't cry any more, Lucy,' he said, feeling very grown up and very daring. 'Let me keep her arm and I'll sort it all out.'

She stared at him, those pretty blue eyes wide with hope – and confusion. 'But . . .'

Joe grinned. 'Best you don't ask any questions,' he said mysteriously. 'Just leave it to me. All right?'

Lucy nodded. She had no idea what Joe was planning, but he was her only hope.

'All right, Joe,' she whispered trustingly.

Chapter Two

Sometimes Annie wondered why she had married Algernon. No, not quite true – she wondered *often*, if not constantly, though she tried to put such thoughts from her mind. They just made her depressed, reminded her of what she had lost. Pointless to waste time and energy on regrets. And it all came back to the same in the end. What choice had she had, with John dead, killed in the terrible accident that had turned out to be no accident at all, and two growing children to support?

She'd been at her wits' end when she'd gone, cap in hand, to beg for more time to pay the rent arrears on the cottage in Fairley Terrace. The house had gone with the job; Sir Montague Fairley, the owner of Shepton Fields, where John had worked as a collier, clearly wanted the bereaved tenants out and had raised the rents accordingly. Sir Montague owned five other collieries locally; Shepton Fields had been the least profitable, and he'd been looking to close it for years. The accident had been for him a blessing in disguise. There was talk now of him expanding and modernising New Grove, another of his pits, and even of sinking a new mine on his land. He would need the houses for his new employees, or so it was being said, and Annie thought it was probably the truth of the matter. Whatever, she'd got short shrift from Clement Firkins, Sir

Montague's agent, when she'd tried to negotiate some leeway on what she owed.

'I'm sorry, Mrs Day,' he'd said, regretful but unyielding none the less. 'It's out of my hands. Sir Montague is insistent all arrears be paid in full by the month's end, or you'll have to vacate the premises, I'm afraid.'

'But I haven't got the money to pay,' Annie had said, frightened at the prospect. 'And we haven't got anywhere to go.'

'Then all I can suggest is that you find some sort of employment so that you *can* afford to pay.' His grim expression softened a little. 'Wasn't John in the Friendly Society?' he asked as an afterthought.

Annie nodded. John had been one of those who had had the foresight to pay into the Society so that Annie wouldn't be left totally destitute in the event of something happening to him, but the little money that had come to her on his death was fast running out. With the two girls to feed and clothe, Annie didn't know which way to turn.

'It's not nearly enough, though,' she said despairingly.

Clement Firkins' features hardened again.

'I'm sorry, Mrs Day. Sir Montague has done everything in his power to assist the families of those who perished . . .'

'Paying for them to be buried in a mass grave, you mean!' Annie said bitterly before she could stop herself.

'. . . and you have been allowed to stay in your houses, even though they are needed for able-bodied working men,' he continued as if she had not spoken.

'What working men?' Annie demanded. 'Who wants to go down one of Fairley's pits after what happened?'

'May I remind you that Sir Montague was not to blame. The rope, as you know, was wilfully severed by a person or persons unknown,' the agent said stiffly. 'But in any case, I can't discuss matters of business with you, and I am now going to call an end to this interview. It is nothing but a waste of my time, and your own. As I suggested, you must either look for some kind of employment, or seek the assistance of the Guardians of the Poor.'

'And a fat lot of good that will do!' Annie burst out. 'Isn't Sir Montague in charge of it round here? I expect he wants us to end up in the workhouse so he doesn't have to see how we're suffering because he wouldn't spend any money on Shepton Fields. That hudge and rope should have been replaced with a proper cage a long time ago. It's a disgrace, Mr Firkins, and you should be ashamed of yourself too . . .'

'That is quite enough, Mrs Day. You do yourself no good with these wild allegations, and I must ask you to leave now or I shall have no option but to call Sergeant Love . . .'

'Don't worry, I'm going.' Defeated, Annie tightened her shawl and almost ran from the room. She was trembling, and close to tears of despair – and anger.

She could hardly believe she'd spoken to Clement Firkins like that. It wasn't in her nature to be confrontational. But sometimes there were things that just had to be said, even if it did no good at all.

'Oh John, John,' she whispered as a biting wind blew clean through her shawl, making her shiver and cooling her anger. 'Whatever am I going to do?'

But really there was only one answer. As Clement Firkins had said, she'd have to find work of some kind, and find it soon, if she, Kitty and Lucy weren't to end up in the workhouse.

But what? Annie was twenty-eight years old. She had no training of any sort, she'd never served in a shop, or worked her way up in domestic service, and in any case, with two little girls to look after, she couldn't be away from the house from dawn till dusk. But she could scrub a floor and wash sheets, she wasn't a bad cook, and she was handy with a flat iron. She'd just have to try to find a way to earn a few shillings while still caring for the children.

A treacherous thought crept into her mind – what would her mother and father have to say if they knew she had come to this? But she could imagine all too well. Wasn't it exactly what they'd warned her of when she'd told them she wanted to marry John?

'But he's a miner!' her mother had exclaimed, horrified, and her father had tried to put his foot down.

'It's not the life we want for you, Annie. A pretty girl like you . . . you could have your pick of much more suitable young men. A professional, perhaps, a doctor or a lawyer. Someone who could give you a secure future and some standing in the community. It's what you've been brought up to, after all.'

This was certainly true – as High Compton's only pharmacist, William Fox was held in high regard in the town, and his family enjoyed a standard of living that far exceeded that of a miner's. But nothing could dissuade Annie. She had fallen in love with John Day the moment she had met him in the queue for the swinging boats at the town fair, and no one else would do.

At last, reluctantly, William had given his permission. He was still disappointed by his daughter's choice, but her happiness was paramount, and he had to concede that John was a likeable fellow, quiet, sober and thrifty, unlike some. William knew of goings-on behind closed doors in some of the most outwardly respectable of households, and not so long ago a bank manager had been convicted of embezzling and stealing customers' money to feed his gambling habit. John Day wouldn't put Annie through any of that, he felt certain. But as he had led her up the aisle on her wedding day, Annie had seen anxiety etched deep in his features and the shadows in his eyes.

Well, at least he hadn't lived to see her come to this, Annie thought. He'd been killed soon afterwards, outside the pharmacy, by a runaway horse and cart, and her mother, broken-hearted, had followed him to the grave just a few years later. But not before she had managed to lose most of what William had left her by putting her trust in an unscrupulous couple – a woman she had taken in as a companion and her handyman brother. Between them they had fleeced her of her money and even persuaded her into signing the house over to them, so that Annie had inherited almost nothing. The little that had come to her had long since gone on trying to give her daughters the kind of upbringing she herself had enjoyed; now she was almost destitute, faced with finding a way of keeping a roof over their heads and feeding and clothing Kitty and Lucy.

Never one to let the grass grow under her feet, Annie bought some postcards, wrote on them in her neat hand details of the services she could offer, and placed them in shop windows in the town, but no replies were forthcoming. There were just too many women ready to take in washing, she supposed. She swallowed her pride and knocked on the doors of some of the more affluent households of the district to enquire if they needed a cleaner, with no more success. Then she tried local business premises, but they too had their regular charwomen.

It was nearing the end of a long morning when she approached the glove factory, which was not in High Compton but in neighbouring Hillsbridge, and it was there that she first set eyes on Algernon Pierce.

Algernon bore the impressive title of Assistant Manager, though his office was little more than a glorified cupboard in the dark passage leading to the big room where the machinists worked. He was portly and bewhiskered, with an air of self-importance; people had always assumed him to be older than he was – now in his middle forties – and he had done nothing to correct the impression. Youth had not sat well with him; status and respect were the attributes that brought him satisfaction.

'I'm sorry, but we already have two regular cleaners, and we aren't looking to take on anyone else at the moment,' he said when Annie told him she was looking for work. 'Do you have any experience as a machinist?'

'Oh . . . no . . .' It hadn't occurred to her before, but now the suggestion gave her a glimmer of hope. 'I do like sewing, though, and I'm sure it wouldn't take me long to learn.'

'Hmm.' Algernon considered. She certainly looked like a bright girl. 'It would be a full-time job, of course, and the hours are long. Seven in the morning till seven at night.'

'Oh.' Annie's face fell. 'I don't think I could manage that. I have two small children to care for. I was hoping for something I could fit in while they are at school, perhaps in the mornings . . .'

'That's not how things are done, I'm afraid,' Algernon said importantly.

'I see. I'm sorry for taking up your time.' But tears were gathering in her eyes. 'Could you at least take my details, and if a suitable vacancy of any kind should come up, consider me for it? I'll do anything, I really don't mind what it is.'

Algernon leaned back in his chair, hands folded in his lap, eyes narrowing speculatively.

For all that he liked to present himself to the world as a man above such things, Algernon had an eye for a pretty face, and a devil that sometimes rode inside him. The congregation of the chapel where he was a lay preacher saw him as a pillar of the community, a man who practised what he preached – abstemiousness and restraint in all things. They would have

28

been shocked to the core if they had known of the dark thoughts, imaginings and urges that simmered, and sometimes raged, beneath the saintly countenance. They had sympathised with him wholeheartedly when his first wife, Jane, had died of consumption, and rejoiced for him when he had married again, a widow from Bath who had been left all alone with a young son, and had not the first idea of what the two women suffered behind closed doors. But Ella, the second wife, was seven months gone now in a pregnancy that had seen her suffering sickness every step of the way and was now not only bloating her body but puffing up her face and making her extremities swell so much that she could no longer get her feet into her shoes. Algernon was repelled by the grotesque transformation, but at the same time finding himself desperately frustrated.

Now, looking at the pretty raven-haired girl who had come to him seeking employment, he felt the all-too-familiar stirrings of lust. His eyes lingered lasciviously on the full red lips, moved slowly down her smooth throat and came to rest on the tantalising swell of her bosom beneath her loosely draped shawl. A sight for sore eyes indeed!

With some difficulty he thrust aside the erotic visions that were exciting him so. Time to revert to his other self – the altruistic man of God. Sometimes it was not only the outside world that was fooled into thinking that was the real Algernon; Algernon had become quite adept at fooling himself.

This was a woman in desperate need, and it was no more than his Christian duty to help her from the Slough of Despond.

'It so happens,' he said magnanimously, 'that my wife is frequently indisposed at present. She is expecting a child and finding it difficult to carry out her domestic duties. What would you say to working a few hours two or three times a week?'

'Oh, that would be wonderful! Thank you so much!'

Her smile was radiant, her blue eyes shining now, not with tears but with joy and relief.

'Shall we say nine pence an hour? Good. Now, when can you begin work?'

Pleased with himself, puffed up with his own importance, Algernon returned her smile. Before long, word would have spread around town of how he, the Good Samaritan, had offered a lifeline to one of the poor souls widowed by the terrible accident. And he would have earned the gratitude of a very desirable young lady.

All in all, Algernon thought, a very satisfactory outcome.

Annie was content, happy even, with her new employment. Besides earning just enough to keep her out of debt to Sir Montague, she found herself enjoying the time she spent at the neat semi-detached house on the hill between High Compton and Hillsbridge. In many ways it reminded her of the home she had left behind when she had married John. The pictures of rural scenes hanging on the parlour wall, the flourishing aspidistra, the chenille curtains at the windows, the upright piano in pride of place: all took her back to a time when life had been safe and simple, with none of the problems she faced now, and none of the sadness of loss that hung over her every waking minute. She liked Ella Pierce, who treated her not as a menial but as an equal. Ella understood her grief, having lost a beloved husband herself, and they would share a cup of tea and a heart-to-heart over the kitchen table before Annie set to work, sweeping and polishing and tidying so that the house looked just the way she'd like it to if it were her own.

She couldn't help being worried about Ella, though – it wasn't right that she should be so swollen. Ella had lifted her skirts one day and showed Annie feet that were fat and shiny as balloons and ankles that had all but disappeared into unnatural folds of flesh.

'I was never like this with Joe,' Ella confided, and Annie thought she hadn't been like it with either of her two children either. But then she'd sailed through pregnancy both times, glowing with health, and she knew not all women were as lucky as she had been.

'What does the doctor say?' she asked Ella anxiously.

'That I need to rest. Keep off my feet as much as I can.' She wriggled her toes, fat as little sausages, and sighed.

'Then what are you doing up and about?' Annie demanded. 'You've no need to be. That's what I'm here for.'

Brooking no argument, she hustled Ella into the parlour, settled her on the sofa with a brocaded footstool under her feet and covered her legs with a crocheted throw.

'Now you stay here and take it easy,' she ordered.

'I will, I promise. At least until Joe gets home,' Ella answered with a rueful smile.

'Even when he does,' Annie insisted. 'He's a big enough boy to get his own tea.'

Usually Joe was at school when she was at the house, but a week or so earlier he'd been at home with a nasty cough and cold, and from what she'd seen of him, Annie liked him too. He was more or less the same age as her Kitty, with a shock of fair curls and a mischievous grin. Knowing how Kitty and Lucy were grieving for their daddy, she felt sorry for him too. He might have a man to call Papa, but no one could take the place of the father he'd lost, especially not a pompous man like Algernon Pierce. She only hoped and prayed he wasn't going to lose his mother too, but she really didn't like the look of Ella Pierce at all.

31

In the event, her worst fears proved justified. One day, only a couple of weeks later, she arrived for her morning stint to find Dr Blackmore's pony and trap outside and the house in uproar. Ella had gone into premature labour during the night and things were not going well. Annie asked if she should go home again – though seriously worried for Ella and the baby, she thought she might only be in the way. But the nurse, a wiry, energetic woman as unlike Dolly Oglethorpe, who had delivered both Annie's babies, as could be imagined, said an extra pair of hands would be most welcome, and Annie set to work looking out clean linen, putting soiled sheets to soak and boiling kettles for endless cups of tea and sterilising instruments.

By lunchtime it was all over. The baby, a little boy, did not survive the birth and Ella lived only a little longer. Annie cried silently all the way home and made sure she was at the school gates when classes ended for the day – though Kitty and Lucy were now considered old enough to come home by themselves in company with Edie Cooper and her older brother Ted, she felt an overwhelming need to have them close to her and to be sure they were safe.

She caught sight of Joe scooting across the playground and out of the gate and her heart turned over. He was going to get home to find his world turned upside down. Whatever would happen to him now? She couldn't imagine that Algernon Pierce would want to keep him – he wasn't his son, after all, and Algernon didn't strike her as the sort of man who would be willing, or able, to cope with a little boy.

In this, however, she was to be proved wrong. Though Algernon was indeed aghast at the prospect, he was too jealous of his reputation as a saintly man, full of the milk of human kindness, to turn Joe out, and actually saw it as a way of being lauded for his actions.

'Just fancy! He's a wonderful man, that Mr Pierce. Keeping that boy and bringing him up all by himself . . .'

'. . . There's plenty would have packed him off to an orphanage or the workhouse, but not Mr Pierce . . .'

He asked Annie if she could work extra hours, and she felt unable to refuse. She took to staying on in the afternoons to be there when Joe came home from school, Kitty and Lucy with him, and she would make tea for all of them and wait for Algernon to get in before going home herself.

The arrangement was, however, far from perfect, and it was not long before Algernon began to consider whether he should make it more permanent. He was still very taken with Annie, and celibacy didn't suit him one bit. Lust consumed him as he watched her going about the most commonplace daily tasks, the curve of her neck as she bent over a sink of washing-up, the way her blouse strained over her breasts as she pegged out washing, the sway of her hips as she walked away down the path, her children skipping along beside her. But her social standing bothered him. Was the widow of a miner really a suitable wife for a man with his position in the community to maintain? Her manners, from what he'd seen of her, seemed perfectly acceptable, but he couldn't imagine that she'd ever learned any social graces.

One day, however, he arrived home unexpectedly and discovered just how wrong he'd been.

The previous evening he'd brought some work home with him, and somehow failed to return all the papers to their file. He'd been too tired to concentrate properly, he assumed. But the very pages that were missing were needed this afternoon – they contained figures needed to strike a deal with one of their most important customers, a big department store in Bath. There was nothing for it but for Algernon to collect them.

Annoyed with himself, he walked the mile and a half or so home during what should have been his midday break. As he strode up the path to the front door, he was startled to hear music wafting out of the front room window, which had been left open to let in some fresh air. It sounded as if someone was playing the piano – and playing it very well. He stopped for a moment, listening. 'Come into the Garden, Maud' had never been one of his favourite pieces, but there was something almost heart-rending in the lilting phrasing, and when a sweet soprano voice began singing the words, Algernon could scarcely believe his ears.

Instead of going in through the front door as he had intended, he walked along the side passage that ran the length of the house, into the little yard, and let himself in through the back door, closing it quietly after him. He crept through the dining room and into the hall; from here he was able to peer around the parlour door and saw that it was Annie who was at the piano, playing and singing along. For a few moments he listened, spellbound, then Annie finished the piece, closed the piano, got up, retrieved the duster she had left on the top, and began polishing the cherry-wood casing.

He stepped into the room, startling her. She had thought she was quite alone.

'Oh, Mr Pierce! You made me jump! Whatever are you doing home?'

He didn't answer her question. 'You were playing the piano,' he said.

Hot colour flooded her cheeks. 'I'm sorry. I shouldn't, I know, but . . .'

'There's no need to apologise,' Algernon said magnanimously. 'But I must confess I am startled. I had no idea you were musical.'

Annie smiled apologetically. 'There's a lot you don't know about me, Mr Pierce.'

'So I am beginning to realise. May I ask – where did you learn to play so well?'

Annie's flush deepened, though she could not have explained the reason. 'We had a piano at home, before I was married. My mother and father both played, and they taught me. And . . . well, actually I did have proper lessons, too, because they thought I had some talent.'

'And I'd agree with them,' Algernon said. 'What I heard was really quite charming.'

'I'm out of practice, I'm afraid,' Annie said ruefully. 'I haven't touched a key for years. But we used to have such lovely times, my mother and father and I. We'd take it in turns to play for the others to sing. "Come into the Garden, Maud" was one of my father's favourites. And "Home Sweet Home". He had a wonderful baritone voice – he was always singing, sometimes even in the shop when he was dispensing pills and potions . . .' She broke off, embarrassed by what she thought of as her own garrulousness.

But Algernon, whose spirits were rising with every word she uttered, was not ready to end the conversation, the first extended one he had ever had with Annie.

'Your father is a pharmacist?' he asked.

She nodded. 'Yes. Or at least, he was. He was killed some years ago now, knocked down by a runaway horse right outside his shop.'

'I'm very sorry,' Algernon said in the voice he reserved for condolences. 'I do believe I remember hearing something of it at the time. So you are his daughter. Well, well. And it was because of his death that you married . . .' *beneath yourself*, he was about to say, but stopped himself just in time.

It was as if Annie had read his mind, however. 'No, I was already married when the accident happened,' she said, defiant suddenly. 'I married for love, Mr Pierce, a wonderful man, and I'm proud of it.'

'Of course, of course . . .' This wasn't a line he wished to pursue. It held too many pitfalls.

'I must get back to the factory, Mrs Day,' he said with his usual pomposity. 'I only returned home to collect some papers I inadvertently left behind this morning. But please, do feel free to play the piano whenever you'd like to. It hasn't had much use in recent years – it belonged to my first wife. I am not musical at all, I'm afraid, and neither was my poor Ella. So I would be only too happy to have it put to good use now.'

'Thank you, Mr Pierce. That's very kind.'

'Not at all. We'll talk again, Mrs Day.'

With that, he'd left her. But she was still very much in his thoughts. What he had learned about Annie Day meant that she was not as unsuitable as a wife for a man in his position as he had previously thought. Her background and breeding were entirely in keeping. And there was no doubt she was a very attractive woman . . .

Algernon waited a further two months before broaching the subject of marriage – he did not want it to be thought that he was acting in unseemly haste. But under the circumstances he didn't think he would be blamed for taking a new wife; he had, after all, to make arrangements for the best possible care for Joe, who was not even his own son. As for Annie, it never even occurred to him that she might refuse his proposal. She was in a similar position, worried as to how she could keep a roof over her head and that of her children. He could offer her security and standing in the community, a life far better than she could ever have expected as the wife of a miner.

Annie wasn't worried about her standing in the community, and she knew she couldn't expect the kind of happy marriage she and John had shared. But she was concerned about her children's future. Never to have to count the pennies at the end of the week to see what food she could afford to put on the table, or to see the girls outgrowing their clothes and not know where new ones would come from, never having to spend sleepless nights worrying that Sir Montague might raise the rent on her house again in order to see her evicted, never having to go cap in hand begging for a remission she knew would not be granted to her: these were the things that mattered. And Algernon was a God-fearing man; he wouldn't ill-treat her or the children, she felt sure.

But she hadn't seen his dark side, the side he kept so well hidden. It was only after they were married and had moved into his house that she had begun to see that Algernon frequently used his godliness as an excuse for ruling their lives with an unbending rod of iron. That he was a man who demanded absolute obedience, and would have life lived in no other way but his own. She accepted his demands in the bedroom because she was, after all, his wife, and she couldn't expect the same loving and tender relationship she'd shared with John, but she didn't like it, dreaded going to bed at all in fact. And she was becoming cowed in other ways too, afraid of putting a foot wrong and incurring his ill temper.

But it was the way he treated the children that she hated most. Take today. Of course Lucy shouldn't have taken the doll to church when he'd forbidden it, of course he was within his rights to chastise her. But to confiscate Victoria when she was the one thing Lucy clung to, surely that wasn't necessary? And to snatch her so roughly that her arms had come off and not show so much as a smidgeon of pity for Lucy's distress just made it a thousand times worse.

Oh why did I marry him? Annie asked herself as she dished up roast lamb, potatoes and peas. She'd done it for the sake of the children, but now she was not so sure that they wouldn't have been better off as they were. If they still lived in the Ten Houses they'd be out playing in the sunshine with their friends, not confined to the house with nothing to do but read the Bible and religious books. And Lucy wouldn't be so dreadfully upset that she'd rushed out of the house and might not even come back when Annie called her for dinner.

But it was too late now. The deed was done. And the only comfort she could find in answer to her question as to why she'd married Algernon had to be the same as it always was. She'd had no choice. If she wavered from that, Annie thought she would go quietly mad.

Chapter Three

Dolly Oglethorpe was in the garden unpegging a sheet from the washing line when Fred Carson's pony and trap turned into the track that ran the length of the rank of the Ten Houses.

Monday was wash day – always had been, always would be, as far as Peggy, and most women like her, was concerned. The copper was lit early so that by the time she'd finished clearing up the kitchen and stripping the beds she could make a start, filling the big stone sink with water as hot as her hands could bear, heaving the sheets into it one by one and giving them a bit of a soak before setting to work with a cake of hard soap and, if necessary, a wash board. When they'd been rinsed in cold water and she'd wrung out as much of it as she could, they had to go through the mangle, which, on fine days, she set up outside the back door with a bowl beneath to catch the moisture.

Luckily today was fine, with a bit of a breeze, and Dolly thought they wouldn't take long to dry. After she'd had her dinner – a nice chunk of tasty cheese and a slice of bread and butter, washed down with a cup of strong sweet tea – she decided to check on the state of the sheets; she didn't want them to get bone dry, as that made ironing difficult, and ironing was Dolly's least favourite chore. She didn't mind the washing, even if it did make painful cracks in her fingers in winter; there was something very satisfying about sloshing the sheets about and poking them with her laundry stick. But ironing was something else. Though she always kept two flat irons on the go, swapping one for the other as it cooled, it seemed to take forever, and standing so long at the kitchen table, which she covered with a thick blanket and an old flannelette sheet kept especially for the purpose, made her back and legs ache.

As she had hoped, the sheets had hardened. She lowered the prop so that she could reach the pegs and took the first one down, folding it roughly under her arm so it wouldn't crease too much when she deposited it in the wicker laundry basket. She had just begun unpegging the second when she heard the clip-clop of hooves on the track, and looked round, curious, to see Fred Carson's pony and trap coming to a halt more or less opposite the entrance to her garden path.

Dolly frowned, shading her eyes against the bright sunshine and trying to see who was in the trap besides Fred. Folk from the rank didn't run to the luxury of a ride unless they had heavy luggage and a long way to go; their usual mode of transport was 'shanks's pony' – their own two legs.

As she watched, the sheet draped over her arm, Fred climbed from the driver's seat on to the track and handed his passenger down.

It was a woman – no, not a woman, Dolly corrected herself, a *lady*. From this distance it wasn't possible to see her features clearly, but Dolly was quite sure she'd never set eyes on her before. Nobody Dolly knew wore a dress like that, all nipped-in waist, frills and flounces at the neck and hem and ballooning leg-of-mutton sleeves, and certainly not such a hat, broad-brimmed and almost as high as it was wide with all the trimming that was heaped upon it.

Who in the world could it be? Dolly hastily finished unpegging the sheet and dumped it unceremoniously in the laundry basket, possible creasing forgotten in her eagerness to get a closer look at the stranger. Oh, she wasn't nosy like Hester Dallimore, she told herself. It was just human nature to be curious.

By the time she reached the track, Fred had moved slowly off, down towards the end, where it was wide enough to turn his trap, and the lady was knocking on the door of number 4, the house next door to her own, the house that had been the home of the Day family and which had stood empty now for the last year and more in spite of the fact that Sir Montague Fairley had claimed he needed it for another miner and his family. Whoever she was, this lady must have made a mistake in the address she was looking for, Dolly thought. And she wouldn't be best pleased to have landed up in a rank of houses with outside privies and wash houses, if Dolly knew anything about it.

'Excuse me!' she called.

As the lady turned enquiringly towards her, Dolly could see that although no longer as young as she had first appeared, she wasn't old either – Dolly would have put her at just the wrong side of thirty. And she'd certainly been right about the quality of her attire: the dress, greeny-blue satin, with lower sleeves of velvet, was embroidered with gold bands around the high white frills at the neck, and the hat – straw – was topped with plumes, flowers and a bird's wing. A veil, tied back at the nape of her neck, revealed a loose pompadour of glossy brown hair.

'You won't get any answer there,' Dolly said. 'That house is empty.'

The lady looked startled.

'Really? Are you sure?' There was no trace of the local Somerset burr in her voice; she sounded . . . not cultured, exactly, like Sir Montague and his sister Lady Elizabeth, but certainly *different*.

Dolly huffed, tucking the laundry basket higher on her hip.

'Sure as I can be. I live next door – this house here – and I can tell you nobody's lived there for the last year or more.'

'Oh!' The lady looked quite nonplussed, raising a gloved hand to her throat. 'I don't understand . . .'

'Who was it you were looking for?' Dolly asked, as much to satisfy her curiosity as from a desire to be helpful.

'John Day. Do you know him?'

Dolly couldn't stop her jaw from dropping. What in the world did a grand lady like this want with the likes of John Day – a miner, like almost all the men of Dolly's acquaintance?

'John Day?' she parroted stupidly.

'Yes. He's my brother.'

Dolly's jaw dropped even further. 'You're having me on,' she said flatly.

A tiny smile quirked the corners of the lady's mouth. 'Why would I do that?'

Why indeed? Dolly was still far from convinced. The laundry basket was slipping down her hip; she hoisted it up again.

'Well in that case, I'm surprised you don't know.'

The lady's eyes narrowed. 'Know what?'

'That he's dead, of course! He were killed two years ago now, in an accident underground . . .' She broke off, uncertain suddenly. The lady's kid-gloved hand had gone to her throat and the colour drained from her face. 'Oh,' Dolly said helplessly. 'Dear, oh dear . . .'

Fred Carson had turned his pony and trap and was walking it back along the track.

'Everything all right then?' he called as he reached them. 'I'll be back at five o'clock like you said.'

'No – wait!' The lady waved in his direction, but she was

still staring at Dolly with that dazed expression. 'John is *dead*, you say?'

'Well, yes, he is, I'm afraid . . .' Dolly was mortified now by what she'd done. Unlikely as it seemed, it appeared the lady had been speaking the truth when she said she was John's sister, and Dolly had broken the news of his death in the most brutal way imaginable.

'Didn't anybody let you know?' she blustered. 'I'd have thought Annie would have, surely? Oh, that sounds awful . . . I didn't mean . . . But I'm really surprised at Annie.'

'It's not her fault. She wouldn't have known where to find me . . .' The lady laughed suddenly, a small, brittle sound that was not really a laugh at all. 'Heavens, she might not even know I exist! John may well have been too ashamed to admit he had a sister.'

Ashamed? Not ashamed of her, surely a fine lady who came visiting in a hired trap. Ashamed by what he'd come to, more like, Dolly thought and realised that in spite of living next door for eight or nine years, in spite of having delivered both Annie's babies and counting her as a friend, she knew next to nothing about the Days. Annie's father had kept the pharmacy in the high street, that much she did know – she remembered a wiry little man, bald, but with a full set of whiskers to compensate, and round wire-rimmed spectacles that were always slipping down his nose. And she remembered, too, that he had been killed by a runaway horse right outside his own shop. She had an idea she'd heard that John had come to High Compton from Pensford way, though why anyone would work down one of Fairley's pits if he had the choice was beyond her. But that was as far as her knowledge of the family went. They were just Annie-and-John-next-door and that was the end of it, and if she had sometimes wondered why they never had family come visiting, not even at Christmas, she was too busy taking care of her own brood to spare it much thought.

'Well I'm sure I don't know,' she said vaguely, still feeling ashamed of herself that she'd broken such terrible news to this poor soul in such a heartless fashion.

'Where is she now then? What has happened to her?' the lady asked, and it took a moment for Dolly to realise that she was talking about Annie.

Dismay filled her as she realised she was going to have to tell John's mysterious sister that his widow had taken another husband, and no more than a year after losing John. Annie had been desperate, Dolly knew, threatened with eviction from her home, and with the two little ones to feed and clothe, and she couldn't find it in herself to blame her. Rather she felt sorry for her, married to that stuffed shirt Algernon Pierce. But John's sister might not see it like that. She might take it as an insult to her brother's memory.

'She's married again.' At long last Dolly put down the laundry basket on the doorstep and folded her arms across her ample stomach. 'She had to do it, ma'am. She had the two girls to think about. It wasn't for lack of respect for John, that I do know. Heartbroken she was when he got killed, and a happier family than they were I've never seen. But Sir Montague, what owns these houses, were going to put her and the children out on the street, and when Algernon Pierce made her an offer, she felt obliged to take it.'

'There are children, then?'

'Yes, the two girls, ma'am.' Dolly wasn't quite sure why she was addressing the lady as 'ma'am' – perhaps to make up, in some small way, for her appalling gaffe. 'Kitty – well, she's going on ten now, and little Lucy's seven.'

'And where are they living?'

'Well, with Mr Pierce, of course.'

'Locally?'

'Well, yes. Between here and Hillsbridge – that's the next place up the road.'

The lady nodded. 'Not too far then.'

'Not far at all. Well, it's quite a step if you're walking it, but—'

'I'd'a know where Mr Pierce do live,' Fred Carson interjected. He had been listening, agog, to the conversation, and he knew the district like the back of his own hand.

'Would you take me there?' the lady asked.

'Ooh ah, if that's what thee d'want.'

'I do.' The lady had recovered something of her composure now. She thanked Dolly – 'Goodness only knows what for!' Dolly said later to her husband, Ollie. 'I must have given her the shock of her life!' – and allowed Fred to hand her up into the trap.

As it moved away, the bird's wing in her hat fluttered as if it were about to take flight once more.

'What a thing!' Dolly said aloud. 'Whatever next?'

She picked up her laundry basket and carried it into the house, and for once the tedious task of ironing the sheets seemed to pass in a flash.

She did, after all, have a great deal to occupy her mind.

For all her finery, for all that every trace of a Somerset burr had long since been erased from her voice, for all that she could still afford to hire a hansom cab in London or a pony and trap in High Compton, Belle Dorne had once been plain Molly Day, and in between whiles, the Contessa di Valerio, though that title, as it had turned out, was as phoney as her stage name.

But oh, in the day, what a name that had been! Its appearance

45

on the playbills outside theatres and music halls up and down the country had drawn in the crowds; for a little while she had even performed in some of the halls in London, where the likes of Marie Lloyd, Vesta Tilley and Lottie Collins had entertained. She'd never quite attained their heights, though she sometimes thought she might have done if it hadn't been for her own foolishness, an infatuation that had ended in disaster. With her striking good looks, with her pure, clear voice – 'the British Nightingale', they'd called her – and her winning ways, Belle Dorne could have been as great as any of them. Even her name sounded as if it belonged at the very top of the bill at the Alhambra or the Shoreditch Music Hall, as, of course, it was meant to.

'You could stick with Molly,' said Spike Trotter, who managed her as well as the Palace of Varieties, where he'd plucked her from the dancing troupe she'd run away from home to join, 'but there's Molly Forde got there before you. You want a name to stand out. What about Salome? Or . . . wait a minute – Belle. The belle of the ball, that's you. But we can't be doing with Day. There's no ring to that. How about Dawn – the start of the day?'

He was a Londoner, sharp as his nickname suggested, with his gaudily checked suits and oiled hair, and his Cockney accent made the name sound like 'Dorn'.

'Dorn?' Molly repeated.

'Nah – Dawn.'

'That's what I said.'

He'd laughed then, chewing on his cigar and watching her narrowly through the spiral of smoke.

'Dorn, eh? You know, I quite like that. Belle Dorn. But we'll spell it with an "e", right? Dorne, with an "e".'

Molly had quite liked it too, but it wasn't that which was uppermost in her mind when agreeing to the change. All that really mattered to her was that it shouldn't be her own name on those billboards. If it was, and her father got to hear of it, she wouldn't put it past him to put in an appearance at the Palace of Varieties and drag her back home.

Sometimes in the early days, when she'd had to share less than salubrious diggings with a motley crew of other performers in the end-of-the-pier shows she'd performed in, she almost wished he would. Tired out from the thrice-nightly performances, she'd think of her old room at home, 'too small to swing a cat in', as her mother had used to say, but cosy and bright with rag rugs on the floor and a patchwork blanket of knitted squares crocheted together on the bed and a pretty jug and basin set on the little wash stand, and feel sick with longing for it – and for her mother and father and younger brother, John. But even then, long before Spike had taken a shine to her and changed her life forever, she'd known she wanted nothing more than to be out on the stage with the glimmer of the lights and the surge of the music, smelling the greasepaint and the sweet nose-tickling perfume of the face powder, seeing the indistinct mass of eager faces in the darkness beyond the orchestra pit, hearing the whoops and the cheers and the applause.

Oh yes, she'd had some wonderful times, and she regretted none of them. Except, perhaps, her Great Mistake. It had not only broken her heart, it had also led to her downfall. To her disastrous venture into vaudeville on the other side of the Atlantic. To her marriage to the Conte di Valerio, who had turned out not to be a count at all, but a crook and a conman. Even so, they'd lived the good life, and she couldn't pretend she hadn't enjoyed it.

Now, though, he was dead, shot through the heart by a man he'd cheated, and she had come back to England hoping to resume her career on the halls where she'd left off ten years earlier. But it hadn't been so easy. She wasn't a bright young thing any more; she was thirty-six years old, and others, just as pretty and talented as she had once been, had come in to take her place like the tide filling the moat of a child's sand castle on the beach at Weston-super-Mare. There were fewer opportunities for artistes too. Stricter licensing regulations meant that the large halls had put many of the small ones out of business. For the most part Belle Dorne had been forgotten, and the pathway back to the stars was further away than it had ever been.

There was one contact, however, who remembered Belle very well. Spike Trotter had always had a mash on his protégée. He had moved up in the world; whereas before he had managed a small hall and a few chosen artistes, now he was the proprietor of the Lyric, the variety theatre in the city of Bath. He had taken her on and given her a contract; though she was no longer billed as the star attraction, at least she hadn't been reduced to the 'dumb act', which opened the show whilst the patrons were finding their seats, or the final turn, which cleared the house, and Belle was forced to be grateful to him for that. There was method in his madness, she knew – he was anxious to keep her close for reasons that had nothing whatever to do with her talents as a songstress and dancer. But she couldn't afford to be choosy in either her professional or her private life. Whilst she was in with Spike, she had a roof over her head and money in her pocket, and if she married him, as she knew he wanted her to, she would be well set up for the years ahead when her beauty and appeal had faded to nothing. Belle had no intention of becoming one of those sad old performers who eked out a miserable existence on the charity of others and spent their days reminiscing about past glories.

Back in Somerset, her thoughts had inevitably turned to her family. She'd not seen any of them since her Great Mistake.

She'd been desperate to keep it from them, for she knew it was only what her parents had been afraid of when she'd run off to join the dancing troupe. 'No good will come of it,' her mother had said, and her father had been even more blunt. 'If you run with those fast types, you'll end up fast yourself, my girl, and bring shame on us all.' They had been to see her perform a few times when she was within striking distance of home, but it was clear they still disapproved of the carmine that made her lips red as cherries, the eye-black that glistened on her lashes, and the saucy petticoats that frothed beneath her costume and showed her ankles – and sometimes more – when she danced. And she had only once been back to the village between Bath and Bristol where she had been brought up. Her appearance had caused quite a stir, she knew, and embarrassment for her mother and father. Even John had been uncharacteristically blunt. He'd been only fifteen when she'd left home, but now he had grown up and was no longer afraid of his sister. 'You know you're breaking our mam's heart the way you're carrying on?' he had said, and though she tried to hide it, Belle had been dreadfully upset by his words.

No, after the Great Mistake there was no way back. She had headed for America and the new life it had promised and she had missed so much. Her parents were both dead now, she knew, and thinking they had died ashamed of her was a barb in her heart, a shadowy sadness she could never quite escape. But at least she could visit John and perhaps rekindle their relationship. Belle hoped very much that he would have come to think of her in a different light now that their parents were no longer around to influence him. He had gone to High Compton to work in the mines there, and had married, that much she knew. In fact she had an address, a last letter that had found her before she disappeared to America. And it was there that she had travelled today, by train from Bath, and then by a pony and trap that had been waiting in the station yard.

Only to find the house locked up and empty, and to be told that John was dead, and had been these last two years . . .

Why didn't I come sooner? she thought wretchedly, tightening her gloved hands in the folds of her skirt until the knuckles ached. But even if she had sought out her brother the minute she had set foot on Somerset soil again, it would still have been too late. The lost years were not just an expanse of desert, but a wall that could never be scaled. It wasn't just her parents that were gone, but John too, dear, solemn little John, who had grown into a man not afraid to speak his mind to her, for which she had turned her back on him.

But at least she had an address for his widow and his two children – her nieces, no less, and her only blood relatives in the whole world. What sort of reception she would be given, Belle had no idea. She only hoped that they, at least, wouldn't judge her, that they would give her some sort of link to a past she now found herself hankering after, a family to make her feel a little less bereft, a little less alone, a little less regretful of the mistakes that had changed her life and haunted her now, and always, she feared, would.

Chapter Four

For Annie, as for Dolly, Monday was washing day. And like Dolly, she was in the garden getting in shirts, undergarments and handkerchiefs when Fred Carson's pony and trap drew up outside. Unlike Dolly, however, she was unaware of it, for her back garden stretched away to the rear of the house, some distance from the main road. It was only when she went back inside with her load of clean laundry and heard someone knocking at the front door that she discovered she had a visitor.

Brushing aside the strands of hair that had been tumbled by the brisk wind, she went to answer it. And was every bit as surprised as Dolly had been to find such a grandly attired lady on her doorstep. For a moment, quite lost for words, she could do nothing but stare.

Beneath her gaze, a faint pink colour rose in the lady's cheeks, so that the little patches of her carefully applied rouge seemed to heighten and spread.

'Annie? Is it Annie? Do I have the right house?' she asked.

'I'm Annie, yes.' Annie was more puzzled than ever.

'You won't know me, of course.' The pink in the lady's cheeks spread even further, staining her neck above the silky flounces. 'But I'm John's sister Molly.'

The old name sounded strange to her ears, but if John had

ever talked about her to his wife, it was the one he would have used.

'Molly!' Annie repeated. John had indeed told her about his sister, who had run off for a career on the halls and broken his mother's heart. But angry though he had been with her, it had also been clear that he had thought the world of her, and the anger was as much for her turning her back on him as on his parents. 'Molly – yes, of course. But I thought—'

'That I was in America? I have been, for a very long time, but I'm home now, and living in Bath. I so wanted to see John again and I went to the last address I had for him—'

'John's dead,' Annie interrupted her, and immediately wished she hadn't said it. Not only was it a cruel way to break the news to his sister, even if she hadn't bothered to contact him in more than a decade, but the words were too bald for her, too. They seared her throat, making her loss all too real again. It was two years now since the accident, yet still a part of her was in denial. There were times when she still expected him to walk in the door, could hardly believe she would never see him again, hear his voice, feel his arms around her. 'He's dead.' Two little words, spoken aloud, and the pain was there in her chest as sharp as ever it had been, as if by voicing them she was losing him all over again.

Molly, as she had once again become, touched a gloved finger to her lips so that a small smear of carmine stained the white silk, and the moment's hesitation betrayed the shock and grief she was experiencing. But when she spoke, her voice was firm and steady, the voice of an actress who has stepped out on the stage into the glare of the limes, leaving her own emotions, her own self, in the wings with her dresser.

'So I understand. I had no idea, of course, until today. I was told by a neighbour. An accident in the pit, she said. And she also mentioned that you had married again, and told me where I might find you. It's a liberty, I know, but I do so hope you don't mind me calling?'

'No, no, of course not . . . Won't you come in?' Annie was still in a flutter of confusion, but she held the door open and stood aside.

As Molly stepped into the hallway, the faint scent of rose water came with her, and Annie was suddenly remembering that her living room, adjacent to the kitchen, was full of the smell of soapsuds from the washing and of yesterday's mutton, the remains of which she was boiling up with some onions and carrots to make a stew. She threw open the door to the parlour, satisfied that that, at least, would be clean and tidy since it was rarely used except for high days and holidays, or by Algernon when he wanted some peace and quiet to compose a sermon.

It was cool and dim in the parlour; Annie hastened to draw back the chenille curtains at the windows, which she kept almost closed so that the sun would not fade the furnishings, and straightened an imaginary crease from an antimacassar on the back of the tapestry-covered chair that stood near the window.

'What a pretty room,' Molly exclaimed.

It wasn't, of course, or at least Annie didn't think so. The overblown red roses on the dark green paper that covered all four walls, the plum-coloured chenille runner that ran the length of the mantelpiece and the matching tasselled lampshades, the black-stained floorboards, the dark, heavy furniture, the abundance of pot plants – an aspidistra with browning leaves and prolific trailing ivies – which forever needed watering, and the copious china ornaments that took hours to dust: Annie found the sum total horribly claustrophobic and depressing. If it weren't for the piano, she didn't think she would ever come into the room at all. Let the plants die and the dust accumulate and see if she cared! But at least it had provided somewhere fit for a lady – John's sister! – and she seemed to appreciate it.

'Won't you sit down?' She could hear the tremor of nervousness in her voice and was ashamed of it. Why should she be nervous meeting John's sister, even if she was still in her working frock at almost three in the afternoon? She had nothing to be ashamed of, unlike her visitor, who for all her fine clothes had brought nothing but disgrace to her family.

'I expect you would like a cup of tea after coming all the way from Bath,' she said, feeling a little more confident.

'I don't want to put you to any trouble.' Molly drew off her gloves, delicately pulling at each finger in turn, and folded them together.

'It's no trouble at all. And it's always easier to talk over a cup of tea, isn't it?'

Annie left her visitor sitting in one of the brocaded chairs and hurried out to the kitchen. The kettle was already singing on the hob; she had intended to make a hot drink for herself when she'd finished getting in the washing. She spooned tea into the pot – the best china one that only came out on Sundays rather than the old brown one she used during the week – and set out matching cups and saucers and a plate of biscuits on a tray. While the tea was brewing, she went to the mirror that hung over the fireplace in the living room and quickly tidied her hair that had been so blown about in the wind. Her face, bare of any powder or rouge, looked strangely naked to her in comparison with Molly's, but she wasn't going to let that worry her. Powder and rouge weren't her style.

When she returned to the parlour bearing the tea tray, Molly was no longer sitting in the chair where she had left her but standing beside the piano, running her fingers lightly over the keys. As Annie came into the room she withdrew them quickly, and smiled apologetically.

'You must think me very rude,' she said ruefully. 'But how lucky you are to have such a lovely instrument! Do you play?'

'A little.' Annie set the tray down on the sturdy leafed table Algernon used as his desk. 'Do you?'

Molly shook her head.

'Unfortunately no. I would have loved to learn, but the opportunity has never arisen. I'm afraid I can only sing.'

'And very well, if what John told me is to be believed.' Annie was pouring milk into the bone-china cups. 'He said you were quite a rage on the halls.'

Molly smiled faintly. 'I expect he was being kind. That's family for you.'

Annie bit her lip. Some of the things John had said about Molly had been far from kind. But he had said she was very talented. And she knew, too, that he had thought a great deal of her, even though he had blamed her for causing his parents so much heartache, and been sad at their estrangement.

'Were you on the halls in America too?' she asked.

'In vaudeville, yes.' Molly returned to her seat and accepted the cup of tea Annie passed to her. 'I was lucky enough to break into the medium time – two performances daily for a moderate wage, and a spot sandwiched between the opening sketch and the allez-oop. But I'm afraid the big time eluded me.'

'The allez-oop?' Annie repeated, puzzled.

'The acrobatic act. You've seen them, I expect.'

Annie shook her head. 'I've never been to a theatre in my life. But I did once see some tumblers at the circus. I suppose that's much the same.'

'I expect so. But Annie – that's enough talk about me and my wasted life.' The cup rattled in the saucer as her hand shook suddenly. 'Please – will you tell me about John? It's come as a dreadful shock to me to find him gone. What happened? And when? I'm sorry if it will upset you to talk about it, but I really have to know.'

Annie experienced a sudden swift rush of resentment. Molly was right: she didn't want to talk about it. Talking about it took her back too painfully to that terrible day when the hudge had gone crashing down the mine shaft, taking John and eleven other men and boys to a horrific death. For months afterwards she had suffered nightmares, waking to find herself bathed in sweat and her face wet with tears, and afraid to go back to sleep in case the awful dream resumed where it had left off. Even now those nightmares sometimes came to plague her. To have to describe what had happened would be to relive it all over again, and to resurrect the terrible grief she tried so hard to bury for the sake of the children.

What right did Molly have to put her through this? She had made no effort to contact John in all the time they had been married, hadn't known or cared whether he was well and happy or poor and wretched, whether he was dead or alive.

But for all that, she was his sister, and Annie didn't think John would have turned her away if he had been here when she came calling. He would want Annie to treat her kindly, tell her everything she wanted to know, and feel sympathy for her. He had been a gentle, forgiving man. For his sake she must control her own feelings of anger and resentment and treat her as if she were her own flesh and blood.

Annie set down her cup and saucer, swallowed at the lump that had risen in her throat, and began the terrible story.

'Mammy! Mammy! We're home! Where are you?'

'Mammy, why is Mr Carson's pony and trap outside?

56

'Mammy – oh . . .'

Lucy and Kitty came bursting into the parlour, then stopped abruptly in the doorway as they caught sight of the visitor.

In the hour or more that they had been talking, Molly had quite forgotten the pony and trap waiting for her, and Annie had not realised that it was time for the children to get home from school. Now she was flustered all over again. The atmosphere, heavy with grief, was not what she wanted Lucy and Kitty to witness; they had suffered enough and were beginning, she hoped, to come to terms with the loss of their father. She didn't want them upset all over again. But neither could she avoid explaining who the strange lady was, and she did not want to. Molly was their flesh and blood, John's flesh and blood, the closest any of them could ever be to him again.

'My daughters, Kitty and Lucy,' she said, with a sudden flush of pride.

Even after a day at school their matching frocks and pinafores still looked bandbox fresh, though she could see a small ink stain that no amount of washing would get out on the hem of Lucy's. With their nut-brown hair falling in shining ringlets round their pretty faces – Kitty's a little sharper-featured than Lucy's, her blue eyes a shade lighter – they might have been models in a newspaper advertisement for Pears soap.

'Girls,' she said. 'This is your Aunt Molly. Your daddy's very own sister.'

The girls' eyes widened and they exchanged a quick surprised glance before turning their attention once more to the glamorous stranger.

'She's a singer,' Annie went on. 'She's made her living – and her name – on the stage. She's even been performing in America. What do you think of that?'

The girls were still staring in awe at the aunt they never knew they had, and she added proudly: 'Kitty is doing very well at her piano lessons, and Lucy has a lovely singing voice. So as you can see, they've both inherited the family traits. I'm hoping they might be able to be part of the programme at the next chapel anniversary.'

'Goodness me! I'd love to hear all about that,' Molly said. 'But first I think I should have a word with my driver. He must be wondering how much longer I will be.'

She stood up and her petticoats rustled as she straightened her skirts.

Annie wondered if perhaps she should invite Molly to stay and have tea with them. If she had still been in her own house in Fairley Terrace she certainly would have done, but she was all too aware that this wasn't her house. She might be married to Algernon, but she still felt more like a housekeeper than the mistress. Algernon wouldn't be best pleased to find an unexpected visitor at his table, and he wouldn't approve of her powder and paint either, though he might be seduced by the quality of her attire.

She went to open the front door for Molly, and the two girls followed her into the hall. The moment Molly was out of earshot, they burst into a volley of questions.

'I'm sure she will tell you everything you want to know, just as long as you behave yourselves and ask nicely.' Annie really didn't feel qualified to provide answers herself. What did she know about John's sister? And in any case, how much was she prepared to share? She had the uncomfortable feeling that there might well be things concerning a life on the stage that were quite unsuitable for young ears; she'd just have to rely on Molly to judge what was right and proper.

'Where's Joe?' she asked as an afterthought. 'Didn't he come home with you?' The children usually all walked to and from school together, Joe charged with looking out for the girls, though he was only a few months older than Kitty and she was beginning to rebel.

'He's gone upstairs,' Lucy offered.

'We don't need him to walk with us anyway,' Kitty said, pursing her lips.

'Perhaps not, but you know I like you all to stay together,' Annie said. 'What is he doing upstairs? I'd have thought on a nice afternoon like this . . .' She broke off; Molly was coming back up the path. And really, it didn't matter whether Joe met Molly or not. She wasn't, after all, his aunt.

'I'm afraid I won't be able to stay much longer,' Molly said as the door closed after them once more. 'Mr Carson – is that his name? – has another booking, and if I wait until he can get back for me, I shall miss my train. But I think there is just time for me to hear the girls sing and play. Will you, girls? I should like that very much.'

'Oh, I'm not sure . . .' Annie was suddenly overcome with nerves. She'd have liked to rehearse them a great deal more before showing off their talents to a professional! 'Perhaps next time . . .'

'You mean you won't mind if I come to visit you again?' Molly sounded surprised but pleased.

'You're more than welcome any time,' Annie said, thinking how nice it would be to get to know John's sister, and for her to get to know them. Their lives might have followed very different paths, but in the short time she had known her, Annie felt very drawn to Molly. Perhaps it was the same charisma that she used to charm her audiences, or perhaps it was that she and John had shared parents, a loving home, their childhood, and was the only direct link Annie still had to the husband she had adored. Or perhaps it was just that she was lonely for female company. She didn't know, and really didn't care. She only knew that she

59

wanted Molly to become part of their lives, and if Algernon didn't like it . . . well, he'd just have to lump it!

'I'm so glad you found us,' she said, and meant it.

'I will come again then.' Molly was drawing her gloves back on, smoothing them up to her slender wrists. 'And perhaps you'd like to come to a performance at the Lyric one evening? You – and your husband, of course. I'll ensure you have some of the best seats in the house.'

'That's very kind,' Annie said, though she couldn't imagine that Algernon would ever be agreeable to an evening at the music hall, best seats in the house or not.

To her surprise, Molly leaned towards her, kissing her lightly on both cheeks before smiling rather sadly at the two girls.

'I'm so pleased to have met you at last. You will keep at your music practice, won't you?'

They nodded, still shy, still overawed, and followed the two women into the hall.

'Isn't she amazing?' Lucy whispered to Kitty as they watched their aunt walk away down the path.

But Kitty said nothing. Truth to tell, she was as impressed as Lucy. But she had not the slightest intention of admitting it.

'Who was that?' Joe asked, coming down the stairs.

Without going into too much detail, Annie explained.

'But I'd be glad if you didn't mention it to Papa until I've had the chance to tell him about it myself,' she added.

The last thing she wanted was one of the children blurting it out. She wanted to think carefully about how she would break the news to Algernon, and just how much of the truth she would tell him. She was fairly certain she could rely on Joe and Lucy – it wasn't of much interest to Joe, and Lucy never spoke to Algernon at all if she could help it. But she wasn't so sure about Kitty. She rather thought her elder daughter wouldn't be above telling

Algernon if she thought it would gain her some favour, and though he barely tolerated the other two children, he seemed to have grown quite fond of Kitty. She rarely caught the brunt of his tongue, and if she was worried about school lessons, sums and spellings, he would take her into the parlour and go over them with her. It would be the ideal opportunity for Kitty to whisper secrets in his ear with no one to hear her disobeying her mother's request. Annie could only hope that Kitty didn't have any such problems to take to him today, when both girls were so full of excitement and curiosity with regard to their new-found aunt.

'Why have we never met her before?' Kitty was asking now, her eyes sharp and narrowed so that they reminded Annie of a cat's.

'Because she has been in America since before you were born.'

But that didn't satisfy them, of course. There were other questions, most of which she either couldn't answer, or didn't want to.

'Why did she go to America?'

'Why didn't Daddy talk about her?'

'Why has she come back now?'

'Why did her cheeks and lips look so red?'

'Why . . .'

'Why . . .'

'Why . . .'

'Oh, I don't know!' Annie was becoming exasperated. The clean clothes from the line were still piled roughly in the laundry basket, and for all she knew, the mutton stew had boiled dry and was burning on the bottom of the pan. 'You'll just have to wait until you see her again and ask her yourselves.'

'Oh Mammy! But isn't she beautiful? She's almost as beautiful as Victoria!'

That was Lucy. But at the thought of Victoria, her lip wobbled and she bent her head so that her chin was resting on the bib of her pinafore.

'Lucy.' Joe caught her arm, gesturing towards the stairs with a little nod of his head. 'Come with me.'

Lucy looked up uncertainly, still biting at her lip in an effort to hold back the threatening tears.

'Come on. I've got something to show you that will cheer you up.'

'What?'

'I'm not going to tell you. You'll just have to come with me if you want to find out.'

Kitty tossed her head and huffed impatiently. It was just like Joe to make a fuss of Lucy with some sort of stupid game.

'I'm not coming with you,' she said haughtily.

'Nobody asked you,' Joe shot back. He caught hold of Lucy's hand, half pulling her up the stairs. Kitty's scathing voice followed them.

'Who wants to play with your silly lead soldiers anyway? Not me!'

As Joe led Lucy into his room, she saw that his soldiers were indeed all laid out in the middle of the floor, as if he had been sending them into some imaginary battle. Truth to tell, she couldn't see that there was much fun to be had playing with soldiers either, but she wasn't going to say so and hurt Joe's feelings. But when he had closed the door behind them, he didn't go down on all fours beside the toy army and expect her to do the same; instead he turned to her with a conspiratorial grin.

'Close your eyes and open your hands and see what God will send you.'

Puzzled, Lucy did as she was told. A moment later she gasped, and her eyes flew wide open.

Lying in her arms was her precious Victoria, miraculously made whole. Her hair was a little mussed from the rough handling she had endured, and her dress was crimped up a bit to expose the lace on the hem of her silk drawers. But her arms were both back in place, poking from the sleeves of her gown, and when Lucy tentatively raised one it didn't come off in her hand. She gasped.'Shh!' He put a finger to his mouth and pointed meaningfully towards the closed door.

'You've mended her! How did you mend her?' She was whispering now, and almost in tears again, but this time tears of joy.

'It was easy really,' Joe said modestly. 'It only took a bit of elastic. But I had to pinch her out of Papa's chest to do it, so keep her out of sight, for goodness' sake, or we'll both be for it.'

'Oh Joe!' Lucy really didn't know what to say, but the look on her face was reward enough for Joe.

'Where can I put her, though?' she asked after a moment. 'She really ought to go to bed in her drawer, but Kitty might find her and . . .' She broke off, not wanting to sound disloyal to her sister, but as uncertain that she could trust her to keep a secret as Annie had been.

'Tell you what,' Joe said, 'you can put her to bed in one of my drawers if you like. I've got far more than I need. You can cover her up with a shirt and nobody will be any the wiser. Just as long as she won't turn her nose up at sharing her bed with a lot of smelly socks,' he added wickedly.

'She won't mind. She won't mind at all!' Lucy was burning with gratitude and – yes – love. 'Nobody would think to look for her in your room, would they? And can I come in and play with her sometimes?'

'Course you can. Just as long as you don't kick over my soldiers.'

'Oh Joe!' Lucy said again. 'Thank you, thank you, thank you!'

'You'd best put her away now, then, before they start to wonder what we're doing up here.'

Joe slid open one of the drawers in his tallboy, tossed a pile of what looked like underwear on to the floor, and found an old shirt that was now too tight in the collar and too short in the sleeve. He kept watch by the door while Lucy laid her precious doll on the makeshift bed and covered her completely so that not even her brown wool hair showed, nor her bare, chipped little toes.

He was glad he'd been able to make Lucy smile. Glad he'd been able to fix Victoria for her. And glad, most of all, to have put one over on Papa. I'd like to kill him, Joe thought. I'd like to hit him and hit him until he's dead. Once, before Kitty and Lucy and their mother had come to live with them, Papa had chased a mouse around the kitchen and thwacked and thwacked it with a walking stick until it could only drag itself, horribly injured, for a little way before he finished it off. Joe had been sickened by the needless cruelty, but now he remembered it with something like satisfaction.

One day I'll do to Papa what he did to that mouse. And then he won't ever be able to take his belt to me again, or make Lucy cry. One day. Just you wait and see if I don't . . .

He opened the bedroom door a crack.

'Coast's clear,' he said to Lucy. 'You go back down. I'll stay here for a bit so they don't get suspicious.'

Lucy nodded and slipped past him, and Joe got down on the floor to vent his fury on the soldiers in the opposing army. They'd better watch out today! They were going to go down like ninepins if he had anything to do with it.

* * *

A week later, Algernon decided Lucy had been deprived of her doll sufficiently long for her to have learned her lesson, and when he opened the chest in his room to find her gone he was, of course, furious. The three children were summoned, and Annie too. She had been in the kitchen preparing the Sunday afternoon tea of bread and butter, stewed rhubarb, and home-made fruit cake, and she stood anxiously in the doorway, wiping her hands on her apron. She had no idea what this was all about, and hoped fervently that it had nothing to do with John's sister's visit. She had told Algernon about it, but nothing of Molly's occupation, saying simply that she was a widow and had been in America, implying that it had been her husband's profession that had taken her there. Now she wondered nervously if Kitty might have spilled the beans – she had been with Algernon in the front room earlier, where he was helping her with the long division that was causing her problems at school.

But it was the three children, lined up in front of him, to whom Algernon was directing his fury.

'Something very serious has occurred,' he thundered. 'One of you is a thief, and I intend to find out which one.'

A thief! Annie was dumbstruck. Neither of her girls would steal, and she couldn't believe Joe would either.

'What are they supposed to have stolen?' she asked.

Algernon ignored her, still addressing the children.

'Someone in this room knows very well. And if the culprit does not own up immediately, all of you will be punished most severely.'

'I don't know what you mean, Papa. Truly I don't!' That was Kitty, her eyes wide with indignation, faint colour rising in her cheeks.

'No, Kitty, I am sure you do not. Or at least, if I thought you did, I would be most disappointed in you.' Algernon turned his

65

gimlet gaze to Lucy and Joe, and Kitty lowered her head slightly to hide the little smirk she could not quite suppress.

'Well, Lucy, and what do you have to say for yourself? If I were to search your room, would I find what I was looking for?'

'What? What is it?' Annie asked again, risking Algernon's anger being turned on her. 'You can't just accuse Lucy of stealing. I'm sure she would never take something that didn't belong to her.'

'Perhaps she thinks it does belong to her. Perhaps she is unaware of the fact that everything under this roof is mine. Especially if that something is in my room, in my chest, put there for a very good reason. Speak up now. Your silence does you no credit.'

Lucy was trembling from head to foot; she knew now what it was Algernon was alluding to, and she was terrified of the consequences. Not so much for herself, but for what he might do to poor Victoria by way of punishing her. Her lip wobbled; she fought back tears.

'I—'

Before she could say another word, however, Joe had stepped forward. His chin was jutting, his hands balled to fists at his sides.

'It was me, sir. I took the doll. It's in my room, hidden.'

Lucy shot him a quick, puzzled glance that was still full of fear.

'But—'

Again he cut her off before the words could leave her lips.

'Lucy doesn't know anything about it. It's not her fault.'

Momentarily the wind was taken out of Algernon's sails. Then he recovered himself. 'And why would you do such a thing, may I ask?'

'I don't know, sir.'

'Come along, you must know.' Perhaps Algernon was hoping to extract an admission that Joe had taken the doll out of spite, to wreak some sort of twisted revenge on Lucy. It was, after all, the kind of motive he understood only too well. But he was to be disappointed.

'I was going to give her back to Lucy, but I haven't,' Joe said, staring down at the toes of his boots.

'Then you had better do so now, hadn't you? And afterwards come into the parlour. Perhaps five stripes of my belt will dissuade you from such wickedness in future. Go along now, fetch the doll. My patience is being sorely tried.'

Joe went, and Algernon addressed the two girls.

'Let this be a lesson to you. If the good Lord's commandments are broken in my house, you will suffer the consequences.'

Moments later Joe was back with Victoria. He gave her to Lucy, his eyes sending her a message to say nothing more, and both of them hoping that Algernon did not notice that the doll's arms were now back in place. Fortunately he seemed not to. Perhaps he had never really registered in the first place the damage that had been done to her; perhaps he was too eagerly anticipating the beating he was about to mete out to Joe.

'Put the doll away now,' he said to Lucy. 'I will not have her played with on the Sabbath day.'

Lucy crept upstairs, hugging Victoria tightly. She was lost in a confusion of gratitude and guilt, relief at having her precious doll back marred by knowing that poor Joe was going to get a thrashing, and all for her sake.

On the landing she lingered. She heard the parlour door open and close again, followed by the swingeing thwack of Algernon's belt across Joe's bare backside, which made her wince and fold her arms tightly around herself. But Joe himself did not make a sound, and imagining his face screwed up against the pain so as not to give Algernon the satisfaction of knowing how much he was hurting, Lucy could hardly bear it. Admiration and gratitude swelled inside her.

Joe wasn't only kind, he was a hero. Her hero. And oddly, that thought was of some strange comfort, and started an unidentifiable yearning deep in her heart.

Joe, I'll never forget, she thought.

She took Victoria to her room, fussed over her for a little while, and put her to bed in the drawer where she belonged before going back downstairs to endure what remained of a miserable and seemingly endless Sunday.

Chapter Five

Throughout the summer Molly visited regularly every couple of weeks. The visits were a little shorter during the summer holidays when the girls were at home, but during term time she stayed long enough to see them when they got home from school. Always, however, she made sure she left before Algernon finished work for the day. Annie hadn't actually had to tell her she'd prefer it that way; Molly herself seemed averse to coming face to face with Annie's new husband – perhaps because she couldn't bear to see another man in her dead brother's place. But whatever her reason, Annie was glad of it.

She'd come to look forward to Molly's visits; not only were they welcome bright spots in the loneliness of her existence since she had moved away from the cosy camaraderie of Fairley Terrace, but they also provided her with a link to her beloved John, and that in itself was an enormous comfort to her. If Algernon took against Molly and forbade any further contact, as she felt he might very well do if he knew the truth about her, Annie didn't think she could bear it.

Strangely, though, she still knew very little about Molly. For all that they'd spent hours now in one another's company, the conversation usually revolved around John – Molly had countless stories of the days when they had been young and growing up together – or around the children, Annie recounting their achievements and their progress at school and in other ways too, how Kitty had shot up by a whole inch since Annie had last measured her against the doorpost, how Lucy was improving at her piano lessons and had been chosen to sing a solo verse of one of the hymns at the school end-of-term concert. Annie had tried a few times to find out exactly why Molly had gone to America, and what had happened to her there, but Molly was always evasive, and adept at changing the subject. Though she was quite happy to talk about her present situation, her twice-nightly appearances at the Lyric Theatre and her friendship with Spike Trotter – Annie suspected he might well be more than just a friend – the past was a closed book.

She had something to hide, Annie felt sure, but there wasn't anything so unusual about that. In her experience, there weren't many people who didn't have skeletons rattling away behind closed doors, even the most respectable of them, and if Molly had spent half her life on the stage it wasn't to be wondered at that she might have more colourful secrets than most. Well, that was her business. Annie wasn't going to let it get in the way of the relationship that was slowly being forged between them.

Algernon, however, would take a very different view of such things. He would be outraged at the very suggestion of impropriety. No, without a doubt, it was infinitely better that the two of them did not meet.

On one occasion, however, she came frighteningly close to being unable to avoid it.

It had long been her hope that Lucy and Kitty would be ready to sing a duet at the chapel anniversary in September. Lucy had such a lovely singing voice, and Kitty, though less blessed, could hold a tune well enough. Algernon had said he would agree to putting their names forward as part of the programme if he thought they were good enough, and Annie had been teaching them a two-part rendition of 'Home Sweet Home'. During the school holidays when Molly was visiting she listened to them singing the number while Annie accompanied them on the piano, praised their efforts, and offered to help them make it even better. Each time she visited she rehearsed them, even taking turns to sing each part herself to show them exactly where they should take a breath, where to place the emphasis, although she had to sing much more quietly than usual in order not to drown out the childish voices. Lucy was entranced, and even Kitty looked at her with a new-found respect.

At last they were ready to perform for Algernon. Annie lined them up and called him in, and though the two girls fidgeted nervously while she settled herself at the piano, the moment she played the introduction they were ready, and they sailed through the number without a single mistake. Their pure young voices brought a lump of pride to her throat, and to her delight Algernon seemed impressed.

'That was very pleasant,' he said, sounding quite surprised.

'And will you put them forward to be part of the programme at the anniversary?' Annie asked, eager that her girls should have a wider audience.

'I see no reason why not.' Algernon tucked his thumbs into the pockets of his waistcoat. 'The Reverend Boody will have the last word, of course. But I must say you have done an excellent job in training them, Annie. They do you credit.'

'They've worked very hard,' Annie said.

'And Auntie Molly has helped us,' Lucy put in. 'We could never have done it without her.'

'Indeed?' Algernon fixed Annie with a quizzical look.

'Well, yes . . . she is a wonderful singer herself,' Annie

blustered, hoping he wasn't going to ask too many awkward questions.

Algernon nodded slowly. 'I see. Then perhaps we should ask her if she would care to attend the anniversary service so that she can witness the results of her tuition.' A faint smirk twisted the corners of his mouth as he anticipated Annie's reaction to his suggestion.

'Oh, Algernon, I'm not sure . . .' she faltered, and Lucy and Kitty exchanged glances – even they could imagine very well what the reaction of the sober and staid congregation would be if a lady such as Molly joined them.

'I'd very much like you to invite her,' Algernon said in a tone that brooked no further discussion. 'Besides, it's high time I made the acquaintance of a lady who has come to play such an important role in your lives. The anniversary will be the perfect opportunity.'

For him the matter was closed. It was quite beyond Algernon's comprehension that the ladies should not hasten to do his bidding. Annie was, of course, horrified at the prospect. There was little doubt but that Molly would doll herself up for the occasion, and Algernon would be quite disgusted by her. Annie could already hear what he would have to say – that he'd been shamed in front of all the respectable folk who looked to him for moral guidance – and she thought it very likely he would forbid any further contact, particularly with regard to Lucy and Kitty. They were young and impressionable girls, he would argue, and shouldn't be exposed to such unseemly company.

She wouldn't say anything to Molly about Algernon's suggestion, she decided. But she had reckoned without Kitty, who wasted no time in raising the subject the next time Molly visited.

'Auntie Molly, you will come and hear us sing at the anniversary, won't you?' she piped.

Molly glanced at Annie, raising an eyebrow.

'And Papa wants to meet you too,' Kitty went on disingenuously. 'He says you would be most welcome.'

Molly smiled. 'When is the anniversary?'

'Next Sunday. It begins at half past two,' Kitty informed her.

'Please come!' Lucy added eagerly. 'We shall sing all the better if you are there to hear us!'

And that, Annie thought wretchedly, was that. While Molly might have been less inclined to come all the way from Bath at Kitty's behest, she had taken a real shine to Lucy.

On the day of the anniversary the children were nervous as kittens at the prospect of their first public performance, and Annie thought the butterflies in her own stomach were at least equal to theirs, if not much worse. Over and over she pictured the scene: Molly sweeping into the dim and musty chapel, all rustling silk and carmined lips, taking centre stage as she must be used to doing. She imagined the scandalised looks she would attract, the whispers, and she imagined Algernon's icy disapproval whilst the congregation's eyes were upon him, and the fury that would be unleashed in private. It would be a total disaster, and she couldn't see that there was anything she could do to avert it.

As she and the children took their places on the end of a pew, towards the front of the chapel so that the girls could get out easily when their turn came, she cast anxious glances over her shoulder. The chapel was filling up – the anniversary always drew a goodly congregation, swelled by those who were not regular Sunday worshippers, but who liked to put in an appearance at least a few times a year – but to her intense relief there was no sign of Molly. The girls were disappointed, she knew. It would have meant a lot to them if their aunt had been there. For once, she couldn't take their feelings into account. They didn't understand, as she did, what the consequences of Molly's appearance might be.

After a short service, in which Algernon assisted the Reverend Boody, the individual contributors to the programme were called, one by one. Hubert Williams, one of the butcher's sons, a weedy lad with a prominent Adam's apple, played a cornet solo, managing to hit only a few duff notes, and he was followed by Miss Broadribb, who recited a monologue. Then it was the turn of Lucy and Kitty. A piano had been brought in from the hall and placed at the front of the chapel; the organ would drown out their little voices, and in any case, as they had rehearsed with her, Annie was to play for them.

As their names were announced, Annie ushered the girls to their place and took her seat at the piano. All thoughts of Molly vanished as if by magic; her only concern was that the girls should do themselves credit and get through without any mistakes – when they'd practised earlier, nerves had made Kitty stumble, completely forgetting words she knew as well as her ABC. But to her immense relief, Kitty and Lucy rose to the occasion. They performed the song as well as she had ever heard them, better, in fact, and as it ended, a ripple of applause echoed around the chapel. Annie glanced at them proudly, and gathered up her music. Only then, as she returned to her place, did she look at the assembled congregation, and the breath caught in her throat.

Standing at the very back of the chapel, close to the entrance porch, was a vision in mauve and purple silk.

Molly.

For a moment their eyes met and Molly nodded, smiling. Her heart thudding, Annie ushered the girls into the pew and took her seat beside them. The next item on the programme was a baritone, a portly, bewhiskered man Annie didn't know, who had brought his own accompanist. Algernon had mentioned him; he had been invited to take part on account of his reputation as a fine singer who did the rounds of chapel anniversaries in the district, and was sure to be well worth listening to. Annie, however, heard not a word of his two sacred songs. Her thoughts were racing, tumbling over one another in a frenzied dance. Arriving late and standing at the back of the chapel had meant that Molly's presence had gone unnoticed by most of the congregation, but that couldn't last. Annie had visions of her sweeping up the aisle when the service was over to congratulate the girls, and the prospect made her cringe inwardly.

The Reverend Boody was leading a set of prayers now, and kneeling on the hard wooden ledge that protruded from the back of the pew in front of her, Annie offered up a prayer of her own.

Please don't let her make a show of us! And then, as an after-thought, hoping to appease the Almighty: *Thank you for letting the girls do so well. But please – don't let her do anything to upset Algernon.*

As the organist began thundering out the introduction to a hymn – 'Our God From Whom All Blessings Flow' – and, along with everyone else, Annie rose to her feet, she glanced apprehensively over her shoulder towards the back of the chapel where Molly had been standing. Unable to see her, she craned further. Still she could see no sign of her sister-in-law. Where had she gone? Had she moved into a spare seat somewhere in the body of the chapel? Throughout the hymn Annie peeked surreptitiously around, but she couldn't see Molly anywhere.

Lucy, too, had seen Molly when they were facing the congregation; now she too was looking for her, and less imperceptibly than Annie.

'Where's Auntie Molly?' she whispered loudly to Annie, who shushed her, but as the service came to an end and the congregation began to file out she asked again.

'I saw Auntie Molly when we were singing, but I can't see her now. Where is she?'

'You must have imagined it, Lucy,' Kitty said scornfully.

'I didn't! She was there! Oh, I want to find her! I want to hear what she thought of our song!'

But Molly had vanished as unexpectedly as she had appeared. Only a faint scent of rose water lingering in the still air at the back of the chapel remained, evidence that neither Annie nor Lucy had been dreaming. Annie half expected to find her on the path as they emerged from the chapel, but she was nowhere to be seen. Lucy was quite upset, but Annie could feel nothing but overwhelming relief.

Her prayer, however imperfect, had, it seemed, been answered.

The puzzle was solved a week later when Molly came to visit.

'I am so sorry I wasn't able to stay for long,' she said. 'Spike and one of his friends were waiting for me in his electric car and one can never be sure how long the battery will last.'

'An electric car?' Annie repeated, almost unable to believe her ears.

'They're quite the rage,' Molly said airily. 'There is even a fleet of them in London, I hear, replacing some of the hackney cabs, though it's so long since I went to town I haven't yet seen them for myself.'

'Good gracious!' Annie shook her head in wonder.

'I expect the pony and trap will soon be a thing of the past.' Molly eased off her gloves and put them on the table. 'And not before time, either. I've always been nervous riding in them, ever since one bolted when I was a child.'

'They can be unpredictable, I suppose,' Annie said, thinking of her father. 'I think I'd be more afraid of riding in an electric car, though.'

'Fiddle-de-dee, it was fun!' Molly declared. 'Spike has been out in it several times since Arthur got it, and when I told him how anxious I was to hear the girls sing, he asked Arthur if we couldn't make a little trip out this way, seeing as how it was a fine Sunday afternoon. But as you can appreciate, I didn't feel I could delay them any longer than necessary. As I say, the battery doesn't last forever, and I would have hated to be responsible for us getting stuck.'

'Well, yes,' Annie said faintly. 'I can't understand why no one has mentioned seeing such a contraption, though. It must have caused quite a stir.'

'The street was quite deserted – that's a Sunday afternoon for you, I suppose.' Molly twinkled wickedly. 'And they didn't stop outside, just long enough for me to get out. Then they drove around while they were waiting for me, heaven knows where. I expect the people in the houses they passed could tell you all about it all right – the engine does make a most peculiar noise. In London they're nicknaming the cabs Hummingbirds.

'Anyway, enough about Arthur's electric car,' she went on. 'It's the girls' performance we should be talking about. They were amazing, Annie – especially Lucy. She has a real talent, that one.'

'I was very proud of both of them,' Annie said, staunchly refusing to differentiate between the two girls, although secretly she could not help agreeing with Molly. It was Lucy who was the star; she would never have thought of suggesting that Kitty should sing in public except as a duo with her sister, and quite honestly Lucy could have impressed just as much if she had been performing a solo.

'I do hope you'll be able to stay until they get home from school so you can tell them yourself how well they did,' she said. 'Lucy in particular was really disappointed not to get your verdict right away.'

'Of course I shall see them today.' Molly smiled. 'And of course I shall tell them how much I enjoyed their performance. As I say, I'm only sorry I had to rush away before I had the chance to speak to them on the day.'

'I'm sure they will understand.' But Annie couldn't help wondering if it had only been concern over the life of the car battery that had made Molly leave before the end of the concert. That might very well be an excuse. Privately she thought it was possible Molly was no more keen to meet Algernon than she herself was for him to come face to face with her glamorous sister-in-law. When the girls arrived home from school, Molly wasted no time in heaping praise on both of them.

'You are quite the professionals, aren't you? I can see that music runs in your blood, and it's my opinion you should be on the halls. You deserve a far larger audience and one of these days you'll get it.'

Lucy's eyes were shining; even Kitty turned a little pink with pleasure at the praise.

'Are you going to sing for me again today?' Molly asked.

'Not today,' Annie said with a smile. She didn't want all this going to the girls' heads.

'But I want to, Mammy!' Lucy cried eagerly. 'I want to pretend I'm on the halls like Auntie Molly! Oh, I do so wish I was! Could I really be, do you think?' she asked her aunt.

Annie shook her head, despairing. 'I don't think so, Lucy. You're far too young for that.'

'Not strictly true,' Molly twinkled. 'We had a little boy on the bill last week who is only four years old. And a huge success he was too.'

'Four years old!' Lucy echoed, her eyes wide with astonishment.

'Well, not on his own, of course,' Molly admitted. 'His father has a song-and-dance routine, and the little fellow joined him for the dance, all dressed up in a miniature matching outfit – topper and tails, don't you know?'

'But where could they get a topper and tails to fit a baby?' Kitty asked doubtfully.

'You'd be surprised what artistes can come up with for stage costumes,' Molly told her. 'And that little boy will have grown up in theatre dressing rooms and waiting in the wings while his parents do their acts. But your mother is quite right, of course. It will be a few years yet before either of you can tread the boards, but when you do you will be quite sensational.'

'I think not!' Annie said quickly. Proud of them as she had been for singing so nicely at the chapel anniversary, she didn't want either of them getting any ideas about following in Molly's footsteps.

'Oh Mammy!'

'It sounds as if your mother wouldn't approve any more than mine did.' Molly sounded a little rueful. 'But I tell you what. You'd like to see inside a real theatre, I expect, wouldn't you? There would be no harm in that, would there?'

She glanced at Annie, raising an eyebrow.

'I'm not sure . . .' Annie said, not liking the way this conversation was going at all, but Lucy was jumping up and down with excitement.

'Oh Mammy, please – please! I'd love to, wouldn't you, Kitty? Please say we can!'

'We'll have to see,' Annie said noncommittally.

'And perhaps you can even ride to Bath in an electric car,' Molly added wickedly.

'Certainly not!' Annie said quickly. 'If we come at all, we shall come on the train.'

'Thank you, Mammy, thank you!' Lucy was taking this as her mother's agreement to the idea, and looking at her eager little face it occurred to Annie that neither she nor Kitty had much fun these days.

'I said we'll have to see,' she repeated.

But already she knew that she was wavering.

Joe was in trouble again. A trail of muddy footprints led across the wood-block floor to where he stood beside the teacher's desk at the front of the empty classroom and water dripped from the hem of his shorts and trickled down his bare legs. The lobe of his right ear felt as if it was on fire; Mr Shearn had dragged him all the way in from the garden by tugging on it, and his head was ringing from the cuff the headmaster had administered when he finally let him go.

'Very well, boy.' Mr Shearn, a short, stocky man not so very much taller than some of the boys in the top class, folded his arms across his chest and glowered at Joe. 'Perhaps you would care to explain what you were doing paddling in my pond.'

'I wasn't paddling, sir,' Joe said indignantly. 'I've got my boots on.'

'Don't be cheeky, boy.'

'Sorry, sir.'

'I should think so too. And I am still waiting for an explanation.'

'I fell in, sir.'

It wasn't the whole story, but Joe was hoping he could get away with it. He was to be disappointed.

'I fail to see how such a thing could have happened,' Mr Shearn growled. 'You had no business being anywhere near the pond. You were supposed to be weeding the flower borders.'

'Yes, sir.'

'So?'

Joe lowered his eyes to the toes of his muddy boots and swallowed hard. He would be given a few strokes of the cane when the truth came out, he knew – and probably a thrashing when Algernon got to hear of it as well. And all for something that had just started as a bit of fun.

Once a week, providing the weather allowed, the boys in Joe's class were sent to work in the headmaster's garden, while the girls did needlework with his wife, who came into the school for that express purpose. The Shearns lived in a house that was part of the school building, and the garden was a large one, extending all the way down to the road and needing far more attention than Mr Shearn cared to give it. The boys provided good free labour, and the headmaster justified the practice by telling himself, and anyone who cared to question him, that they were learning a valuable practical lesson.

In spring they dug over the vegetable patch and planted seeds, potatoes and onion sets, in summer they Dutch-hoed between the rows of growing vegetables, banked up potato haulms and harvested peas and beans, and those who were big enough to handle the mower cut the lawns. For the most part they enjoyed the break from spelling tests and times tables and handwriting practice, though of course it was almost obligatory that they grumbled about it amongst themselves, but things got tedious at this time of year. There wasn't much to do except weeding flower borders and digging up the clumps of dandelions that were constantly springing up along the concreted kerbs and in the cracks between the paving stones, or pulling up the stumps of broad beans that had come to the end of their productive life and piling them up for a cooch fire.

Usually Mr Shearn kept an eye on them, strutting about and dispensing criticism, advice and praise where it was due. But today, suffering from a toothache that had built from a niggle into a painful throb, he'd left them to their own devices and gone into his kitchen in search of some oil of cloves he kept handy for just such an eventuality – Mr Shearn was a martyr to toothache.

No sooner was his back turned than the boys began larking about. Blackened bean stalks were used as missiles and an impromptu game of chase began.

The headmaster's pond was in a far corner of the garden, and nearby were a couple of gnarled old apple trees. In autumn the falling leaves clogged the pond, but clearing it out was one job Mr Shearn never asked his pupils to do. In his experience boys and water did not make an advisable combination and he always saw to it himself, fishing the dead leaves out with a net attached to a long pole. Although the leaves hadn't yet begun to fall, a gusty storm a couple of weeks earlier had brought down some twigs and even a few small branches, and Mr Shearn had used the net to clear them from the pond, then left it propped against the trunk of one of the trees.

The boys' game of chase had taken them to this very spot, although they knew it was out of bounds, and the sight of the apples, rosy and red and just waiting to be picked, proved too great a temptation for them. With the help of the pole they rattled the branches, bit into the fruit that cascaded down, and stuffed what they could into their pockets.

Just out of reach was a clump of apples that looked even bigger and riper than any they had so far – wasn't it always the way? But even though they tried jumping, there was no way the pole would reach the branch they clung to.

'Tell you what,' Joe said, 'if you were to give me a leg up, I reckon I could get them.'

Two of the bigger boys knelt down on the grass, making a step of their backs; Joe clambered up, raised the pole above his head and thrashed about.

'Yes!' he whooped as he struck lucky and the coveted apples came tumbling down. But it was there that his luck ended. In the excitement, the boys providing his platform shifted, and Joe wavered madly, arms outstretched, before completely losing his balance. He landed awkwardly on the rough ground and catapulted sideways. For a long moment he teetered on the edge of the pond and then, almost before he knew it, he was in the water.

The pond wasn't deep, but it was deep enough, reaching almost to his knees. Joe swore, a word he knew he wasn't supposed to use but which rolled readily off his tongue. The other boys thought it hilarious, of course, and did nothing to help him out. He was just struggling to pull his boots out of the mud and silt at the bottom of the pond when Mr Shearn appeared on the scene, and wasted no time in marching Joe off in disgrace.

'Well?' he said now. 'What were you doing by the pond, I would like to know.'

'Just fooling about, sir.' He didn't want to implicate the other boys; he wasn't a telltale or a sneak.

Mr Shearn had not become a headmaster through being stupid.

'You were after my apples, I suppose. Don't you know that is stealing?'

'Yes, sir.'

'Oh Joe, Joe, what are we going to do with you?'

Joe raised his eyes, surprised to be addressed by his Christian name.

'I have such high hopes of you, and then you do something as stupid as this.' Mr Shearn rubbed his jaw as he spoke; so far the oil of cloves had done little to ease his throbbing tooth.

'Sorry, sir.'

'It's no use being sorry unless you change your ways,' Mr Shearn continued. 'This foolish behaviour does you no credit at all. And you will never achieve your full potential unless you knuckle down and work hard.'

'No, sir.'

'I mean it, Joe.' Mr Shearn met his gaze full on. 'I believe you are an ideal candidate for a scholarship so that you can continue your education in the best possible environment – the first boy I've considered for such a thing in a good many years. It was my intention to speak to your father about it. I would be very sorry to see you waste your life in a menial job. You could achieve so much more than that. Become a lawyer, perhaps, a commissioned officer, or even a teacher. But this sort of nonsense will have to stop. Do I make myself clear?'

Joe's head was reeling. He simply couldn't take it in. He'd realised long ago that Algernon would never countenance him going down the mine when he was old enough to leave school, as so many of his contemporaries would do, but he'd envisaged his stepfather finding him some sort of clerical job, perhaps even in the glove factory where he was assistant manager. The prospect hadn't appealed to him, but had seemed far enough away in the future for him not to worry unduly about it. Now Mr Shearn was telling him that all sorts of other possibilities could be open to him if he would only apply himself. It was truly mind-boggling.

'Go and get yourself cleaned up, then, and you can fetch a

mop and bucket and wash the floor you've traipsed mud over too.' Mr Shearn's fingers closed over the vial of oil of cloves in his coat pocket; he could hardly wait to rub some more on to his aching tooth in the hope that it would have more effect than the first dose had. 'Off you go now, boy.'

'Yes, sir.'

Joe's overwhelming feeling was one of relief that he'd been spared a caning. But a little thread of excitement bubbled inside him too, though he could scarcely identify it. Life as Algernon's stepson wasn't a lot of fun, and Joe could only dream of a future when he'd be free. Suddenly that future seemed a whole lot more attainable than he'd ever imagined.

Chapter Six

It was, Lucy thought, the most exciting day of her entire life. At last – at last! – Mammy was taking her and Kitty to Bath to visit the Lyric. Ever since Aunt Molly had suggested it, Lucy had nagged and pleaded until Annie, against her better judgement, had given in.

They went on a blustery Saturday in November – Molly had said the best day would be a Sunday, when there were no performances, but a Sunday was out of the question: Papa would never have allowed it. So a Saturday was decided upon, and after an early dinner – a quarter to twelve instead of the more usual half past – they set out to walk to the station, Lucy and Kitty wearing the new tartan capes that Annie had made for them and been up half the night finishing. Annie herself was wearing her best cloak and bonnet, which added to the sense of occasion, since they only came out for chapel or on high days and holidays.

Neither of the girls had ever been to Bath before – though it was only ten miles away, there was never any cause for going there – and they had only ridden on a train a handful of times, on summer outings to the seaside. As they waited on the platform Lucy hopped up and down with excitement, and when the train steamed into the station Annie had to hold on to her hand to keep her from scrambling into the carriage whilst passengers disembarked.

'But I want to sit by the window!' she squealed.

'So do I, but I'm not pushing,' Kitty said primly.

'I'm sure you'll both be able to,' Annie said. 'But getting overexcited will do no good at all.'

She was right. There were two window seats vacant, and though there was a bit of an altercation over who would face forward and who backwards, it was soon resolved.

'Kitty can have first choice now, and you can on the way home,' Annie decreed.

Lucy was too excited to argue, and then it was only out of habit. Throughout the journey she gazed intently out of the soot-blackened window, kicking the heels of her boots against the seat and keeping up a running commentary on everything she saw, from the stations they stopped at to the cows in the fields they passed, and chanting 'I think I can . . . I think I can . . . I know I can . . . I know I can . . .' in time with the chugging of the engine and the rattle of the wheels on the track.

'Why is it called Bath Green Park?' she asked, disappointed, when the train eventually came to a halt under the glass canopy of the station. 'It's not green at all!'

'I expect it was a park once,' Annie said, her words drowned out by a hiss of steam from the engine. 'Come on now, make haste. We don't want to keep Aunt Molly waiting.'

The girls did not need telling twice. They scrambled down on to the platform so eagerly that Lucy took a tumble and Annie had to brush the dust from her hands and knees.

She held tight to Lucy's hand as they left the station and headed out into the busy street, afraid she might dart out into the path of one of the horse-drawn vehicles in her excitement. At least she could trust Kitty not to do anything so foolish!

'I think this is the right way,' she murmured, trying to remember the directions Molly had given her. They were walking along a street as wide again as the high street in High Compton, bordered by tall, gracious houses with brightly painted front doors and low iron railings hemming in basement windows.

Once they must have taken a wrong turn, for they found themselves on one side of a tree-lined square of park, but after Annie had asked directions of the driver of a brougham that was waiting outside a grand hotel, they turned down a narrower alleyway and there, almost directly in front of them, was the Lyric.

To reach it they had to pass directly by another theatre – the Theatre Royal. Its doors were open for a matinee performance, and Lucy peered eagerly inside at red plush and sparkling chandeliers. But the billboards outside advertised not a music hall but a play by a Mr Robert Buchanan and a Mr Charles Marlow – *The Strange Adventures of Miss Brown* – and Lucy quickly turned her gaze to the more flamboyant bills that flanked the entrance to the Lyric on the other side of the road.

The main doors of the Lyric were closed; as instructed, Annie led the girls to another, much smaller door to one side of the grey stone building. She knocked on the flaking paintwork, and when no one answered, turned the handle and tentatively opened the door.

As they stepped into the dim interior, Lucy's heart was thudding with anticipation, but she stopped short, overawed suddenly, as she breathed in the smell of a theatre for the first time in her life.

The air in the passage was thick with dust and tobacco smoke that tickled her nose and made her want to sneeze. Overlaying it was a scent she didn't recognise at all, though later she would come to know it as the sweet, cloying smell of greasepaint and powder, a scent that would forever have the power to excite her and fill her with a glorious sense of anticipation.

A man appeared in the passageway, heading towards them, a man so large and beefy he seemed to fill the narrow corridor.

'Hey – what y'doing? You're not allowed in here.' His voice was rough and threatening.

Annie lifted her chin. 'We are here at the invitation of Miss Molly Day. Could you tell me where we might find her?'

'Who?' The man's tone became even more aggressive. 'There's no Molly Day here, missus. I don't know no Molly Day.'

'She's appearing here. She's a singer, and she's my sister-in-law,' Annie said, determined not to be intimidated.

'I told you – we don't have no Molly Day. Never heard of her, right? So off you go now.' He moved towards them, appearing quite capable of manhandling them out of the theatre.

Lucy's heart leapt in alarm, her fertile imagination creating some unimaginable drama in which her dream of an aunt who was a music hall star came tumbling down about her ears. But Annie was standing her ground.

'I assure you—'

And suddenly: 'Annie! Girls! There you are!'

Aunt Molly.

The belligerent man looked bemused, but made no sign of moving.

'They say they're looking for a Molly somebody, Miss Dorne. I told them—'

'Just get out of the way, Warren, and let them pass.' Molly's voice had the ring of authority, and the man stepped aside, scratching his head.

'Follow me.' Molly turned, leading the way. 'I am sorry you

had to come in by way of the stage door,' she said over her shoulder. 'It's not the most beautiful part of the theatre.'

But Lucy thought it was wonderful. This would be the way the artistes would enter and leave, which made it so much more exciting than the grand entrance and foyer. Doors bearing old and scratched brass numbers with hand-written cards tacked beneath them flanked the corridor; one of them was open, and through it Lucy glimpsed what she felt sure must be a dressing room – there was a looking glass, a table and chair, and a folding screen over which was hanging a scarlet gown, all lace and flounces. The public might pay for a seat to watch the show, but they would never get to see what she was seeing.

The same feeling of awe, of being especially privileged, bubbled inside her as Molly gave them a guided tour of the theatre. It was empty but for the man, Warren, who had returned with a broom and was now sweeping the stage, and a couple of men who were scrambling about high above, lithe as monkeys, on wooden beams Molly said were called battens, but Lucy could feel the charged energy of the place, a hushed air of expectancy. As she stood on the bare boards looking out at the rows of plush seats in the stalls, the gallery above and the little boxes set to each side of the stage, she imagined them filled with an eager crowd, and though the light was dim she could picture the glow of the limes illuminating the plain canvas backdrop. She could almost hear the swish of the curtain when it was opened and closed by the man or boy who would operate the pulley Aunt Molly showed them, and the whoops and shouts of an appreciative audience as an act concluded. Sometimes, of course, there were jeers and catcalls, but they had no place in Lucy's vision.

This, she knew, was where she wanted to be. Here, on a stage, like Auntie Molly. It was, of course, only a distant dream, something that would have to wait for years and years, until she was quite grown up. But that didn't matter. Just the thought of it transported her to a place she had never been before. Lucy could not wait to make that dream a reality.

But the day was not over yet. Molly took them to Hands Tearooms, where they tucked into delicious scones with jam and thick yellow clotted cream that she said was made on the premises – an unimaginable treat.

And then it was time for their train home. Molly kissed them all goodbye on the cobbled street in the shadow of the Abbey and pointed out the way back to the station.

It had been, Lucy thought, the very best day of the whole of her life.

The carriage was full to overflowing with folk who had been to Bath for the afternoon, perhaps for a spot of early Christmas shopping, and the window seats were all taken by the time Annie and the girls climbed in, but Lucy was too happy to mind much, though Kitty looked sulky. It began to empty, though, as the train stopped at the stations along the way, and by the time they reached Wellow, there was no one left but themselves and a gentleman, perhaps in his mid-thirties, who was attired in a voluminous checked overcoat with a matching cape and cap, the like of which Annie had never seen before. His face was narrow and pale, and it was clean-shaven but for a handlebar moustache, the corners of which curled stiffly as if fixed with wax.

As the girls scrambled for their preferred seats, he smiled at Annie, a small, amused smile that quirked the corners of his mouth beneath that impressive moustache and crinkled his eyes.

'They're overexcited,' Annie said apologetically. 'A train ride is something of a novelty for them.'

He said nothing, merely smiled again and raised an eyebrow, but every so often Annie noticed he was watching them with the same look of amusement. When they squealed, pointing out the same cows in fields adjoining the track as they had on the way in, he spoke for the first time.

'I don't suppose they see many farm animals, living in Bath.'

His voice was cultured, much like Molly's, with only the faintest trace of a Somerset burr.

'Oh, we don't live in Bath,' Annie said. 'We live in the country, so they see plenty of cows every day. We even have some sometimes in the fields at the back of our house. As I said, it's just that they're excited.'

'Really? I imagined they were city children, visiting relatives, perhaps.'

Annie felt a flush of pride. It must be the new capes, she thought, that had made him think they looked too smart to be country children.

'No, it's the other way round,' she said. 'We've been visiting a relative in Bath.'

Lucy, overhearing the conversation, couldn't resist joining in.

'Auntie Molly is a singer at the Lyric,' she offered enthusiastically. 'We've been to see her there. We went on the stage and everything!'

Annie's flush deepened, in embarrassment now.

'That will do, Lucy. She's my husband's sister,' she said to the gentleman. 'Well – my first husband. The children's father. He's no longer with us, I'm afraid. He passed away,' she added, wondering how all this must sound to him, and hastening to try to put the record straight.

To her relief the gentleman did not look in the least shocked.

'You've been to a theatre! How exciting!' he said to Lucy.

'You should go to London, where I live. There are dozens of theatres there.'

'Dozens?' Lucy's eyes were round with wonder. 'Oh Mammy, can we go and see them?'

Annie shook her head, despairing. 'No, Lucy, we can't.'

Lucy turned her attention to the gentleman. 'Have you ever been on a real live stage?'

The gentleman laughed. It was a nice laugh, a deep, throaty chuckle. 'No, I haven't. But I do live in a very big house. Have you ever heard of Buckingham Palace?'

'Buckingham Palace?' Lucy echoed. 'But that's where the Queen lives!'

'Don't tease her, please,' Annie implored him. 'You'll only make her worse.' She took Lucy by the hand, urging her back into her seat. 'That's quite enough, Lucy. Sit down, there's a good girl, and stop bothering the gentleman.'

Lucy wrinkled her nose but did as she was told. She couldn't contain herself for long, though.

'Do you really live at Buckingham Palace?'

The gentleman gave Annie an apologetic look. 'I do. But only because I work there.'

'For the Queen?'

'In her household. It's not nearly as grand as you'd think, I'm afraid. I spend most of my days in a very small office and I almost never get as much as a glimpse of the Queen. What does your daddy do? I expect his job is much more interesting than mine.'

'He was a miner,' Lucy said, and Kitty, who had been listening in silence, piped up:

'Papa is the assistant manager of the glove factory.'

Annie glanced at her sharply. It was almost as if she was ashamed of her real father.

'My husband likes the children to call him Papa,' she said by way of explanation.

The gentleman had sat forward a little in his seat, his head cocked to one side, his eyes narrowed.

'He's not Algernon Pierce by any chance, is he?'

Annie nodded, surprised. 'Yes.'

The gentleman shook his head wonderingly. 'This is extraordinary! My parents live next door to Algernon Pierce. I was brought up in that house. You must be the new neighbour my mother has mentioned in her letters.'

'Mrs Latcham?' Annie asked in disbelief, unable to reconcile the elderly, and very ordinary, couple next door with this fashionable gentleman. She knew there was a son who lived and worked in London, but for the Queen, at Buckingham Palace . . .

He nodded. 'Yes.'

'She's very deaf,' Lucy said.

'Lucy!' Annie was mortified.

But the gentleman was merely smiling.

'It's quite all right. Yes, I'm afraid she is rather, my dear. That happens sometimes to people when they get older.'

'It was very rude of you, Lucy,' Annie scolded. 'I don't want to hear another word out of either of you until we get home. Is that understood?'

Lucy bowed her head, chastened.

'I'm so sorry,' Annie said. What in the world must he think of them? And he'd almost certainly pass on his impression to his parents, though not the bit about his mother being deaf, presumably. Annie thought she would die of shame, and if Algernon got to hear of it there would be the devil to pay.

'Really, it doesn't matter. Children will be children, and all the better for it, I'm sure, though I can't say I speak from personal experience.'

'You haven't any?' Annie ventured.

'Unfortunately not. But then again, perhaps it was for the best. I lost my wife when she was very young, and it would have been difficult for me to give them the sort of home life they would have needed and deserved.' A shadow had fallen over his face.

He still loves her, Annie thought, feeling her own grief for her beloved John a sudden knot in her throat.

The train had stopped at Hillsbridge, and was now chugging beneath an embankment. Soon it would arrive in High Compton.

'Is your husband meeting you at the station?' The question took Annie by surprise.

'Oh, I don't expect so. It's not far to walk and the road is well lit . . . Well, of course, you know that! You probably know it better than I do.'

'Not these days, I'm sure. I don't get home to visit my parents as often as I'd like. But it's reassuring to know they have such good neighbours.'

Annie flushed a little. She barely knew Mr and Mrs Latcham.

'The least I can do is ensure you get home safely,' the gentleman continued. 'I'm Marcus, by the way.'

'Annie,' she said. 'Kitty is my eldest, and this pickle is Lucy.'

The train pulled into the station. Marcus Latcham opened the door and helped Annie and the children down on to the platform, then walked with them until they reached the adjoining houses.

'It's been very nice to meet you,' he said courteously as he unlatched the gate. 'And so strange that it should have been on a train rather than over the garden fence.'

Annie didn't point out that it was a hedge that separated the two gardens at the front and nothing at all in the back.

'It's a small world.'

'It is indeed.'

Algernon was less than impressed when she told him of the chance meeting, and disparaging when Lucy imparted the bit about Buckingham Palace.

'He's some sort of jumped-up clerk, I believe,' he said stiffly. 'A confirmed bachelor who can't find the time to come and see his parents.'

'He's actually a widower, I believe,' Annie said, and was rewarded with a glare from Algernon.

'I must say you seem to have learned a great deal about him in a very short space of time,' he said disapprovingly.

'We were just chatting,' Annie said hastily, glad, however, that the thrill of meeting someone who worked for the Queen had at least thrust the visit to the Lyric further down the list of topics the girls would enthuse about. Though Algernon had allowed them to go to the theatre, she knew he had strong reservations, and Lucy chattering on and on about it would only exacerbate the situation.

'Upstairs now, girls, and change out of your best clothes before you dirty them,' she instructed.

As she laid the table for supper – bread, tasty cheese and some of the shallots she'd pickled – Joe came clattering down the stairs.

'Is it true the man next door lives at Buckingham Palace? Or is it just one of Lucy's stories?'

'He's just a jumped-up clerk,' Algernon said, reiterating his earlier remark. 'It's something to brag about, that's all. It doesn't make him better than anyone else.'

He wasn't bragging, Annie almost said, then thought better of it. Algernon hated to be contradicted.

But she thought it all the same, and thought too that Marcus Latcham was more of a gentleman than Algernon would ever be. Kinder, too. More tolerant. And really very charming . . .

She was still thinking about him as she buttered bread and made a pot of tea, and still seeing that pale, interesting face with the waxed handlebar moustache, still hearing his beautiful cultured voice as she cleared away the supper things and saw the children into bed.

And wondering why, after a day so filled with action and new experiences, it should be a chance encounter with a stranger, who had turned out not to be a stranger at all, that she couldn't stop thinking about.

One morning in late November, when Annie had gone into town to buy a few necessary items, she happened to run into Hester Dallimore. Hester had always been known as the gossip of Fairley Terrace, and she was more than delighted to see Annie, since she guessed she would not have heard the latest news that was causing a stir in the rank.

'You'll never guess what!' she began, her mean little face twisted in a smirk of pleasure. 'Such goings-on with folk living right next door to us! Scandalous, it is!'

'What's that then, Hester?' Annie asked. She knew she would never escape until Hester had told her all about it, and in any case she was always pleased to hear news of her old neighbours, even if it was a version Hester had embellished.

'Well, for a start, Ewart Donovan has come back home from Yorkshire and he's living in number ten. Going to marry Cathy Small, or so I hear – you know, she serves in the drapery shop and was friendly with his sister Maggie? That's got to be a rush job, if you ask me – that Cathy was never any better than she should be.' She paused, then added triumphantly: 'Not, of course, that Maggie was any better when push came to shove.'

Annie said nothing. She didn't like casting stones at the people who had been her neighbours, and though the Donovans had not been the most respected family in the rank, she had always got on well with them. They had suffered badly as a result of the tragedy at the pit: Maggie had lost not only her father but her fiancé, Jack Withers, too, and now her mother Rose was gone, having died just as Maggie was giving birth to her own son, Patrick.

'And that's not the half of it,' Hester went on, getting into her stride. 'You know she married that Lawrence Jacobs from Hillsbridge, and had a baby? Well, it turns out Mr Jacobs wasn't the father at all – no surprise there, an old man like him – and who do you think was? Only Josh Withers, that's who, Jack's own brother! And him hardly cold in the ground!'

Annie was beginning to feel uncomfortable; she really didn't like the way Hester was glorying in all this.

'I ought to be getting home,' she said, but Hester wasn't going to let her go so easily.

'And now they've gone off to America, if you please! Something to do with stained-glass windows Lawrence Jacobs made for a cathedral in New York before he died. I can't make her out. Carrying on like that with Josh straight after Jack got killed, and then doing the same again when her husband kicks the bucket. But then I suppose it's only what you'd expect from folk like that, and Josh Withers always was a wild one too. His poor mother and father had to send him away to keep him out of trouble when he was just a boy! Not that Florrie will own to him doing anything wrong. She had the nerve to come knocking on my door saying she'd thank me not to tell stories about her son. I ask you! I told her straight, not a word had passed my lips that wasn't the truth, and she had no answer for that.'

This was not strictly true. Florrie Withers had told Hester in no uncertain terms that neighbour or not, there would be a serious falling-out if she continued to spread unpleasant stories about Josh and Maggie. But trying to stop Hester gossiping was like King Canute sitting in his chair and trying to stop the tide coming in, as Florrie had said later to her husband, Gilby, and she was right.

'I expect they're just glad to have each other after everything that happened,' Annie said, jumping at last to Maggie's defence. 'I really don't think it's for us to judge.'

'I was just saying . . .' Hester's tone was huffy. 'I thought you'd be interested, that's all.'

'I must go now,' Annie said. 'It was nice seeing you, Hester.'

She walked quickly away up the street, digesting what Hester had told her, and, in spite of her disapproval of the woman's attitude, acknowledging how much she missed living in the rank, where everybody knew everybody else's business, but were, for the most part, good friends and neighbours who shared celebrations and happy occasions and looked out for one another in times of trouble. She thought wistfully of the chats over the washing lines, the cups of tea on the doorstep when work was done, the feeling that if something went wrong, help was no more than a few steps away.

It wasn't like that in her new home. Her only neighbours were the Latchams, who kept themselves to themselves, and whom she scarcely saw from one week's end to the next.

But fancy them having a son like Marcus! Annie thought. And felt the colour rising in her cheeks.

For goodness' sake! Whatever is the matter with you?

She'd spent less than an hour in his company, and not so much as set eyes on him since. He'd gone back to London now, and given that he visited his parents so rarely, it was likely to be

99

a very long time before she saw him again – which, given the way she couldn't get him out of her head, was really just as well.

You're thirty years old, a married woman with two growing girls, and you're acting like a silly schoolgirl!

But for all that she knew it was no more than a foolish flight of fantasy, and would soon be forgotten, Annie couldn't help a secret smile as she made her way home.

Chapter Seven

The girls were both ill and had been since Christmas. Kitty had been the first to succumb, and within a few days Lucy had followed, and they were far from being the only ones. An outbreak of diphtheria was raging through High Compton and before long it had claimed three victims, two small children and a baby. Panic had set in, and speculation was rife as to how it had started. Annie always boiled milk in a big pan so that it kept for longer and, as she had long ago heard, was safer to drink. But not everyone took that precaution, drinking it straight from the jug it came home from the farm in, and diphtheria spread so easily, especially at this time of year when there were big gatherings at parties and concerts and church services, and nobody thought anything of someone sneezing or coughing because ordinary head colds were rife.

That, of course, was before the diagnosis of diphtheria was confirmed in the first patients, and everyone became so cautious that children were kept home from school and parties cancelled.

It was, Annie thought, the most horrible disease she'd ever come across. The girls both started with chills, high fevers and sore throats, and before long they found swallowing so difficult she could get no solid food into them. Even broths and egg custard refused to go down and Annie was horrified when she saw the thick grey membrane that had formed on their tonsils. The sound of their coughing and gasping seemed to fill the house, and the bluish colour of their skin added to her anxiety.

Though she had been a day or two behind Kitty in succumbing to the infection, Lucy was the first to begin to recover, and she was moved into Joe's room so that she could get some rest without being disturbed by her sister. Joe was in any case already sleeping on the sofa downstairs – so far he had escaped catching the terrible disease, and Annie wanted to do all she could to keep him out of the way of their germs. If he fell ill too she didn't know how she would cope, and she had the horrible feeling that Kitty was deteriorating. The infection was spreading, to her nose, her windpipe and voice box, and her neck was swelling badly, which was making it difficult for her to breathe.

Eventually there was nothing for it: Kitty had to be taken into hospital so that she could be intubated and nursed by professional staff. That night Annie couldn't sleep a wink; she paced the house and continually checked on Lucy, fearing that she might suddenly have a relapse. Then there was the problem of getting away so that she could visit Kitty. Algernon had gone to work as usual, and reluctant as she was to leave Lucy with Joe, there was really no alternative. She didn't think Lucy was still infectious, but she told Joe he was to go no closer to her than the bedroom door, and he must run for help if she showed any signs of worsening. Worried half to death, and wishing with all her heart that she was still living in the Ten Houses, where any of the neighbours would have been only too pleased to help out, she walked the couple of miles to the cottage hospital.

Thankfully, Kitty was responding. Now that she had been intubated she was in no danger of choking to death, but she was still dreadfully ill, and the doctor Annie spoke to warned her that they were far from out of the woods yet. There was really nothing more that could be done; they could only wait and pray that the infection would clear of its own accord, and that Kitty would be strong enough to survive all the rigours the dreadful illness had placed on her heart.

Those days felt to Annie like the longest she had ever lived through. The aura of nightmare hung in the air like a noxious cloud, and for the first time since she had married Algernon, she fell willingly to her knees when he led the nightly prayers. She was praying most of the rest of the time, too, as she went about the unavoidable tasks that made up her daily routine, the words catching in her throat and lodging there like the morsels of food on Lucy's still inflamed tonsils, her breathing almost as ragged as the girls' had been at the height of their sickness.

At last it seemed her prayers had been heard. Kitty began to improve and was able to come home, though she was still dreadfully weak, and the doctors were afraid her heart might have suffered some irreparable damage. For the moment Annie couldn't find it in her to worry about that. Kitty was going to pull through. Really, that was the only thing that mattered.

'Oh Mammy, I was so scared she was going to die!' Lucy whispered to Annie. 'And I thought it was all my fault.'

'Why would you think that, Lucy?' Annie asked, trying to comfort her, though truth to tell she felt that she must be to blame herself for what had happened to Kitty. 'It wasn't even as if it was you who caught the diphtheria first and gave it to her.'

'No, but . . .' Lucy hesitated, her lip wobbling. 'Sometimes I've thought I don't like her very much. And God was going to punish me by taking her away.'

'Oh darling . . .'

'I promised him that if only he'd let Kitty be all right I'd never have a mean thought about her again, ever. And I'd be really, really good . . .'

103

'You are good,' Annie said, hugging her. 'And I know you'll do all you can to help me get Kitty well again.'

Lucy nodded seriously. 'I will. Oh, I will. And Joe said he'd help too. He said he'll clean out the grate for you every morning, and riddle the cinders, and get in the coal from the shed, and light the fire . . .'

'I don't know about him lighting the fire,' Annie said. 'I don't want him burning himself or setting fire to the house. But the rest of it . . . that would be really nice.'

She passed a hand across her eyes, trying to smooth out the tired ache that had seemed to be there for weeks now. And thought that even if Algernon was far from perfect as a husband, at least she was blessed as far as the children were concerned.

At the beginning of April 1899, Lucy was going to be nine. Every year for as long as she could remember she had really looked forward to her birthday, which Annie always tried to make a special day. This year, however, it was going to be quiet; Kitty was still convalescing, and in any case, there could be no party, as Algernon would never have given his approval.

He had, though, agreed somewhat reluctantly that Edie Cooper could come for tea, and Molly had also promised to try to be there, and in all honesty Lucy couldn't think of anything she would enjoy more. Though she and Edie were still insepar-able during school hours, they rarely saw one another after they parted at the gates, and Molly was still Lucy's heroine, glamorous and exciting and always interested to hear what she had been up to since she had seen her last.

As it was a school day, Edie's mother had agreed that Edie should go home with Lucy and Joe, and Wesley, her father, would collect her at six thirty. By the time the children got home, Molly had already arrived; she and Annie were having a cup of tea in the living room with Kitty tucked up under a crocheted blanket on the sofa.

Lucy came dancing into the house, Edie following a little shyly.

'Auntie Molly! You're here!'

'I promised I would be, didn't I? Happy birthday, Lucy! My, I swear you've grown at least an inch since I saw you last! And prettier than ever!'

Lucy flushed with pleasure.

'Now, I've something for you.' Molly reached into her beaded handbag and drew out an envelope and a small package and handed them to Lucy. 'You must open the card first, or I fear you won't open it at all, and I chose it especially for you.'

'Oh!' Lucy cried excitedly. She perched on one of the dining chairs and laid the package on the table beside her whilst she tore open the envelope.

Inside was the most beautiful card she had ever seen, shaped like a fan, and edged with fine paper lace. The delicate segments were decorated with oval miniatures, each of a pretty girl.

'That one reminded me of you,' Molly said, pointing to one of the girls. 'She has brown curls and blue eyes, just as you have.'

'I don't have a hat like that, though,' Lucy said wistfully, and they all laughed.

None of them noticed Joe slip away and run upstairs, but he was back by the time Lucy began tearing the wrapping from Molly's present, and Annie saw that he was carrying a small parcel wrapped in brown paper. She'd seen him rifling through the oddments drawer in the chiffonier, and wondered what he was looking for; now she knew. He had a gift for Lucy too, and had wanted something to wrap it in. She smiled to herself; he really was a very good boy, and very fond of Lucy.

Molly's present, of course, was not wrapped in anything so

ordinary, but the palest blue tissue, and she had secured it with a ribbon of darker blue. Lucy slid it off, almost reluctant to spoil the pretty effect, but also eager to discover its contents. Then she gasped again.

Inside a little pillbox, an oval locket lay on a bed of velvet. Reverently Lucy lifted it out, holding it in the palm of her hand while the fine silver chain draped through her fingers.

'It's beautiful!'

'It opens, and I've put a miniature of myself inside,' Molly said, sitting forward to show her. 'But you can change it if you like, or put another in the other side.'

'I wouldn't change it!' Lucy couldn't think of anyone whose picture she would rather have in the locket.

Annie was shaking her head. The locket must have cost as much money as she had to spend in a month.

'Molly, you shouldn't have!'

'Nonsense. I wanted to. It will remind her of me, I hope. And perhaps she will wear it the first time she sings in a theatre – to bring her luck.'

'I will, I will! I'll wear it every single time!'

A little uncomfortable with the direction the conversation was taking, Annie turned to Joe.

'Do you have something for Lucy too, Joe?'

To her surprise, instead of stepping forward with his gift, Joe shuffled awkwardly, his fist clamped tightly over the little parcel.

'It's nothing . . . it's not worth having . . .'

'Come on, Joe,' Annie encouraged him, and Molly cried gaily, 'Don't be shy!'

Lucy tore her eyes away from the silver locket. 'What is it, Joe?'

'You won't want it. Not now.' Joe had turned red, and Annie

thought he looked as if he might be going to cry. She was astonished. She'd rarely, if ever, seen Joe in tears, even when Algernon took the strap to him.

'I'm sure she'll love it, whatever it is,' she soothed.

Backed into a corner, Joe reluctantly handed the parcel to Lucy.

'I don't mind if you don't like it,' he said defiantly.

Joe had tied the brown paper with a length of kitchen twine, held in place by a blob of sealing wax. Lucy had some difficulty tearing it open, but at last a little box was revealed. She lifted the lid. Inside was another locket, not silver, but perhaps pewter. It was heavier and clumsier than the one Molly had chosen, and obviously nowhere near as valuable.

'It was me mam's. There's a pressed flower in it,' Joe blurted. 'I cleaned it up 'cos I thought you'd like it, but you won't want it now . . .'

'Of course I like it!' Lucy exclaimed, much to Annie's relief. 'It's lovely, Joe! Thank you!'

Her heart was swelling as she opened the locket and saw the tiny sprig of forget-me-not behind the glass. How lucky was she?

Joe's locket might not be as beautiful or as expensive as Molly's, but even at nine years old, Lucy knew how much it must have cost him to give it to her, something so precious, something that had belonged to his dead mother.

She held the lockets, one in each hand.

'I love them both! And this is my very best birthday ever!'

'Why don't you give us a song, Molly?' Annie suggested.

The birthday cake she had baked had been cut and eaten, Joe, a little bored, had slipped off to his room to play with his toy soldiers, taking an extra slice with him, and Annie was anxious to keep the celebration going for Lucy's sake.

107

Molly grimaced, but when Lucy begged: 'Oh yes please, Auntie Molly!' she relented.

'Very well. But only if your mama will play for me.'

'My goodness, my playing is not up to that!' Annie protested, but Molly would have none of it.

'You play very well, Annie.'

'But not the songs you sing.' Annie was doubtful, suddenly, whether Molly's songs would be suitable for young ears. Though she'd never been to a music hall performance, she knew that many of the numbers were ribald, to say the least of it, and full of innuendo. Hadn't Marie Lloyd been called up before the so-called Vigilance Committee when one of the ladies of the Purity Party had made a public protest about her vulgarity from the stalls of the Empire during her act? She'd got away with it, so Annie had read, by singing her songs with a perfectly straight face and none of her usual wicked nudges and winks, so hopefully Molly would be just as restrained.

'It's the deal,' Molly said, smiling, and Lucy was begging again, 'Please, Mammy! It's my birthday! And what I want most is for Auntie Molly to sing!'

'Well, you mustn't blame me if I go wrong.' Annie went to Kitty, lying on the sofa, pale and listless. 'Can you manage to walk into the parlour if I help you, my love? You're a big girl to carry now.'

'I can do it, I'm sure.' Molly crossed to the sofa and turned back the blanket. 'Put your arms round my neck, Kitty – yes, that's the way.'

'Mind your fingers aren't sticky, Kitty!' Annie was worried Kitty might mark Molly's fine dress – as if she wasn't already worried enough that Molly might strain herself. But Molly lifted Kitty as easily as if she was still a toddler, carried her into the parlour and deposited her on the sofa with no trouble at all.

She was much stronger than she looked, Annie thought – perhaps from her days as a dancer.

'What shall we have, then?' she asked, spreading her arms.

'Well, I know "Come into the Garden, Maud",' Annie suggested.

Molly pulled a bit of a face, then laughed. 'Go on then, if you must.'

So 'Come into the Garden, Maud' it was, and Molly's powerful voice filled the little room, soaring and true.

'More! More!' Lucy cried when it was finished. Edie clapped, even Kitty was smiling wanly, and Joe appeared in the doorway with one of his lead soldiers still in his hand and cake crumbs round his mouth.

'Let's have something a bit brighter!' Molly urged. 'Can't you play by ear at all, Annie? What about "Oh! Mr Porter"?'

'Well, I'll try . . .' Annie had tinkled it out a few times when she had been alone in the house.

She began tentatively, then gained confidence as Molly belted out the song, every bit as well as Marie Lloyd in Annie's opinion, and Lucy, Edie and Joe joined in with the chorus. Only poor Kitty remained silent. Her throat had not recovered enough for her to be able to sing – if, indeed, it ever would, something that worried Annie.

Things were going swimmingly, and Annie forgot her inhibitions as one song followed another. The tunes were all familiar to her and she was able to follow Molly well enough.

Enjoyment was making them all merry – as if we'd been on the Christmas port! Annie thought, though of course Algernon would not have so much as a drop of liquor in the house.

'What next? What next?' Lucy squealed eagerly, and Molly laughed.

'Has your pa got a hat and cane I could borrow? There's the

one the mashers sing – well, it's Charles Coborn's song really, but some of the girls have it in their act.'

For a moment, Annie tensed. She didn't want one of the children asking what a masher was and having to explain they were male impersonators. But there was no harm, surely? It was only a bit of fun, of no more consequence to them than borrowing her shoes and hats or even an old curtain to play at dressing-up.

'I'll get them – I know where they are.' Lucy disappeared into the hall, returning a moment later with Algernon's Sunday-best bowler and his ivory-topped cane.

'Oh, Lucy – no!' Annie protested, but too late. Already Molly had patted the bowler on to her head, where it sat like a pea on a rump of beef, as Annie's mother might have said, and was twirling the cane expertly.

'Ready, Annie?'

'I don't know what . . .'

'"The Man Who Broke the Bank at Monte Carlo"!' Molly's tone was carefree and gay. 'You must know that, surely?'

She began to sing, and after a moment Annie joined in, her fingers miraculously finding the right notes.

> As I walk along the Bois Boolong
> With an independent air
> You can hear the girls declare
> 'He must be a millionaire'
> You can hear them sigh and wish to die
> You can see them wink the other eye
> At the man who broke the bank at Monte Carlo.

They couldn't sing the verses, of course, they didn't know the words, and Molly belted those out, strutting her stuff as if she were in the glow of the limes on stage at the Lyric.

They were enjoying themselves so much, none of them heard the front door opening.

Algernon Pierce had not been feeling well all day. A tickly throat had grown steadily worse until it burned uncomfortably when he tried to speak, and even when he swallowed, his eyes were sore and itchy, and though he had resorted to putting on his overcoat, he couldn't stop shivering. Common sense told him that the germs that had caused the girls' infection had long since lost their potency, and in any case, he had never heard of a case of an adult suffering from diphtheria – as far as he was aware it was a childhood disease – but the spectre of their sickness loomed large anyway, and halfway through the afternoon Algernon decided he would go home early.

The longish walk from Hillsbridge to High Compton did nothing to improve the way he felt, and by the time he turned in at the gate, all he wanted to do was to have a cup of tea and retire to bed.

As he walked up the path, however, voices raised in song wafted out to greet him, and he grunted bad-temperedly to himself as he remembered that today was Lucy's birthday, Edie Cooper was coming to tea, and Molly, whom he had never met, had promised to visit too. Other folk in his house was the last thing he wanted, and certainly not ones making this unholy racket. The purpose of music was, in Algernon's view, for the praise of the Lord, and the cacophony coming from his parlour was most certainly not a hymn or sacred song.

'Intolerable!' he muttered. Well, he'd soon put a stop to that. He slammed the door hard behind him, thinking that might put a stop to the awful caterwauling, but no, it continued unabated.

Algernon's jaw tightened. He strode along the hall purpose-fully, his aches and pains momentarily forgotten, then stopped short in the doorway, shocked and outraged at the scene that greeted him.

Annie was at the piano, her back towards him – that was only what he had expected – and the children, Lucy, Joe and Edie Cooper, were capering excitedly. But it was the woman in the centre of the room – Molly, he assumed – who was the cause of his disbelief and outrage. Not only were the words she was singing quite unsuitable for young ears, they were positively blasphemous!

> *I patronised the tables at the Monte Carlo hell*
> *Till they hadn't got a sou for a Christian or a Jew;*
> *So I quickly went to Paris for the charms of mad'moiselle*
> *Who's the lodestone of my heart – what can I do.*

Still worse, on her head was perched his Sunday-best bowler, and she was twirling his ivory-topped cane.

'What in the world . . . !' Algernon roared, and though his voice gave out before he could utter another word, it was enough to alert the revellers.

Edie Cooper stopped mid-caper, staring at him with big startled eyes, Lucy and Joe followed suit, and Annie turned around on the piano stool, her hands still hovering over the keys, a look of alarm replacing her smile. But the woman making free with his hat and bowler seemed utterly unfazed.

She took her time about turning, first looking over her shoulder coquettishly. Then, as if remembering that she was doing a male impersonation act, she jammed one hand on her hip and with the other tipped the bowler at him so that it sat at a rakish angle and, to his utter disbelief, treated him to a slow and meaningful wink.

'Algernon, I presume,' she said languidly. 'We meet at last.'

'How dare you!' The words rasped in his sore throat.

'Algernon!' Annie was on her feet now, flustered and frightened. 'We're only having a bit of fun. We didn't expect you home yet . . .'

'Clearly!'

'Molly is entertaining us . . . for Lucy's birthday . . .'

'With my cane. And my best hat. Have you any idea how much that hat cost? And how easily it can go out of shape?'

'There's no harm done, Algernon . . .'

'No harm, you say? Making use of *my* piano to accompany profane songs in *my* home, in front of young children? Have you no shame? And you, madam' – his chest swelled as he addressed Molly – 'you are no better than a common showgirl, or worse. There are names for women like you, but I would not lower myself to use them. Get out of my house!'

Molly drew herself up to her full height, raising her eyebrows and regarding him in mock amusement.

'Where's your sense of humour, Algernon? There's no need to spoil Lucy's birthday. Let's all have a cup of tea and another slice of cake, and behave like good girls and boys. Agreed?'

Algernon was trembling now with fury. This woman, this *tart* – perhaps worse, a tom! – dared to stand there in his parlour wearing his hat and laughing at him! It was beyond endurance.

'I said get out!' he repeated. 'And don't come back. You are not welcome here. I won't have the children corrupted by the likes of you. Or by disgusting, dirty songs. Do I make myself clear?'

'Abundantly.' Molly's own temper was flaring; the man was quite impossible. She threw the cane down into a chair, took off the bowler and thrust it at Algernon. 'Here you are, have your hat, you silly old fart.'

Annie caught her breath, the children stood frozen, though Joe looked suspiciously close to having to stifle a giggle. Molly paused only to touch Lucy's hair, smile at her and murmur an apology before striding straight-backed from the room. Annie hurried after her.

'Oh Molly, I am so sorry . . .'

'Never mind about me. My skin's thick as an elephant's, don't worry. But that man!' She retrieved her bag from the living room, and her parasol from the hall. 'How in the world do you live with him?'

Annie shrugged helplessly. There was nothing she could say, and in any case Algernon had appeared in the parlour doorway, arms folded, chin jutting, clearly determined to see the object of his fury off the premises without further delay.

'Your transport's not due yet, is it?' Annie dared to say, and anticipating a further outburst, Molly raised a gloved hand.

'It won't be long. Time's flown. And I can wait outside. Goodbye, my dear. I'm sorry for the upset.'

'And I'm sorry . . .'

'I meant what I said,' Algernon said as the door closed after her. 'I will not have that woman in this house. Is that understood?'

'But Algernon . . .'

'I cannot believe I have been so naïve as to imagine she was a respectable lady! She will not come here again, and you and the children will have nothing more to do with her.'

'But . . . she is John's sister, Algernon! She's their only living relative, their only flesh and blood . . .'

'And quite an unsuitable person for them to be associating with. She is, Annie, nothing more nor less than a common harlot. She may pretend to be a lady, but it is quite clear she is not. The song and her behaviour aside, surely the language she

114

used towards me is proof enough of that? No – I'm sorry, but I won't have it.'

'Algernon, please . . .'

'My decision is final, Annie. I will not have you associating with such a person. And if you choose to defy me and continue to allow your daughters – who I must remind you are now my daughters also – to walk in the paths of iniquity, then I am afraid I can no longer offer you a home here. I will not be seen to be condoning such disgraceful behaviour. The choice, my dear, is yours.'

Annie was staring at him in horror. She couldn't believe he was forbidding her to see Molly again, depriving her of the one spark of brightness in her wretched world. And Lucy was going to be so upset . . .

But at the same time, she could believe it all too well. This was Algernon the tyrant, Algernon the man she had been desperate enough to tie herself to for life. Annie felt tears gathering in her eyes, not just for herself, but for all of them.

Algernon was rubbing his throat now, and swallowing with obvious effort. All the yelling and shouting had done him no good at all.

'Make me a cup of hot milk and bring it up to me,' he ordered. 'I am not well and I am going to bed.'

Make it yourself, Annie longed to say. But, of course, she did not dare. If she crossed Algernon, she and the girls might find themselves without a roof over their heads, or worse, he might turn her out and keep the girls to raise himself, as he was raising Joe. With his standing in the community to uphold, it wasn't beyond the realms of possibility, and Annie didn't dare take the risk.

Full of hatred for him, and feeling wretched for poor Lucy, whose birthday had been ruined, she went to warm the milk.

* * *

Lucy simply couldn't believe it. When Edie's father had collected her – a very subdued little girl, considerably frightened by the scene she had witnessed – Lucy had gone to her room, thrown herself on her bed and wept. She could imagine nothing worse than being banned from meeting Auntie Molly, whom she idolised. When her tears subsided, she reached for the locket Molly had given her and prised it open, staring avidly at the tiny miniature within.

It wasn't enough. It could never be enough. But for now it would have to do.

Though Lucy did not know it at the time, and would have been even more distraught if she had, it would be another eight years before she would see her beloved Aunt Molly again.

Chapter Eight

When as a youth I thought and talked
Time walked.

1906

Joe was in love. In the blink of an eye his uncomplicated world had turned upside down. To discover emotions that seethed and bubbled like a volcano on the brink of erupting would have been a shock to him no matter who was the object of his affections. But it was Lucy he had fallen in love with, and the realisation had hit him as squarely in the stomach as if he'd been in the way of one of the cows that lived in the field at the back of his home when it became frisky and decided to kick out.

Joe was staggered, disbelieving almost. He'd always loved her and wanted to protect her, but in a brotherly way. But this . . . this was quite different. How could he not have realised the way his feelings for her were changing to something much deeper? It must have happened gradually, he supposed, and concentrating first on his studies and then on his new career and the independence it had brought him, he just hadn't stopped to notice that the pretty little girl had turned into a beautiful young woman.

Now, suddenly, he could think of nothing but her. She filled his head and his heart, sent his senses reeling. And totally confused, he did not know how to handle it.

Until now, for all the bad start he'd had, Joe's life had been unfolding very satisfactorily. Under the tutelage of Mr Shearn, the schoolmaster who had seen his potential and helped him fulfil it, he had gained a scholarship to a grammar school in Bath. When the offer was first made, Joe had wondered anxiously whether he would be able to take it up – although his education would be paid for, all the extras such as uniform, books and various items of equipment would come at a considerable expense, not to mention the cost of travelling to the city every day. But once again, Algernon's desire to be seen as a man of standing within the community had come to the rescue; he enjoyed boasting that his stepson had achieved far more than most High Compton lads could hope for, and liked the philanthropic status he felt it bestowed on him.

In his new environment, Joe had thrived, and when he had sat his Higher National it was suggested he should try for a place at a university. But the idea hadn't appealed to him. He'd had enough of being dependent on Algernon, and was eager to begin earning some money of his own.

It was Annie who came up with the suggestion that he should train as a pharmacist, and the more Joe thought about it, the more enthusiastic he became. Annie spoke to the chemist who had taken over her father's business, and he agreed to take Joe on as a 'student associate', the official name, now, for apprentices. Whilst he studied for his exams, he would make up prescriptions under supervision. If he was successful, he would eventually become a registered pharmacist; if not, he could always find employment in a hospital, asylum or prison as a dispenser. But Joe was determined not to fail.

Besides the prospect of an interesting career, the offer provided him with an opportunity to move out of the family home and get away from Algernon and his domineering ways. There were a few rooms above the pharmacy well suited to living accommodation, but Richard Penny, the chemist, had purchased a pleasant villa on the outskirts of town and the rooms remained empty. 'It would ease my mind if the premises were occupied,' he'd told Joe. 'I'm constantly worried that some young thug might try to break in and steal the drugs or poisons; if you were living there, it's far less likely such a thing would happen.'

So Joe had moved his few possessions into the back room and upper storey, where the only furniture was a table, a sideboard covered with scratches, a few ancient chairs and a rickety bed, and though it was much less comfortable than the house he'd called home, he was enjoying the freedom it afforded him. He still went back at least twice a week for what Annie called 'a good square meal', and he and Lucy, who had begun work in the office at the glove factory when she left school, often shared a chat before he went back to his new-found bolt-hole.

But still it had not occurred to him that his feelings for her were mutating into something far from brotherly. Until that cold and frosty evening in the November of 1906. And when it did, it hit the eighteen-year-old Joe with all the force of a hurricane.

The eureka moment happened in the upper room of the town hall, where the local concert party, led by Stanley Bristow, was giving a performance. Stanley's concert parties had been entertaining around the district for the last ten years or so, and everyone loved the mixture of comic turns and music hall songs. Stanley himself would sing 'Burlington Bertie' – just right for him, since he was considered a bit of a toff – and recite

119

monologues; Horace Parfitt dressed as a country yokel in smock and battered hat and told the sort of jokes that had everyone groaning – 'An' he said ter I: "You'm wearing one black shoe and one brown!" An' I said to he: "Ah, I d'know, and I got another pair at home what's just the same . . .".' Then there was little Grace O'Halloran, no more than six years old, lisping 'Daddy Wouldn't Buy Me a Bow-wow', and a girl named Ethel Talbot, who had a pretty soprano voice.

Tonight, however, Ethel had been unable to appear. She was suffering from a nasty cold and chesty cough, and wouldn't have been able to sing a note. With a big hole to fill in his programme, Stanley had asked around, and Lucy Day, who it seemed was well known for singing at chapel anniversaries, had been recommended to him. The proud owner of a brand-new Thornycroft motor car, he drove to High Compton and called at the house where he'd been told Lucy lived.

His knock at the door was answered by Mrs Pierce – Annie, he'd taken the trouble to learn she was called, so that he could slip it in during the course of the conversation. She told him Lucy was not at home, but she was sure she would love to sing in the concert. He could find her in the office at the glove factory, and Algernon too, whose permission she would need. Stanley gained the impression she was not overly confident it would be granted, but undeterred, he drove back to Hillsbridge and parked his magnificent motor in the narrow road outside the factory.

If it had been anyone but Stanley suggesting such a thing, Algernon would have been most unlikely to agree, as Annie had feared. But Stanley was a genial and very persuasive man, and, more importantly as far as Algernon was concerned, just the sort of person with whom to form connections. He was the owner of a successful iron foundry, which had been started by his father, though he left the day-to-day running of it to a trusted manager, and moved in circles Algernon longed to penetrate.

Though Stanley knew Algernon only by reputation, he was canny enough to understand the best way to approach him. Before so much as mentioning the reason for his visit, he praised Algernon's good works, his connections with the church, the wonderful example he set to one and all by his commitment to his family, and in particular his generous decision to raise Joe as his own son after the tragic death of his mother. He enthused over Lucy's wonderful contribution to chapel anniversaries, and said what a credit she was to Algernon, and then called on him to help out a fellow businessman in his hour of need.

'You see what a fix I'm in, Algernon. I feel sure I can rely on you to save the day.'

Flattered and, in spite of his misgivings, unable to resist the opportunity to get in with the likes of Stanley Bristow, Algernon had felt obliged to agree. He introduced him to Lucy, who was, it seemed, employed as a trainee secretary and bookkeeper, and was at her desk in a tiny cupboard of an office next door to Algernon's own. Her eyes had lit up like blue beacons in her pretty face when he told her the reason for his call, and Stanley thought she would go down very well with his audience. He was not to be disappointed.

On the night of the concert, he stood at the foot of the two steps that led up to the low stage, smiling to himself as he listened to her sweet voice filling the hall.

> *The boy I love is up in the gallery*
> *The boy I love is looking down at me . . .*

Well, there was no gallery here, only rows of chairs set out on the creaky wooden floor beneath the stage, but the hush as she sang and the roar of appreciation as she finished was every bit as enthusiastic as if the town hall had been one of the great palaces of variety. She was good, very good, and Stanley decided there and then that he'd try to get her to join his little band of performers on a regular basis, even if it did put Ethel Talbot's nose out of joint.

In the second row from the front, sitting between Annie and Kitty, Joe was staring mesmerised at Lucy. The moment she had come on stage, something very odd had happened to him. It was almost as if he had never seen her before, and now his chest felt tight, his pulse raced, and a sensation midway between excitement and yearning had begun in the pit of his stomach. Surely this beautiful young woman couldn't be one and the same as the sad little girl he'd championed? He'd always been fond of her, of course, drawn to her in a way he'd never been drawn to Kitty. She's OK for a girl, he'd thought when they were children. But she wasn't a child any more, and neither was he. The heat in Joe's blood, the ache in his loins, excited yet unnerved him.

Overwhelmed by the enormity of the unfamiliar feelings he was experiencing, Joe wondered what in the world he was going to do about it.

'You were marvellous, Lucy!' Annie said.

They were walking home up the high street, quite slowly, since Kitty got dreadfully out of breath if she hurried. She'd never been a well girl since the bout of diphtheria, and Dr Blackmore had said he was afraid her heart had been damaged by it. In fact, Annie wasn't at all sure she should be out on such a cold night, but she'd wanted to come with them, and Annie hadn't had the heart to put her foot down about it. Kitty missed out on so much that other girls of her age could enjoy.

She was panting a little now and Lucy glanced anxiously at her sister. The fear that she might lose her had made her realise just how much she cared for her. There might have been friction between them in the past, she might sometimes have felt she didn't like Kitty very much, but she was still her sister, and Lucy knew she couldn't bear it if anything happened to her. She'd even come to feel oddly protective of her, as if she herself were the older sister instead of the younger.

Tonight, however, she was too fired up with the excitement of her performance to worry about Kitty for long. Exhilaration was singing in every vein and nerve ending; she felt that if she spread her arms wide she'd be able to fly, high above the rooftops of the grimy shops and houses that lined the high street, up, up into the velvet darkness, until she could touch the stars.

'Was I really all right?' Her voice trembled with that exhilaration.

'More than all right, my love,' Annie reaffirmed. 'Mr Bristow wouldn't have asked you to sing with them again if he hadn't been pleased, would he?'

'No, I suppose not . . .' A fresh rush of warmth flooded Lucy's veins at the thought; she could hardly wait to do it all again.

'What did you think, Kitty? Didn't you wish you were up there with me?'

'No I didn't. I don't like the limelight like you. But you did well. You're cut out for it, Lucy. You reminded me of Aunt Molly.'

'Really?' Lucy was thrilled; this was praise indeed. Though Molly still kept in touch with Annie, they hadn't seen her since that awful day when Algernon had thrown her out of the house, but the distance somehow only added to her aura as a glamorous and romantic figure.

'Joe?'

Joe was stomping along a step or two ahead of them, chin tucked down into the collar of his coat. He hadn't said a word since they'd left the hall. Now Lucy did a little skip to catch up with him and linked her arm through his.

'What did you think, Joe? Did you think I was good?'

'Yeah . . . yeah.' His tone was short and he pulled back from her a little, turning so that his shoulder made a barrier between them.

'Well don't sound so enthusiastic!' Lucy retorted, stung. 'Didn't you like it?'

'I said it was good, didn't I?' Still snappy, cool.

'No you didn't. Come on, Joe!' She pulled on his arm.

'For goodness' sake, Lucy, don't keep on! Everybody's told you, but you won't shut up about it.'

In the dark his face was flaming; the unfamiliar emotions were churning, and her arm, interlinked with his, was unsettling him even more.

'Be like that and see if I care!'

Lucy dropped his arm and fell back, linking up with Annie instead. But Joe's offhandedness had cast a shadow over her excitement. He meant a great deal to her, always had. When she was little, he'd been her hero; as they'd grown up, she'd shared her secrets with him, taken her troubles to him, and he'd always been there for her. Even when he'd got the scholarship and gone to Bath to school he'd still had time for her, though he had to leave early in the mornings to catch his train and was busy with homework in the evenings and at weekends. Since he'd left home to live in the rooms over the chemist shop she missed him dreadfully, and she'd been delighted that he had said he'd like to come to the concert. Now she simply couldn't understand why he was behaving so strangely. He'd been his usual self when he'd come home for tea so they could all go together, even joking with her about Algernon allowing her to perform.

'What's got into him? Is he going soft in his old age?'

'I don't think so,' she'd said ruefully. 'He's just as bad as ever, and now I'm working in the office at the glove factory I have to put up with him all day too. But you know how he likes sucking up to people, especially toffs like Stanley Bristow.'

'Got his eye on a motor car like his, has he?' Joe chortled. 'He'll be lucky!'

He'd wished her good luck, too, though she'd assured him she wouldn't need it because she was going to wear Aunt Molly's locket as a talisman, and then quickly added that she often wore the one he'd given her too, though that was not strictly true. Though she treasured it, it was nowhere near as pretty as the one Aunt Molly had given her.

Perhaps that was it, she thought now. Perhaps she'd upset him by choosing to wear Aunt Molly's locket for luck and not his. But it was such a long time since he'd given it to her; surely it wouldn't even have entered his head. Though of course it had been his mother's, and he'd always kept a likeness of Ella on the table beside his bed . . .

Oh, I don't know what's wrong with him, Lucy thought crossly, and tried to ignore the set shoulders and bent head of the young man stomping along a couple of steps ahead of them.

Joe might be in a bad mood, but she wasn't going to let it spoil what had been a wonderful and memorable evening.

Christmas was fast approaching, and amongst the cards that fell through the letter box each day was one from Molly. She still sent every year and Annie sent to her, though Algernon was unaware of it, and they hadn't met again since he had banned her from the house all those years ago. Annie always tucked the card away out of sight after she'd showed it to Lucy, but not to Kitty, since she couldn't be sure Kitty wouldn't make it her business to mention it to Algernon.

This year, as there so often was, there was a letter inside the card. Annie sat down at the kitchen table to read it, eager, as always, for news of her sister-in-law.

And this year what news there was! Molly, it seemed, had finally married her theatre-owning friend, and was now Mrs Daniel Trotter. There was an address, too, for her new home, in what Annie knew was a sought-after area on the outskirts of Bath.

Perhaps she was coming to the end of her career on the halls, Annie thought. She must, after all, be well into her forties by now, and though the big stars continued to work into middle age, Molly had never quite made that grade.

It looked as if she'd done well enough for herself, anyway, and Annie was pleased for her. She only wished that John's sister was still a part of their lives.

Kitty was at the dining table, painting.

It was one of the things she loved to do to fill her days – her ill health as a result of the diphtheria meant that going out to work as Lucy did was out of the question, just as it had been out of the question for her to pursue the education she'd been eager for. For one thing she'd missed a great deal of schooling, and though Algernon had spent as much time as he could helping her to catch up, Mr Shearn doubted she would make the grade, and even if she had, Annie didn't think she was well enough to travel all the way to Bath each day. So when she reached school-leaving age she simply stayed at home, sewing, crocheting, and helping out with the cooking and baking when she was up to it, and resting on the sofa with a book when she was not.

Later she'd expressed an interest in sketching and painting. Algernon had bought her a palette of watercolours, and she'd soon shown a real talent. 'I don't know where she gets it from!' Annie, who couldn't draw anything that didn't look like the efforts of a rather backward three-year-old, remarked in amazement as she admired the fine work Kitty produced – flowers so lifelike you could almost feel the dew on their velvety petals, fruit you'd have sworn you could pick up and eat.

Today she was painting a spray of holly that Annie had cut from a bush in the garden to put over one of the pictures in the living room. Though the colours of the dark green leaves and scarlet berries were much more vibrant than the delicate shades she usually favoured, her light touch was still there, and the berries and leaves seemed to gleam softly against the matt cream of the paper Algernon had managed to get for her – very expensive, Annie imagined, more like the vellum solicitors used to write wills on than the pages to be found in an ordinary drawing book.

'It's beautiful, darling,' Annie said. 'We should have it framed and hang it on the wall where everyone can see it. It's much nicer to look at than those dark old landscapes.'

'I haven't quite finished yet.' Kitty was adding tiny details.

'Well, I need the table cleared so I can set it for tea,' Annie said. 'Why don't you take everything into the parlour and work on Papa's desk – just as long as you cover it with newspaper first. You don't want to mark it with your water pot.'

Kitty did as she suggested, and was still there perfecting her painting when Algernon got home from work, along with Lucy.

'Where's Kitty?'

They were almost his first words when he had taken off his coat and was standing in front of the living room fire, jacket raised to warm his backside, just as they were almost every evening if she wasn't there to greet him. He worried about Kitty, Annie thought, in a way he never worried about her or Lucy or Joe. But then, she was very delicate, and she'd always been his favourite, presumably because she was more biddable than Lucy, and showed him a respect that bordered on sycophancy – not that Annie knew the word, but if she had she would have used it to describe the way Kitty behaved towards Algernon.

'She's in the parlour, finishing off a painting,' Annie said now. 'I told her she could work on your desk as long as she was careful not to make water marks. It's really lovely, Algernon, her best yet, I think. I told her we should hang it on the wall instead of those dreary old landscapes.'

Algernon scowled, offended by the implied criticism. 'Those dreary old landscapes as you call them are originals, and probably worth a pretty penny.'

'Kitty's is an original too!' Annie protested. 'And who knows, one day her paintings might be worth a pretty penny.'

She was, she thought, getting bolder in talking back to him, something she hadn't dared to do in the early years of their marriage, though there were still boundaries she knew better than to overstep, such as any mention of Molly.

When Algernon had warmed his buttocks to his satisfaction, he headed for the parlour; to make sure Kitty hadn't damaged his desk, Annie thought.

'What have we got for afters?' Lucy asked as she helped Annie set the table for tea – she'd already sniffed appreciatively at the pot of mutton stew that was bubbling on the stove.

'I thought we'd open a bottle of plums,' Annie said. 'I'll get them now.'

The plums she'd preserved were stored on a shelf in the cupboard under the stairs. After she'd fetched them, she went along the hall towards the front room intending to tell Algernon and Kitty that tea was almost ready. But in the doorway she stopped short, disturbed suddenly and almost inexplicably by the scene that met her eyes.

Kitty was seated at the desk, paintbrush poised over the picture, head bent. Algernon stood behind her, his hand resting on her shoulder. As Annie watched, Kitty turned her head, looking up at him, cheeks flushed, expression eager, and something about the intimacy between them sent a chill of unease through her.

For the moment she simply couldn't understand it. There was nothing remotely untoward in the little tableau; Algernon might have been any father admiring his daughter's work, Kitty any daughter relishing her father's approval. It was only later, worrying about it, that she realised what it was that had made her so uncomfortable.

Algernon was not Kitty's father. Kitty was not his daughter. And there was something not quite right about the way they had been looking at each other, the impression that they were in a little world all their own.

All evening, as she busied herself with making the rich fruit cake that would be the centrepiece of Christmas Day tea, the memory of it nagged at her, and Annie found herself remembering so many other little things – things that taken individually had had no real significance, but which, when put together, made her even more uncomfortable.

The times when she'd seen them whispering together. The occasions when Kitty was too poorly to come downstairs and Algernon went to her room and sat in the basket chair by her bed. The times when he scooped her up in his arms to carry her from one room to the other. The expensive art materials he had got for her. And, most of all, the way they were together, Kitty all flushed adoration, Algernon . . . well, Annie could barely find words to describe the way Algernon looked at Kitty when she came to think about it. Until recently she'd only ever seen that feverish glint in his eye when he was proclaiming the will of the Lord, but there was something guarded about it too, as if he was concealing a dark secret.

Algernon was a lustful man, she'd learned that to her cost. His predilections in the bedroom were much at odds with the sanctimonious and very proper man-of-God image he presented to the outside world. She'd told herself she couldn't expect every man to be as gentle and considerate as her beloved John had been, and in any case, she had loved John, enjoyed every moment of their intimacy, whilst she was still repelled by Algernon's touch, even more so now than she had been in the beginning.

Now, Annie felt a chill finger of fear touch her heart. Could it be that Algernon was tired of the coldness towards him that she was never quite able to hide? Could it be that he was looking elsewhere to satisfy that dark side of his nature he strove so hard to conceal from the outside world but which she knew only too well?

Surely not! He, of all people, would never stoop to defiling a child – her child! But then again, Kitty was no longer a child. She was nineteen years old, a young woman. The diphtheria might have damaged her heart and destroyed her hopes of a future that should have included a life outside these four walls, and perhaps a husband and children, but it had left no mark on her pretty face, nor stopped her from developing the body of a woman, albeit a delicate one. Which had, in some ways, given her a fragility that some men might find alluring.

I'm being stupid. Imagining things, Annie told herself.

But the anxiety still hovered at the edges of her consciousness, and, busy as she was, it would not go away.

Chapter Nine

On Christmas Eve, Joe was hard at work in the pharmacy, serving customers and making up medicines under the eagle eye of Richard Penny, the pharmacist, but for once his mind was not on the job.

'Think about what you're doing, lad,' Mr Penny admonished him as he fumbled with a phial. 'If you were to make a mistake with that dosage, you could cause the death of the patient.'

'Sorry, Mr Penny.'

'I should think so too! I don't know what it is you're so excited about. It's not as if you were a little boy waiting for Father Christmas to come down the chimney any more.'

Joe flushed. It wasn't Father Christmas who was on his mind. It was Lucy. Truth to tell, he'd thought about her almost constantly since the night of the concert. The difference was that today he was wondering if he dared do something about it. When the shop shut at five that evening, he would be going home for the holiday and he would be there for two whole days and nights, under the same roof. The thought of it filled him with apprehension. He didn't know how he could hide his new-found feelings for her, and he didn't know that he wanted to. It wasn't comfortable behind the defensive wall he'd erected when he'd realised the effect she was having on him. They'd grown too close over the years, and he knew Lucy was hurt and puzzled by the way he'd been behaving towards her in the first throes of confusion and embarrassment.

What he really wanted was to make a clean breast of it and find out if there was any chance she felt the same way. But at the same time the very idea frightened the life out of him. How would she react? She'd be taken by surprise, that much he was sure of. But what then? Dismay? Disgust even? Or, worse almost, supposing she laughed at him? His stomach contracted every time he imagined the moment. Once the words were spoken there could be no taking them back. Lucy, and the closeness they had shared, would be lost to him forever – unless, of course, by some miracle, she felt the same way.

But if he said nothing, then he almost certainly would miss his chance. He wouldn't be the only lad to fancy her; there would be plenty of others who'd set their cap at a pretty girl like her, and they wouldn't be so shy at trying their luck. If he lost her because he lacked the courage to make a move, he'd never forgive himself. Faint heart never won fair lady . . .

Hard as Joe tried to decide on a course of action, he felt as if he were caught in a crazy fairground from which there was no escape. Emotions whirling as if he were a gingerbread horse on a merry-go-round, elation and despair a see-saw powered by resolve and hope at the one end, fear of the consequences of speaking out at the other, and all the while his stomach churning with the perpetual pendulum motion of a swinging boat.

He had to do it. He had to tell her, and maybe the rewards would be everything he hoped for. And if not . . . His stomach churned again, but he tried not to think about that.

It would do no good at all if he made a bad mistake in dispensing the medicines and Mr Penny gave him the sack.

Time enough to worry about it when the shutters came down and the shop door was locked behind him.

With a supreme effort Joe tried to put his dilemma to the back of his mind and concentrate on his work.

Joe was not the only one dreaming romantic dreams that Christmas Eve. Annie, too, was in something of a dither, and the reason for it had nothing to do with her anxiety about Kitty's relationship with Algernon, which in any case she'd managed to convince herself was all a figment of her imagination.

As she used a taper to burn away the tiny nibs left on the skin of the cockerel for tomorrow's dinner – Mr Wright, the fowl man, had plucked it before delivering it to their door earlier in the day, but little bits of feather still clung to the carcass in places – Annie's mind was free to wander, and she allowed herself to dip in and out of the froth of delicious, but forbidden, emotions that were bubbling inside her.

Marcus Latcham was home for Christmas. She'd seen him arrive mid-afternoon with a suitcase that looked as if it held enough luggage for a stay of a few days – unless, of course, it was full of Christmas presents for his parents.

Since that long-ago day when she and the girls had met him on the train from Bath after Molly had given them a tour of the Lyric, she'd seen him only a handful of times, but when she did, her heart always missed a beat, and she was left with a glow inside that lifted her spirits and set her dreaming.

The thoughts she hardly dared articulate were the purest fantasy, of course – she knew that – but they were an oasis of pleasure in the monotonous and sometimes downright wretched pattern of her daily life with Algernon. She shouldn't entertain them for a moment, she knew, but still they prickled at her, and where, she asked herself, was the harm in that?

133

It wasn't as if there was the slightest chance of them ever becoming reality. Not only did Marcus live in London and only visit once or twice a year, he'd never given her the slightest indication that he saw her as anything other than the woman who lived next door to his parents. He never said a word that could be construed as anything but neighbourly, never looked at her in a flirtatious manner. And yet Annie had stored away every word that passed between them, every glance, to be taken out and relished when she was feeling low, and the muted excitement that suffused her when she thought of him was her guilty secret pleasure.

Take the time last summer when Edith Latcham's canary had escaped. The poor woman had been distraught, running up and down the road with the cage, calling the bird's name to no avail. And then Annie had seen him, a little flash of yellow, cowering in the corner of their back yard. She'd approached him cautiously, afraid he'd take fright and fly off again, and everyone knew the fate of brightly coloured little birds who braved the world outside their cages – they would be attacked by bigger wild birds and pecked to death. But Polly – as Edith had inexplicably named him – must have been exhausted; Annie had managed to catch him and carry him, carefully cupped between her hands, back to his delighted owner.

Edith had been almost too overcome to thank her properly, though her delight was recompense enough, but the next time Marcus visited, he had made a point of coming round to express his gratitude. The surprise of opening the front door to find him standing on the step had sent Annie into a tizzy, and though she'd managed to make all the normal responses – that it was nothing, no more than anyone would have done, and she was glad she'd been able to help and that Polly was safely back where he belonged – she couldn't help feeling she'd sounded garrulous and foolish, and that Marcus must have noticed her pink cheeks and flustered demeanour.

Then there had been the time when the prop with which she hoisted up her washing line had fallen down. Her clean sheets had been draped across the garden, dragging in the mud, and she had been struggling to rescue them when he'd appeared.

She hadn't even known he was home for a visit, but he must have seen what was happening from his bedroom window and come out to help her. On that occasion it wasn't to be wondered at that she was flustered – anyone would be, when the whole of the week's wash would have to be done again – but she knew it wasn't just the filthy sheets that were the cause of her inner turmoil. He'd helped her fold them into the laundry basket, rescued the prop, which was lying across the garden, and dug it in more securely, so that the smaller items that hadn't fallen into the dirt began blowing again, and commiserated with her over the minor catastrophe. And as she went through the unwelcome palaver of having to boil up the copper, wash the sheets and put them through the mangle once more, Annie had found herself singing, all the old favourites, as she hadn't done for years.

It was, she thought, as if she was a young girl again, besotted with her first beau. Silly, almost euphoric, with a head full of dreams and the marvellous feeling that something wonderful was hovering just around the corner.

Now he was home again for Christmas. Just the other side of the wall that divided their two houses. She probably wouldn't get to see him, much less speak to him, and even if she did it would be no more than to wish him a happy Christmas, and to entertain the hope of something more was not only foolish but downright wrong.

But a person could dream, couldn't they? Sometimes Annie thought that the moments when she fantasised about Marcus

Latcham were the only times that were hers and hers alone. Her secret, and all the more precious for it. When, for just a little while, she could almost become the woman she had once been, before the trials and tragedies of life had turned her into an abused wife and a drudge. Annie could lose herself in those moments, and guilty as they made her feel, foolish as she knew they were, yet they made all the rest more bearable.

Joe was no closer to deciding how he was going to approach Lucy by the time he reached the house on the outskirts of High Compton that he had long ago learned to call home. If anything he was in more of a turmoil than ever, and rather than going in by the front door, he unlatched the tall and solid wooden gate at the entrance to the side passage and walked past the sheds and the coal house to the back yard.

The kitchen window was open, letting out steam and an aroma that reminded him of all the Christmases he had ever known. As he turned the heavy handle and opened the back door, the evocative smells encompassed him. Hot sugar and spice, baking pastry, and the pungent, lingering stink of singed feathers.

'Joe! You're here!' Annie straightened, holding a tray of mince pies fresh from the oven with a tea cloth to protect her hands.

'Just at the right moment by the look of it!'

He dumped his carpet bag, containing a change of clothes and the gifts he'd brought for the family, on the tiled floor, and reached for a pie, then gasped, dropping it just as quickly.

'Ouch! They're burning hot!' he complained, blowing on his fingers.

'Serves you right for being so impatient. You can jolly well wait like everyone else,' Annie said tartly, but she was smiling too, her mouth curving irrepressibly in her flushed face, a face he'd grown to love. Nobody could ever replace the mother he had lost, but Annie had come as close as anyone ever could. Ella was just a sweet sad memory now; Annie was the one who'd been there for him in sorrow and in joy.

A sudden unwelcome thought struck him. What would Annie have to say if she knew how he felt about Lucy? What if she thought badly of him for it? For all her gentleness, if something upset her Annie wasn't afraid to speak her mind.

Though not to Algernon. Never to Algernon. She was like a different person when he was around. Meek, afraid almost of saying the wrong thing. Joe hadn't really noticed it until he'd left home, but he noticed now . . .

'Happy Christmas, Joe.' Kitty was at the kitchen table, rolling out pastry for yet more mince pies. She too was flushed from the heat of the kitchen, but unlike Annie, it was not a healthy flush. It sat on her pasty-pale cheeks like badly applied rouge.

Joe didn't really notice, though. He had other things – someone else – on his mind.

'Happy Christmas, Kitty. Though it's not until tomorrow.'

'And we've still got a thousand things to do.' Annie was sliding a knife under the mince pies she'd just taken out of the oven and upending them where they stood until they were cool enough to put on the wire tray she had ready. 'Take your things upstairs out of the way, and then you can help.'

'Help?' Joe grinned. 'I wouldn't want to eat the mince pie I'd make!'

'And nor would anybody else, I should think. But you can give Lucy a hand putting up the holly and mistletoe for a start. You're taller than she is, and I don't want her falling off a chair and breaking an arm or a leg.'

All Joe's turmoil returned with a rush, an unsettling combination of eagerness and panic.

'Where is she?'

'I don't know. We've not seen hide nor hair of her since we started baking. She's no more of a pastry cook than you are.'

Joe grinned. No, domestic skills weren't among Lucy's attributes. It was one of the things that made her different from most girls.

'I'll get out of your hair then,' he said, picking up his bag.

He went through the living room and into the hall. No Lucy. The front room door was ajar; through the crack he could see Algernon at his desk, finalising his notes for his part in tomorrow's service at chapel, no doubt. Joe didn't call out a greeting; relations between him and Algernon were as strained as they had ever been, and in any case, Algernon hated any interruption when he was working.

He hoisted his bag over one shoulder and ran up the stairs, taking care not to let it swing into the aspidistra that stood on the sill of the window near the top. Four bedrooms led off a narrow landing, two large ones, and two small ones, hardly bigger than box rooms, one at each end. His was at the front of the house, with a view of the road when the sycamore tree wasn't in full leaf; when it was, the branches sometimes slapped against the window and made the room dim and, some might say, gloomy, but Joe liked it. When he was a little boy, he'd pretended he lived in a tree house.

Although he stayed in the apartment above the chemist shop all week, Annie had ensured that his room at home remained exclusively his, and all his old things were still there – his books, a draughts board and men he'd made himself in woodwork class, and even the box containing his toy soldiers were still stacked on the shelf above the narrow bed.

There had been one change in the family's sleeping arrangements since the old days, though. Whereas the two girls had once shared the second of the two big bedrooms, Kitty now had it to herself. Following her illness, Annie had cleared all the clutter from the little back bedroom and Lucy had moved in there. It made sense, since Kitty was so often poorly, and likely to keep Lucy awake at night with her coughing and struggling for breath, and besides, now they were grown up, they both valued their own space.

As he rounded the bend in the stairs, Joe could see a glimmer of light coming from Lucy's room. He took the last two stairs more hesitantly, wondering what to do. In the old days he'd have barged in without even bothering to knock, though since they'd grown up he'd come to respect her privacy as she did his. But now the very thought of entering the room where she slept, dressed and undressed made his face redden and he was overcome with uncharacteristic self-consciousness. Stupid – stupid! He'd never been shy – it was a feeling he scarcely recognised. All he knew was he felt horribly awkward and indecisive.

'Joe – is that you?'

Her voice cut through his confusion, his heart thudded in his chest.

'Yeah, it's me. Can I come in?'

'Of course you can! Don't be silly.'

He pushed the door open. She was sitting on the bed, surrounded by an assortment of wrapped Christmas gifts. One lay in her lap; she was attaching a label with a length of red twine to the ribbon around it.

'I'm just finishing these off,' she said, then quickly grabbed up one of the packages, pushing it under the pillow. 'You're not supposed to see that one.'

'For me, is it?' He made a playful dive for the pillow; she slapped his hand away.

'Don't you dare! You've got to wait till tomorrow like everyone else.'

'I don't know!' he grumbled. 'Presents, mince pies, seems I'm not allowed any of it.'

'No, you're not. Until tomorrow.' She cleared a space on the bed beside her and patted it. 'Sit down and tell me what you've been up to.'

And suddenly all his self-consciousness was back, making his neck prickle beneath the tight collar of the shirt he wore for work, the easy camaraderie of the last few moments dispelled as if it had never been.

'I'm going to get changed out of my best suit. Then your ma wants us to put up the holly and mistletoe.'

'Oh bother!' Lucy complained. 'I hate doing that. I always prick myself on the holly, and what's the point of mistletoe?'

'Well, it's for kissing under,' Joe said, surprising himself with his daring.

'Chance would be a fine thing! Nobody's going to kiss me.'

There was something in her tone, mock rueful yet almost teasing, that brought Joe up short. He glanced at her, head cocked to one side, eyes wide and guileless, lips pursed slightly, almost as if they were ready to be kissed. Was she flirting? He was probably imagining it. But Joe's heart gave a little thud all the same.

'You never know,' he said jokingly.

Then, before she could reply, and before he could give away the fact that he wasn't joking at all, he backed out the door and went along the landing to his own room, elation and determination taking the place of his earlier confusion.

He might have got it all wrong, it wouldn't be the first time, but at least he'd seen a way to find out if there was a chance for him without having to spell it out. She might knock him back, he'd have to be prepared for that, but he wouldn't lose too much face; he could always pass it off as a bit of horseplay.

Joe dumped his bag on the narrow bed, took off his coat and hung it up behind the door. For the first time all day he felt purposeful and optimistic. Perhaps it would be a happy Christmas after all.

They did the holly first, selecting the best-shaped branches from the bunch that Annie had picked from the garden and a tree in the field at the back of the house, tucking it behind the pictures that hung in the living room and hall and putting what was left into the tall china vase on the chiffonier.

The mistletoe Annie had bought from a gypsy who'd come selling it door to door. It was tied neatly into sheaves, but the berries were beginning to turn a little brown and drop off. They'd harvested it too soon, Annie suspected, but beggars couldn't be choosers. It grew far too high in the trees for her to be able to collect any herself, and Christmas wouldn't be Christmas without mistletoe.

'Be careful with it,' she warned Lucy when she collected it from the back yard where Annie had put it to stand in a jug in the hope of reviving it. 'And do try not to drip water everywhere.'

'Where do you want it?' Lucy asked, pocketing a ball of twine and the kitchen scissors.

'The usual places – you know. In the doorways. The nails are still there from last year.'

'Couldn't we hang some from the lamp in the hall?'

'No, we could not. We don't want to set the house on fire. And just be careful. Let Joe do the climbing. Though I expect he can reach anyway, if you make a loop in the twine before you start.'

'I think we can manage to hang a few bunches of mistletoe,

Mam,' Lucy said pertly. 'Joe, let's put one up here, between the kitchen and the living room. Then Mam can see for herself that we're perfectly capable.'

She tied off a bunch, and, as Annie had said, Joe was able to hook the loop over the nail in the doorway with no effort at all.

'See?' Lucy said. 'Is that to your satisfaction, madam?'

'Very good.' Annie thought that if the berries began falling off they would be right in the treadway and she'd have to make sure and sweep them up before they got trodden into a mush, but she wasn't going to say so.

Lucy and Joe went into the living room, where they hung another bunch in the doorway leading into the hall. They still had some over.

'I really would like to put some on the lamp,' Lucy said in a low voice.

'Your mam said—'

'I know what she said, but where's the harm? It's not going to catch fire as long as we make sure it's not anywhere near the flame. And when you see pictures of grand houses decorated for Christmas, they always have bunches of mistletoe hanging in the hall. Come on, Joe! Don't be a spoilsport!'

'Well . . . we'll try if you like, but she's not going to be best pleased.'

'She probably won't even notice, and if she does, she'll see it's perfectly safe. Bet you she doesn't make us take it down again.'

They went into the hall. The parlour door was closed now; perhaps Algernon had heard Joe come home and was making sure he would not be interrupted. Joe pulled on the cord to extinguish the gas before attempting the decoration; enough light spilled out from the living room and in through the glass panel in the front door for him to be able to see what he was doing. Lucy twisted twine round the last remaining bunch of mistletoe and tied it securely, leaving two ends long enough to loop around the gas bracket. Joe took it from her and reached up. Tall as he was, this was more awkward than the doorways had been. He fetched a chair from the living room and climbed up on it, his head almost brushing the ceiling as he tied the ends of the twine round the bracket.

'How's that?'

'Perfect!' Lucy stood back to admire the effect, hands clasped, laughing.

In the dim light, the curves of her upturned face looked soft and delectable; though there was no gas flame to reflect in them, it seemed to Joe that her blue eyes were shining the way they had when she'd been on stage in the town hall. His stomach clenched. He reckoned it was now or never.

He stepped down from the chair too quickly – one of his feet caught a strut and it almost toppled over.

'Careful!' Lucy reached out to save it; Joe regained his balance and, before he could lose his nerve, made a grab for her.

'Oh!' It wasn't a cry, more a startled little gasp. And then his mouth was on hers, stifling even that tiny sound.

For a moment she was stiff in his arms, unresponsive, and he thought she would push him away. Then her arms went round his neck, her small firm breasts pressing into his chest, her lips moving beneath his. He drew back a little, lifting his mouth from hers, looking down at the soft curves of her face, feeling the love exploding inside him.

'See?' he teased. 'I told you you might get kissed under the mistletoe, didn't I?'

Her lips curved; she opened her eyes, smiling up at him.

'Only the once?'

'You want some more?'

For answer she lifted her face and pulled his down. This time there was no hesitation, her mouth moving instantly beneath his, though it was still a chaste kiss.

And then the rattle of the door handle just a few feet away from them broke the spell. They jumped apart hastily – just in time before the door opened and Algernon emerged.

'Why is the light out?' were his first words.

'We've been putting up mistletoe . . .' Lucy sounded a little flustered, but Algernon appeared not to notice.

'Mistletoe? Christmas is a Christian festival to celebrate the birth of our Lord Jesus Christ. Mistletoe is purely pagan, a symbol of lust and depravity.'

'Oh, don't make us take it down, please!'

Algernon grunted, an exasperated shake of his head leaving them in no doubt as to his feelings on the matter. But he said no more about it, merely turning his back on them and disappearing into the living room.

Lucy clapped her hands over her mouth, suppressing the giggles that threatened to betray her, and quite suddenly Joe wanted to laugh too, the laughter that came with relief and the release of the tension that had been plaguing him all day.

'Silly old killjoy,' Lucy whispered from behind her hand.

'You've got to feel sorry for him,' Joe replied.

And for perhaps the first time in his life he really meant it. Algernon seemed only to find pleasure in sanctimonious misery. 'Killjoy' was a good word for him.

But just at that moment, not a single thing Algernon could have said or done would kill the joy Joe was feeling. He'd kissed Lucy, and she'd kissed him back. She hadn't pushed him away in disgust or laughed at him.

Just a kiss under the mistletoe it might have been, but to Joe it felt like the whole world was opening up before him. Algernon Pierce and his funny, miserable ways could not matter less. He thought he stood a chance with Lucy, and that trumped everything.

Algernon stalked away from Lucy and Joe and into the living room, seething with righteous disgust. Did they really think he was so stupid he didn't know what they'd been up to? That he hadn't seen them jump apart, all pretended innocence? Did Joe think he hadn't noticed the lustful looks he cast at Lucy, or her provocative behaviour when she was in his presence? He didn't entirely blame Joe – he was fast becoming a man, and base instincts were part of the nature of men, God help them, though he accepted such depravity as part of the Almighty's plan for procreation.

He remembered too well the lusts and longings that had plagued and shamed him when he had first begun to notice the temptations of a female form, the nights when he had been unable to resist the urge to relieve the unbearable tension by pleasuring himself, and then climbed from his bed where the evidence of his sin was growing cold upon the sheets, and fallen to his knees to beg the forgiveness of his Maker.

Those days were gone now; he'd ensured there was always a woman in his bed to give him satisfaction, but the dark urges still possessed him, even he, a man of God. Sometimes he despised himself for them. If he had been an old-style priest he would have willingly donned the hair shirt as penance and taken perverted pleasure from the pain of skin rubbed raw and bleeding flesh; as things stood, he took out his disgust on those around him. But when the lust was in him, he gloried in it, savouring every moment. Men were blessed and cursed, not a doubt of it, though not all, he knew, had the grace to be ashamed of it, and he feared that Joe, who never attended chapel any more, who had taken up smoking, and partook of the demon drink, might well be one of those.

Lucy, though – Lucy was a different kettle of fish and he feared for her. The signs had been there since childhood: the lack of proper respect for authority, the mischievous streak that all too easily became outright naughtiness or disobedience. He had hoped her mother's influence would set her on the right path; Annie was, for the most part, a decent enough woman, though there had been times when he'd had to discipline her so as to mould her into the wife he required her to be. But those traits he believed he had successfully eradicated in Annie were all too apparent in Lucy. She was destined for trouble, that one, if he was not much mistaken.

Why could she not be more like her sister, who was in the kitchen now, baking, as a woman should, not flirting and acting up with a young man? He stood in the doorway looking at Kitty, prettily pale, as demure as he could wish. The little girl who had sat on his lap as he taught her her sums. The adolescent he had carried in his arms when she was sick. The young woman who looked at him now with the same adoration in her eyes as she had when he'd first rescued the three of them from the penury of the life that would almost certainly have been theirs following the pit tragedy that had taken her father's life.

Dark pleasure stirred in Algernon's gut as it always did when he could feast his eyes on her.

Kitty. Kitty the pure. Kitty the biddable. Kitty, whom he'd trained as he might have trained a puppy or a kitten, if he had ever had one. There had been no imperfections ingrained in her when he had begun to teach her; he had no fear that beneath her compliant manner rebellion might lurk, as he felt might be the case with her mother. And the consequences of the dreadful illness that had so nearly taken her from him that long-ago Christmas now kept her confined to the home. She would never be sullied by the evils of the outside world – just so long as the evils of the outside world did not come to her. He'd seen off the aunt long ago; she had been the living epitome of everything he wanted Kitty protected from. But Joe he couldn't bar from the house, not unless he wanted to forfeit the respect of the townsfolk who admired his generosity and goodness in raising the boy as his own. He would need a reason for that which everyone could understand and sympathise with.

Perhaps he should be grateful to Lucy for her flighty ways. Perhaps, without knowing it, they were playing into his hands, and providing him with good reason to bar them both from the house. That way he would be able to keep Kitty safe. For her sake – and for his own.

Chapter Ten

Lucy was floating through Christmas Day on a cloud of mystery and magic, so that she felt a little as she had used to in those long-ago days when she had still believed in Father Christmas. But the reason for her happiness was, of course, quite different, and the sharp little prickles of excitement that tingled inside her were unlike anything she'd ever experienced before.

Last night Joe had kissed her, and it had been wonderful. She kept remembering the way it had felt, his mouth on hers, his arms around her, her heart beating so hard she'd thought it would burst out of her chest. Joe had kissed her, and it was exactly what she'd been longing for him to do, though she'd scarcely acknowledged it. For weeks now she'd felt a sort of yearning deep inside, a restless ache she couldn't really identify except that she knew it had to do with Joe. She missed him, she'd supposed, now that he was living over the chemist's shop; he'd been her friend and champion for so long and the house felt empty without him. Yet at the same time she knew instinctively it was more than that. There was an aura about him now that was unfamiliar; he seemed to her to have become a little like a fairy-tale hero, not a prince exactly, but certainly of that ilk.

And then, all of a sudden, he'd begun acting strangely, cutting her off, avoiding her, it seemed, and Lucy had been hurt and puzzled. She'd done everything she could to tease him out of it, but nothing had worked.

Last night when he'd come home he'd seemed more his usual self, coming to her room to see her, but he had still been tense and awkward somehow, quite unlike the old easy-going Joe. It was almost, she had thought, as if he had something on his mind, and the dreadful thought struck her – had he met a girl? Was that why he was acting differently, because he'd fallen in love and was embarrassed to tell them? Suddenly she was quite sure that must be it and she was shocked by how much it upset her. She couldn't bear the thought of him with another girl, it made her feel quite sick and totally wretched, though she'd tried to hide it under the guise of her usual gay banter. Even worse would be if Joe knew the way she was feeling; her pride could not allow that.

And then he'd kissed her and everything had come suddenly, miraculously right. At first so happy was she, she could hardly think straight, then, gradually, the little doubts had come creeping in, because she simply couldn't believe this euphoria was real. What if he'd done it only in fun? What would he think of her for kissing him back the way she had? Colour rose in her cheeks as she remembered just how she'd responded.

She'd been almost afraid to face him this morning, but she need not have worried. Joe was back to his old self, the same happy-go-lucky lad he'd always been, except that now there was something more, some frisson between them that crackled and fizzed. When their glances met she could feel herself flushing all over again, this time from pleasure, and when they took their places at the dinner table and his hand brushed hers, her flesh tingled with sudden awareness. Lucy covered the spot where his fingers had touched with her other hand, as if she could somehow freeze the delicious sensation in time, and keep it safe forever.

The whole of the day had been touched by magic; she felt as if she was floating on a cloud somewhere in a world that was new and exciting and full of promise. She was in love – with Joe, her childhood friend, her protector, her champion. And perhaps he was in love too, not with some unknown girl, but with her. Lucy could think of nothing more perfect.

'Why don't we go out for a walk? It's a nice afternoon, and I reckon we could do with some exercise after that great big dinner we've just had,' Joe said.

'Oh Joe, I really think I'd rather just sit down and put my feet up,' Annie sighed, and Algernon mumbled something non-committal.

Lucy, though, was on her feet in an instant.

'What a good idea!'

'Kitty?' Joe felt obliged to ask, though what he really wanted was to be alone with Lucy, and he was mightily relieved when she shook her head.

'I don't think so, Joe. I'll only slow you down.'

Not half as much as I intend to slow down if I get my chance with Lucy! Joe thought, but he couldn't help feeling sorry for Kitty, always being left out of things.

'We can go at your pace,' he said.

'No, really,' Kitty said. 'I'm a bit tired. I think I overdid things yesterday.'

'You did,' Annie chided her. '*I'm* tired out, and I don't have your bad heart. You'll sit here and take things easy, my girl. And you be sure to wrap up warm, Lucy,' she added. 'The sun might be shining, but it's a bitter wind, and you don't want to go catching a chill. You've got the New Year's concert next week, don't forget.'

As if she would! Lucy was really looking forward to it, but she didn't think it was wise to talk too much about the concert in front of Algernon any more than it would be to let him see how eager she was to be alone with Joe. Algernon had a nasty habit of spoiling everything.

'I'll get my coat,' she said.

They left the others relaxing by the fire and set out. As Annie had said, though the sun was shining there was no real warmth in it. The wind had dropped, thankfully, but the chill in the air foretold a bitter frost to come later. By the time they reached the gate leading to the track that ran along beside the river, Lucy's cheeks and ears were tingling. She made to thrust her hand into the pocket of her coat – gloves were no real protection against the cold – but Joe caught it with his own, a simple, almost friendly gesture, but one that set her pulse racing.

They crossed the river by way of a rickety wooden bridge, Joe helping her down the steep bank and up the other side, then taking her hand again as they walked along the path on the edge of the woods that ran all the way down to the riverbank. Dead leaves crunched beneath their feet – luckily it had been quite dry lately, for in wet weather there would have been swampy patches to negotiate. After a while the woods ended abruptly and the path led up the outskirts to a gate into a farmer's field. In summer it would be closed, and tied with a chain or a hank of rope, to keep in a herd of cows, but today it stood half open.

'Perhaps we've gone far enough,' Joe said. 'It will start to get dark soon.'

'I suppose.'

'Anyway, there's something I want to give you.'

Lucy was surprised. 'But I thought I'd already had my Christmas present.'

The family had exchanged gifts this morning sitting around the living room fire after they'd got back from chapel and while they were waiting for the cockerel to finish roasting and the potatoes and Brussels sprouts to come to the boil. Joe had given Algernon a propelling pencil; the miserable man had only grunted and examined it to test its quality, and Lucy had seethed inwardly, guessing the purchase had cost Joe a lot of thought – since Algernon was far from being the easiest man to buy a present for – not to mention a good deal of money he could ill afford. There had been little bottles of perfume for her, Annie and Kitty: rose water for Annie, lavender for Kitty and something a little spicy for her – Lucy was not sure what it was, but she thought it smelled a little like wallflowers. They'd begun selling perfumes in the chemist's shop, so they were an obvious choice of gift for Joe to make really, but she'd thanked him profusely and dabbed some on her wrists and behind her ears right away so that he would know she was pleased with it.

Now, though, Joe delved into the pocket of his coat and pulled out a small box. It wasn't wrapped – Lucy imagined that wrapping it would have been a fiddly job, and in any case, Joe would probably have thought it unnecessary.

'I didn't want to give you this in front of the others.' His awkwardness was back; she could see he was a bit embarrassed. 'It's nothing really, but I saw it and thought of you.'

'Oh Joe!'

Lucy took off her gloves, stuffed them in her pocket, and opened the box. Inside, nestling on a bed of jeweller's wool, was a cameo brooch set in a surround of what looked like silver.

'Oh Joe!' she said again. 'You shouldn't have!'

'Don't you like it?' He sounded anxious.

'I love it! It's beautiful! But—'

'Remember I gave you my mam's locket years ago? And your Aunt Molly gave you one a thousand times better? Well I wanted to get you something special, and I reckoned at least this time she wouldn't be around to top it.'

'But I love that locket!' Lucy's heart was melting. 'And it was your mam's, and that makes it more special than if it was the Crown Jewels. You shouldn't have spent so much money on me, that's all.'

'I wanted to,' he said, his tone gruff. 'Because *you're* special, Lucy. To me, anyway.'

'And you're special to me. But I haven't got anything nice for you.'

'That scarf you gave me is nice.'

'But not like this . . .'

'And you're here, aren't you? That's all I wanted really.'

Unexpectedly, there was a lump in Lucy's throat and her eyes filled with tears.

'Don't go crying!' Joe said, embarrassed. 'There's nothing to cry about. Do you want to put it on?'

Lucy nodded wordlessly and unbuttoned her coat. But her fingers felt clumsy from the cold and she didn't trust herself not to drop the brooch.

'Can you do it for me?'

'I'll try.' Joe fumbled awkwardly. 'Oh, I'm worse than you. P'raps we'd better leave it.'

'No, I want to wear it.' Lucy took the brooch back from him, managed to flip the catch, slip the pin through the fabric of her dress and secure it. 'There – how does it look?'

Joe nodded. 'Yeah, fine.' He reached out, pretending to straighten it, then his fingers moved from the brooch, tracing a path to her shoulder and upwards until they reached the soft skin of her neck. Lucy stood motionless, scarcely able to breathe, then, as she felt his breath warm on her cold cheek, she leaned towards him.

It wasn't just two quick kisses this time, it was a dozen or more, each deeper and more lingering than the last. Not a single word was spoken; none were needed. They clung together like two people drowning in a storm. Lucy loved the feel of Joe's arms around her, loved the taut muscles of his back and the slight rasp of the skin of his neck beneath her fingers, loved the excitement of the new sensations coursing through her, loved the warmth, the closeness, the feeling of togetherness.

But most of all she loved the kisses. For now she wanted nothing more.

Lucy and Joe had scarcely left for their walk, and Annie was brewing a pot of tea in the kitchen, when she saw a shadow pass the window and a moment later there was a knock at the back door. Her heart leapt into her throat. Marcus Latcham! It had to be. Visitors rarely came by way of the back garden, but a little trackway led between the rear of the two houses.

Flustered, Annie opened the door, and sure enough, it was Marcus, looking suave and handsome as ever. He hadn't bothered to put on an overcoat and he stood on the doorstep chafing his arms against the cold so that the sleeves of his shirt ruffled up and down over the smart gold wristlets that held them in place.

'I hope I'm not disturbing you, but we wondered if you and your family would like to join us this evening for a glass of sherry and a mince pie.' He smiled, that smile that crinkled his eyes, the smile Annie pictured so clearly in all her foolish daydreams. She'd love to accept the invitation, but she knew Algernon would never agree.

'It's very kind of you,' she said, 'but I don't think my husband . . . He's very much against alcohol, I'm afraid.'

Marcus raised an eyebrow. 'Surely sherry hardly counts as the demon drink?'

Annie laughed nervously, concerned that she'd offended him, both by her refusal of his invitation and by the suggestion that a glass of sherry was somehow immoral if not downright wicked.

'It's his religion,' she said apologetically. 'And he's a stalwart of the Temperance League.'

Marcus's eyebrow quirked again. 'That's a shame. I always think a drink is one of the pleasures of Christmas, along with the plum pudding and the carol singing.'

'Oh, I do agree.'

It's not me, it's him, Annie wanted to say, but of course she didn't. That would be dreadfully disloyal. But a sudden thought struck her, and before she could lose her nerve, she said what had popped into her head.

'We shall be having carols later. I play the piano a little, and we always have a sing-song. Why don't you and your mother and father join us?'

'Isn't a sing-song a little frivolous for your husband?' Marcus enquired blithely.

Annie didn't think there was any need to point out that carols, being religious in nature, didn't count amongst Algernon's many taboos.

'Do come, please!' she urged him. 'It would be so nice to have company.'

Marcus smiled, that nice smile that lit up his rather serious face.

'Well, I can't speak for my mother and father. My mother is, as you know, very deaf, and would probably throw everyone else out of tune anyway. But I'll accept your kind invitation. What time shall we say?'

The way he'd worded that flustered Annie all over again. Not 'What time shall I arrive?' but 'What time shall we say?' as if it was an arrangement just between the two of them.

'About half past seven?' she suggested.

When he had gone, she closed the door and leaned against it, hands pressed to her mouth, trembling at her own daring. What was Algernon going to have to say about it? But she didn't think he'd object too much – he was very impressed by the fact that their mostly absent neighbour was employed at Buckingham Palace; Marcus was exactly the sort of person he liked to associate with. And even if he did object, for once in her life she really didn't care.

The winter sun was pale and low in the sky before Lucy and Joe got home. No holding hands now, once they were in sight of the house; they weren't ready yet for anyone, least of all Annie and Algernon, to see the evidence of their new-found closeness. It was still their secret, too precious and tender to be shared, and besides, they were shy, ashamed almost, of their turbulent emotions. They hadn't done anything wrong, they weren't brother and sister, but others might not see it that way, and although neither articulated as much, even to themselves, the unacknowledged reservation hung somewhere in the back of their minds like a tiny cloud in the azure sky of a sparkling summer's day.

For all their caution, however, there was no hiding it from Annie. She'd begun to be concerned that they had been gone so long, though she couldn't imagine what harm could have befallen them, but the looks that had passed between them hadn't escaped her, and when they eventually returned, her suspicions were confirmed. There was a flush to Lucy's cheeks that wasn't solely due to coming into a warm house from the cold outside, and a glow about her that was new. And Joe – well, Joe looked conspicuously pleased with himself.

Then, of course, there was the brooch. Annie noticed it the moment Lucy took off her coat, but stopped short of mentioning it. But when she went into the kitchen to cut bread and butter and rich fruit cake, and put the kettle on to make a fresh brew, Lucy followed her and pointed it out.

'Joe gave it to me, Mam,' she said proudly. 'Isn't it beautiful? But he didn't want to give it to me in front of Kitty, because he couldn't afford one for both of us, and he didn't want her to feel left out.'

'That was very sweet of him,' Annie said, 'but what will you say when Kitty sees it and asks where it came from?'

Lucy's face clouded; she felt sorry for Kitty, who never went anywhere and who was never likely to have a boy like Joe to share kisses with.

'Do you think I should take it off?'

Annie hesitated, torn between her two daughters. 'I don't know, Lucy. You must do what you think is right.'

Lucy's hand went to the cameo, but she didn't unfasten it, just ran her fingers over the raised silhouette, the expression on her face leaving Annie in no doubt as to what it meant to her.

'Joe will be ever so hurt if he sees I'm not wearing it.'

'Then I'm sure you'll find a way to explain it to Kitty,' Annie said.

Suddenly, glad though she was for Lucy, she was overcome with a wave of almost unbearable sadness.

She'd been not much older than Lucy was now when she'd fallen in love with John, and she could still remember so clearly the way she had felt, the dizzying happiness, the delicious anticipation, the feeling of a whole new world opening up for her. Why, oh why, had it all had to end so soon and so tragically? Even when that first magic had faded a little they had still been so very happy and she had loved him so much.

John, oh John! her heart cried, and for a moment she felt she would burst with the wanting of him.

But John was gone forever. Annie gave herself a little shake and pulled herself together. Wallowing in long-buried grief would do no good – it never had, though in the beginning there had been times when she could have drowned in it. But she'd had the girls to provide for, and she thought she'd managed that pretty well. They'd grown up wanting for nothing, except, of course, a father's love, and she was proud of them both. It had cost her dear, but now she had to get on with her life as it was and make the best of it. And if entertaining a few foolish fantasies about Marcus Latcham helped her survive, she didn't think John would begrudge her them.

All she could hope for now was that fate would deal Lucy, Kitty, and Joe a kinder hand than it had dealt her.

They were her world; their happiness was the only thing that really mattered.

* * *

In the bleak midwinter
Frosty wind made moan
Earth stood hard as iron
Water like a stone . . .

The voices, raised in unison, filled the parlour. Lucy's, sweet and strong, Kitty's, melodic but much softer, Joe's, enthusiastic when he could remember the words, Annie singing along as she played, even Algernon joining in, though his delivery was rather disconcerting, a low mutter that occasionally boomed out in a stentorian roar. And leaning casually against the corner of the mantelpiece, Marcus, who had arrived promptly at seven thirty as arranged, had surprised them all with a pleasant baritone voice. Algernon seemed to have accepted his presence with good grace, and there was hot fruit punch to make up for the lack of alcohol, which they sipped between carols.

'I hear Lucy is making quite a name for herself locally,' Marcus said during one of the pauses. 'Perhaps she could give us a solo while the rest of us get a second wind.'

Lucy flushed with pleasure to think her reputation was spreading so that even deaf old Mrs Latcham had heard about her, but a glance at Kitty told her that her sister was less impressed.

'Kitty and I used to sing together at chapel anniversaries,' she said quickly. 'We could do a duet.'

'Oh no . . .' Kitty protested.

'"Silent Night". You can do the tune and I'll do the harmony. Come on, Kitty! It's ages since we sang together.'

'Oh . . . all right.'

Lucy wasn't sure if her sister's reluctance was genuine or pretended, but she tugged on Kitty's hand, drawing her over to the piano.

Annie played the introduction and they began, watching one another at first, then gaining confidence. Lucy tempered her strong voice so as not to overpower her sister, and their voices blended perfectly as they had used to do. As the haunting melody came to an end, there was a moment's complete silence, then Marcus began to clap, and Joe joined in. Annie was beaming with pride. Only Algernon remained mute, scowling, and rasping his fingers over the knees of his trousers.

159

A perfect rendering of a beautiful Christmas carol it might have been, but seeing Kitty performing with her sister had raised his hackles none the less, reminding him that corruption was never far away. An unwelcome vision rose in his mind of that long-ago day when he'd come home to find the whole family joining in the disgraceful rendition of 'The Man Who Broke the Bank at Monte Carlo' with that shameless woman Molly Day, decked out in his best bowler hat and swinging his cane, and Algernon was determined Kitty should not be sucked back into that kind of depravity by her flighty sister.

Marcus Latcham was calling for more; it was the moment to intervene.

'You are overtiring yourself, my dear,' he said to Kitty (she was the only one to whom he ever used any term of endearment). 'Let us retire to the living room and leave the merrymaking to those strong enough to endure it.'

'Oh Algernon!' Annie remonstrated. 'She's enjoying herself, aren't you, Kitty? And it is Christmas!'

'And what better day to ponder the story of the nativity? Come, my dear, we'll read from the Gospels.'

He crossed to the door, holding it open.

'I am a bit tired,' Kitty said, following him.

The discomfort Annie had begun to feel about the relationship between the two of them stirred, and her eyes followed the compliant figure anxiously. This was not the moment to confront it, but even as she began to pick out the notes of 'O Come, All Ye Faithful', the misgivings remained, a cloud over her enjoyment of the festive gathering.

'When am I going to see you again?' Joe asked Lucy.

It was Boxing Day, the crisp cold weather was holding, and they'd gone for another walk.

'Oh – I don't know.' Lucy hadn't thought beyond the moment. She and Joe were alone together again, the magic was singing all around her and the strange sensations, more familiar now, were quivering in her stomach and sending little flare paths shooting to the deepest parts of her.

They'd held hands, stood close together in a gateway far from prying eyes and kissed. He'd blown gently on her fingers to warm them when she'd complained they were freezing, and then tucked them inside his coat so she could feel the beating of his heart. They'd lived only for the moment. Now, with a little shock, she realised that tomorrow he would be gone, back to his billet over the chemist's shop, and being together wasn't going to be easy at all. She went to work each day with Algernon, and home again at night, and at this time of year, when it was dark by four o'clock, there was no reason to go out again, unless it was for one of her concerts. And even then Annie would accompany her, even if Stanley Bristow picked them up in his motor car as he had promised to do if the venue was further afield. Annie would never countenance Lucy going alone – she was far too young, and some audiences could become a bit rowdy.

The concerts, though, provided the only excuse she could think of for getting out of the house. One had been arranged to take place at the town hall in a couple of weeks' time – perhaps when she'd finished her turn, she could slip away and meet Joe outside for a little while, just as long as she was back in time for the grand finale.

She suggested it now, tentatively, but Joe was unimpressed.

'Two weeks? That's ages away, Lucy! And anyway, I don't like all this creeping about. We're just going to have to tell them, then I can come and meet you properly.'

'I don't know . . .' Lucy broke off, chewing her lip. The thought of telling anyone was a daunting one; she wasn't at all

sure what Mam's reaction would be, and as for Algernon . . .
'Tell them what, anyway?' she asked.

'That you're my girl, of course.'

His words sent a thrill through her.

'You are, aren't you?'

'Am I?' She was flirting now, albeit unconsciously.

'I certainly hope so!' He caught her arms, turning her to face
him, leaning forward so that his forehead lay against hers. 'Well
– are you?'

The burst of joy gave her new confidence. 'You know
I am.'

He pulled away slightly, kissing her cold nose, her flushed
cheek.

'Well then?'

'I'll tell Mam,' she said with determination. 'I'm not sure
about Papa, though. Do you think we could keep it from him
for a bit longer? You know what he's like.'

'Only too well – the bastard.' His tone was bitter, but it was
the swear word that shocked Lucy. She'd never heard anyone
say it aloud before, especially not Joe.

'Do as you think fit, Lucy. Just as long as we can see one
another properly and not have to sneak about and tell lies.
Though,' he added, 'if that's the only way, I suppose I'll have to
put up with it. Anything would be better than not seeing you at
all.'

'I'll tell Mam,' Lucy promised. 'And I'll see what she says.
Perhaps she'll tell Algernon, and perhaps she won't. I would feel
bad about deceiving her, but him . . . well, I couldn't care less.'

Joe was silent for a moment, then his chin came up.

'You can leave Algernon to me. I'll tell the bastard myself.'

That word again! But this time it was the least of Lucy's
worries.

'Oh Joe, no!'

'He doesn't scare me. I'm not a kid any more. He can't take a strap to me now, and if he tried, I'd give as good as I got.'

Lucy shook her head, full of admiration, but frightened by the prospect.

'You're not the one who has to live with him.'

'And nor do you if you don't want to. You're sixteen now – you don't have to do everything he says. Working with him, living under his roof . . .'

'And where would I go, I'd like to know?'

Joe's expression was mutinous. 'We'd think of something. It's time that bugger learned he can't have everything his own way. And I'd like to be the one to teach him!'

'Don't rock the boat, for goodness' sake, Joe. Not yet,' Lucy begged. 'Let me speak to Mam first, see what she thinks is best. And Algernon might not be as against it as we think. Now if it was Kitty . . .' She broke off. Algernon's overprotective ways with her sister hadn't escaped her notice.

Kitty had always been his favourite, of course, but then she'd never been the one to cross him. Now, though, the difference in his attitude towards the two of them was unmissable. And the way he looked at Kitty – it was almost the way a miser might look at his gold. Except that sometimes there was something in his expression that was even darker than that, and it was something that Lucy found inexplicably sinister.

Joe sighed, nodding. 'All right, we'll do it your way. But if he tries to stop you seeing me, then we'll do it mine.'

'Oh, Joe . . .' Lucy leaned against him, loving the way his determined stance made her feel. It reminded her of the way she had used to feel when she was a little girl and Daddy had hoisted her up, his arms strong and protective around her, his shoulder a rock to cling to when she was upset or frightened. So safe. So cherished. Knowing that while he was there nothing could harm her.

Then Joe's breath was warm on her cheek, his mouth moist on her ear, his teeth biting gently at the tender lobe, and all thoughts of childhood were forgotten. A tremor ran through Lucy, igniting all the mysterious sensations and desires. She pressed herself against him and lost herself in a delicious haze of wonder.

Chapter Eleven

Annie was in the kitchen, peeling potatoes, when Lucy appeared in the doorway.

'Can I do anything to help?'

Annie was a little surprised; it wasn't like Lucy to offer her help with household chores, unless it was to dry dishes or lend a hand with changing bed linen, a task which was too tiring for Kitty. Today Kitty wasn't even up to preparing vegetables – the Christmas festivities seemed to have taken it out of her, and she was resting in bed. But here was Lucy, hovering and apparently willing.

'You could go and get some more sprouts,' she said. 'We've used all the ones I picked to last us over Christmas.'

She could tell at once from Lucy's face that that wasn't at all what she'd had in mind, and she couldn't say she blamed her. The bitter weather had turned the sprouts into balls of ice, and Lucy's fingers would be frozen by the time she'd harvested enough for dinner. But she got the bowl from under the sink anyway and shrugged into Annie's thick old coat that she kept hanging on a hook behind the door for just such eventualities. She fetched a knife from the drawer, then hesitated, twisting it round and round between her fingers.

'Mam . . .'

Annie, fishing another potato out of the bowl, looked up, guessing from Lucy's tentative tone that giving her a hand in the kitchen wasn't the real reason her daughter was here now.

'What's wrong, Lucy?'

'There's something . . .' Lucy chewed her lip. 'Something I wanted to talk to you about.'

I knew it! Annie thought. And she could guess, too, what it was. That something was going on between Lucy and Joe was so obvious a blind man could have seen it. But she wasn't going to say so. She didn't want Lucy to be embarrassed thinking they'd made a show of themselves.

'Go on then, this is as good a chance as any,' she said, hiding a smile.

Which of course it was. The glove factory had reopened today after the two-day break and Algernon had gone to work as usual, but Lucy had been granted an extra day's holiday. With Kitty upstairs in bed, the coast was clear for confidences.

'It's just that . . .' Lucy was still hesitant. 'Me and Joe . . . we want to go out sometimes . . .'

'You and Joe?' Annie feigned surprise.

'Yes. I really like him, and he likes me. We want to see one another.'

'But you see one another every Sunday,' Annie pointed out. 'And sometimes in the week as well.'

'But not on our own. Not usually.'

You seem to have managed pretty well the last couple of days, Annie thought, amused.

'We want to meet on a week night, after we've finished work. He's going to come and call for me on Wednesday and . . . well, I wanted to tell you first. You don't mind, do you?'

Annie decided it was time to take pity on her daughter.

'Of course I don't mind. I knew it was only a matter of time before you found yourself a young man, and I can't think of anyone I'd rather it was than Joe.'

'Oh Mammy!' Lucy's face lit up with relief and joy. 'Thank you!' Then it clouded over again. 'But what about Papa?'

'Don't worry about Papa.'

'But he'll have to know, won't he? What if he forbids it? He's so fond of forbidding things.'

'Only because he wants the best for you,' Annie said, with a generosity she was far from feeling.

She made up her mind. If Algernon did object – though she couldn't see how he could – she'd be firmly behind Lucy and Joe. This was one of those occasions when she absolutely must stand her ground and take the consequences. She wouldn't stand by and see Lucy's heart broken and her dreams shattered.

Young love was a tender and delicate plant, and so precious while it lasted. She didn't suppose it would last long. First fancies seldom did, more was the pity. She had truly meant it when she had said she couldn't think of anyone she'd rather Lucy had chosen for her first love. She loved Joe like a son, always had, and he had grown into a fine young man. He wouldn't take advantage as some might; he'd loved Lucy too well for too long. Not that Annie could imagine Joe behaving cruelly or treating any girl as a plaything. He was too principled for that, even if the tenets he lived by did not spring from any religious creed, and in her experience, sometimes religious zealots were the worst of all . . .

Dear God, don't let Lucy ever end up with someone like Algernon, she prayed silently.

Lucy had picked up the bowl again and dropped the knife into it; with a smile at Annie that outdid the wintry sun that slanted down at this time of day directly into the kitchen, she went out the door, closing it after her, and Annie could not help but smile at the lightness of her footfalls as she ran up the steps to the back garden.

In years to come, when Lucy looked back, it was those early months of 1907 that she remembered as the happiest time of her life. A time when every day was filled with magic, when the world around her sang with joyous mystery, and the future was an uncharted adventure. A time when anything and everything seemed possible.

She and Joe spent every moment they could in each other's company. They walked together on crisp evenings when frost glistened white on hedgerows and the ground crunched beneath their feet and the moon was so big and bright you felt you could reach up and touch it. They stopped frequently to share those kisses Lucy loved so much, Joe resting against a hoar-encrusted gate or tree trunk, Lucy leaning into him, her hands tucked inside his coat so that the heat of his body warmed them, and trembling, not from cold, but from the sharp prickles of desire deep inside and the strange hot yearnings that possessed her as their bodies pressed together.

Sometimes Joe took her up to his rooms above the chemist's shop – a tiny kitchen, a bedroom she had glimpsed only through the half-open door, and a big living room with an oilcloth-covered table, two dining chairs with sagging seats, a faded armchair and a scratched sideboard. There they would sit in front of the guttering gas fire, which didn't really give out enough heat for them to be able to take their coats off, and Lucy was quite glad of that, for she was somehow less comfortable with her strange feelings and desires here with the door locked against the outside world than she was when they were out in a public place, however deserted that might be.

Sitting on his lap or in the circle of his arms, she would

168

tell him about her day – not that there was much to relate – and he would tell her about his – much more interesting, since he came into contact with all sorts of people in the shop, and had so much to learn about the business. Sometimes they relived memories, harking back to dramatic or amusing incidents in their shared past, or talked over a family matter. Algernon they mentioned as little as possible. He had not raised the objections Lucy had feared, though he made his disapproval clear in the ways she knew so well – the glowering stare, the tight lips, the impatience of his tone, the set of his shoulders, all of which made for a poisonous atmosphere that was almost tangible the moment he walked through the door and lingered long after he had gone out again. But Lucy was used to that; she could shrug it off just as long as he didn't stop her from seeing Joe.

One night, however, while they waited for milk to come to the boil on the little gas ring in the kitchen – always a tediously lengthy process – so that they could have a hot drink before he walked her home, Joe broke the unspoken rule.

'I don't know why your mam ever married that bastard,' he said.

Lucy was no longer shocked by the word; she'd discovered that away from the confines of home Joe was prone to using it, but she was surprised that he had raised the subject of Algernon.

'She didn't have any choice,' she said. 'We were left with nothing when Daddy was killed. Sir Montague would have thrown us out of our house because we couldn't pay the rent and we'd have had nowhere to go. We'd probably have ended up in the workhouse.'

'I suppose. But I'd have thought she could have done better than him. Not that I'm not glad she didn't look elsewhere, of course. She's been like a mother to me, and I might never have met you if she'd finished up with someone else.'

That triggered another few kisses, then Joe returned to his theme.

'She deserves somebody who treats her nicer than he does,' he said. 'Somebody who gives her a bit of respect, not uses her like a skivvy and a . . .' He broke off, not wanting to speak the word that was on the tip of his tongue. 'Whore' wasn't one to use in front of Lucy, especially when he was talking about her own mother.

Lucy knew what he had been on the point of saying, though. She'd heard the disgusting sounds that came from the other side of the bedroom wall when she'd shared the room next door with Kitty. It had been one of the reasons why she'd been only too glad to move to the tiny room at the end of the corridor, though even there, when she couldn't sleep, she could sometimes still hear grunts and roars, and the creak of the bed springs. As a child, though she hadn't understood, she'd been disconcerted, frightened even, and pulled the covers over her head to shut out the sounds. Now she understood only too well, and knew too that what was going on was not the pleasurable, intimate experience it should have been. If she was in any doubt, her mother's haunted expression next morning, the dark circles under her eyes and the red weals on her arms, and even her throat, confirmed her worst fears – Algernon used Mammy in ways no man should use his wife, or any woman.

She didn't want to think about it, let alone talk about it; she wished Joe hadn't raised the subject.

'I think that milk is going to boil at last!' she said, pushing herself up from the sagging sofa. 'I'll fetch the cups.'

It wasn't only her wonderful new-found love for Joe (Lucy was in no doubt but that she loved him) that made these months so special. There were also the concert parties, when she was able to take to the stage and indulge in her other passion, singing – and performing – for an appreciative audience. Every couple of weeks, sometimes more often, she joined the other members of Stanley Bristow's talented little band to put on their show at halls around the district. Her popularity had grown and she had come to be regarded as one of the star turns, along with Horace Parfitt, who everyone agreed was a scream when he put on his smock and did his comic routine, and, of course, Stanley himself. Now, instead of just one spot, she had two, and had increased her repertoire to include such numbers as 'She's Only a Bird in a Gilded Cage', while Stanley had suggested they should learn a duet to perform together.

She had two new dresses especially to wear on the stage, one pink and one blue, and a pretty little straw boater for a brand new song, 'I Do Like to Be Beside the Seaside'.

Joe now accompanied her to the concerts in place of Annie, sitting towards the back of the hall so that the prime seats in the front rows were left free for those who hadn't seen the show as many times as he had, then waiting patiently while she changed out of her finale costume in some cramped dressing room in whatever hall they were performing in. And his patience was certainly called for – the troupe, high on the sweet flush of success, usually spent quite some time talking and laughing together before they finally emerged. More often than not Stanley produced a bottle of something alcoholic – a drop of sherry, 'good for the voice', before a performance, a flask of whisky afterwards – and Lucy had been tempted into taking her first sips; the sherry she liked, the whisky she didn't. Joe had begun keeping a bag of Fisherman's Friends in his pocket and making her suck one on the way home.

'If Algernon smells your breath you'll be for it,' he warned, and though she hated the taste of the lozenges, Lucy knew she'd better do as he said.

Winter turned to spring and early summer, the evenings stayed lighter for longer, and Lucy, now seventeen, wished she could stop time. The concerts would be fewer and farther apart as the weather improved; folk would have things they wanted to do outdoors rather than sitting in a stuffy hall for two or three hours, however good the entertainment.

One evening when they were once again performing at High Compton town hall, Lucy came off stage in the ivory gown she wore to play the bride in the wedding procession that formed the grand finale to find Joe waiting for her at the foot of the three steps that led down from the stage. She was surprised and a little alarmed; Joe never came through the closed door that separated the stage from the main hall until the audience had all left, and even then only if she was taking an extraordinarily long time to emerge.

'What's the matter?' she asked, fearful that something awful had happened at home and Joe had been sent a message.

He grinned. 'Nothing. Only don't take too long getting changed tonight. There's somebody here wants to see you.'

Lucy was blocking the narrow stairs; Horace Parfitt, who had been following her off stage, tapped her on the shoulder.

'Go on then, sweetheart. Some of us want to get home tonight.'

Lucy moved out of the way to let him and the others past.

'Who is it?' she asked Joe, curious. She had little idea of who was in the audience; the curtains at the windows of the hall had all been drawn so that it was quite dark inside, and with the flare of the stage lights in her eyes she could not see beyond the first few rows even if she had been looking.

'Wait and see. We'll be in the hall when you've changed.'

Lucy was tempted to peek out straight away, but Stanley had very strict rules, and one of them was that his performers should not be seen offstage in their costumes. It spoiled the illusion, he said, though just what illusion they were supposed to be preserving when they'd only been feet from their audience moments before, Lucy was not sure.

She hurried to the dressing room, changing as fast as she could, and passing her dress to Stanley's housekeeper, Ada Perrett, who was in charge of the wardrobe. Stanley already had his flask out, and he waved it in her direction, but she shook her head.

'Not tonight, thank you. I've got someone waiting to see me.'

'Not a fine lady, by any chance?' Stanley had been one of the last to leave the stage and with the house lights up had seen Joe heading towards the stage door, a woman behind him.

A fine lady? Lucy's heart leapt with sudden impossible hope. She grabbed her shawl, half ran along the narrow passageway and yanked open the door to the hall. It couldn't be . . . not here, in High Compton after all this time, surely . . .

But it was. Sitting on one of the chairs in the now empty front row was the aunt she had not seen in almost ten years. As Lucy emerged, she rose and came forward, gloved hands outstretched.

'Lucy! My dear!'

'Aunt Molly!' Lucy cried, both surprised and delighted. 'What are you doing here?'

Molly laughed, the same throaty laugh Lucy remembered so well, gay, and just a little naughty.

'Watching you perform, of course! When your mama wrote to tell me you were singing in concert parties, I was determined to come and see for myself what kind of artiste my talented little niece has turned into.'

173

'Mam wrote to you?' Lucy was amazed; though Annie had told her she still got Christmas cards and news from Molly, she hadn't realised they were actually corresponding.

Molly's mouth twitched. 'Oh, your wicked stepfather isn't as powerful as he thinks, thank the Lord! Now, there's someone you must meet. My husband, Mr Daniel Trotter.'

Lucy had been so overwhelmed to see her aunt, she hadn't noticed the man who had been sitting beside her. Now he materialised at Molly's elbow, offering a hand in greeting, a big, flashily dressed fellow with mutton-chop whiskers, a flushed complexion and a large red-veined nose.

'Pleased to meet you, my dear. A stunning performance, if I may say so. A true professional in the making.'

Lucy was almost speechless that a real live theatre manager should have come to listen to her sing, let alone praise her so highly.

'Thank you so much,' she managed.

Molly was beaming proudly. 'What did I tell you?'

'Indeed. She reminds me very much of you at her age. I see a great future ahead for you, Miss Day.'

Chairs clattered suddenly behind them: old Gaston Weeks, caretaker of the hall, was making a great show of wanting to clear up so that he could lock the door and go home.

'I think we're in the way,' Molly said, flashing the caretaker an apologetic look. 'Perhaps we should leave.'

Lucy was less impressed by Gaston's pantomime. She was used to it by now, and in any case she knew it would be some time before the other performers emerged from the dressing room.

'Don't go yet, Aunt Molly, please!' she begged. 'It's so long since I saw you!'

Joe spoke for the first time. 'Why don't we go back to mine

so you and Lucy can have a proper catch-up? It's a bit of a dump, but . . .'

'I expect I've seen worse,' Molly said, smiling. The lines between her nose and mouth were much deeper than Lucy remembered, and her jaw sagged a little. But that smile was exactly the same, just as her laugh had been. 'Theatrical lodgings are far from salubrious, especially when one is just starting out,' she added when she saw Joe's expression of disbelief.

Leaving Gaston Weeks to clear up in peace, they went down the stairs and into the warm still evening. Daniel Trotter's motor car was parked outside the town hall – not the strange electric contraption Molly had arrived in when she had come to see Lucy and Kitty sing at the chapel anniversary, but a shiny black Daimler, spanking new, with headlamps like giant eyes and red leather upholstery. When Daniel saw Joe's admiring glance, he walked him around it, pointing out the luxurious features, and Lucy knew Joe would give his eye teeth for a ride in it. But with the chemist shop only just across the street, there was no chance of that.

'It's just over there,' Joe said, indicating with a nod of his head, and Molly laughed.

'Very convenient! Lead on!'

It was late when the party at last broke up. Lucy had made drinks for them all, and Molly and 'Spike' had sat uncomplaining on the sagging furniture while they all chatted.

An hour slipped by almost unnoticed, and it was with regret that Lucy realised she would be in deep trouble with Algernon if she didn't get home soon.

As they had to pass by her home on their way back to Bath, naturally Lucy was offered a ride, and she climbed on to the high rear seat, happy and a little overexcited, waving to an envious Joe as the car moved off.

'Don't forget, my dear, if ever you decide you'd like to make a career of your singing, just let me know,' Daniel said, as he pulled up outside the house.

'I think Lucy has more sense than to go down that road,' Molly said tartly, but as she kissed Lucy good night, she whispered in her ear: 'I'm very proud of you, Lucy. Do keep in touch.'

'I will,' Lucy promised. 'And thank you so much for coming to see me.'

'The pleasure is all ours,' Molly said.

Oh no, it was mine! Lucy thought as she watched the car disappear down the road.

The world, it seemed, was at her feet.

There was something different about Joe. It was almost, Lucy thought, the way he'd been in those weeks leading up to Christmas, before they'd discovered one another. He was moody, silent and uncommunicative, going into himself, lost in a place where she couldn't reach him. She'd tried every way she knew to tease him out of it, with no success. He didn't even seem to want to kiss her – well, certainly he didn't want the long, tender sessions she loved so much.

'What's the matter, Joe?' she asked one evening when he'd almost pushed her away from him. 'Don't you like me any more?'

'Don't be daft.'

'Why don't you want to kiss me then?'

'We can't be kissing all the time.' His voice was rough, impatient.

'You didn't used to say that.'

'Oh, just leave it, can't you, Lucy?'

She couldn't, of course. But the more she persisted, the more Joe retreated into his shell, and Lucy could only think that his feelings had changed and he had grown tired of her. She shrank inwardly at the awful thought. If he told her he didn't want to see her any more, she couldn't bear it. But she couldn't understand why else he would be acting this way.

Something else had changed too – they rarely went to his rooms over the chemist's shop now either. Joe always seemed to have some excuse why they shouldn't, none of them very plausible. And one evening his reluctance was more obvious than ever.

The rain that had been threatening all day began in earnest not long after he'd called for her, a thick drizzle that soon became a downpour.

'I'd better get you home,' Joe said.

Lucy's heart sank.

'We're a lot closer to your place,' she objected – they'd been walking in the direction of town when the downpour began.

'And all the further for you to get back if it's set in for the night.'

'I don't think it has. Look, I'm sure the sky's lighter over there . . . Let's not go home! We haven't been to your place for ages.'

'Have it your way.' It was typical of the way he'd begun speaking to her, and Lucy wanted to weep.

'Don't you want to be with me any more?' she asked wretchedly.

'Course I do.'

'Well you've got a funny way of showing it.' She pulled her hand from the crook of his arm – that was something else that had changed. He'd taken to thrusting his hand into his pocket instead of holding hers, so she could only tuck her arm through his as they walked.

'Oh Lucy.' Joe sighed deeply, a sigh of frustration. 'You just don't understand, do you?'

'No,' she said. 'I don't. I love you, Joe. I'd do anything for you. But you . . .'

He grunted, took her hand now, but without any of the old tenderness, more as a way of hurrying her through the rain, which had begun to fall harder than ever.

'Come on. We're going to get soaked.'

It was hot and muggy in the apartment. A meat fly buzzed against the window pane and the smell of the bacon Joe had fried for his breakfast hung heavily in the stale air. Joe took off his coat, brushing the moisture off the shoulders before draping it over the back of a chair, and Lucy spread her wet shawl over another.

'Can't you open a window?' The smell of the bacon was making Lucy feel a bit sick.

'It doesn't open very far.'

Lucy already knew that. When the apartment was empty, before Joe had moved in, a cautious Richard Penny had fixed the window to make it impossible for burglars to break in. Now Joe twisted the swivel catch and pulled the sash down the few inches that the brackets Richard had fitted allowed.

'And can't we get that poor fly out?' Lucy hated to see any living creature suffer, even a dirty meat fly.

Joe huffed, but he took out his handkerchief and tried to catch it, unsuccessfully. Dozy the meat fly might be, but there was still enough life left in it to evade capture.

'It will have to find its own way out,' he said, conceding defeat.

His tone was ill-tempered, and the atmosphere between them

was tense and unpleasant. Lucy felt tears gathering in her throat, and she went up behind Joe, putting her arms around his waist and laying her head against his back.

'I can't bear you being like this, Joe. Please tell me what's wrong.'

'Nothing.' His shoulders were set, his whole body stiff with a tension she couldn't begin to understand.

'But there is. What have I done wrong?' Though she was trying very hard not to cry, a small hiccuping sound escaped her, and Joe huffed, almost despairingly, before turning abruptly, putting his arms around her and resting his chin on her damp curls.

'Don't cry, Lucy, please.'

She swallowed her tears, but they still swam in her eyes as she lifted her chin, looking up at him.

'I love you so much, Joe. I can't bear it when you're like this. I just want—'

Before she could finish, Joe was crushing her to him, his mouth hard on hers. Lucy gasped at the fierceness of his kiss, so different to the sweet and gentle ones she'd grown to love, but even more darkly exciting. It made her prickle with awareness, magnetised her, so that she moved her hips closer to his, pressing against him and feeling shudders of delight and a desire she barely understood twisting deep inside her.

Then, with shocking suddenness, he pushed her away roughly. 'Bugger it, Lucy.' He strode past her, not even looking at her.

'What have I done now?' she sobbed, the tears welling again.

He sank on to one of the dining chairs, head bowed, hands clasping the back of his neck.

'You really don't know, do you? You don't know what you do to me. You're a tease, Lucy. I don't suppose you mean to be, but that's what you are, and it's more than flesh and blood can stand.'

The shock of his words dried Lucy's tears; she gazed at him, wide-eyed and horrified.

He looked up, his face set.

'You want to know what's wrong? I'll tell you. The way you act, I don't think I can control myself. I want you too much. So there you have it. We can't get into situations like this or I'll do something we'll both regret. Satisfied now?'

The realisation of what he was saying dawned on her in a blinding flash. Suddenly Lucy was remembering a night when his hand had gone to her breast and she'd pushed it away, nice as the sensations it aroused had been. *Stop it, Joe!* She could hear herself now. *Stop that this minute!* But she'd still put her face up for his kisses, pressed her body close to his, selfishly wanting more. How could she have been so blind, so stupid that she hadn't realised what she was doing to him? And of course it explained why the more she'd tried to win him back with hugs and kisses, the more he'd shut her out.

'Oh Joe . . . I'm sorry,' she whispered.

He shrugged. 'No need to be. It's my fault for wanting what I can't have.'

Lucy chewed her lip, wondering why she was so reluctant to let him touch her. Didn't she want it too? Yet something had held her back, the part of her that was still a child, the part that was not ready to move on from the simple pleasure of a first love that was pure and innocent and sweet.

'If you want to touch me, Joe, I won't stop you,' she said, shy and a little hesitant.

For a brief moment his face softened, then he brought one hand crashing down on his knee.

'Of course it's what I want. But it wouldn't stop there. Not for long. It won't be enough, and before we know it, it'll go too far.'

'I don't mind,' Lucy said desperately. 'I just want things to be the way they were.'

'No.' His voice was hard, determined. 'What if I got you into trouble? I could never face your mam again.'

The very suggestion made Lucy curl up inside. But the thought of losing Joe was even worse.

'It might not come to that.'

'It's too much of a risk, even if I was careful. No, it's just best we don't get in situations like this until I've got enough put aside so we can get married. I don't earn much, but I'm saving what I can.'

Lucy's hands flew to her mouth, scarcely able to believe she'd heard aright.

'Married!'

'We're both young, I know, but it's the only way I can think of to have you for my own.'

The tears started to her eyes again, not from bewilderment and hurt now, but from soaring joy. Joe wanted to marry her. All the time she'd thought he was going to finish with her he'd been planning and saving.

'You do want to marry me, don't you?' he asked roughly.

'Of course I do! More than anything in the world!'

He reached out and took her hand.

'Come here, then. But no more teasing, OK?'

She nodded. He pulled her down on to his lap and kissed her tenderly, the old, gentle Joe, and Lucy's heart swelled with love.

'And now,' he said, 'if that rain's stopped, I reckon we'd better get out of here before I forget myself again.'

The rain *had* stopped, the black clouds had moved on and the patch of sky visible through the sash window was clear blue.

181

And the meat fly was no longer buzzing impotently about the pane. Had it flown off elsewhere in the apartment, or had it escaped through the narrow vent? Lucy had no way of knowing, but she hoped it had escaped. Given her elated mood, that was only fitting. With happiness and relief buoying her up, she wanted every single living creature in the universe to be happy too.

Chapter Twelve

As Lucy went in the front door, she heard the sound of voices coming from the living room. Annie and Algernon. They had usually gone to bed before Lucy got in, though Lucy knew her mother never went to sleep until she was sure Lucy was safely home. Lucy wished they hadn't broken the habit tonight of all nights, when she was all abuzz over Joe's proposal. They'd agreed not to tell anyone for ages yet, though Lucy thought she might be unable to resist confiding in Annie, but not tonight. Definitely not tonight.

'I'm home!' she called, and at once the voices fell silent, as if she had interrupted a conversation she was not meant to hear.

She went into the living room and was immediately aware of a strained atmosphere. Algernon was standing in front of the hearth, scowling; Annie, sitting stiffly, looked anxious and embarrassed. As Lucy took off her still damp shawl and draped it over the back of one of the dining chairs, Annie leapt up, all consternation, as if looking for a diversion to fill the awkward silence.

'Oh, Lucy, did you get caught in the storm? Let me put that shawl on the airer to dry . . .'

'Do stop fussing, Annie!' Algernon sounded even more exasperated than usual.

'I'm fine,' Lucy said. 'It did rain hard, but we went to Joe's to shelter.' The memory of what had happened there made her cheeks burn suddenly, and she added hastily: 'I'm off to bed now, though. I'm really tired.'

She turned for the door, but Algernon's voice, sharp with the all-too-familiar ring of authority, stopped her.

'Wait! I have something to say to you.'

'Algernon, no . . .' Annie laid a hand on her husband's arm, but he shook it off impatiently.

'She has to be told, and it might as well be now.'

Lucy turned back, puzzled and a little apprehensive now, looking at Algernon, who stood ramrod straight, his thumbs hooked into the pockets of his waistcoat. He might have been about to address the chapel congregation, Lucy thought.

'Something has occurred – or at least come to my notice. Belatedly.' He spat the word, as if it disgusted him. 'As a result of what I've learned, I have to tell you that you will not be performing in any more of Stanley Bristow's concert parties. It is, I am afraid to say, a hive of depravity, and you cannot be associated with it.'

Lucy's jaw dropped. Her first thought was that Algernon must have somehow learned about the bottle of sherry and the flask of whisky Stanley shared around the dressing room. She flushed again, this time from guilt.

'I don't . . . honestly . . .' she lied. But Algernon was in full flow and she might as well not have spoken.

'I have to say that allowing you to take part at all was against my better judgement, and I was only swayed by the fact that Bristow was such a well-respected gentleman in this town. Now it appears he is no gentleman, and certainly not entitled to respect. He is, in fact, an abomination before God.'

Still thinking Algernon was talking about the alcohol, Lucy

was quite shocked. 'Oh Papa! That's an awful thing to say! Stanley might have a little drink now and then, but so do lots of other people. It doesn't make him a bad person.'

Algernon harrumphed in disgust. 'A drink is one thing. This, I'm afraid, is something else entirely.'

Lucy was mystified now. 'What are you talking about? Whatever is it he is supposed to have done?'

A vein throbbed in Algernon's temple.

'*Don't ever again speak his name in this house.*' He spat out each word for added emphasis. 'I do not wish to hear it cross your lips. That man is the very devil. As to what he has done, it's not a subject to be discussed.'

'Mam?' Shocked and bewildered, Lucy turned to her mother. But Annie only shook her head.

'Papa's right, Lucy. It's not something for your ears.'

'But I don't understand!' Lucy said. 'Whatever it is, it can't be so terrible, surely? He's a lovely man! Kind, and funny, and—'

'And *that* is a fine example of how easily the young are corrupted,' Algernon stated triumphantly. 'That is why I will not allow you any further contact with that man.'

'But . . .' So taken aback had she been at the assassination of her mentor's character that Lucy had for a moment forgotten Algernon's ban. Now she realised he had meant every word he said. 'Papa, you can't stop me singing in the concert party! Please . . . you can't!'

Algernon drew himself up to his full, impressive height.

'After this,' he said, 'I very much doubt there will be any concert party. And if there is, no decent person will attend. There is no more to be said on the matter.'

With that he crossed to the window, drawing back the curtains to let in the last of the fading light before extinguishing the gas lamp in the centre of the room.

'Mam . . .' Lucy pleaded, hoping desperately that Annie would intervene, but she said nothing, simply stood, hands tightly clasped together at her waist, shaking her head.

Algernon crossed to the door, holding it open. 'Go to bed now, Lucy. Put this whole matter out of your mind. And pray to God for salvation.'

Once again Lucy looked appealingly at her mother; once again Annie failed to respond.

'It's for the best, my love,' she said gently. 'Go on, there's a good girl, get some sleep or you'll be fit for nothing in the morning. And make sure your hair's properly dry before you lie down or you'll end up with a stiff neck, or even the shingles.'

Lucy gazed from one to the other of them in confusion. Why were they behaving like this? How could they ban her from the thing she loved most without a proper explanation? It was so dreadfully unfair! But with her mother siding with Algernon there really was no point in arguing any more tonight.

In a kind of daze she turned away. She'd forgotten all about Joe now, and what had happened earlier. All she could think of was that for some mysterious reason she was not to be allowed to sing and perform with the concert party any more. And that was so devastating it eclipsed everything else.

Within days the whole of High Compton and Hillsbridge was abuzz with the same news that had so incensed Algernon, though it was mostly passed on in shocked whispers and behind fanned fingertips. It was only the men squatting in groups at the pitheads or gathered over a pint of ale in the pubs and bars who mentioned it openly, though they expressed their disgust in terms that would never have passed Algernon's lips.

'Well, who'd-a thought it? Stanley Bristow a poofter!'

'I al'us thought t'were funny, him never having a woman

that we heard of. And very friendly with a lot of young chaps . . .'

'Well I'll be buggered!'

'Not so much you, my cocker. *'Im*, you'da mean, I reckon . . .'

Hearty laughter all round.

Though she heard whispers, Lucy still had no idea of what lay behind the gossip, though it was clearly something scandalous. Not even Joe would explain when she asked him.

'He's been arrested for gross indecency, that's all I know. They reckon he'll go to prison.'

'Gross indecency? But what does that mean?' Lucy asked, perplexed.

'Oh, you don't want to know,' was all Joe would say.

A few weeks later, much to the disappointment of the gossips, and the relief of all those who liked and respected him, the charges against Stanley were dropped. The accusation, it seemed, had stemmed from a complaint made by a Bristol businessman who had claimed Stanley had been cavorting with rent boys and taking them to a hotel room in the city. But no real evidence was forthcoming to back up his claims of debauchery. Though Stanley's name did appear regularly in the register of the hotel in question, none of the staff there were prepared to say they had seen boys going up to his room. Ada Perrett, his housekeeper, up in arms at the suggestion, had vowed to take the stand and swear that she had never witnessed anything untoward at home – 'Mr Bristow's not like that!' And the list of influential local gentlemen willing to appear as character witnesses was impressive and growing. Discovering that Stanley's accuser had been trying to acquire the Bristow foundry business in order to expand his own empire and been sent packing was the last straw for the investigating officers, and with the case against him falling apart, Stanley was released from custody.

187

'It was all very interesting,' he remarked in his sanguine way to the well-to-do cronies he drank with in an upper room at the George Hotel, though he was, in truth, very shaken by the experience.

'We always knew there couldn't be anything in it,' his supporters proclaimed.

But there were those who disagreed.

'No smoke without fire,' was their verdict.

Algernon was one of the latter.

The concert parties resumed almost at once – Stanley was anxious to brazen it out and show the world he had nothing to hide. But Algernon would not be swayed from his decision that Lucy would no longer be performing with them. When Stanley came calling to ask her to attend a rehearsal, Algernon gave him short shrift, berating him roundly before slamming the door in his face.

Lucy, who had been in Joe's room where they were looking for a book he wanted, had seen Stanley's car draw up outside, and hurried down eagerly. From the foot of the stairs she had heard the whole unpleasant altercation, and mortified as well as shocked and upset, she fled back up to Joe's room.

'Oh, Joe – something terrible! Papa has sent Stanley packing!'

Joe looked up from the books scattered across the bedroom floor.

'Is that any surprise? You don't think he's going to change his mind, do you?'

'But Stanley's name has been cleared of whatever it was he was supposed to have done. He has to be innocent, or he'd still be in prison!' Lucy argued. 'And Papa said the most terrible things to him. It was awful – awful!' She sank on to the bed, trembling. 'I'm so ashamed! How could he say those things?'

Joe got up from his knees and sat beside her, putting his arm round her.

'No point getting upset. You know what he's like, and Stanley does too.'

'He'll never have me back in the concert party now. And I couldn't face him even if he did . . .'

'Well, it's not going to happen, Lucy, so you might as well stop worrying about it.'

For once Joe's pragmatism infuriated Lucy rather than calming her. She beat her fists hard against the counterpane.

'Why does Papa have to spoil everything? I hate him! I hate him!'

'Come here.' Joe pulled her towards him, kissing her, but it was of no comfort to Lucy, and she pushed him away, feeling betrayed and resentful. Joe didn't understand how much singing meant to her. The thought of not being able to perform was more than she could bear.

'He's not going to stop me,' she vowed. 'He's not!' A thought struck her; a way to escape Algernon's dominance. 'Can't we get married now, Joe? You wouldn't stop me, would you? If we were married . . .'

'Oh Lucy, you know that's out of the question,' Joe groaned. 'I can hardly support myself, let alone you too. And in any case, neither of us is old enough to marry without permission. Can you imagine Algernon allowing it?'

He was right, of course, but Lucy had gone beyond reason.

'We could run away.'

'Now you're just talking silly. Come on, Lucy, buck up, do!'

'Oh . . . I hate him, and I hate you too.'

She didn't mean it, of course – well at least she certainly didn't hate Joe. She loved him – didn't she? But in that moment Lucy knew it wasn't enough. She wanted more from life than to marry and settle down to life as a wife and mother. The stage held too great an attraction for her. If she couldn't perform, she might as well be dead. In that moment, she made up her mind.

She wouldn't be dictated to. She was going to sing again with the concert party, and to hell with the consequences.

Lucy was walking into town as fast as her legs would carry her. The nervousness that had been getting worse all day was making her tremble inwardly, and she felt guilty too, but she was as determined as ever. Much as she hated lying to her mother, there had really been no alternative. If she'd told her what she planned, it would have placed Annie in an impossible position, so instead she'd pretended she was meeting Edie Cooper, her childhood friend.

She hadn't told Joe, either. He'd only warn her that defying Algernon was asking for trouble, and there'd be sure to be an argument. She and Joe seemed to argue a lot these days, and she hated that. Their unofficial betrothal hadn't really helped at all, and the strain of avoiding physical intimacy was telling on them both. So for the first time, Lucy was heading for the concert party alone, and not even sure what sort of reception she could expect. But some things had to be faced up to. If you wanted something badly enough you had to take risks, and Lucy wanted this very badly indeed.

When she reached the town hall, she saw that Stanley Bristow's car was parked outside. So he was already here, as she'd expected, though it was a good hour until the concert was due to begin. She hoped none of the other performers had arrived yet. She didn't want anyone else there when she faced Stanley for the first time since the awful contretemps with Algernon, and she certainly didn't want them to witness her humiliation if Stanley sent her packing.

She crossed the road outside Freeman's drapery shop, for once not stopping to look in the window at the display of hats, scarves and bolts of cloth, and pushed open the door of the town hall. Nerves tangled and knotted in the pit of her stomach and she gripped the handrail tightly as she climbed the stairs to the upper hall.

Please don't let Stanley turn me away!

The door at the top of the stairs was pegged open, and a card table with a pottery basin and wooden cash box on it stood just inside, ready for whoever was to be on the door. Lucy went into the hall, which felt hot and muggy from the heat of the day. The windows were seldom opened except when the hall was in use, for too often a swift, one of the many that nested under the eaves, would find its way in and become trapped. Besides the mess it made, this inevitably caused a high drama as the next users of the hall tried to catch it and persuade it out again.

No swift swooping low then fluttering up out of reach tonight, thank goodness. But as she went into the hall, Stanley himself appeared from the wings of the stage carrying an aspidistra in a china pot.

He stopped short when he saw Lucy.

'My dear! What are you doing here?'

Lucy went towards the stage, swallowing at the tightness in her throat.

'Can I talk to you, Mr Bristow? Please?'

'Yes, of course. Just let me get rid of this . . .'

He carried the aspidistra to a corner of the stage and set it on a tall wooden plant stand that was already in place.

'Come into the dressing room.'

Lucy went through the door beside the stage, where Stanley was waiting for her in the narrow passage.

'Ah – on second thoughts, perhaps that's not such a good idea.'

Through the open door into the tiny dressing room Lucy could see a buxom figure – Ada Perrett, who was busy unpacking costumes from a tin trunk and hanging them on a clothes rail. Her heart sank. She'd forgotten Mrs Perrett would be here, transported along with the costumes and props in Stanley's car.

'We'll go into the hall. No one else will be arriving just yet.' Stanley ushered her back into the empty room. 'I didn't expect you tonight, Lucy.'

'No, I know. Mr Bristow, I am so sorry . . .'

Stanley shook his head, his thin, agile face regretful but surprisingly kind.

'You can't be held responsible for your stepfather, Lucy. But he did make it quite clear that he would not allow you to perform with my little band again.'

Lucy lifted her chin.

'He has no right. Please, Mr Bristow, I do so want to!'

'But my dear . . . I've arranged for Ethel Talbot to take your place. She's rehearsed her old numbers and she will be arriving at any moment. I can't possibly turn her away.'

'Oh.' All Lucy's bravado dissipated like the air escaping from a popped balloon, leaving nothing but hollow emptiness. She should have known that a concert party without a pretty girl soloist would be no concert party at all, and that Stanley would have to replace her. But she'd had such high hopes, risked so much to be here tonight . . . Tears of disappointment were gathering in her throat; she turned away, not wanting Stanley to see her cry.

'Lucy, Lucy, let me think.'

Stanley was swiftly running over possible solutions. Lucy was by far and away the most talented performer he'd ever worked with, and a thousand times better than Ethel. Besides which, he felt dreadfully sorry for her. He, more than most, knew how much it meant to her, and he couldn't begin to imagine what sort of a home life she had living with that pompous boor Algernon Pierce.

'Does he know you're here?' he asked.

Lucy gave a tiny shake of her head; she still couldn't trust herself to speak.

'Hmm.' An imp of wickedness landed on Stanley's shoulder, tempting him. Never mind that Lucy would have been his first choice as soloist, it would be very satisfying to put one over on Algernon.

It was enough to prompt him to make up his mind.

'I'll tell you what we'll do, Lucy. I can't change the programme at this late stage, and I can't disappoint Ethel. But I dare say we could slot in one of your numbers.'

'Oh, Mr Bristow!' Lucy's eyes, which a moment ago had been bright with tears, now shone with delight.

'Ethel will have to play the bride in the finale, of course, and all the other items we've rehearsed . . .'

Lucy nodded eagerly. Seeing Ethel take her place wouldn't be easy, but at least she would get to sing, even if it was only one song.

'And if Algernon gets to hear of this, I wouldn't want to be in your shoes,' Stanley added, giving her a straight look.

'I don't care!' Lucy said recklessly.

And she didn't. Really she didn't.

Even though it was a fine, warm summer evening, the hall was packed, the audience boosted, no doubt, by Stanley's recent notoriety. Along with his diehard supporters, there were those who were curious to see the man who had so nearly become their very own Oscar Wilde, and Stanley played shamelessly to the gallery, with dry quips that had them in stitches.

Ethel, however, was not best pleased to find Lucy in the dressing room when she arrived; she shot her a filthy look and turned her back, ignoring her rival. Things went from bad to worse when she took to the stage in what should have been Lucy's spot. Some wag called out: 'Where's our little Lucy?' and a few others took up the cry.

Stanley hurried out on to the stage, anxious to nip this unrest in the bud.

'Don't worry, "our little Lucy" will be singing for you later. Tonight you have a double treat – two lovely young ladies for the price of one. Now, please, a round of applause for our delightful soloist – Miss Ethel Talbot!'

The objectors, a little shamed, fell silent, the pianist played the opening bars, and Ethel began her number. But she was upset by her reception, and nerves were getting the better of her. She failed to reach several of the high notes, and muddled her words, singing the same verse twice. As she finished, the applause was muted, and people were muttering to one another.

Ethel looked close to tears, and as she began her second number, it was obvious to Stanley that she was about to forget her words again. He turned to Lucy, who was standing beside him in the wings, watching.

'If she muffs it, go on and help her out,' he instructed in a low voice.

Lucy needed no second telling. As Ethel stumbled, looking to be on the point of turning and fleeing, she picked up her skirts and ran on to the stage. Beaming prettily at the restless audience, she caught Ethel's hand and joined her in the song.

A cheer had gone up from the audience when Lucy appeared, then they fell silent, until the last soaring notes filled the hall, Lucy's strong voice drowning Ethel out, just as she had drowned out Kitty all those years ago until she had learned how to sing more softly so as to blend her voice with her sister's. The rapturous applause was music to her ears, but she was canny enough to draw Ethel with her to the front of the stage to take their bow. She wasn't going to make it obvious that she knew very well she was stealing the limelight.

Ethel's hand trembled in hers, and the moment they were in the wings she tore it away and ran weeping to the dressing room. Lucy sighed impatiently, though she was glowing with triumph. Stanley squeezed her arm appreciatively before stepping out on to the stage to announce the next act, and Horace Parfitt, waiting to go on, gave her a wink and a broad, toothless grin.

In the dressing room, Ethel had collapsed on to a chair, her hands covering her face, shoulders shaking. As Lucy entered, her head jerked up.

'What do you think you were doing? That was my spot! Mine!'

'I was helping you out,' Lucy said shortly. 'You were dying out there.'

'I was not! I was in this concert party long before you! You had no business—'

'Oh, have it your way.' Lucy couldn't be bothered to argue; besides, Stanley was in the doorway.

'Are you going to do your next turn, Ethel, or do you want Lucy to do it for you?' It was clear from his tone what he hoped her answer would be, and Ethel promptly burst into tears again.

'That's settled then,' Stanley said. 'Mrs Perrett, will you help Lucy change into her costume?'

He strode out again, and Lucy presented her back to the house-keeper, allowing her to undo the fiddly buttons of her blouse, then slip her into the gingham dress she wore for the seaside medley, which would be next on the programme. Her face was flushed as she settled the cute little boater on her head and checked her appearance in the mirror that was propped up on the make-up table. A tiny part of her felt sorry for Ethel, but equally she was impatient that the girl had made such a pathetic show of herself, and too high on her own success to care much about Ethel's humiliation.

The audience had wanted *her*, called for *her*. They'd fallen silent for her, and clapped and cheered when she finished. Lucy felt she was almost bursting with exhilaration. This, more than anything in the world, was what she wanted. This was where she was meant to be. And if another, less talented girl had to be hurt for her to get it, that was too bad.

As for that monster Algernon Pierce . . . there was no way, no way at all, that she was going to let him stand between her and her destiny.

Chapter Thirteen

It was well past ten o'clock, and Lucy was beginning to become a little anxious. Stanley had offered her a lift home and she had accepted, with the proviso that he dropped her off further along her road so that no one would see her getting out of his car. Now, however, as he lingered, chatting to Horace and the others, she was beginning to wish she had set out and walked; if she was very late home she would have some explaining to do.

At last Stanley pocketed the flask, which he had been passing around as usual.

'Right. Time to go, I think. Can you give me a hand down with some of the gear, Lucy? The plant, perhaps? Horace and I will take care of the heavy things.'

Lucy obliged, picking up the potted aspidistra, and Stanley hefted the tin trunk, awkward but reasonably manageable since it contained only costumes, cradling it to his chest like an oversized parcel. At the foot of the stairs, she held the door open with her foot for him to follow her out.

It was dusk, but not yet dark. Lucy was heading for Stanley's car when a figure materialised out of the shadows, and an all-too-familiar voice boomed out her name. Lucy froze, her heart leaping into her throat.

'I knew it!' Algernon approached, triumphant and furious. 'I knew you were lying, you wicked, deceitful girl!'

'Papa . . .' For once, Lucy was lost for words.

'How dare you disobey me? And you have been drinking too! No, don't bother to deny it. I can smell it from here!'

A sudden recklessness, born of her recent success, and perhaps the very alcohol that Algernon so despised, overtook Lucy.

'What if I have?'

For a moment, Algernon stared at her, scarcely able to believe his ears. Then, with a grunt of fury, he raised his hand, striking Lucy a sharp blow across the cheek. She stepped back in shock, her hand flying to her stinging face. The aspidistra went crashing to the ground, the china plant pot smashing to a thousand pieces on the pavement.

'My dear fellow, there's no need for that!' Stanley, who had been keeping his distance, stepped into the fray to protest, and for a horrible moment Lucy thought Algernon was going to strike him too, but he thought better of it.

'Don't you "my dear fellow" me, you disgusting little man,' he roared instead. 'I made myself quite clear when you came calling. I will not have Lucy disporting herself with the likes of you.'

'She's done nothing wrong.' Stanley was still being eminently reasonable. Lucy marvelled at his composure, but Algernon was apoplectic.

'Nothing wrong? Do you not call lying to her mother and me wrong? Flouting my express instructions and creeping out on a pretext to flaunt herself in public? Imbibing the demon drink like a common whore? Nothing wrong? You, sir, have a strange interpretation of the word "wrong". But this is nothing less than I would expect of a man with morals that belong in the gutter.'

'I'm sorry you feel that way, Algernon.' Stanley's tone was

mild and placatory. 'And I do think you are being a little hard on poor Lucy. Look – why don't we agree to differ and I'll give you both a lift home. I have to pass right by your house.'

'Indeed you do. And if passing by is not exactly what you do in future, you'll live to regret it,' Algernon stormed. 'Any more attempts to contact Lucy and I shall be going straight to the police to have molestation and attempted child abduction added to your record. Which, I may say, is already something of which you should be heartily ashamed.' He caught hold of Lucy's arm. 'Home, miss. Now!'

With that, he began to drag her across the road and Stanley could do nothing but watch them go, concerned though he was for Lucy. Her eyes smarting with tears of shock and humiliation, she was trying to struggle free, but Algernon was too strong for her. Up the high street he propelled her, past a group of youths who stopped their joshing and turned to stare, amused by the unexpected entertainment. Not another word was uttered until they reached the chapel, which fronted on to the street. Then Algernon stopped, fumbling in his pocket without relinquishing his hold on Lucy's arm, and drawing out a bunch of keys, one of which he inserted into the lock.

'What are you doing?' Lucy cried, frightened.

'You, my girl, are going to prostrate yourself before your Maker and beg his forgiveness.'

'Let me go!'

She was struggling again, terrified now, but Algernon was a man possessed. Somehow he managed to turn the key and shove the heavy oak door open with his shoulder whilst still keeping a tight hold of her arm. He pushed her inside, kicked the door shut behind them, and thrust home a heavy bolt above Lucy's head.

Inside, the chapel was hot and airless as the town hall had

been, and the smell of wilting flowers hung heavy – not the sweet perfume of roses or stocks, but the strangely woody smell of chrysanthemums, a smell that for some reason had always made Lucy think of funerals. Up the aisle Algernon propelled her, between the rows of pews, until they reached the plain altar, unadorned but for a linen cloth lovingly stitched by one of the ladies of the congregation and two pewter vases filled with those horrid-smelling chrysanthemums. He pushed Lucy down on to her knees on the wooden surround, and only then did he let go her arm. It was too late for escape, she knew. The door had been made fast with a bolt that was out of her reach, and even if it hadn't been, Algernon would have reached her long before she could slide it open and get away.

'Pray!' he ordered her.

Lucy's teeth were chattering, her cheek throbbing, her knees hurting from the rough way he'd pushed her down on to the altar surround. Never in her life had she been more afraid. She opened her mouth, but no words came, only a small, panicked sob.

'Pray!'

'I . . . I don't know what to say . . .' Lucy managed.

Algernon towered over her, a giant of a man in the dim light, like some monstrous ogre of a thousand nightmares. For a moment Lucy thought he was going to strike her again, and she cowered away, looking up at him in terror. Then, unbelievably, he folded his hands as if in prayer before flinging his arms wide, an evil avenging angel.

'Repeat after me. Dear Father, I have sinned . . .'

'Dear Father, I have sinned . . .' The words came stumbling from Lucy's trembling lips, little more than a whisper.

'Louder!' Algernon commanded. 'Dear Father, I have sinned grievously.'

'Dear Father, I have sinned grievously.'

'I am no longer fit to be called your child.'

'I am no longer fit to be called your child.'

'Forgive me. Purge me of my wickedness so that I may once again dwell in your house.'

'Forgive me . . . Purge me of my wickedness . . .'

'That I may once again dwell in your house.'

'That I may once again dwell in your house.'

'Dear Father, I crave your love and forgiveness.'

'Dear Father . . .'

In the vast chapel, Lucy's voice was barely audible. Her head and shoulders were bowed; tears ran down her cheeks and splashed on to her clasped hands.

As he swelled with religious fervour, a sense of power unlike anything he had experienced before, and intoxicating as any of the hard liquor he despised, possessed Algernon. He might be God himself, towering there over the terrified girl, holding out his arms to rescue her if – when – she genuinely achieved a state of repentance. And she was truly his child, addressing him as Father, begging, pleading for his forgiveness. The madness that for the most part he kept carefully hidden beneath an outward show of piety and respectability reared in him now, the delusion of himself as synonymous with the Almighty fanning the fires of his darkest desires and the depraved compulsions that had plagued him all his life. Algernon's body throbbed and ached with it now, blood coursed through his veins in a scalding tide and his desire rose to fever pitch.

Total domination. He needed to exercise it with every aspect of his being. Nothing less would do.

He grabbed Lucy by the arm again, yanking her to her feet, and dragged her to the open space between the carved lectern and the front pews.

'And now,' he growled, his voice low with crazed fervour, 'you will do your penance.'

He took her there, on the cold flagged floor. Her head had cracked against it as he threw her roughly down, half dazing her, and she was too petrified to fight against the greedy hands tearing at her clothing and the hot hard shaft driving into her. He would kill her if she didn't let him do as he wanted. As pain knifed through her, she gasped and spasmed, but his weight pressing down on her pinned her to the ground like a butterfly on a board, and when it was over she lay sobbing softly, but otherwise silent and still.

'Get up. Cover yourself.'

She heard the order as if through a haze and still she couldn't move or speak.

'Get up, I say!' He caught her arm, jerking roughly at it.

As if in a trance, she obeyed. Every bit of her, it seemed, hurt. Her head, throbbing from the sharp crack on the flagged floor, her cheek, burning still from Algernon's slap, her wrists and arms where his fingers had dug into them as he held her spread-eagled whilst he satisfied his crazed lust, and worst of all, the searing pain between her legs as if the most tender parts of her were on fire, and an ache low in her belly that made her want to double over against it. As if in a trance, she allowed herself to be led back down the chapel aisle, curling into herself as he released her to unbolt the door and lock it behind them. As if in a trance, her feet moved to carry her along the road towards home, propelled by a surly and silent Algernon. But a wave of shame engulfed her as he opened the front door and pushed her inside, as if she had been the one who had committed the terrible crime.

'Mam?' It came out on a trembling sob, the first word

she had spoken since Algernon's frenzied attack.

'Your mother is in bed. She wasn't feeling well.' He gave Lucy another push. 'Go and wash yourself. Don't even think of disturbing her.'

For that, at least, Lucy was grateful. Much as she longed for Annie's comforting arms, she shrank from the thought of facing her. Still so numb that she could take only one moment at a time, she went to the kitchen, drew water in a bowl in the stone sink, and did as he said, all the while afraid he might be watching from the living room, or even that he might burst in and take her again.

He was standing by the fireplace when she returned, his face set in a scowl.

'I hope,' he said, showing not the slightest regret or shame, 'that you have learned your lesson.'

He extinguished the gas lamp and followed Lucy up the stairs, waiting until her bedroom door closed behind her before going into his own room.

Lucy began to undress, still clinging to routine as some semblance of normality. But when she stood in nothing but her undergarments, hysteria began to bubble up in her. She ripped off her soiled drawers, throwing them aside, and felt her legs give way beneath her. She sank on to the bed, huddling into a ball as if somehow she could belatedly protect herself, trembling as violently as if she had a fever, and sobbing soundlessly.

Coherent thought was still beyond her, but the sense of shame was stronger than ever. How could she have allowed that terrible man to do what he did to her? Had it all been her fault – was she really all the dreadful things he had said she was? Though she had washed herself she could still smell him, and with every painful throb of her poor bruised body she could feel him thrusting into her. She'd never forget it as long as she lived. Never feel clean again.

She thought of Joe, refusing to allow them to be in a situation where things might go too far, restraining himself for the sake of her chastity, and sobbed aloud. She thought of Annie, so proud of her, so loving, the best mother in the world. She thought of Kitty, who would die, she felt sure, rather than let a man touch her. How could she face any of them ever again?

And Algernon . . . the thought of simply seeing him was nauseating. To have to face him over the breakfast table, go to work with him, sit at her desk in the little office next to his was beyond endurance.

Bile rose in Lucy's throat and her stomach heaved. She uncurled all of a rush and dived for the wash stand, where she vomited copiously into the china basin. Then she returned to the bed, climbed in just as she was, and pulled the sheet over her tormented, aching body.

What was she going to do? Lucy was still too shocked and upset to be able to even think about it. But one thing she knew. She couldn't, wouldn't, stay here under the same roof as that evil monster. Somehow she would find a means of escape.

By the next day, the red mark on Lucy's cheek had faded. When she looked in the mirror above her dressing table, only the faintest imprint of Algernon's fingers remained, and she was greatly relieved. She didn't want Mammy asking where she had got it. She couldn't bear to think about what had happened, let alone talk about it.

The days passed and still Lucy couldn't bring herself to confide in anyone. The shame and the feelings of guilt were too great. She'd die before she could tell Mammy, and though she and Kitty were closer now than they had ever been, there was no way she could divulge something so dreadful. As for Joe . . .

She shrank even more from the thought of telling him what had happened, just as she shrank away now when he tried to kiss her, or hold her. There was no way she could find the words, and besides, heaven only knew what he would do if she did. The ensuing scene had the quality of a nightmare in her imaginings. Joe storming to the house, the violent confrontation that would follow, Mammy and Kitty learning of it in the most dreadful way . . . She couldn't risk such a thing happening. And there was no way she could marry him now either. He'd know, he'd be bound to, that she was no longer a virgin, and in any case she couldn't bear the thought of him touching her, let alone doing . . . that thing that Algernon had done.

She couldn't tell him, but she couldn't keep her secret from him either. The only answer was to end it, to set him free, and that meant the end of her hopes of a future together. Lucy almost wept with despair when she thought of it.

But one dream remained to her, one dream that was miraculously untouched by the terrible events of that summer night and which grew ever more important to her as she struggled to keep up the pretence of normality whilst her world fell apart around her.

In the last months, her passion for performing had vied with her love for Joe as the most important thing in her life. Now, it seemed, it was all she had left, and it was something to cling to in her darkest moments. She would never again sing with Stanley Bristow's concert party, that much she knew, but perhaps much greater opportunities lay ahead of her. And they would offer her a way of escape from the living hell she had found herself in if she was brave enough to take it.

Not so long ago – though after what had happened it might

have been in another lifetime – Aunt Molly's husband, theatre owner and impresario, had praised her as a music hall star in the making, and told her that if ever she should decide to make a career of it she should contact him. Supposing she did just that? The very thought scared her a little, but the prospect of singing every night, not just once or twice every few weeks, and in real theatres and halls, to bigger crowds, was an exciting one.

Lucy lost herself in her imaginings – of seeing her name on playbills, of being accompanied by a proper orchestra, not just blind Nobby Parker on the piano, of curtsying to a stamping, cheering crowd rather than a handful of local people seated on hard upright chairs in some town hall. If she closed her eyes, she could recall the smell of greasepaint and dust, see the plush seating in the stalls and the ornate carvings on the balcony above, feel the swish of the curtain as she stood in the wings of the stage – the things that had so excited her when Aunt Molly had shown them around the Lyric all those years ago.

A little drunk on her own daring, Lucy made up her mind. She couldn't stay here under the same roof as that monster who had done such unspeakable things to her and pretend nothing had happened. She couldn't marry Joe and either deceive him or break his heart. But she could try to carve out a new life for herself, one that she had always longed for. Fate, it seemed, was pushing her towards it.

But how to set about it? Mammy would be totally against the idea, she felt sure. She'd be worried that such a life would bring Lucy into close contact with all kinds of undesirables, men who would try to take advantage of her, and women who were no better than they should be. Ironic, really, since Lucy had encountered far worse in the supposed safety of her own home. Algernon, undoubtedly, would forbid it, and do everything in his power to scupper her plans, but Lucy no longer cared what Algernon thought. And Joe, of course, would be dreadfully upset and probably try to persuade her to marry him right away, the very last thing she wanted.

No, best that none of them knew until her new life was a *fait accompli*. Aunt Molly had run away from home to go on the stage, hadn't she, and made a tremendous success of it? Then why shouldn't she, Lucy, do the same?

In the privacy of her room, Lucy wrote three more or less identical letters on the lavender-scented notepaper she'd been given for her birthday: one to Mammy, one to Kitty and one to Joe. As she wrote her sister's, a sudden awful thought occurred to her – supposing when she had gone Algernon turned his attentions to Kitty? She didn't think it was likely – Algernon was always kind to Kitty, and almost respectful – but just in case, she added a carefully worded warning at the bottom of her letter: *I know you get on well with Algernon, but do be careful of him, Kitty.* It was the best she could do without revealing the truth, and she hoped Algernon would not get to see it.

He undoubtedly would read Annie's letter, of course, and he would know that ambition wasn't the whole reason for Lucy's going, but he'd never admit it. The shame of having his stepdaughter run away to become a music hall singer would be a lesser evil than having the world know him for the monster he was. He would simply shake his head, say he'd always known she would come to no good, and no doubt pray for her eternal soul. But he would know, and she was glad. He would know, and chafe under the knowledge, though she doubted it would stir him to real remorse. He was too practised at shifting the blame elsewhere for that.

The letter to Joe was the hardest of all to write. She explained, as she had in the others, that she wanted to try her luck on the stage, and that if she didn't she would spend the rest of her life wondering what might have been, regretting that she hadn't given it a go and yearning for a star she'd failed to follow.

Then she added another paragraph, especially for him.

You will be hurt, I know. But please don't think any of this is your fault. I do love you, very much, but it's not enough. I have to give myself the chance to do what I've always wanted before I can even think of settling down to a life of domesticity as a wife and mother. I don't expect you to wait for me, Joe. You'll find another girl who can be the wife you want, as I never could be. One day you'll be glad of it, that we parted before life could turn our love sour like last week's milk, and that's what would have happened, believe me. I wish you every happiness and I am sure you will find it, for you deserve far better than me.

In order to drive home to him that there could be nothing more between them, she signed the letter: *Your ever loving sister Lucy.* And when a tear splashed on to the page and blurred her name, she copied it out on a fresh sheet. She didn't want Joe to know she'd been crying as she wrote it.

She planned her escape like a military exercise, which somehow helped her to forget the way her heart contracted every time she thought of leaving all the people she loved most in the world without so much as a goodbye. She packed the things she would need into her big soft carpet bag, making sure there were enough clothes left hanging in the wardrobe so as not to arouse Annie's suspicions should she go to it to hang a freshly laundered blouse or skirt. Into a small attaché case in which she had kept birthday cards and her collection of postcards she packed a few sheets of her favourite music (she didn't possess many, since Nobby's blindness forced him to play by ear), the brooch Joe had given her at Christmas, and the two lockets – Aunt Molly's long-ago gift, and the one that had belonged to Joe's mother. One day she'd return it to him so that he could give it to some other girl, the girl who would become his wife. But for the moment she couldn't bear to part with it.

She found out the times of trains to Bath and decided on one in the early evening. That, she thought, would give her the best chance of getting away without arousing suspicion. As long as the weather remained fine, she could pretend she was going for a walk.

She wouldn't be able to leave in broad daylight carrying her carpet bag and attaché case, of course, so the night before she planned to go she crept down when the rest of the family were in bed and asleep and hid them in the bushes at the bottom of the garden. She'd have to make sure the coast was clear before she retrieved them, and hope she didn't meet anyone she knew on her way to the station who might wonder why she was laden with luggage. For the first time, she was glad she didn't still live in the Ten Houses; she'd never have got away with it there, where everyone knew everyone else and made it their business. But then, of course, if she'd still been living in the Ten Houses, this would never have happened at all.

Lucy felt a sharp pang of longing for her dead father. Strange how after all this time she could still miss him so much. Still smell the tobacco and coal dust on his skin. Still remember the wonderful feeling of safety when he lifted her into his arms. Still ache with love for him.

Well, she was going to his sister. She hoped he would approve of that. And she hoped that in time she would be able to make enough of a success of herself to make him proud.

A tiny sharp imp of excitement darted in her stomach.

Perhaps after all the despicable Algernon had done her a favour. If he hadn't made it impossible for her to remain under his roof, she might never have been brave enough to take this step, much as she might have wanted it.

As things stood, a whole new life awaited her. There was a rainbow now in the storm-dark skies, and her future was the pot of gold at its end.

Chapter Fourteen

When I became a full grown man
Time ran.

Lucy had to ask directions several times before she found the Lyric. She had only been there the once, all those years ago, and she had been far too young – and too excited – to notice which way they had walked to get there. Her carpet bag was weighing heavily by the time she rounded a corner and saw it ahead of her, its square, unprepossessing facade jutting carbuncle-like from the tall buildings next to it.

She paused for a moment, putting down her attaché case and bag in order to change arms. A mixture of nervousness and excitement knotted her stomach as she gazed at the theatre, light spilling pale from the open doors into the still day-lit street. Should she go in that way, or through the stage door as she, Kitty and Mam had when Molly had given them the guided tour? How was she going to announce herself? And what would Molly say, or, for that matter, do, when Lucy told her why she was here?

Well, too late to turn back now, even if she'd wanted to. Taking a deep breath, Lucy hefted her bag again, waited for a motor car to splutter past, and crossed the road.

She went first to the stage door, deciding that unless she was actually on stage, Molly would most likely be in her dressing room. When she tried it, however, she found it locked, and when she rang the bell alongside it, and rapped on the blue-painted wooden panels, there was no response.

Picking up her bag again, she went back to the front of the theatre. The small foyer was empty but for a girl in the ticket booth. Her hair was obviously hennaed, and the neckline of her dress – shocking pink – was lower than any Lucy had ever seen, exposing the hollow between her full breasts.

Lucy approached the window and set her bag down yet again, and the girl looked up from a novelette open on the counter in front of her, her expression conveying that she was none too pleased at the interruption.

'The show's nearly half over.'

'I haven't come to see the show,' Lucy said. 'I've come to see . . .' She hesitated, remembering that the name of Molly Day meant nothing here. 'Belle Dorne,' she finished.

'Belle Dorne?' The girl's lips tightened into a little sneer. 'You mean Mrs Trotter?'

'Well . . . yes . . .'

The girl smirked.

'You're out of luck then, dearie. Mrs Trotter isn't here. She don't work any more.'

'Oh!' Lucy was totally taken aback and dismayed. This wasn't something she'd anticipated.

As she tried to gather her thoughts, the girl returned to her book, casually flicking over a page and presenting Lucy with the top of her hennaed head.

Left with no alternative, Lucy made up her mind. Daniel – or Spike – was Aunt Molly's husband, and hadn't he told her to come to him if she decided to make a career on the halls?

'Mr Trotter then,' she said.

The girl huffed.

212

'Mr Trotter don't see just anybody.'

'I think you'll find he'll see me,' Lucy said, with more confidence than she was feeling. 'I am Mrs Trotter's niece, and I'd be glad if you would get a message to him.'

The girl looked up again, curious now, and a little uncomfortable – afraid, no doubt, of losing her job.

'Well why didn't you say so?' She shifted the cheap-looking book to one side as if, too late, she could pretend it had never been there. 'I can't do nothing while the show's on, though. I'm not to leave my post.'

'Then perhaps you can tell me where I can find him,' Lucy said, frustrated. The tensions of the past days were starting to tell on her and she was very afraid everything was going to go terribly wrong. The last thing she wanted was another hour or so of uncertainty.

'He's in the house, I expect. Or backstage. Could be anywhere really.' The girl was recovering her equilibrium, and, Lucy thought, beginning to enjoy herself.

'I'll go in then,' she said.

'Not without paying you won't. How do I know you're who you say you are? D'you want the gallery or the stalls? Ninepence or one and six. It's up to you.'

'Oh, the stalls.' Lucy was reluctant to part with the money since she hadn't had very much to bring with her and had no idea how long it would have to last her, but if the only way to get to see Spike before the end of the show was to pay to go into the theatre, she really had no choice. And the gallery would be of no use to her. She couldn't imagine that the theatre owner would watch the show from up there amongst the hobbledehoys who couldn't afford better. She found her purse and counted out the coins, then, clutching her ticket between her teeth, she bundled her way into the hall.

Even before the door swung open she could hear the orchestra, or at any rate, the rapid rattle of a drum, and a sudden excitement kicked in her stomach. Then, as she stepped into the garish half-light, the drum rolls reached a crescendo and the rest of the ensemble joined in a triumphant flourish. The act on stage was just finishing, she realised – a troupe of tumblers in spangles and tights dismounted from a pyramid with all the grace of the waters of an ornamental fountain and leapt to the front of the stage, where they took their bow holding hands in a line just behind the footlights. The crowd erupted then, cheering, whistling and stamping so loudly that they almost drowned out the orchestra.

It wasn't just the enthusiastic applause that made excitement kick in her stomach again, and her pulses race, but the atmosphere that seemed to swallow her up. The air was thick with cigarette smoke, and the smell that hung in it was just as intoxicating as she remembered it from that long-ago visit, but multiplied a thousandfold, greasepaint wafting from beyond the footlights, beer and body odour. Shafts of light with their clouded miasmas pierced the murky darkness, changing colour as the linesman swapped his filters, and for a moment Lucy wanted nothing more than to slip into a seat and soak it all up. But the places on the ends of the rows closest to her were already taken, and she couldn't squeeze past their occupants with her bulky luggage.

A man approached her, coming up the aisle. With the light behind him she couldn't see his face, but the bulk of him told her he was one of the heavies employed to restore order should the crowd become rowdy.

'You can't stop 'ere, miss. You need to sit down.'

Lucy decided to take the bull by the horns.

'I'm looking for Mr Trotter. I'm his niece.'

The man snorted. 'Oh yes, I've 'eard that one before. Move on now.'

'I am!' Lucy protested. 'He's in the hall, I understand. Could you please tell him Lucy Day is here and wants to see him.'

The big man studied her closely in the beam of the limes. In her demure dress, and with her hair tucked into a neat coil at the nape of her neck, she didn't look like a dollymop, or even one of Spike's lady friends. Perhaps she really was his niece; he'd come across stranger things. In this line of work you saw it all

'All right, I'll tell him,' he grunted. 'But keep to the side, and don't block the gangway. And if Mr Trotter don't know you from Adam, you'll have to either find a seat or be on your way.'

He turned, walking down the aisle toward the stage with a swaggering gait as if he were a mariner negotiating a rolling deck, and Lucy waited, anxious now. Supposing Spike had forgotten her – and his invitation? Suppose her name meant nothing to him? What would she do then? But Molly's real name was Day, or had been before she'd married him. Surely that, at least, would ring bells with him?

The numbers beside the stage had changed, and the spot was now on a man in full evening dress with an extravagant moustache and sideburns who sat behind a small table.

'And now, for your delectation, I give you the most stylish masher ever to grace the boards of a stage. Eat your hearts out, boys and girls, ladies and gentlemen, and raise the roof for the exquisite, the most delightful . . .' His sonorous tones rose to a crescendo, 'Miss Lally Deneuve!'

The drum rolled again, the orchestra struck up, and into the rosy beam of light strolled a girl who was dressed not at all as a girl dressed, but in a tailored black evening suit, starched white dickey and top hat. In one hand she carried a cigarette in a long holder, and an ivory-topped cane was tucked beneath her arm.

Lucy's eyes widened. Never before had she seen a girl dressed as a man, but she recognised the introduction the orchestra was playing and was transported back to that birthday when Molly had borrowed Algernon's hat and cane to sing for them in the front parlour.

Had Molly once dressed like this to perform in front of an audience? Lucy couldn't imagine it somehow; Molly's hair was thick and luxuriant, while this girl's was close-cropped about her elfin face, and her aunt had a figure that was unmistakably womanly, while this girl was flat-chested and slim as a boy. But the actions she was performing were much the same. As for the saucy way this girl was phrasing the lyrics, she was making Lucy blush in the semi-darkness as she divined a meaning to the words that had never occurred to her before. No wonder Algernon had reacted the way he did, she thought. Even if Molly hadn't been flouncing about in his best hat, those words would have enraged him, an affront to his professed piety, and ones that a man with such a terrible dark side to his nature would understand all too well . . .

It was hot in the theatre; Lucy's dress was clinging damply to her back and her armpits, and the flesh beneath the rise of her breasts felt sticky with it. But still she shivered, a chill prickling over her skin as she remembered that dreadful night in the chapel, and what Algernon had done to her.

She'd been right to run away, and she would never go back. No, not even if Spike Trotter refused to so much as see her.

As the girl's song came to an end and the cheering, stamping and whistles erupted again, even louder than before, Lucy felt a tap on her shoulder. She whirled round, expecting an irate member of the audience or even another of the security men. But to her surprise, it was neither.

'Well, little Lucy.' Although she couldn't hear the words

over the thunderous applause, she was able to lip-read them well enough, and relief flooded through her.

'Mr Trotter.'

'Come with me.'

He placed a hand about her waist, steering her back up the aisle. As the door closed behind them, the noise became fainter and more muffled, but he said no more as he led her through the foyer, where the henna-haired girl gawped at them from behind her window, out of the main doors and around the building to the stage door, and neither did he make any attempt to relieve her of at least one of her bags. The stage door was now on the latch; he pushed it open and ushered her into the narrow passageway beyond.

The doors of the dressing rooms they passed were ajar. Through one Lucy caught a glimpse of the back of an elaborately coiffed woman sitting at a mirror set on a bare board table; through another, some men she recognised as the tumblers, though they were now wearing everyday clothes instead of their spangles, and were obviously preparing to leave. They passed the top-hatted man who was the MC so close that Lucy could smell the fresh sweat that ran in rivulets down his face; he made to speak to Spike, but Spike brushed him aside.

'Not now, Walter. And why aren't you on stage? Not caught short again, I hope. If this goes on . . .'

'Have a heart, dear boy . . .'

Spike ignored him, and swept on with Lucy in tow.

The little room at the far end of the passage that he led her to was, she guessed, his office. Playbills littered a desk badly marked by white rings left by beer glasses and cigar burns, and the walls were hung with photographs – one of them was of Molly in a low-cut gown, smiling provocatively over a highly decorated oriental fan. Spike closed the door after them and indicated that Lucy should take the single upright chair that stood in the corner. He lowered himself into a padded swivel chair in front of the desk, and pivoted around to face her.

'Well, this is a surprise!'

Lucy set down her luggage and settled herself on the upright chair, smoothing her skirt over her knees with hands that she couldn't keep from trembling a little.

'I thought I'd find Aunt Molly here,' she said, struggling to keep the tremble from creeping into her voice.

'And why were you looking for your Aunt Molly, may I ask?' His eyes went to the carpet bag and attaché case, stacked on the floor beside her chair, then returned to her face. A small smile was barely concealed, and he raised a quizzical eyebrow.

He knows, Lucy thought. He knows very well why I'm here. There was no point beating about the bush, then.

'I've left home,' she said boldly. 'You remember you told me to come to you if I decided to make a career on the halls? Well . . . here I am!'

Molly was sitting in the garden of the house she now shared with Spike – or Daniel, as she preferred to call him. 'Spike' reminded her too much of the old days, a life she was trying, without much success, to put behind her.

Oh, but she missed it so! Missed the thrill of performing and the adulation of the crowd, missed the surge of adrenalin that came with walking into the beam of the limes with the orchestra playing her intro, even missed the sharp, stomach-churning fear when she stood in the wings waiting to make her entrance. For all her years of experience, that fear had never left her; in fact it had grown sharper with the passage of time. Yes, she missed it all dreadfully, and neither the life of luxury and leisure she had enjoyed since marrying Daniel nor the grand house he had bought for them to live in could make up for that.

She knew, though, in her heart of hearts, that retiring from the stage had been the right decision. Had she risen to the heights and achieved the cult popularity of Marie Lloyd or Vesta Tilley it would have been different, but she hadn't, and she had only herself to blame for that. She might never have become a shining star like them, of course, though she had thought once that was within her grasp. But she'd lost sight of her goal, or perhaps fooled herself into thinking she could have it all, and her chance had slipped away. Her fame and popularity had been lost in the wilderness years, and though thanks to Daniel she'd still had a reasonably successful career, she had realised it had to come to an end. She was no longer young; others, prettier and not so long in the tooth, had been snapping at her heels for years now, and they were what audiences wanted, not a fading talent with a thickening waist and wrinkles that took ever longer to disguise with powder and paint.

Her voice wasn't what it had once been either. Years of singing in smoky halls had taken their toll, and she could no longer hit the soaring high notes that had been her trademark. Molly hadn't wanted to outstay her welcome and hear the cheers and raucous applause of her heyday turn to catcalls and jeers. She'd seen it happen to others and knew it would destroy her, and sour all her cherished memories of her glory days. So at last – at long last – she'd given in and accepted Spike's oft-rejected proposal of marriage, only surprised that he hadn't given up on her and decided he'd prefer a younger model in his bed as well as on stage as the star of his shows.

His loyalty and devotion were, she supposed, his saving grace, for she didn't love him, never had. Well, she loved him, maybe, but more as a friend. He'd never made her heart turn over in her breast the way Anthony had, never made her so crazy with desire that she was prepared to risk everything to be with him. And perhaps that was just as well, considering how badly that affair had ended . . .

Molly gave herself a little shake now as she found the memories – and the great gulf of aching sadness they unleashed – creeping over her like the lengthening shadows on the lawn. That was another thing about retirement: it gave her too much time for thinking, and for regrets. She reached for the glass of beer that stood on the little garden table beside her and took a long pull, trying to push those troublesome thoughts to the back of her mind. She had a great deal to be grateful for: this house, with all its comforts, when she might well have been forced to languish in some seedy home for retired artistes had it not been for Daniel; the garden, which she loved, long and broad, bright with hollyhocks and perfumed with Sweet William at this time of year, and a pear tree, its branches dripping with ripening fruit. And Daniel was generous; he was happy for her to spend whatever she liked on nice clothes and shoes, perfume and trinkets. She must count herself as lucky, and stop this stupid hankering for the past, try to ignore the ache of longing that never quite left her, only slept, waiting like some hibernating animal to be aroused to unbearable pain – the longing for what she had lost and could never have again.

She wouldn't think about him tonight. But what else was there to think about now? Where was he? Was he well and happy? What did he look like? Heavens, she could pass him in the street and not know it . . .

Molly's hand trembled a little and she reached again for her glass. The beer was warm now, but she drank it anyway, savouring the taste of hops on her tongue. She'd always liked beer – Anthony had used to tease her about it. How could she prefer beer to champagne, cognac or fine wine? Daniel understood, though. He liked his beer too – it was their roots, she supposed. His in the East End of London, hers in a Somerset mining community.

Yes, she was lucky. He loved her and they understood one another. It was more than she had any right to expect. More than she deserved.

The sound of a motor car engine broke the stillness of the evening. Molly tilted her head, listening. Though motor cars weren't entirely unusual in this affluent district of the city, they were still enough of a novelty to attract attention. As she listened, the engine cut, and after a moment's silence she heard the slam of a car door. It sounded quite close. It was too early for it to be Daniel home from the theatre; perhaps one of their near neighbours had a visitor. They certainly didn't own motor cars themselves. The wondering provided a welcome diversion and the unwelcome thoughts of a few moments ago receded.

She'd fetch a fresh cold beer, Molly decided. She got up from the garden bench, smoothed down her rumpled dress, enjoying the satisfying rustle of the taffeta underskirt, and picked up her glass. To her surprise, as she turned toward the house two figures emerged from the path that ran from the little front garden along the side of the mellow stone building.

Daniel – and a young lady! A young lady in a modest green day dress, carrying a carpet bag . . . Molly stared, scarcely able to believe her eyes.

'Lucy!'

'Aunt Molly.' Lucy sounded nervous, quite unlike her usual bubbly self.

'Quite a surprise, eh?' Daniel, Molly noticed, was carrying a battered brown leather attaché case. 'She turned up at the Lyric, so I thought I'd better bring her home.'

'But . . .' Molly was lost for words. 'What are you doing in Bath, Lucy?'

Lucy was clutching the carpet bag with both hands, holding it in front of her so that it squashed the fabric of her skirt between her knees.

'I've left home,' she said in a small voice. 'Please, Aunt Molly, can I stay with you?'

'My goodness . . .' Molly was completely taken aback. 'But . . . what about your mam? Does she know you're here? Won't she be worried about you?'

Lucy swallowed hard.

'I've left her a note. She'll find it when she goes to bed. Oh, Aunt Molly – please! I couldn't stay there any longer . . . I couldn't! Not with *him*.'

Molly's mouth tightened. 'Your charming stepfather, you mean?'

Lucy nodded. Her lip trembled, and she caught it between her teeth. 'Don't make me go back there, please.'

Molly sighed. Fond as she was of Lucy, having her turn up like this, unannounced and without her mother's permission, was rather a worrying situation. But here she was, and something very bad must have happened to drive her to it.

'Of course you can stay, Lucy. But will your mam be happy about this? And I really think we are owed some sort of explanation . . .'

'She wants a career on the halls,' Daniel interrupted. His tone was jovial; he looked rather pleased with himself. 'Isn't that explanation enough? And isn't it just what you did yourself? Ran away to go on the stage?'

Molly grimaced. He was right, of course – how could she condemn Lucy for doing exactly what she had done? But there was more to it than that, she was sure of it. Lucy wasn't the wild type of girl she had been. And she'd seemed to be very much in love with the boy Joe. Algernon was a dreadful man, of course – she couldn't understand why someone as nice as Annie should have married him, and living with him couldn't be easy for a personable young girl like Lucy. But even so, running away was a pretty extreme course of action. What on earth had happened to drive her to it? And how was she, Molly, going to answer to Annie for conniving in it?

'You must be hungry and thirsty,' she said to Lucy. 'Let's find you something in the way of sustenance and then we'll sit down and talk about this.'

Lucy looked to be on the verge of tears.

'Oh, thank you! Thank you . . .' was all she could manage.

'You'd better come inside,' Molly said. She was still full of misgivings, but she couldn't turn Lucy away, at least not tonight.

Well, she'd wanted a distraction, she thought ruefully. It seemed that fate had sent one, but not at all in a manner she might have expected.

After Molly had shown Lucy to a spare room where the bed was made up, and Lucy had unpacked a few bits and pieces, they talked over a platter of cold meats and cheeses, washed down by yet more cold beer. But by the end of the evening Molly was still none the wiser as to the real reason for her niece's unexpected arrival, nor why she was so obviously in a state of distress.

Daniel, however, red-faced with enthusiasm at the prospect of launching a new act, was happy to accept her explanation of wanting to make a career on the halls and having met with not just disapproval but downright obstruction.

'Papa wouldn't let me perform with the concert party any longer, and in any case I wanted more,' was all Lucy would say. But the dark circles beneath her eyes spoke volumes, and Molly was still far from convinced that there wasn't more to it than that. She didn't feel this was the right time to press her, though, and in any case, she could hardly find a gap in the conversation to voice her suspicions that something was seriously wrong, or, for that matter, her misgivings about taking Lucy in when her mother had no idea where she was. Spike was already full of plans to rehearse Lucy and give her a spot as soon as he thought she was ready.

'We'll see how you do at the Lyric, and if you go down well I'll get a couple of manager friends in to hear you. There's my pals from Bristol and Weston-super-Mare – they might well give you a spot. They're always looking for fresh talent. But the one I really want to introduce you to is Spanker Barnes. He fixes bookings all over the country and he's well in with a lot of the London halls.'

'London!' Lucy was looking a little dazed; this was all moving at a much faster rate than she'd expected, Molly guessed.

'That's where you need to be if you're going to make a name for yourself.' Daniel took a long pull of beer and wiped the froth from his whiskers with the back of his hand.

'But I thought I'd be at the Lyric . . .'

'Gotta keep my bill on the move,' Daniel told her. 'Can't pull in the punters with the same old acts week after week.'

'I suppose not . . . I didn't realise . . .'

'No, London's the place to be,' Daniel asserted. 'You'll start small, of course, and you'll have to work hard. Two, maybe three shows a night, running between halls. But if they like you, the better-class places will take you, and the world'll be your oyster. Why, you might even get a season in panto. I can just see you as Cinderella or Snow White.'

'Aren't you getting a bit ahead of yourself, Daniel?' Molly chided. She was used to his enthusiasm and optimistic predictions, but she didn't want Lucy to be carried away only to be disappointed.

Daniel banged his beer glass down on the table and laughed. 'You'll see, my dear. The world's her oyster, mark my words. I look at her, I see you, thirty years ago. She'll go far, mark my words.'

Molly looked down at the beringed hands holding her glass. They were blue-veined now, not smooth and pale – ageing, just like the rest of her. Then she looked up at Lucy, her pretty face bright, her eyes shining, her lips still full, not thinning to a whisper, with the carmine bleeding into the fine lines around them, as Molly's were.

Yes, Lucy did remind her of herself at that age, all soaring hopes and youthful promise. Perhaps she would be luckier than she, Molly, had been. But before she embarked on a course she might live to regret, Molly would have a heart-to-heart with her, warn her of the hardships and the pitfalls, the disappointments and the temptations, the exploitation, and the unscrupulousness of some of the people she would come into contact with. She didn't want Lucy to make the same mistakes she had made.

And she would talk to her too about her reasons for leaving home so unceremoniously.

But not tonight. Suddenly Molly was very weary. She rose from the table.

'In the morning,' she said, 'I shall write to your mama and tell her you are here. And we really need to discuss exactly what it is you will be getting yourself into. But for now, I'm going to bed, and I suggest you do the same.'

'I'll be up in a bit, my dear.' Daniel winked conspiratorially at Lucy. 'It's early yet. You're not tired, are you?'

Lucy shook her head, but a shadow had fallen into her eyes,

and she suddenly looked as downcast as she had done when she had arrived.

'I expect Mam's found my note by now,' she said softly, and, Molly thought, rather sadly.

She crossed to the door, then paused, looking back at the two of them. Daniel was always a late bird, as she herself had once been. They'd be there, like as not, until the wee small hours, discussing his plans for Lucy's future. A future she hoped would be bright, with none of the misfortunes and heartache that had marred her own life.

'Good night, Lucy. Sleep well,' she said.

And the sadness was back, a thick river mist drifting over her heart.

Chapter Fifteen

The note Lucy had left for Annie lay on her pillow. The moment she saw the lavender-coloured envelope addressed to her in Lucy's handwriting, a feeling of dread began in the pit of her stomach and washed over her in a chill wave.

All evening she'd been uneasy – Lucy had gone out as soon as she'd finished her tea, saying she was going to meet Joe. But she'd seemed edgy, as if she was hiding something, and Annie had been afraid she might be sneaking off to sing with Stanley Bristow's concert party again. If she had, and Algernon found out, there'd be hell to pay.

But Lucy wouldn't leave a note if that was where she'd gone, she'd just creep in and hope she'd got away with it. And in any case, she would have been home by now. Annie's fingers were already trembling as she tore open the envelope.

Dearest Mam,

Please don't be angry with me, or too upset . . . I am going to try my luck on the stage . . . More than anything I want to be a singer, and I know Papa would never allow it.

I'm sorry, but it's something I have to do.

Take good care of Kitty, and don't worry about me. I promise to write and let you know how I am getting on. But please, please don't try to stop me . . .

The words blurred before Annie's eyes; the iron rim of the bedstead was sharp against the back of her legs, which seemed to have turned to jelly. She sank down on to the bed and stared, transfixed, at the letter. She was scarcely able to believe what she was seeing, yet at the same time the sinking feeling in her stomach was telling her it was true.

'Oh Lucy!' she groaned. 'What have you done?'

It made sense now, of course, the way Lucy had been this last week or so. Annie had known there was something wrong – her daughter had been so unlike her usual sunny self. Why, oh why, hadn't she asked her what was troubling her? But she'd thought that perhaps Lucy and Joe had had a lovers' tiff, or that her strange mood stemmed from having been forbidden to sing with the concert party. Since there was nothing she could do to help on either score, she'd left Lucy alone to work things out for herself. Now, however, she wondered how she could have been so complacent. She should have talked to her at least, and asked her what was wrong. Now Lucy had done something really stupid, and heaven only knew what would come of it, or what repercussions there would be.

I can't let her go like this! Annie thought. All very well for her to ask me not to try to stop her. I'd be failing in my duty as a mother if I didn't at least try to get her to see sense. She's been carried away on a dream; she isn't thinking beyond the excitement and glamour. She's just a child; she has no idea of the dangers and the hardships, the unscrupulous men who will prey on her and take advantage of her innocence.

She shivered at the thought, her stomach turning and anxiety rising like bile in her throat. She swallowed it, trying to force herself to be calm and to think rationally.

Though she didn't say so in the letter, Lucy would almost certainly have gone to Molly, and for the moment, at least, she'd be safe there. Molly wouldn't let any harm come to her . . . would she?

Suddenly Annie was unsure. What did she really know about John's sister? She'd been a wild one, for sure, running away herself to go on the stage. She'd lived for years as Spike Trotter's mistress – Annie was fairly sure of that – which didn't say a great deal for her morals. And she'd encouraged Lucy, who would probably never have even thought of such a thing if the idea hadn't been put in her head.

Annie felt a flash of anger towards her sister-in-law, and at herself for having allowed her to become part of their lives. She'd been so pleased to be able to make the connection to her beloved John, she'd never for one moment stopped to think what a bad influence Molly might be on the girls – Lucy in particular. Even after she'd showed herself in her true colours and been banned from the house, Annie had surreptitiously kept up contact. And all the while Molly had been grooming Lucy to follow the same chancy path as herself. Worse, maybe that man, Spike Trotter, was behind it. He'd seen a pretty, talented young woman when he and Molly had attended one of Lucy's concerts, and made up his mind to inveigle her into his murky world with promises of stardom on the halls. And who knew what he might want in return?

Furious, worried half to death, but suddenly determined, Annie made up her mind. Still clutching the letter, she rose on legs that felt shaky and weak, and went downstairs to break the news to Algernon of what had happened – and what she intended to do about it.

* * *

Algernon had been sitting at the living room table reading a chapter of the Bible as he always did before going to bed. Though he knew many of the passages off by heart, he could always find new meaning in the familiar words, meanings that struck chords with him, and seemed to have particular relevance to whatever was going on in his life, or the lives of those around him.

The grim stories of the Old Testament in particular resonated with him: the plagues of Egypt, Lot's wife turned to stone for disobedience, a sinful world covered by water by a vengeful God whilst Noah, the chosen one, was led to build an ark so that he might survive – Algernon, of course, saw himself as the living embodiment of Noah. Most of all, however, he gloried in the Revelation of St John the Divine. He had heard, he believed, the voice from heaven as the voice of many waters, the harpers singing with their harps, and drunk from the fountain of the water of life.

Tonight, however, it was the vision of retribution that was occupying him and giving him satisfaction at the opprobrium heaped on sinners, most of whom he could recognise in those he knew: '. . . the fearful, and unbelieving, and the abominable, and murderers, and whoremongers, and sorcerers, and idolaters, and all liars, shall have their part in the lake which burneth with fire and brimstone, which is the second death . . .'

He glanced up, annoyed, at the sound of Annie's footsteps on the stairs. She should know better than to interrupt when he was reading. He straightened in his chair, his place in the text marked with his finger, ready to castigate her, but as she appeared in the doorway, the sight of her shocked him into silence. She was, he saw, pale as a ghost, her face contorted in an expression of anguish.

'Annie?' he said sharply. For a moment her mouth worked but no words came. 'Annie?' he said again. 'Are you ill?'

'It's Lucy.' Her voice cracked. 'She's gone.'

Algernon stared at his wife, uncomprehending. Half his mind was still on the vision of St John the Divine.

'Gone? Gone where? What are you talking about?'

'Lucy! She's run away.'

As her words sank in, the colour drained from Algernon's own face, then returned in a scalding flood as the spectre of what he had done rose, apparition-like, before his eyes.

Dear God, no! Ever since that night in the chapel, the shadow of repercussion had hung over him. The devil had been in him, he knew that, tempting him, filling him with lust, not only for sexual gratification but also for power, and, weak mortal that he was, he had succumbed. He had prayed every day to the Lord his God for forgiveness, and even inflicted small tortures on himself by way of atonement – deliberately dragging his bare arm through the rosebush in the front garden when he passed it; scraping his neck with his cut-throat razor until it bled.

But the prayers had also been for Lucy's silence. Algernon was more afraid of being exposed than he was repentant. And it had seemed those prayers had been answered. The days had passed and Lucy had said nothing. Algernon had begun to breathe more easily and pray less fervently about something he would have preferred to forget.

Now . . .

'She's out with Joe, I thought,' he said, his tone abrupt and almost aggressive. 'Why should you think she's run away?'

'She left me a letter. It was on my pillow.'

For the first time he noticed the sheet of notepaper Annie was clutching, and the flood of ice surged through his veins again and turned his stomach to liquid. A letter. Explaining why she had gone. Accusing him . . .

'What does it say?' He could feel the muscles in his back and

231

shoulders tightening, and in his jaw and neck too, as if by his very steeliness he could withstand the expected onslaught of blame and disgust.

It did not come.

'She says she's going to try for a career singing on the halls.' Annie's voice cracked again, her distress taking her to the verge of tears. 'The halls, Algernon! But she's just an innocent young girl! She has no experience of that kind of life. You know as well as I do the sort of place many of them are!'

Algernon's eyes narrowed. Surely, if Lucy had accused him, it would have been the first thing Annie mentioned?

'I do indeed!' he said forcefully, feeling himself to be on more familiar, safer ground. 'They are nothing but dens of iniquity!'

His relief, however, was to be short-lived.

'I have to go after her!' Annie said distractedly. 'I've got to find her and bring her home.'

The fear leapt in him again. If Annie went after her, Lucy would undoubtedly tell her mother the reason for her going, even if she hadn't written it in her letter.

'I see little point in that,' he said shortly. 'If her mind is made up, she'll do as she pleases. She has always been wilful, and, I am afraid to say, wild too.'

'That's not so!' Annie protested. 'She's a good girl, and really scarcely more than a child. Heaven only knows where it would end. I can't let her go through with this.'

'And how would you know where to find her? She could be anywhere.'

'She's gone to Molly, I'm sure of it. Molly will have taken her in.' She saw his scowl deepen as she said it, saw the way his beetling brows drew together over his hard, cold eyes so that they almost met above the bridge of his nose, but nothing would stop her now. 'I shall go to Bath, first thing in the morning. I'll talk to her, make her see sense.'

Algernon brought his fist down on the table with a thud that made the glass vase that stood in the centre jump in its bowl.

'You will do no such thing.'

'I have to. You must understand that, Algernon.'

'It would do no good whatsoever,' Algernon declared. 'She's made her choice, Annie, and you have to accept that.'

'I'm sorry, but I can't. If she's still set on it in a couple of years, well, I dare say I shall have to let her spread her wings. But she's only seventeen, Algernon. Far too young yet to deal with the sort of situations she may well find herself in. I'd be failing in my duty as a mother if I didn't at least try to get her to change her mind.'

Algernon had rarely seen Annie so determined. He was used to her obeying his every command, and his temper began to rise, fuelled too by the anxiety that was beginning to become something close to panic. Annie must not find Lucy; she must not talk to her; the consequences didn't bear thinking about, yet they hovered like an ominous black thundercloud, a storm that would sunder the heavens and his reputation, his world, with it. With Lucy gone, his secret was safe. If Annie tried to bring her back, it would almost certainly be revealed.

He half rose from his seat, banging the table again with the full force of his weight behind his fist.

'You will not have anything to do with that woman,' he roared. 'You know I forbade it long ago. She is nothing but a cancer on the flesh of humanity. If Lucy is with her, then she is beyond saving – as she has been, no doubt, since you allowed her to spend time with the filthy whore before I was fortunate enough to discover her true nature.'

Annie took a small step backward, but her jaw was as set as ever.

'You're being ridiculous! Molly is certainly not a whore, and even if she was, one night in her company wouldn't corrupt Lucy. I just don't want her going on the halls at her age, and if I can stop her, then I shall.'

Algernon pushed himself away from the table and approached Annie. His face was flushed to a purplish red and he was apoplectic with rage.

'You will not go to the house of that woman! I forbid it!'

Annie stood her ground, frightened as she was.

'I will go, Algernon. You cannot stop me.'

'You would defy me?'

'Yes – I would. I will!'

Deranged now with fury, Algernon did what he had always stopped short of before. His hand shot out, so fast that Annie had no time to sidestep or duck. The blow caught her square on her cheekbone, just beneath her eye, with such force that she staggered backwards. The carpet must have rumpled; the heel of her slipper caught in a fold of it and she fell, unable to do anything to save herself. The back of her head cracked against the arm of a chair and she rolled into a foetal position, but with one leg trapped beneath her and the other twisted out awkwardly at an angle behind her.

'Whore!' Algernon kicked out viciously, and the toe of his boot caught her between the legs. She gasped, a gasp that would have been a scream had she had any air left in her lungs, and curled tighter, thinking, in dazed fashion, that he would kick her again. He did not. He towered over her, his eyes narrowed in his purpled face, lips twisted in a snarl. A dribble of spittle ran down his chin and splashed on to the lobe of her ear.

'Get up, whore!'

For a moment Annie was unable to move. She lay, sick and shaking, aware of nothing but the pain that burned like fire between her legs. As yet there was no feeling in her injured face, which was temporarily numbed by the force of Algernon's vicious blow, but the back of her head throbbed in pounding waves and her neck, when she tried to move it, was stiff and aching.

'Get up, I say!'

Dazed and shocked though she was, Annie knew she must do as he said. To defy him now would be to invite yet more violence. Somehow she struggled into a sitting position. Then, and only then, did he take her by the arm, jerking her to her feet.

Annie cowered away from him, her hand covering her cheek where the feeling had suddenly begun to return, a stinging that would soon build to a crescendo of pain, and she felt her fingers sticky with blood. Algernon's signet ring must have cut into the skin and she hadn't even realised.

'How . . . how could you?' she whispered.

'You needed to be taught a lesson, my lady.' The uncontrollable fury had died from his voice now; he was the old, domineering Algernon. 'Look at the state of you! I'd like to know what Lucy and your precious Molly would think if they could see you now. Going to Bath, are you? I rather think not!'

Tears rose in Annie's eyes. She knew if she tried to speak she'd begin to cry in earnest, and she was determined not to give him that satisfaction.

'Get to bed,' he ordered.

Trembling, hurting, too shocked to be capable of forming any coherent thought, Annie did as he said. But the determination to find Lucy and bring her home burned as brightly as ever. She couldn't, she wouldn't, let this monster she had married stop her.

Another wave of anxiety for her daughter overcame her, eclipsing her own pain and distress. Where was Lucy now? She'd meant to go to Molly, Annie felt sure. But supposing she hadn't been able to find her? She'd only ever been to Bath the once, and it was a city, not a small town like High Compton or Hillsbridge. Did she even know Molly's address? She'd seen it on the letter that had come with the Christmas card, but to Annie's knowledge she hadn't noted it down.

She'd go to the Lyric, perhaps. But what if Molly wasn't there? Would her husband agree to take her in? And suppose neither of them was there? What if they were away, travelling, on holiday, or in some other town where Molly was appearing on the bill? What would Lucy do then? Where would she spend the night? Where was she now?

The tears Annie had managed to suppress in front of Algernon flowed now, tears of frantic worry and desperation as well as pain from the cruel beating.

But her mind was made up. She was going to go to try to find Lucy tomorrow whatever Algernon might say. Another beating would be a small price to pay if only she could get her beloved daughter back where she belonged.

Chapter Sixteen

By next morning, however, it was plain even to Annie that she was in no fit state to go to Bath. She felt dreadfully ill, sick and shaky, and a pain in her stomach that had begun during the night to add to all the other pains and discomforts that had kept her from sleeping had grown much worse, making her double over as it gripped her. As for her face . . . Looking at herself in the mirror that stood on top of the dressing table, Annie was horrified. One eye was almost closed, but through the narrow slit she could see it was terribly bloodshot, and the whole of her face beneath it was swollen to twice its normal size, with a lump like a billiard ball on her cheekbone and an enormous bruise, purple, black and a muddy green, spreading from beneath the half-closed eye in a huge ugly blotch.

Algernon made no mention of it, merely grunting and turning away when he looked at her, but Kitty, when she came downstairs, started, and gazed at her mother in horror.

'Mam! Whatever . . . ?'

Annie's hand flew to her face. 'Oh, Kitty . . .'

'Your mother had a fall last night.' Algernon, dressed ready for the office, set down his teacup and adjusted the stud in the starched collar of his shirt, the only sign that he was feeling any discomfort.

'A fall? But how?'

'She tripped on the rug and caught her face on the back of the chair.' Algernon answered before Annie could say a single word. 'And there is something else. Before you ask where your sister is, she's gone. Run off to sing on the halls. Your mama found a letter from her when she went to bed and she was naturally upset. That, I imagine, is the reason why she was careless enough not to notice that the rug was reeved up.'

It was an approximation of the truth that Annie did nothing to correct. She didn't want Kitty to know what had really happened.

As for Kitty, though she had heard the raised voices last night, it never occurred to her for a moment to question Algernon's explanation, and the shocking news about Lucy was all she could think about for the moment.

'Lucy's *gone*?' she gasped in disbelief. 'You mean she's run away?'

'It would seem so, yes.'

Kitty looked at her mother for confirmation.

'It's true, Kitty,' Annie said quietly. 'I think she has gone to your Aunt Molly. For the moment, anyway.'

'Then we must go after her!'

'No one is going after her,' Algernon said. He spoke softly enough, but there was no mistaking the ring of steel in his voice. 'Lucy has made her choice. We must let her go her own way, and if she falls into the gutter then she has no one to blame but herself.'

'But Papa . . .'

'She has gone and that's an end of it.' Algernon was getting into his stride. 'There is no place for a defiled woman under my roof. Lucy is wild, and, I am afraid, quite lacking in standards of common decency. She is disobedient, disrespectful of both me and, more importantly, our Lord. She has been tempted by the demon drink, and she flaunts herself in public and thinks nothing of it. In short, your sister is past saving, and I would prefer not to hear her name mentioned in this house again. Do I make myself clear?'

Kitty's lip trembled, and for a moment she seemed on the verge of arguing with Algernon. But the years of unquestioning subservience had conditioned her against such a thing.

'Yes, Papa,' she said miserably.

She and Annie exchanged an agonised glance, then, as if it were any normal morning, Annie said: 'Would you like another cup of tea, Algernon?'

Lucy's absence was not mentioned again until he had left for work. The moment the front door closed behind him, however, Annie took Kitty's hand, holding on to it as if she would never let it go.

'It's just awful, my love. I'm going out of my mind with worry.'

'I can't believe it.' Kitty's eyes were full of tears. 'I can't believe she'd go like that, and not a word to anyone.'

'She left me a letter . . .' All of a sudden Annie remembered what she had forgotten before in all that had happened. 'Oh – there's one for you too. I'll get it in a minute, but I expect it says much the same as the one she left for me . . . that she wants to try her luck as a professional singer on the halls. But I can't let her do that, Kitty – not until she's older, anyway. I was going to go to Bath today to try and talk her out of it, but . . .' her hand went to her face again, 'how can I, looking like this?'

She didn't add that in any case she felt too ill – she didn't want to give Kitty cause to wonder if there was more to her injured face than a simple trip on a ruffled-up rug.

'You can't, Mam,' Kitty agreed. She hesitated, then added

tentatively: 'Perhaps I could go.'

Annie shook her head. Such a thing was way beyond Kitty in her precarious state of health. And besides, Algernon had forbidden it. The last thing she wanted was for Kitty to feel the full force of his wrath if he was defied. She'd tried to do just that, and look at what had happened! Though she couldn't imagine Algernon raising a hand against Kitty, she simply could not take the risk.

'I was wondering if perhaps Joe . . .'

'Does he know Lucy's gone?' Kitty asked.

'I don't know.' Annie shook her head and winced as the muscles of her neck protested. 'I'm thinking that if she left notes for you and me, then surely she would have got one to Joe. But if not, he'll have to be told. And he's going to be in an awful way about it.'

She was silent for a moment. She simply couldn't understand how Lucy could have done this to Joe, even if she'd been able to justify leaving her home and her mother and sister. She had been so in love with Joe, or so Annie had thought. Oh, she'd loved her singing, been distraught when Algernon had forbidden her to appear with the concert party, but Annie had been confident Lucy loved Joe more.

'If anyone can persuade her to give up this foolishness and come home, it's Joe,' she said. 'I'd go into town and see him myself, but . . .'

But there was no way she could parade her injured face in front of neighbours and townsfolk. Kitty mentally completed the unfinished sentence.

'I'll go and see him,' she said.

'Oh Kitty . . . I don't know . . .'

'It's not too far for me to walk if I take it steady.'

'But Algernon . . .'

'There's no need for him to know, is there?' Kitty's pale face reflected her anxiety at the thought of going against her step-father's wishes, but there were some things more important than that, and this was one of them. 'Give me Aunt Molly's address, and I'll give it to Joe. He'll want her home every bit as much as we do.'

Tears welled in Annie's eyes. She knew what this was costing Kitty.

'Thank you, my love.'

Kitty half smiled, the tiniest movement of her lips that was almost a grimace.

'No need to thank me. She's my sister, isn't she?'

Annie nodded, feeling that at least part of the load had been lifted from her shoulders.

Kitty might be in thrall to Algernon, though for the life of her she couldn't understand why, but in the last resort it was the ties of blood that counted.

'Yes, my love, she is,' she said.

Joe was feeling as if the bottom had dropped out of his world.

The letter had arrived with the morning's post; he'd found it on the floor of the chemist's shop amongst the invoices, pay-ments and advertising matter from would-be suppliers, and had been staggered to see the envelope addressed to him in Lucy's handwriting.

He'd opened it right there in the shop, and turned cold when he'd read what it had to say. Yet in a strange way he was not as surprised as he might have been.

Lucy hadn't been herself for the last week or so. She'd seemed withdrawn somehow, lost in a world of her own, and she'd been different with him too – the girl who had always been so eager for his kisses and embraces seemed not to want him to so much as touch her. He'd felt her flinch when he took her hand, pull away when he tried to hug her. He'd wondered about it, a little anxiously, but not too much. Joe was not one of life's deep thinkers. Perhaps it was her time of the month – that was probably it. But he couldn't ever remember her acting this way before. The one thing he really didn't want to consider was that she might be having second thoughts about marrying him. But she'd been so excited, so happy . . . it couldn't be that, could it?

Well, now he knew that it was. He'd always known how much her singing meant to her; now she'd decided she wanted it more than she wanted to be with him. The knowledge was a pain in his heart, sharp as a barbed arrow, an ache deep inside that seemed to spread and grow until it consumed him.

As for the things she'd written in the letter . . . Joe could hardly bear to think of them. She hadn't asked him to wait for her, which he would have done, willingly; she'd told him to find someone to take her place. She hadn't said she loved him, except as a brother. Perhaps it was that that had hurt him most of all.

'What's up with you?' Richard Penny asked when he arrived on the dot of eight thirty. 'You look as if you've lost a guinea and found a threepenny bit.'

'I'm all right,' Joe said, and though it was perfectly clear he was not, Richard did not press him.

He was measuring cough medicine into a bottle when the doorbell jangled, and he looked up to see Kitty entering the shop.

'Kitty!' he exclaimed, surprised. She'd never been to the chemist's before in all the time he'd been working here; Annie always collected the prescriptions she needed.

'Joe.' She sounded breathless, gasping a little as she spoke, and there were high spots of colour in her otherwise parchment-coloured face.

'You look as if you need to sit down.'

He put down the medicine bottle and measuring cup, lifted the flap in the counter and came through. There was an upright chair in a corner of the shop, kept there especially for the use of patients who were too unwell to stand as they waited for their medication, and he pulled it out for her.

Though he guessed her unexpected visit had to do with Lucy's departure, he couldn't understand why it was she and not Annie who had come to the shop.

'What's up?' he asked, concerned. 'Is it your mam? Has all this made her bad?'

It took a few long minutes before Kitty could catch her breath enough to answer, but when she did, it came in the form of a question.

'You know, then? About Lucy running away?'

A muscle worked in Joe's cheek. 'Yes, I know. I got a letter off her this morning.'

'She left letters for us as well.' Kitty pressed a hand to her chest, where her heart was still beating uncomfortably fast. 'Mam found hers last night, though she only gave me mine this morning. It's been a terrible shock for us and Mam's in an awful way about it.'

She made no mention of the cryptic warning Lucy had included in her letter to be careful of Algernon; that had made no sense at all to her.

'I expect she is,' Joe said bitterly, glad that Richard Penny was not in the shop but in his cramped little office sorting paperwork and placing orders. He wouldn't have wanted his employer to be party to this conversation.

'She'd have come to see you herself,' Kitty went on, 'but I think she must have fainted, or had a funny turn last night, with all the upset. She fell down and caught her face on the arm of

243

the chair, and it's a real sight, black and blue, and her eye . . . well, it's all closed up and swollen.'

Joe was a little surprised. He'd never known Annie to faint. But if she was upset enough, he supposed it could happen. Or maybe she just hadn't been looking where she was going.

'I'm sorry to hear that, Kitty, but it's the doctor you want, not a chemist.'

'Oh no, that's not why I'm here. The thing is, Mam wanted to go to Bath to see Lucy – we think she's gone to Aunt Molly's – but she's in no fit state, and in any case, Papa has forbidden it. We wondered . . . Oh Joe, will you go? Tell her not to do anything so silly?'

Joe's face set into hard lines.

'I'm at work, Kitty. I can't just walk out any time I please.'

'Tonight, then. She'll still be there, I expect. I've got the address and everything . . .' She fished into her bag and pulled out a folded sheet of paper. 'Mam's written it down for you. Or if it's in the evening, you could try the Lyric.'

'No,' Joe said.

Kitty frowned, puzzled. 'What?'

'No,' Joe said again. 'I'm not going after her.'

'But . . . we thought . . . She'd listen to you, Joe, I'm sure of it.'

Joe snorted. 'I doubt it. She's made it pretty clear I'm not what she wants. I'm sorry you've had a wasted journey, Kitty. You know I'd do pretty well anything for your mam. But not this. I'm not going chasing after Lucy and begging her to come home. I've got more pride than that. I'm sorry, but there it is.'

'Oh dear . . .' Kitty's breathing was becoming ragged again, and now that the high spots of colour had faded from her cheeks she was deathly pale.

Joe looked her over anxiously. 'Are you taking your medicine?'

'For all the good it does . . .' Her hand flew to her mouth. 'I didn't this morning, though. In all the to-do I quite forgot.'

'I'll have a word with Mr Penny – see if he'll make up a dose for you. He knows you have a regular prescription,' he suggested, though he wasn't at all sure Richard Penny would do any such thing. He was a stickler for the rules and regulations of the profession.

'No, you mustn't bother him. I'll have it as soon as I get home.'

Joe eyed her doubtfully. 'And how are you going to get there? You can't walk all the way back in this state. I'll go and see if Cyril Short is about.'

Cyril Short, the bicycle shop proprietor, had recently bought himself a motor car and was offering a taxi service. Often the car was parked outside his premises, two doors down from the chemist's, in the hope of advertising his new venture.

'I can't afford a taxi!' Kitty protested.

'You don't have to. I'll pay for it.'

'I can't let you do that.'

'Well I'm going to. My peace of mind is worth a lot more than Cyril will charge for the journey.'

Kitty still wasn't giving in. 'I've never been in a motor car, and I'm not sure I want to. They frighten me.'

'Better than collapsing on the way home.' He could have said 'dropping down dead', which was what he was thinking, but of course he didn't. 'I'm calling Cyril Short and that's that.'

As he went towards the door, it opened, the bell jangling, and a portly woman in a wide-brimmed hat trimmed with silk daisies came into the shop.

'I won't be a minute, Mrs Taylor,' Joe said to her. 'I've got someone here who's not well and I'm going to get the taxi for her.'

He hurried down the two stone steps and along the street. As he'd expected, the car was parked at the kerb outside the bicycle shop. He went in, told Cyril that his services were required, asked what the fare would be, and paid it.

'If you'd just pull up outside the chemist,' he said, then went back to help Kitty out. She was still protesting as Cyril gallantly handed her up into the rear seat, but more feebly, and when she was installed and Cyril was climbing into the driver's seat, she leaned over to Joe, who was standing on the pavement.

'Please, Joe . . . Won't you change your mind and go and find Lucy?'

But his jaw was set as tight as before, and his eyes as hard.

'I'm sorry, Kitty, but no. I shan't change my mind.'

She acknowledged that with a tiny tight nod of her head, as if she didn't trust herself to speak.

'Take care,' he said. 'And tell Mam I'm sorry.'

Before the car had even pulled away, with Kitty sitting bolt upright on the highly polished leather seat, clutching her bag with both hands so tightly that the knuckles turned white, he turned away and went back into the shop.

He had a customer waiting to be served, and Mr Penny wouldn't be best pleased if he came out of his office and saw her there with no one to attend to her. He'd done what he could to make sure Kitty got home safely. But beyond that he would not go. Lucy had made her feelings abundantly clear. Though Joe felt more wretched than he could ever remember feeling in his life, his pride simply would not allow it.

Annie was distraught when Kitty arrived home, helped right to the door by a solicitous Cyril Short.

'He won't do it,' Kitty told her bluntly when she had recovered her breath. 'She's hurt him really badly, I think.'

'I expect she has. Well there's nothing for it. I'll just have to go myself.'

'Mam – you can't!'

'I'll go and get changed,' was all Annie said in reply.

But simply climbing the stairs required the most dreadful effort, and when she got up from the bed where she'd sat to put on her boots, the room spun around her and she thought she was going to faint.

Kitty was right, she was in no fit state to catch a train and go to Bath. To even consider it was folly.

Annie sat down again, lowering her aching head between her knees, and tears of utter helplessness gathered in her eyes.

'What a useless woman I am!' she muttered to herself.

But she had no choice in the matter. The visit to Bath would have to wait. And really, if she thought about it sensibly, what difference would a day or so make? Molly would make sure Lucy came to no harm. Wouldn't she? Just as long as she was with Molly . . . and that Molly didn't encourage her to do something foolish . . .

As the panic began to mount again, Annie tried to get a grip on herself. Worrying herself to death would do no good. All she hoped was that when she did manage to get to Lucy, she could make her see sense. But knowing her daughter's obsession with the stage, and her strong will, she wasn't overly confident that she would succeed.

Chapter Seventeen

Molly was enjoying having Lucy about the house. Her niece made her feel almost young again, and the planning of her future career gave her something to think about, relieving the monotony of her days since she had decided to retire from the stage.

She did, it was true, feel a little guilty that Lucy was here, with her, and not at home with her mother and sister, but she told herself that if the girl was so set on pursuing a career on the halls, she would have left anyway, just as Molly herself had done.

Molly remembered only too well the hardships and pitfalls she had encountered. There had been the seedy lodging houses with rats scuttling behind the skirting boards, stairwells that smelled of overcooked cabbage, and the girls sleeping two, or even three, to a narrow bed. There had been the days when she'd gone hungry, with not a bite to sustain her but a bowl of greasy broth from some soup kitchen. And always the managers who had wanted her to trade her virginity for a five-minute spot on their bills. As things stood, Lucy had a roof over her head, clean sheets on her bed and good food to eat. And with Spike to promote her, the worst of the lechers who worked in the business would keep their distance and treat her with caution, if not respect.

Besides all this, Molly had written to Annie promising to look after Lucy, and had given the letter to Spike to post. Really, there was nothing more she could do, and she told herself she had nothing whatever to feel guilty about.

Nevertheless, when Annie turned up at her door a few days later, the niggling guilt raised its head again, though it was almost lost in her shock at the sight of Annie, who was scarcely recognisable as the personable woman her brother had married.

'Whatever has happened to you?' she cried, staring in horror at the face that was swollen to twice its normal size, an eye so puffed it was almost closed, and an enormous livid bruise, black, green, and now beginning to turn ochre in places, extending the length and breadth of her cheek.

'Never mind me,' Annie returned shortly. 'Is Lucy with you?'

'Well, yes . . . Didn't you get my letter?' Molly replied, defensive now.

'I haven't had a letter, no. Except the one Lucy left for me.' There was an aggression in Annie's voice that Molly had never heard before.

'I did write to tell you Lucy was here,' Molly insisted. 'It must have been delayed in the post.'

'I want to see her,' Annie said in the same aggressive tone.

'She's not here, I'm afraid. She's at the theatre with Daniel. They're rehearsing some numbers . . . Look, you'd better come in,' Molly added belatedly. She held the door open and stood to one side, but Annie made no move to accept the invitation.

'If she's at the theatre, I'll go and see her there.'

'I'm not sure that's such a good idea,' Molly said, anxious now. 'Daniel won't want to be interrupted—'

'Do you really think I care what Daniel wants?' Annie demanded. 'What *I* want is to talk some sense into my seventeen-year-old daughter, and I mean to do it.'

She was shaking, Molly noticed, trembling from head to foot, and besides the awful black eye and swollen face, she really didn't look at all well.

'Why don't you come in anyway and have a cup of tea and we can talk?' she said. 'Lucy and Daniel should be home for lunch soon and you'll see her then.'

A puzzled expression crossed Annie's damaged face, and Molly realised that to her, 'lunch' probably meant a snack of bread and cheese, or crackers, in the middle of the morning.

'A midday meal,' she added by way of explanation.

'I know what you mean by lunch,' Annie said huffily. 'Just because we call it dinner doesn't make me completely ignorant.'

'I never for one moment thought you were.' Molly hastened to try and soothe Annie's ruffled feathers. 'So why don't you come in and wait? And in the meantime I can reassure you that we are looking after Lucy exactly as you would wish.'

'What I would wish is that she should be at home where she belongs.' But Annie was softening a little, Molly could see, and she touched her sister-in-law's arm.

'Come on, my dear. I know you're upset about all this, but let's talk it over and try to sort things out.'

Annie was beginning to feel rather ill again; the train journey, the long walk from the station to Molly's home and the confrontation had tired her more than she could have believed possible.

She allowed Molly to show her into the parlour. It was grander than any room Annie had ever been in in her life, large and sunny, with velvet drapes at the big bay window, floral-patterned wallpaper, a lace runner along the mantelpiece above the ornately tiled fireplace rather than the shawl that humbler households used to drape their mantels, and yet more lace everywhere, crisp and creamy – a cloth spread over an occasional table, and doilies on the stands that supported aspidistras and trailing ivies.

'Sit down, my dear,' Molly invited, and Annie perched herself on one of the fat armchairs. 'I'm sure this must have come as an awful shock to you, and the fact that you haven't received my letter won't have helped. But I assure you, I knew nothing of what Lucy planned until she turned up here with Daniel – she'd found him at the theatre. It was entirely her doing. I haven't encouraged her at all, truly I haven't. But since she seemed so set on a career on the halls, I thought it best to keep her here, rather than let her go off to try her luck on her own.'

'Thank you for that, at least,' Annie said. 'I do think you've encouraged her, though. She's always admired you so, and didn't your husband tell her to come to him if she wanted to sing professionally?'

'He did, yes,' Molly agreed reluctantly. 'I don't suppose for one moment, however, that he expected her to do what she's done.'

'He shouldn't have said it then,' Annie retorted.

'Perhaps not, but what's done is done. Look, Annie, she's made her decision, and I'm happy to have her here and keep an eye on her while she discovers for herself if it's the right one. That's for the best, don't you think?'

'I suppose. But I'm worried half to death about her, Molly.'

'I can understand that, but I'm sure there's no need,' Molly said briskly, with more confidence than she was feeling. She knew only too well how easily a girl who thought herself sensible could be led astray . . . and the consequences. 'Now, how about that cup of tea?' She lifted a small bell from the table at her elbow and rang it sharply.

Annie looked at her in surprise.

'My daily woman should have finished the bedrooms by now and be in the kitchen preparing lunch. I saw you from the window – that's why I answered the door myself. If I hadn't, she would have done it for me.'

It hadn't occurred to Annie that Molly might have servants, but then again, she couldn't imagine her rolling up her sleeves and cleaning this huge house herself.

A girl, neatly attired in a grey frock with an apron tied around her waist, appeared in the doorway.

'You rang, Mrs Trotter?'

'A pot of tea, if you please, Millicent. And a glass of my usual . . .' She glanced at Annie. 'Unless, of course, you'd like a home-brewed too, my dear?'

'Oh, no, thank you!' Annie said. Beer in the middle of the morning – what would Algernon have to say about that? But hopefully Algernon would never know.

'Tea for my guest it is then.' As the maid disappeared, Molly turned again to Annie. 'I have to ask you, my dear. What on earth happened to your face?'

'I fell.' Annie repeated the same lie she had used to explain her injuries to Kitty. 'I was so upset about Lucy running away, I wasn't looking where I was going. I must look a fright, I know,' she added, a faint flush tingeing her cheek below the bruise.

'Really?' Molly wasn't sure she believed her. She'd seen enough black eyes in her time on both men and women to hazard a guess that the cause of Annie's was something quite different. Besides, she well remembered Algernon's vile temper. But things were awkward enough between her and Annie already without her voicing her suspicions. If Annie wanted to tell her the truth, she would, and if she chose to stay with a man who could treat her so, she would. There was nothing she could do about it, and it wasn't her place to interfere even if she could.

Though what on earth dear gentle John would think of it if he knew, she hardly dared imagine.

She felt a flush of fury towards the man her sister-in-law had taken as her husband, and, irrationally, towards Annie for putting up with such punishment and covering up for the monster who had inflicted it.

'I'm sorry you're so upset,' she said, swallowing her anger and pretending to believe Annie's explanation. 'Let me tell you what Daniel has planned for Lucy, and perhaps it will set your mind at rest a little.'

Annie sat forward in her chair, hands clasped in the folds of her skirt.

'And what does he have planned?'

'At this very moment he is rehearsing Lucy with the intention of giving her a spot on the bill as soon as he can fit her in. Then he's inviting a chum from Bristol to come and see her, and he's sure she'll get a booking there.'

'Bristol!' Annie exclaimed. She'd never been to Bristol, but she knew it was a big city, and a port. Visions of Lucy being accosted by drunken sailors or dock workers swam before her eyes.

'She'll be quite safe, I assure you,' Molly said. 'Daniel will drive her there each evening and bring her back here when she's finished her turn.'

Annie nodded, biting her lip. It was the best she could hope for, she supposed, but even so . . .

'He will, won't he?' she pressed Molly. 'I wouldn't like to think of her there all alone.'

Molly suppressed a flash of irritation. 'She's seventeen, Annie, not a baby any more. Heavens above, I was fending for myself when I was younger than her. Really, I think you are worrying unnecessarily.'

All the same, she decided it would not be wise to mention the pier at Weston-super-Mare, and certainly not London at this stage. If Annie was baulking at Bristol, goodness only knew what she would make of that!

Just as she was wondering what else she could say to set Annie's mind at rest, the sound of a motor car engine drifted in through the open window.

'Do you know, I think that's them now.' She got up and peered out of the window. 'Yes, it is! Well there you are. You didn't have too long to wait, did you?'

Millicent, the maid, came into the drawing room with a pot of tea, a jug of milk and a bone-china cup and saucer on a silver tray. In her other hand she carried a glass of foaming beer.

'Here you are, Mrs Trotter.' She put the beer down at Molly's elbow before setting the tray on a low table close to Annie. 'And would you like me to pour, madam, or would you prefer to do it yourself?'

'Oh – you pour,' Annie said faintly. She was afraid to trust her shaking hands to carry out even that simple task.

As the maid did as she'd asked, the front door opened and she heard Lucy's voice, eager and excited.

'Do you really think . . . ?'

'I do.' That was Spike, his theatrical delivery echoing in the tiled hallway. 'You did well, my dear. You are going to be a sensation.' Then: 'Molly!' he called.

'In here,' Molly called back.

But it was Lucy who came bursting into the room.

'Aunt Molly, what do you think . . . ?' She broke off mid-sentence as she saw Annie sitting there. 'Mam!'

'Lucy.' Annie's throat was tight.

Lucy was gazing at her, shocked. 'Whatever is the matter with your face?'

'Never mind that,' Annie said shortly. 'It's you I want to talk about. Whatever were you thinking of, running off like that?'

Lucy's face fell. She looked the picture of guilt.

'Didn't you know how worried I'd be?'

'I'm sorry,' Lucy said dejectedly. 'But there wasn't any other way.'

'You couldn't have talked to me about it first?'

'You'd never have agreed. Papa would never have let you . . .' She was still gazing in horror at Annie's injured face. 'Did he do this to you?'

'No,' Annie lied. 'I tripped.'

'I don't believe you. He's a monster. You should leave him, Mam.'

A moment's awful doubt assailed Annie. Why should Lucy assume so readily that it was Algernon who had inflicted the injuries? Had he been violent towards her? He was often furious with her, after all. But no, she'd never seen a mark on Lucy. And if he'd struck her, surely Lucy would have told her about it, not just run away.

'I'm really disappointed in you, Lucy,' she said, and immediately knew it was the wrong thing to say. Lucy's expression became mutinous, her bottom lip jutting stubbornly.

'It's what I want to do, Mam. Please don't try to stop me, because I'm not listening.'

Annie flinched inwardly. 'If you don't care about upsetting me, what about Joe? You've hurt him terribly, you know.'

Lucy ducked her head, unable to meet Annie's eyes.

'I'm sorry. Please tell him I'm sorry. But it's for the best.'

'I don't understand, Lucy,' Annie protested. 'I thought you and he . . .'

'Well, we're not. I don't want to marry him, all right? At least, not yet.'

Annie's eyes widened. This was news to her.

'This is what I want, Mam. Mr Trotter has promised me a spot on the bill at the Lyric. I'm going to sing, on a proper stage, with a proper orchestra . . . Tell her, Mr Trotter.'

Spike was looking a little uneasy, but he stepped into the breach gallantly. 'Your daughter, Mrs Pierce, is a very talented young woman. You should be proud of her.'

'I am proud of her, Mr Trotter!' Annie flared. 'But not when she behaves in this way. Causing all this trouble, worrying us half to death, thinking of nobody but herself . . .'

'Do let's all calm down, please!' Molly implored. 'Your mother has agreed, Lucy, that you can take the spot at the Lyric, and in Bristol, too, if it's offered to you. So can we not all be civilised about this?'

Annie drew a deep breath. She didn't remember agreeing to any such thing. But she didn't want to cause an irreparable rift between herself and her daughter, and that, she was very afraid, was where this was headed unless she backed down.

'Let's take it one step at a time,' she said. 'Just as long as you have Aunt Molly to look after you.'

'I don't need looking after,' Lucy said mutinously.

'And just as long as you know you must come home if things don't work out,' Annie continued as if she had not spoken, but as the words left her lips she remembered Algernon's furious diktat that he would never take Lucy back under his roof after what she had done. Well, time to worry about that if the occasion arose and he refused to relent. She'd work something out.

Lucy was looking a little ashamed again.

'I will, Mam, I promise. And I'm truly sorry if I've upset you. But it will work out. I know it will!'

'Very well. In that case you have my blessing.'

'Thank you, Mam!' Lucy ran to her, throwing her arms around her mother and hugging her.

Over her head Annie caught Molly's eye, and didn't care for the expression she saw there. Molly wasn't as confident as she liked to make out about Lucy's prospects. But what else could she do but trust her – and Lucy – to do the right thing?

'You will look after Kitty, won't you?' Lucy said, raising her head.

'Of course!' Annie was puzzled that Lucy should think it necessary to say such a thing, and she'd mentioned it in her letter too. 'You know I always do.'

Lucy nodded, but there was a shadow of anxiety in her eyes.

'And please tell Joe I'm really sorry,' she said after a moment.

Annie sighed inwardly. 'I'll tell him.'

Then there really was nothing else to do but finish her tea and head home, braving the curious stares from strangers who were startled by the state of her face. To tell Kitty she had failed. To pass the message that was not really a message at all to Joe. And to hope against hope that Algernon never discovered that she had defied him.

Lucy woke from the nightmare with a jolt and lay for long moments with her hand stuffed against her mouth, suppressing the scream and the sobs that were choking her.

It was a dream, she told herself, only a dream. But oh, it had been so real! Algernon towering over her like some evil ogre, holding her fast so she had no hope of escape, ripping at her clothing. The odour of him, and of burnt candles, damp stone and chrysanthemums, was all around her; she could smell it even now, stronger, far stronger than the lavender scent of Aunt Molly's bed linen, an odour that made bile rise in her throat.

257

Stop it, stop it! Only a dream! But she was afraid to close her eyes for fear she would drift back to sleep and it would all begin again. She pushed aside the sheet, climbed out of bed and crossed to the window.

The garden below was dappled with moonlight; a cat crept slowly across the lawn, then streaked into the bushes; on the bench beneath the pear tree she could see Aunt Molly's shawl where she had left it, draped across the latticed timber.

Gradually her breathing grew steadier and the nightmare began to recede. But still the aura of it was all around her, filling her with dread.

They'd come, these horrors, ever since that terrible night when Algernon had raped her, not every night, but often enough to make her afraid to sleep. Only since she'd got away from his house and come to Bath had she been free of them. But not tonight. Tonight the terror had come again, vivid as ever, and Lucy thought she knew the reason for it.

Today, when Mam had come looking for her, all the reasons behind her flight had been resurrected and she had no longer been able to hide behind the pretence to herself that the sole reason she was here was to pursue a career on the halls. Besides which, there was Mam's injured face. Lucy did not for one moment believe it was the result of an accident. *He* had done that to her, she was sure of it, and it made him all too real again instead of the shadowy monster she'd managed to get away from. The monster her mother and Kitty still lived with, God help them. But what could she do about it?

Lucy shivered again, and wrapped her arms around herself. She wouldn't think about it – she wouldn't.

And she wouldn't think about Joe either. The longing for him was a physical ache in her stomach and around her heart – she missed him so much, and she knew how much she'd hurt him. No, she'd concentrate instead on the opportunities that were opening up to her, her hopes for the future.

But this evening something of a cloud had been cast over that, too. When Spike had left for the theatre, Aunt Molly had sat her down and warned her of the dangers and pitfalls, the disappointments and hardships that might well lie ahead of her.

'It's understandable your mother is worried about you,' she said. 'Life on the halls is not all glamour, you know. It can be very hard in all manner of ways, when you're not in the spotlight – and sometimes when you are in it, too. You won't always be basking in adulation. Some audiences can be tricky and even hostile. If a drunkard starts to heckle and call out rude things, you have to be ready to take him on and give as good as you get. However upset you feel inside, you must never show it.'

Lucy thought of Ethel Talbot, and how she'd had to rescue her when she'd almost fled the stage in tears when the audience had turned restless.

'I'd think of something.'

'You'd have to,' Molly said. 'If you can't handle a difficult crowd you won't last very long. And it's no good you thinking you're going to become a star overnight, whatever Daniel might tell you. You won't. You have to work long and hard to establish yourself, and even then it's no guarantee of the sort of success you're dreaming about.'

'I know.'

Molly shook her head, a little sadly. 'I'm not sure you do, my dear. Oh, at first you'll be satisfied with the provincial halls like the Lyric, and the less well-known London ones. But it won't be long before you want more. To top the bill at the Haymarket, or even the Empire, or the Alhambra. And it may never happen. It's only the lucky few who achieve that sort of success.'

'But I have to try!' Lucy said earnestly. 'If I don't, I shall wonder for the rest of my life if I could have done it. I don't want to regret letting the chance slip through my fingers.'

'I can see your heart's set on it,' Molly said.

'It is! It is! I'm not afraid of hard work, Aunt Molly, and I don't mind if I don't have time for anything else. I'm prepared to do whatever it takes.'

'You won't always have a comfortable room to come home to,' Molly warned. 'Theatrical digs can be pretty grim if you're not earning enough to be able to afford better. You might even go hungry. Daniel and I can't be there all the time for you.'

'I wouldn't expect you to be.' Lucy was a little dismayed, though – she'd somehow imagined that as Mr Trotter's protégée she would always have a roof over her head and a good square meal after she'd performed.

'There are other things too.' Molly hesitated, wondering how to explain those 'other things' to a naïve girl like Lucy, who had led such a sheltered life and would, she felt sure, have no idea of the ways of some of the men she would come into contact with.

'You'll have to deal with some awkward situations,' she went on, choosing her words with care. 'There will be men who want to take advantage of you. Some of them will offer to further your career in exchange for favours. They'll promise you the earth in return for a kiss, but believe me when I say it is a great deal more than a kiss they want, and you might find yourself in a situation you are unable to handle. Your reputation, maybe your whole life, could be ruined. And for nothing. The promises would never be fulfilled; they were idly made to suit the chap's purpose. Do you understand what I'm saying?'

Lucy gazed down at her hands, tightly knotted in her lap, unable to meet Molly's eyes. Oh, she knew what her aunt was saying all right! Not that Algernon had made her any promises; what he'd done to her he'd done by brute force alone, and if Aunt Molly thought for one moment she'd do anything that might land her in a similar situation, she was very much mistaken.

Molly, of course, knowing nothing of what Lucy was thinking, assumed she had embarrassed her niece.

'I'm sorry to speak so bluntly, Lucy,' she said, 'but I'd be failing in my duty if I didn't warn you of some of the dangers. I don't want you making the same mistakes I made, and living to regret them.'

Lucy's head jerked up, her eyes wide and startled, and Molly chuckled mirthlessly.

'Oh, I wasn't taken in by any of the lecherous managers. I was sharp enough to see through their sweet talk, and I hope you will be too. But they are not the only source of danger, I'm afraid. There will be other men, especially as you become better known. Men who will place temptation in your way, rich men, *gentlemen*, who will flatter you with their attentions, make you feel so very special you will find it hard to resist. Their promises will be quite different, but even more seductive, especially if they find a way into your heart. But those promises are just as unlikely to be fulfilled. Especially if the gentleman in question already has a wife.'

There was a bitterness in her voice now, but she was no longer really looking at Lucy. The expression in her eyes was distant, and Lucy became uncomfortably aware that she was speaking from personal experience.

For long moments there was complete silence, Molly lost in a world of her own, Lucy too shocked by the revelation to know what to say. She'd always thought of Aunt Molly as the epitome of sophistication and success. To discover there might be dark episodes in her past that even now cast a long shadow was disconcerting to say the least.

'Well, there you have it, Lucy.' At last Molly came out of her reverie. 'I don't suppose the stage is the only route to making a mistake one will regret for the rest of one's life, but it is certainly one that is conducive to putting temptation in one's way. And the unreality of it all makes it easy to lose one's head. The spell it casts can reach far beyond the footlights. I know that only too well, and I suspect your mama knows it too, even though she's never set foot on a stage. It's why she's worried for you.'

'She need not be, honestly.' Lucy wanted to say there was no chance of her losing her heart to a stage-door Johnny, that it belonged to Joe and always would. She wished she could unburden herself as to the terrible thing Algernon had done to her, the reason she had cut herself off from Joe. But the secret was locked inside her; there was no way she could bring herself to speak of it.

Molly had said then that they had talked quite enough for one night, and it was time to go to bed if Lucy was to be fit to rehearse at the Lyric tomorrow, and they had said their good nights.

But now, standing at the bedroom window and looking down on the moonlit garden, Lucy wondered again just what it was that had happened to Molly.

Some so-called gentleman had broken her heart, that much was clear. But it seemed strange that a love affair from so long ago should haunt her still, even if it had ended sadly. She was married to Mr Trotter now, and had been with him, as Lucy understood it, for many years. Surely a hankering for an old love wouldn't affect her so deeply? She might feel sad in a wistful kind of way, but the torment in her eyes had spoken of more, much more than that, a pain that belonged in the here and now, not the distant past.

A breeze crept in through the partly open sash window, whispering over her skin, and Lucy shivered.

The world, it seemed, was full of heartache and wrongs. Her mother, tied to that monster Algernon; Kitty, her whole life marred by a single bout of illness; and now Molly, bearing some kind of mysterious cross. And Joe, dear Joe, whom she loved so much, and whom she'd hurt so badly. Joe, who had lost his mother when he was a little boy just as she had lost her father . . .

At the thought of him, tears sprang to Lucy's eyes.

'Oh, Daddy, Daddy . . .' she whispered, and the wanting of him was as sharp and painful as it had ever been. 'Where are you, Daddy? I need you so!'

The breeze stirred again, and this time it seemed to Lucy to feel very like her father's touch. She closed her eyes, embracing it, and feeling suddenly comforted. If Daddy was here, watching over her, she could cope with anything.

At last she went back to bed, and was asleep almost as soon as her head touched the pillow. And this time there was no nightmare to disturb her, only a sweet dreamless slumber.

Chapter Eighteen

Sunday. The day Joe always went home for the midday meal. But this week he was dreading it. He couldn't face sitting around the family table and eating the roast that Annie would have prepared with Lucy not there; the very thought of it made him sick to his stomach. And he didn't want to have to face Annie either. She'd likely ask him again to go to Bath to talk to Lucy, and he didn't want to have to tell her no. He loved Annie as a mother; he'd do pretty well anything for her but that. The wretched days he'd spent since he'd received Lucy's letter had done nothing to change his mind. She didn't want him, she'd made that crystal clear, and he wasn't going to go chasing after her. His pride simply wouldn't allow it, no matter how much he wanted her back, on any terms at all.

It was late on Saturday afternoon and he was tidying up in preparation for weekend closing when a man he recognised, but for the moment couldn't place, came into the shop. The man seemed to know him, though.

'It's Joe, isn't it?' he said.

Joe studied the thin, interesting face, and was still unable to think where he'd seen it before.

'Last Christmas?' the man prompted him. 'We had a jolly

time singing carols in your front room. Marcus Latcham. My parents live next door to yours.'

'Yes, of course. I'm sorry . . .'

'Don't worry about it. It's not easy to place a face out of context.' Marcus smiled, a wicked little twist of his mouth. 'Besides, I think you may have had other things on your mind.'

Joe swallowed hard at Marcus's innocent words. The memory of how ecstatic he'd been that evening was a sharp pain in his gut, a prickly rash creeping over his skin. No wonder he hadn't recognised Marcus immediately; the one time he'd met him he'd had eyes for no one but Lucy.

'How can I help?' he asked now.

Marcus held out a prescription. 'This is for my mother. I'm sorry to be making work for you so late on a Saturday, but she's not at all well, and the doctor would like her to start taking the medicine right away.'

'It's no trouble – it's what we're here for,' Joe said automatically. 'I'm sorry to hear your mother is poorly. I'll just take this through to Mr Penny.'

Richard Penny was in the back room and Joe was not permitted to make up prescriptions without his supervision, though this one looked pretty straightforward – a tincture for settling an upset stomach and some pills that only needed counting out.

Mr Penny, however, said he would make up the prescription himself; Joe could carry on with tidying up. He was anxious to get away promptly tonight, Joe guessed. Perhaps he and his wife had a social engagement to get to; they often did, as they had a large circle of friends in the locality.

As Joe went back to the shelves he'd been setting straight, it occurred to him that Marcus Latcham's appearance in the shop had provided him with the perfect opportunity to get out of his regular visit home tomorrow. He couldn't have simply not turned up; Annie would be expecting him, and would worry if he didn't arrive.

Marcus was browsing the shelves as he waited for his mother's prescription to be made up, and Joe approached him, still holding a tin of tooth powder.

'I don't suppose I could ask a favour of you, Mr Latcham? Could you give Annie – Mrs Pierce – a message for me?'

A sudden alertness came over Marcus, but of course Joe was too preoccupied to notice it.

'Could you tell her not to expect me for dinner tomorrow? I've . . .' He hesitated. 'Something's cropped up, and I won't be able to make it.'

'Just that?'

'Just that.' Annie would draw her own conclusions, Joe knew. 'I hope your mother's feeling better soon,' he added out of politeness.

'I hope so too.' A worried frown creased Marcus's forehead. 'My father should have called the doctor to her days ago from what I can hear of it, but she didn't want him to. You know how stubborn old people can be.'

Joe nodded, though his experience of old people and their stubborn ways was sorely lacking.

'It's a good thing I came home this weekend,' Marcus went on. 'I dread to think what might have happened had I not. I'm going to have to try to get back more often and keep an eye on things.'

'Your mother's prescription, Mr Latcham.' Richard Penny's tone was brisk and businesslike; yes, definitely anxious to close the shop and get away, Joe thought. Besides which he might well disapprove of his trainee chatting to a customer when he should be working.

But for once Joe really didn't care what his employer thought. He'd got out of having to go through the ordeal of going home tomorrow, which was a huge relief. But it didn't do anything to lighten the cloud of misery that hung over him.

Oh Lucy . . . Lucy . . .

Joe slammed the tin of tooth powder back into its place on the shelf and wished he dared thud his fist into the whole display and send it crashing down. He might have managed to postpone that first Sunday dinner, but that wasn't going to change anything. Somehow he had to get used to living the rest of his life without her, and he wasn't at all sure that he was going to be able to do that.

Annie was in the living room laying the table for tea when she heard someone coming down the back steps. She had no idea who it might be – no one but the baker's boy came to the house that way, everyone else called by way of the front entrance. But whoever it was, she couldn't see them, not in her state. Her face was still horribly swollen and the bruise under her eye looked worse than ever now, a motley of warring colours, as if they had been mixed on an artist's palette for a storm scene.

Annie darted out into the hall. Kitty, she knew, was in the front room, working on her latest watercolour.

'Kitty!' she called in urgent but hushed tones. 'Kitty! There's somebody at the back door! Can you go? I can't see anybody!'

Kitty emerged, paintbrush in hand. There was a smear of paint on her cheek and several on the apron she wore over her clothes to protect them. As she went through to the kitchen, Annie lurked behind the living room door; though it was unlikely any visitor would peer in through the window, she didn't want to take the slightest chance of being seen.

When Kitty opened the door, she heard her surprised 'Oh,

hello!' and craned forward to listen, but could hear nothing beyond that the answering voice sounded like a man.

Whoever it was didn't stay long. A few minutes later she heard the back door close and Kitty came back through into the living room.

'Who was it? Have they gone?' she asked, still whispering in case the visitor was within earshot.

'It was Marcus Latcham, and yes, he's gone. It's all right. You don't have to hide any more.'

'Marcus Latcham! I didn't even know he was home!' Her heart gave an unsteady beat. Thank goodness she hadn't answered the door! She'd have died if he'd seen her looking like this. 'What did he want?' she asked.

'He had a message from Joe. He's not coming for his dinner tomorrow. Apparently something's cropped up. But we can guess the real reason, can't we?'

'Yes, we can,' Annie said miserably. 'But how on earth did he come to have a message from Joe?'

'Apparently his mother's not well and he went to the chemist's to pick up a prescription,' Kitty said.

'Mrs Latcham's ill?'

'So it seems. Anyway, Joe asked him to tell you not to expect him tomorrow.'

'To tell the truth, I'm not surprised. I don't suppose he could face me after refusing to go to Bath to look for Lucy.' Annie smoothed her apron over her hips. 'It's all a fine how-d'you-do, isn't it?'

Kitty regarded her mother a little curiously. Annie was worried about Lucy, of course, and cross with Joe for not doing what he could to persuade her to come home, and she was understandably reluctant for anyone to see her with her face in the state it was. But there was something else, Kitty was sure of it, something almost distracted about her, and Kitty had not the faintest idea what it might be.

'Did I hear someone at the door?' Algernon had been upstairs whilst all this had been going on. Now he came into the room, a book in his hand, his place in it marked by his forefinger.

'Marcus Latcham,' Annie said. 'He had a message from Joe. He won't be home tomorrow.'

Algernon harrumphed. 'And not in chapel either, I suppose. That boy, I am afraid, is beyond redemption. As, I may say, is your daughter.'

'Oh Papa, don't say such things!' Kitty cried.

'I'm sorry, my dear, but it's no more than the truth.' Algernon swept out, heading for the front room, but was back almost immediately. 'Could you clear your painting things from my desk, please, Kitty? I need it to prepare my address for tomorrow's service.'

'I'm sorry, Papa.' Anxious as always to do his bidding, Kitty hurried into the front room and Annie went back to making the tea. Her heart was still thudding unevenly and the throb of forbidden excitement pulsed in her veins. How was it that the very thought of Marcus Latcham could do this to her? It was totally insane, especially given that she had so much else on her mind, and all of it Algernon's fault.

How she hated him! And she was beginning to be afraid of him too. *I wish he were dead*, Annie thought, and though she was instantly ashamed of thinking such a thing, she couldn't be sorry for it. If Algernon were dead, it would be an end to all their problems.

And it would get Kitty out of his clutches, too. She was still in the front room with him; Annie could hear the murmur of their voices, though she couldn't make out what they were saying, and the pervasive feeling of unease that she could never quite shake off stirred in her again along with all the other emotions.

She should be grateful, she thought, that Algernon was fond of Kitty. He'd never hit her in a million years – at least she didn't think he would – and he was never likely to bar her from the house as he had Lucy, because she would never give him cause. But still Annie didn't like it. Though she couldn't put her finger on the reason for her unease, she felt instinctively that there was something unhealthy about the relationship between them.

What would Kitty do, she wondered, if she were to leave Algernon? Would she go with her, or would she want to stay here with him? Simply asking herself the question made Annie more uneasy than ever – how could she think for a moment that Kitty might choose that brute? But it was hypothetical in any case. She couldn't leave – she had nowhere to go – and even if she had been prepared to take her chances had she been a free agent, the irony was that she couldn't do it because of Kitty. In her precarious state of health Kitty needed a roof over her head, a room where she could rest, comfort, warmth, nourishing food. Though she was no longer a child, her condition meant that really nothing had changed since Annie had married Algernon in order to provide her two little girls with some security. Lucy had flown the nest – Annie's heart ached every time she thought about it – but worried though she was for Lucy's welfare, she was in no doubt that she would fend for herself. Kitty was another matter entirely. Without care and home comforts she wouldn't last the year.

No, unless she could provide properly for Kitty, leaving Algernon was simply not an option, and neither was leaving her here alone with the horrible man.

And if you did go, you'd never see Marcus Latcham again . . .

Given the serious nature of her troubles it was such a frivolous thought that Annie had to smile.

Well there you are, my girl. Always looking for the silver lining . . .

But if she wasn't able to do that, Annie thought, she'd buckle under the stress of it all and go quite mad.

'You're going to need some costumes, Lucy,' Molly said.

They were sitting in the garden, enjoying the cool of the evening after what had been yet another warm, dry day. As usual, Spike had gone to the theatre and she and Lucy were quite alone.

'I've got my gingham.' It was one of the few dresses Lucy had been able to fit into her carpet bag, and perhaps her favourite from her days with Stanley Bristow's concert party. She'd asked Molly if she might press it, but Molly had insisted Millicent would do it for her. As yet, however, that hadn't happened, and Lucy had resorted to putting it on a hanger and hoping the creases would drop out.

'It's a very pretty frock,' Molly said now, 'but not altogether suitable for the Lyric. If things go well we'll see about getting some proper costumes made for you, but for the moment I'm wondering if I might have something to fit the bill.'

'One of your dresses?' Lucy looked doubtful, and, reading her mind, Molly smiled.

'I wasn't always as fat as I am now. And I've kept the things I couldn't bear to throw away. Shall we at least take a look?'

'Oh yes!' Lucy said, eager to see the costumes Aunt Molly had worn, if nothing else.

Molly led the way upstairs, but not, as Lucy had expected, to the room she shared with Spike. Instead she went to a door at the end of the landing and opened it.

'Let's see what we have here.'

As Lucy followed her inside, she gasped in surprise and

delight. The little room was an Aladdin's cave – countless dresses hung on a rail, feather boas and delicate chiffon scarves were draped from hooks on the wall, and hatboxes occupied their own shelves. In yet another rack pretty silk slippers and high laced boots of polished leather and silky suede were piled neatly in separate compartments.

'Are these really all yours?' she asked wonderingly.

Molly laughed. 'I'm afraid so. A lifetime treading the boards, Lucy – and every one of these things has its own special memory.' She pulled out an emerald gown, tight-bodiced and with a flounced skirt rucked up at one side by a black velvet ribbon. 'I wore this one at the London Pavilion. My, what a night that was! And what a hit I made!' Her eyes went a little faraway; she hurriedly turned back to the rail. 'And this one . . .' she held up a gown of hunting scarlet, edged with scalloped black lace, 'I had this specially made when I appeared at the Trocadero Palace. Those were the days . . .'

'They're beautiful!' Lucy murmured in awe.

'They are. I haven't been able to fit into them for years, but as I said, I couldn't bear to part with them.'

'Can I try them on?' Lucy asked.

'Certainly. But neither of these is the one I have in mind for you. With your colouring and your song – it is "The Boy I Love Is Up In The Gallery" you've been rehearsing, isn't it?'

Lucy nodded, and she went on: 'Then I think this would be the perfect dress for you.'

She rehung the scarlet and the emerald numbers and pulled out a dress of cornflower-blue silk, trimmed with creamy ivory lace. 'Let's see how it looks on you, shall we?'

Lucy took off her skirt and blouse and Molly lifted the blue dress over her head, waiting for Lucy to slip her arms into the little puffed sleeves before letting it drop to the floor. Then she fastened the tiny pearl buttons at the back and smoothed the fine fabric over Lucy's hips.

'Hmm – yes.' She stood back, eyeing her niece critically. 'As I thought, the colour is just right. But it needs taking in a fraction on the bust. I was always what you might call curvy, even in the days when my waist was a mere eighteen inches. Just wait there and I'll get my sewing things.'

Lucy did as she was told. Though she longed to go to a mirror and see how she looked, for the moment she had to be content with enjoying the feel of the silk against her skin and the swish of the skirt about her bare legs.

Molly returned with a cushion of pins and a needle and thread.

'You'd better stay very still if I'm not to prick you,' she warned as she set to work, pulling the bodice more tightly around Lucy and fastening it at the seams. A few little tucks beneath the swell of Lucy's small breasts, and she stood back, nodding critically. 'That's much better. Now, I think maybe an inch or so off the hem . . .'

She dropped to her knees, folding up the skirt a little and working her way around.

'I'll leave the pins in the hem, but I'll just tack what I've done to the bodice so that the seamstress can see exactly how it should be . . . Now, shoes. You'll need stockings, too, of course, but we won't bother about those for now. And gloves . . .'

The shoes she pulled from one of the racks were dainty and low-heeled, fastened with bows of blue ribbon that matched the dress perfectly. Lucy had expected that they, like the dress, would be a little too big for her, but to her surprise they were actually a fraction small, crushing the first two toes on her right foot, though her left felt quite comfortable. She didn't mention it, though; they were just so pretty, and she was more than

273

prepared to put up with some slight discomfort in order to wear them. Last of all, Molly pulled wisps of creamy lace, folded into a ball, from a drawer – they were, Lucy discovered, fingerless mittens that reached to her elbow.

Molly nodded, satisfied. '*Now* you can look, my dear, and tell me what you think.'

Almost afraid to move in case she split Aunt Molly's tacking stitches, Lucy followed her along the landing to the bedroom she shared with Spike. There, in a corner, sandwiched between a heavy oak wardrobe on one side and a chest of drawers on the other, was a tall mirror, angled slightly on its stand. As she faced it and saw her reflection for the first time, Lucy's eyes widened.

Was that really her? She wasn't used to seeing herself full length; at home they had only hand mirrors and the ones that stood on the tallboys or dressing tables. As for the dress . . . It was fit for a fairy-tale princess. The only recognisable bit of her outfit was the locket hanging around her neck – the locket her aunt had given her so long ago, and which she never took off.

'I think you'll do,' Molly said, sounding quite proud. 'We'll have to do something special with your hair, and you'll need make-up, but we won't bother with that for the moment. I don't want to risk getting powder and paint on the dress before you've even worn it properly. I shall send it to the seamstress first thing tomorrow.'

'Tomorrow's Sunday,' Lucy pointed out.

Molly laughed. 'Not everyone can afford the luxury of a day of rest. Don't worry, she'll be well paid. I've known enough poverty in my time to do what I can to help those less well off now that I'm in a position to do so. And we want the dress to be ready for when Daniel finds a spot for you on the bill, don't we?'

Lucy prickled with excitement – and also nervousness. It was really happening. She was going to appear in a proper hall, wearing this beautiful dress.

'Thank you, Aunt Molly!' she said, going to hug her only to have a pin jab into her midriff.

'No need for thanks. It's no use to me any more.' Molly's tone was brisk, but at the same time Lucy thought she looked a little wistful.

How odd it must be, she thought, to be old, and see someone young wearing the dress you had once worn. To know they were going to perform on stage in it as you once had. What memories would it evoke? Happy ones, or sad – the ones Aunt Molly had hinted at when she'd talked of her past mistakes? A tiny shiver ran over Lucy's skin; a goose walking over her grave, Mam would have said.

'Let's get you out of this then.' Molly moved behind her, undoing the tiny pearl buttons, and Lucy could no longer see her face, only the sleek dark hair, streaked now with grey, reflected in the mirror.

What she was thinking and feeling, Lucy could only imagine.

Chapter Nineteen

Annie was sitting on the wooden bench in the back yard –'the form', they called it – peeling apples for a pie with the little black-handled knife she'd brought with her when she married Algernon.

'Why do you want that old thing?' he'd asked impatiently. 'It's had its day – I've got far better ones than that.'

But Annie had kept it anyway. Perhaps the blade had been sharpened so often it had worn down to little more than a stub, but she'd had it all her married life and before that it had been her mother's and maybe even her grandmother's. She liked it, it felt comfortable in her hand and took the peel off apples and potatoes too in long, satisfying strips.

She dropped a curl of peel into the bowl on her lap and sliced expertly through the core. The sun was warm on her face, and sitting here with only birdsong and the sound of church bells waxing and waning as the wind rose and dropped to break the Sunday morning silence, she could almost forget her troubles.

She'd been excused chapel this morning – Algernon didn't want her parading her bruises in front of a curious congregation who would, no doubt, express sympathy to their faces but whisper behind their backs – and Annie intended to make the most of the couple of hours she would have to herself.

She was slicing the apple into a dish, taking care not to let the knife slip and cut her fingers, when a crunch of gravel made her glance up just as a man rounded the corner made by the apex of the kitchen roof and started down the steps.

Annie's heart gave an uncomfortable leap. Marcus Latcham! Well, there was no way she could avoid him today as she had done yesterday – he'd seen her now – and ashamed though she was of the state of her face, she wasn't sure she wanted to avoid him.

'Morning!' he called breezily.

'Good morning! You've really caught me this time . . .' Her voice was breathy and unsteady, and . . . what a stupid thing to say! Annie thought, embarrassed.

'That's what I was hoping to do.' He reached the foot of the steps and stopped, staring at Annie. 'Oh dear. That's a nasty bruise. Have you had an accident?'

'I tripped.' Annie trotted out the well-worn lie, but to her own ears it sounded totally unconvincing.

Marcus Latcham, however, seemed to accept her explanation.

'You'll have to be more careful,' he said easily.

'I know.'

'I was coming to ask a favour, but perhaps you won't feel up to it.'

'Oh, I'm perfectly fine in myself. It's just that I look such a sight.'

'Not at all,' Marcus said gallantly.

To her amazement, Annie found herself laughing. 'You're very kind, but I do know how awful I look. I'm not even allowed to go to chapel this morning for fear I'd frighten the horses.'

'Ah, chapel, of course. I'd forgotten your husband is a regular worshipper.'

'More than that. He likes to think it would all collapse in

277

ruins without him.' She broke off, feeling horribly disloyal. It was one thing for her to have hateful thoughts, quite another to disparage Algernon to a neighbour.

'I shouldn't have said that,' she added quickly. 'He's very dedicated to serving the Lord, that's all.'

'I'm sure.' But there was a wicked twinkle in Marcus's eye.

'You said you wanted to ask a favour,' Annie said, anxious to change the subject.

'Well, yes. It's Mother. As I told your daughter yester-day . . .'

'Kitty.'

'Yes, Kitty. How she's grown up, by the way! To think of her now as the little girl on the train the first time we met . . . it makes me feel my age! It was quite a shock when I came around at Christmas to see that she's now a beautiful young lady. I don't think I'd seen her in the intervening years.'

'She doesn't go out a lot. She's rather delicate,' Annie said. 'And of course, you're not at home very often.'

'I'm sorry to hear that,' Marcus said sympathetically. 'And speaking of my not being at home brings me to the favour I wanted to ask. I have to go back to London on the afternoon train, and I'm somewhat concerned about leaving my mother. Father does his best, of course, but Mother does rather tend to rule the roost. She can be very stubborn when it comes to things like calling the doctor, and Father takes her at her word when she says it's not necessary. If you could keep an eye on things, and send for Dr Blackmore if you think she needs him, I'd be truly grateful.'

'Of course I will. And would you like me to let you know if I think there's cause for concern?'

'I would, yes. You can reach me at—'

'Buckingham Palace. I know,' Annie said with a smile.

'I'll give you a telephone number.'

'Oh, but I couldn't!' Annie had never used a telephone in her life.

Marcus smiled, that lovely smile that crinkled the corners of his eyes. 'Don't worry – you wouldn't find yourself talking to the King. An operator on the switchboard would either put you through to my office, or take a message.'

'But I don't know anyone with a telephone . . .'

'Ah. I can see that might be a problem. Well, you could always send me a wire.'

'Yes, I suppose I could.' She'd never sent a telegram either, but there had to be a first time for everything. 'Anyway, let's hope it doesn't come to that.'

'Let's hope not. But it would set my mind at rest to know there's someone keeping an eye on things. Now, I mustn't take up any more of your time.'

Suddenly Annie was reluctant to see him go.

'Would you like a cup of tea?' she asked. 'I was just about to make one.'

'Thanks, but I'd better not.' Marcus sounded regretful. 'I'm home so seldom I really should spend what little time I am here with my parents.'

'Of course,' Annie said, disappointed.

'I'll try to get home again soon. In fact, I intend to manage things so I can come much more often. Perhaps I can take you up on your kind offer then.'

'You'd be very welcome.'

But it wouldn't be the same. She wasn't likely to be alone next time. Algernon would most likely be there, anxious to entertain the man who actually worked for His Majesty. And Kitty. Maybe even Lucy . . . though that was a vain hope, she rather thought. Lucy had made it perfectly clear she wasn't coming home, and even if she changed her mind, Algernon might refuse to allow it.

'George! George! Where are you?' There was no mistaking the shrill voice that came floating over the pitched roofs of the adjoining kitchens. 'George? Marcus?'

Marcus raised an eyebrow, smiling wryly.

'Poorly or not, my mother certainly knows how to make herself heard.'

'She does,' Annie agreed.

'I'd better go and see what she wants. Goodbye for now, Mrs Pierce.'

'Annie.'

'Annie. And thanks for agreeing to keep an eye on Mother.'

And then he was gone, running back up the steps and disappearing around the corner.

'Oh there you are, Marcus! Where have you been?' Those querulous tones, loud enough to wake the dead, annoyed Annie at times. Today she merely smiled.

No wonder he doesn't come home very often, she thought. All that shouting was bad enough when it came from next door. For anyone in the same house it must be enough to drive them crazy.

But she couldn't imagine Marcus would think like that. He was too nice a man. And really very, very attractive . . .

With a little sigh, Annie returned to her apples. The one she had been cutting up when she'd been interrupted had turned quite brown. She'd have to throw it away and do another. But she didn't care. Those few minutes spent with Marcus more than made up for it.

Lucy had spent the morning at the Lyric with Spike, who had persuaded the pianist, Windy Bray, to come in and run through a few numbers – though they had more or less settled on 'The Boy I Love Is Up In The Gallery' for her debut, he was anxious for her to have a wider repertoire in readiness.

But for the three of them, the theatre had been empty. Sunday was a well-earned day of rest for performers and backstage crew alike. Tomorrow morning all would be bustle as props were wheeled into place, tabs changed and lights set up, and there would be competition amongst the various acts on the week's new bill to run through their routines on an unfamiliar stage. But today all had been quiet, giving Spike the opportunity to try out some of his ideas for Lucy without interruption.

It was the sweet, soulful numbers he had in mind for her; later, when she had gained experience, he hoped she would be able to introduce a little light comedy, but for the moment he thought that would be beyond her. Better to present her as an innocent young soprano than stretch her to something that might miss its mark. No one knew better than he what a risk that could be. Lucy needed cheers and applause to boost her confidence; he didn't want her having to ward off rude comments with the sort of repartee that came naturally to a more seasoned performer.

The rehearsal had been a great success; by the end of it, when Windy closed his piano lid and announced that he was ready for a pint or two, they'd identified three more numbers that would suit Lucy and her image well.

'You know what? I think you're ready, my darling,' Spike announced triumphantly. 'What do you say, Windy?'

'I'll say whatever you like, Spike, as long as I can get to my pint.' Windy reached for a half-smoked cigarette that he had tucked behind his ear while they rehearsed and pulled a book of matches from the pocket of his waistcoat.

'Come on, pal, you can do better than that!'

'Okey-doke. I think the little lady's doing fine, just so long as she don't dry up when she's got a full house.'

'You're a hard man, Windy.'

'Well we don't want it going to her head, do we?' The match flared; he touched it to his cigarette. 'But I reckon she'll do,' he added through a stream of smoke.

'Coming from Windy, that's a compliment,' Spike told Lucy. 'I've heard him say worse about some of the best artistes I've ever had here. Go on, get your pint, you old rogue. P'raps it'll put you in a better humour.'

To Lucy's surprise, as the pianist passed her, he gave her a broad wink.

'You'll do all right, my sweetheart. Just keep going, and I'll follow you. Right?'

She nodded. When he had gone, she turned to Spike.

'When are you going to put me on?'

'I'm thinking next week, soon as the costume Molly's fixing you up with is ready,' he said, collecting his coat from a chair at the side of the stage and draping it over his arm.

'Next week!'

Breath caught in Lucy's throat. From the front of the stage where she stood, the auditorium stretched vast and empty before her, much, much bigger than it had ever looked before. Row upon row of plush-covered seats raking all the way up to the very back of the theatre, and above it the gallery, all hazy and dim. But next week those seats would be full, cigarette smoke would make a thick haze in the light of the limes, and the orchestra would be assembled in the pit below the stage, not just Windy pounding the keys of the piano, but the drummer, the clarinettist, and all the others. All eyes would be on her. Everyone waiting to see if the new performer could cut the mustard. Lucy felt a moment's blind panic. When the spotlight was on her, when she could hear the expectant murmurs, when the orchestra struck up the first notes of her intro, how would it feel? Could she do it?

'Don't worry about it, my dear. They're going to love you.' Spike was behind her; the smoke of the cigar he'd lit drifted past her nostrils.

'I hope so!'

'You'll be fine.' He touched her arm, squeezing it gently.

What a nice man he was. How lucky Aunt Molly was to have him. The thoughts flittered through Lucy's head without her really acknowledging them.

She drew a deep breath, imagining the moment to come, and seeing it not as something to be feared, but a golden opportunity, her passport to the world of her dreams.

'Yes,' she said. 'I'll be fine. I will be!'

The midday meal was cold poached salmon with watercress sauce and a salad of new potatoes, all prepared the previous day by Millicent and quite delicious, but it seemed wrong, somehow, for a Sunday, and thinking of her mother's roasts, Lucy experienced another of the pangs of homesickness that could catch her unawares.

When lunch was finished, Spike settled into one of the big easy chairs and Molly another for their afternoon nap, something Lucy had come to realise was a habit of theirs.

'Why don't you go and have a rummage through my costumes, Lucy?' Molly suggested. 'Try on anything that takes your fancy. You're going to need more than the blue dress soon, and it will be quicker to have alterations made than to start from scratch.'

'Cheaper, too,' Spike grunted. For all that he was now a wealthy man, he had never forgotten his humble beginnings, nor the creed of 'waste not, want not' that his parents had lived by. 'And we could do without more costumes cluttering up the place.'

'They are not clutter!' Molly protested indignantly.

'If they're no use to man nor beast, that's just what they are. My, Molly, you could fill a stately home with all the stuff you refuse to part with. If Lucy can take some of them off our hands, so much the better.'

'That's what I said, isn't it?' Molly said, annoyed. 'She can have what she likes.'

Lucy smiled at their mild bickering. The next thing they'd be arguing about was who snored the loudest. But there was no mistaking the ease and affection between them, and Lucy thought again that whatever troubles Aunt Molly had experienced in the past, things had worked out well for her in the end.

She left the two of them relaxing in their matching chairs, climbed the stairs, and opened the door to the Aladdin's cave.

For a while she flipped through the dresses of every imaginable hue, and all in silks and satins that shone as they reflected the afternoon sun slanting in through the window. How much more gorgeous they must look in the beam of the spots or the limes! Some, the newer ones, would be far too large for her, Lucy knew. But even they could easily be taken in by the seamstress without too much trouble, she imagined.

She tried one on, a brilliant turquoise trimmed with black, but the neckline hung very low, exposing far more of her cleavage than she was comfortable with, and since she couldn't manage the back fastening herself, she had to be content with holding it together behind her, not the ideal way to see how it would look on her if it was altered. She'd have to wait for Aunt Molly to help, and also, of course, to advise. Besides which there might be some that held special memories for her that she'd prefer Lucy not to wear.

Replacing the hangers on the rail, she turned her attention to the accessories. The shoes, like the ones Molly had already picked out for her, were all a little on the tight side, but they were so pretty Lucy thought that a five-minute spot wearing them would hardly cripple her for life. There was no such problem of course with the hats and headdresses, and she spent a most enjoyable ten minutes trying them on – wide-brimmed straws trimmed with flowers and even a stuffed blue tit – poor little thing! Lucy thought, stroking the soft breast feathers – and best of all, the headdresses of feathers, of which there seemed to be one to match every one of the gowns. Several times she tripped along to look at herself in Aunt Molly's full-length mirror and was mightily pleased with the image that looked back at her – inches taller than she used to be, she thought, and a good deal more grown up.

The headdresses exhausted, she turned to the drawers of scarves, gloves and stockings, shaking out the scarves to look at them before carefully refolding them and placing them in a neat heap on the floor.

At the very bottom of one drawer was something packaged in tissue paper and fastened with a length of pale blue ribbon. Lucy hesitated before taking it out. This must be something extra special. But hadn't Aunt Molly told her she could rummage to her heart's content? Carefully she lifted the package into her lap, slipped off the blue ribbon and unfolded the white tissue paper, yellowed now with age.

There were two items inside, both neatly folded. On top was something made of white cambric, which Lucy thought at first must be a chemise, but when she lifted it out she saw to her surprise that it was a baby's christening gown, long and flowing,

285

with a yoke of tiny pin-tuck pleats and puffed sleeves. Beneath it lay a little crocheted shawl. Both appeared to have been unused – certainly they'd never been in a wash tub: the cambric gown was still stiff with 'dress', and there was no sign of matting to mar the appearance of the intricately patterned shawl.

Lucy stared at them, curious and a little awed. What were they doing here amongst the accoutrements of Aunt Molly's heyday? Had she once been expecting a baby, a baby for whom she had lovingly crocheted a shawl, but who had not lived to use it, or to wear the christening robe? She couldn't think of any other explanation.

So engrossed was she that she didn't hear the footsteps on the stairs, and since she had left the box room door open, there was no creak of the handle being turned to warn her. It was only when she heard a gasp that was no more than a sharp intake of breath that she looked up and saw Aunt Molly in the doorway. For a moment her aunt stood motionless, one hand clutching the door jamb, the other pressed to her mouth, then all at once she flew into the room, snatching the shawl from Lucy's lap and tugging the christening robe from her hands.

'Give me those!'

Her tone, her whole demeanour, was quite unlike the Molly Lucy knew. Gone was the cool sophistication, the air of amusement. In its place was passion, and something close to hysteria.

'I . . .' Lucy began, but Molly wasn't listening. The shawl and the gown pressed tightly to her bosom, she turned and half ran along the landing and into her bedroom, slamming the door behind her.

Lucy got up, standing shocked and uncertain amid the piles of scarves and shawls on the floor around her. Her pleasure in her wonderful finds was forgotten now; all she could think of was that she'd upset Aunt Molly dreadfully, and she wouldn't have done that for the world. It really wasn't her fault: Molly had given her carte blanche to look at whatever she liked. But Lucy felt terrible just the same, and every bit as guilty as if she'd been prying where she should not.

Leaving her finds where they lay, she crept out on to the landing. She had to apologise to Aunt Molly, explain that she'd found the baby things by accident, try to make things right. But from behind the closed door of Molly's bedroom came the sound of frenzied weeping; not sobs, but terrible wails, such as might be made by a wounded animal, punctuated by gasps and small throbbing silences.

Lucy stood stock still, not knowing what to do. She couldn't possibly intrude, she wasn't close enough to Molly for that, but she had to do something. Distressed, flushed with shame at having been the cause of all this, she fled downstairs.

Spike was still asleep in his armchair, but as Lucy came rushing into the room, he stirred, blinking and spluttering.

'What the blazes . . . ?'

'Oh, Mr Trotter, I think I've done something terrible!'

Spike shook himself, hawked at a glob of phlegm that had lodged in his throat.

'Whatever is the matter? What's going on?'

'It's Aunt Molly. She's terribly upset. There were some things in the drawer – baby things. I found them and—'

'Aw, Christ!' Spike groaned. 'You haven't set her off, have you?'

Lucy couldn't answer. Tears were filling her own eyes.

'I'm sorry . . . I'm really sorry . . .'

'You weren't to know.' He pulled himself more upright, but made no attempt to get up and go to Molly, as Lucy had thought he would.

'Shouldn't you . . . ?' she began.

'She's best left alone when she gets like this. I'm the last person she'd want to see till she's calmed down a bit,' Spike said, disgruntled but strangely unmoved. 'Put the kettle on, there's a good girl. I could murder a cuppa, and I expect Molly could do with one too when she comes down.'

'But . . . what is it, Mr Trotter? What did I do to upset her so?' Lucy wailed.

Spike stretched, easing the waistband of his trousers.

'There's some things we don't talk about, Lucy. And I'm not the one to tell you. Molly might in her own good time, or she might not. Either way, it's up to her. Now, how about that cup of tea?'

Lucy went to the kitchen, upset and perplexed. If Molly had lost a baby, that was really sad. But it must have been years and years ago; surely she should have got over it somewhat by now? And why did Spike talk as if, rather than comforting Molly, his interference would only make things worse? Lots of people lost babies, sometimes even before they were born, and there was scarcely a family she knew who hadn't buried a child. There was no way Spike could be held to blame for such a tragedy; it was just a part of life. But the way Molly had reacted . . . well, anyone would think it had happened just yesterday.

Oh, why did I have to unpack that parcel? Lucy groaned to herself.

But there was nothing she could do about it now. The genie was out of the bottle, Pandora's box had been opened and the mischiefs – whatever they were – were flying free. All the wishing in the world wouldn't put them back again.

Chapter Twenty

Dear God, how could she bear it? How could she live with the pain, the longing, the uncertainty and the loss that never entirely left her, only slumbered? How had she borne it all these years? Once she'd thought – hoped, prayed – that time would heal. But it never had. It was as sharp now as it had ever been. As all-consuming as the last time she had held him in her arms, knowing she would never see him again. Never again feel the softness of his skin against her cheek. Never again smell the warm, milky scent of him.

Molly rocked back and forth on the edge of the bed, clutching the bundle of shawl and robe close to her, arms wrapped around herself, tear-stained face buried in it, and fancied she could smell him still in the soft fabric, though of course that was impossible. He'd never worn it. A fresh wave of agony and regret, undimmed by the years, washed over her and she cried out again, squirming against the physical pain in her chest, her stomach, her heart.

Oh David, where are you now? Are you well? Are you happy? It was, she sometimes thought, the not knowing that was the worst part of her torment.

If she had buried her baby, maybe she could have found some measure of acceptance, some sort of peace. But she didn't bury him. He was out there somewhere, God willing. The son whose childhood and growing-up years she had missed. A man she could pass by in the street and not know . . .

How could she have done it? How could she have brought herself to part with him? She never would have done it if it hadn't been for Daniel. It was his doing, all his doing . . .

Molly's mouth twisted into an ugly line that was almost a snarl as the little nugget of blame she would forever harbour in her heart swelled and grew, as it always did when the grief overcame her. It was Daniel's fault her baby was lost to her forever. He had only meant it for the best, she knew that. But all the same, how could she ever forgive him for his part in it? How could she forgive herself?

At last, at last the agonised wails quietened to sobs, and the terrible anguish turned to familiar despair. Molly lifted her head and caught sight of herself in the long mirror. What a sight! Her hair had come loose from its pins, hanging Miss Havisham-like about her shoulders, the grey streaks plainly visible. Her eyes, puffed from weeping, were huge dark circles in her tear-streaked face; her agonised expression emphasised the deep lines around her mouth and the sag of her once firm jawline.

I'm old, she realised. I've lived almost a whole lifetime, and what have I to show for it but pain and regret?

She buried her face once more in the soft blanket she had crocheted with love in every stitch, and let the memories flow.

She had been twenty-one years old when she'd started down the path that had led to this. Old enough to have known better. But is one ever old enough to be wise when one falls in love?

He had been so handsome, so tender, so generous with his favours and his not-inconsiderable fortune, and she had loved him so much she hadn't stopped for a moment to consider where the affair might lead her. All she had known was that he made her pulse race and her limbs tremble, that he filled her up, body and mind, heart and soul, so she could think of nothing but him. When she was with him she felt complete; when they were apart she wanted nothing but to be by his side once more.

Not even the love of her career on the halls that had once consumed her could hold a candle to the way she felt for Anthony. When she sang now, every word was for him, whether he was in his usual box, looking down at her, or not. He was her life, every breath she breathed, and it was wonderful.

She hadn't known, of course, in the beginning that he had a wife, but somehow she doubted even that could have stopped her. After all the long years she had devoted to building a career, running from rehearsal to rehearsal and hall to hall with not so much as a single minute to spare for anything else, least of all a beau, the force with which this passion engulfed her was as unstoppable as a tide driven by a tempest.

She could recall still so clearly the night she met him. She was of course working the London circuit by then, her days of provincial touring thankfully behind her. She'd moved up steadily from the dives of the East End to the better-class halls of the suburbs, her name rising slowly up the notices, and the number of her admirers had grown, so that invitations to dinner and gifts of flowers and chocolates had become almost common-place. Molly had paid no attention to any of them, any more than she paid attention to Spike Trotter, who had come to London with her to act as her manager. He was in love with her, she knew, but she could think of him only as a dear friend, and laughingly rebuffed his advances. Her only mission in life had been to achieve star billing at the famous halls, the ones where the likes of Marie Lloyd strutted her stuff.

But everything had changed that night in 1882. Spike had

secured her an engagement at the Pavilion, and Molly had been thrilled to appear at the famous theatre. No matter that her name was in very small letters at the bottom of the bill, no matter that she had the least coveted spots on the programme, the ones when the audience might be still arriving or even leaving early – Molly was sure that at last she was on the road to the kind of success she had always dreamed of.

She had a new costume – emerald green, trimmed with jet-black lace, daringly low-cut at the front and with a flounced skirt that, when hitched up with a black velvet ribbon on one hip, gave the audience a glimpse of shapely leg right up to her garter, also emerald and black, and black button boots of the softest leather that reached just above her ankles. She had a wonderful headdress of emerald-green feathers dotted with tiny bits of diamanté that caught the light when the spot lit on them, for all the world like the feathers of a peacock in full display. And she had a new number, especially written for her by a musician chum of Spike's, which was not a little saucy – certainly saucier than any song she had ever sung before – but which she thought was great fun.

And what a success she had been! When she finished her set, the audience had cheered and whistled and shouted for more. She came off stage thrilling to the applause that was ringing in her ears, laughing and crying too from sheer exhilaration. Spike was in the wings, waiting. He swung her up into his arms and twirled her round so that the next act, a Scottish comic singer, swore at them and the boy in charge of the curtain made urgent gestures for them to get out of his way. But Molly was too happy and excited to care. She didn't even object, as she usually did, to Spike's arm about her as they made their way to the dressing room she was sharing with a lady contortionist.

'You did the business all right!' Spike planted a smacking

kiss on her cheek. 'Didn't I say you'd knock 'em dead?'

'Went well then, did it?' the lady contortionist said, but there was a slightly sour tone to her voice – she'd heard the applause and was feeling a little jealous.

'You can say that again!' Spike took a half-smoked cigar from behind his ear and lit it, filling the tiny room with aromatic smoke.

'Do you have to?' the lady contortionist complained, and her dresser joined in.

'You'll make her cough. Very funny about smoke, she is. And we can't have her coughing when her legs are up round her neck, can we?'

Molly and Spike exchanged a look and went out into the corridor, where they both burst out laughing at the picture the dresser's words had conjured up.

It was there that Seamus O'Connor, the theatre manager, found them, sitting on a wicker trunk full of costumes while Spike smoked his cigar and Molly a cigarette. He had been out front, watching Molly's act; now he was beaming broadly.

'Ah sure, me darlin', that was grand,' he enthused.

'Not sorry you gave her a spot then, Seamus?' Spike asked.

'An' how could I be, with her driving the punters wild? There's one in particular wants to meet you, Miss Dorne. I was with him in his box for your set, and let me tell you he was most impressed – most impressed. He wants to meet you, and I've promised he shall, right after the show.'

Molly saw Spike stiffen.

'Belle doesn't entertain gentlemen admirers, Seamus,' he said shortly.

'Ah, but this one she will.' The Irishman's beaming smile was still in place, but there was no mistaking the ring of steel in his voice. 'Isn't he a friend of mine, and a very good patron to boot? I'm sure Miss Dorne would not want to disappoint such a man, now would you, Miss Dorne?'

Molly glanced at Spike, who was shifting uncomfortably, only too well aware that this was not a question but a command.

'I suppose it can do no harm,' he conceded, knowing that to upset an influential theatre manager would do Molly's career no good, no matter how impressed he might be with her performance.

When Seamus had gone, leaving them alone, Spike patted Molly's arm reassuringly.

'Don't worry, I won't leave you alone with him.'

'Oh, I'm not worried,' Molly said gaily.

In fact, the idea of a grand gentleman having been so taken with her was adding to her euphoria. Spike was only against the meeting because he was sweet on her and jealous of her so much as talking to another man. Well, he'd have to learn he didn't own her, and this was as good a place to start as any.

Molly had thought that Seamus would bring his friend to the dressing room, which was hers alone once the lady contortionist had finished her turn and she and her dresser had left, heading off for yet another hall – girls whose bones were seemingly made of rubber were fewer and farther between than singers and dancers, and consequently much in demand. But when the show was over and the manager appeared in the doorway, he was alone.

'Changed his mind, did he?' Spike said, looking pleased, but the smile was quickly wiped off his face as Seamus informed them that they were meeting Molly's admirer in a restaurant frequented by theatre folk that was just around the corner.

It was a cold and foggy February night. As they emerged on to the street, Molly shivered and pulled her coat up high around her throat; she couldn't afford to catch a chill with a week's engagement at the Pavilion ahead of her. But as Seamus had promised, it wasn't far to the restaurant, and as they stepped inside, a blast of smoky warmth enveloped them.

The dining room was full to overflowing, every table, it seemed, occupied by parties of men in fancy waistcoats and women, some whose faces looked bare and shiny from the gloopy cream with which they had removed their greasepaint, but whose lips were still stained with carmine, some who had left it all on, reluctant to relinquish the glamour of it and not realising it looked horribly garish in the flickering candlelight and gas flares.

'We'll never get a place here.' Spike sounded hopeful, even now, of avoiding this unwelcome assignation. But Seamus ploughed on, undeterred.

'I made a reservation,' he said over his shoulder. 'My usual table. And by the look of it . . . yes, Anthony is here already, waiting for us.'

He gesticulated for Molly to go ahead of him; there could be no mistaking now which booth was the one to which he had been heading. It was the only one unoccupied but for a lone figure.

He rose as she approached, a man of medium height, more formally attired than anyone else in the restaurant. A lick of fair hair fell across a high forehead; beneath it his features were finely chiselled and his eyes dark, though that, of course, might have been because they were in shadow.

Seamus stepped forward.

'Anthony, may I present the delectable Miss Belle Dorne? Miss Dorne – the Honourable Anthony Thorpe-Bleasedale.'

'My dear Miss Dorne.' He took Molly's hand, which was still clutching the collar of her coat, and brought it to his lips. 'I do hope you will pardon me for pressing Seamus for an introduction, but I so enjoyed your performance I absolutely had to meet you and tell you for myself. You possess, Miss Dorne, the sweetest voice I have ever had the pleasure of hearing, and also the sweetest face I have ever seen, if you will allow me to say so.'

The blood was rushing to Molly's cheeks.

'Oh, sir, you are too kind!'

'It is nothing but the truth. And now I intend to order a bottle of the finest champagne the house has to offer. Nothing less would be appropriate to celebrate your triumph.'

Looking back, the remainder of the evening was little more than a blur to Molly, with snatches standing out like crystalline vignettes against a background of heady pleasure. The champagne, the first she had ever tasted, the bubbles bursting on her tongue and tickling her nose and throat. The supper, sweet, rich pheasant that Anthony ordered for her because she was quite bemused by the waiter's recitation of the bill of fare. The jollity that surrounded them – someone had begun to play a harmonica, and other patrons, determined not to be outdone, joined in, some jangling spoons, others with combs covered with tissue paper. And all the while Anthony catching her eye across the table and smiling, a Puckish smile that seemed to tickle inside her just as the champagne bubbles had done.

Had she fallen in love with him that night? Molly rather thought she had, though at the time he was just a part of the magic that had begun the moment she had stepped out on stage into the glare of the limes and the murmur of the waiting audience. The light still sparkled in her eyes and she could still hear the rapturous applause.

And then there was Anthony.

He wooed her with flowers and hand-made chocolates in boxes tied with ribbon. He took her to supper after performances in restaurants much grander than the theatrical one where they first met, but where the champagne flowed even more freely, and for carriage rides on cold, crisp nights when the pavements glittered with frost and the stars studded the inky velvet sky like a thousand diamonds. As the horse's hooves slithered on the icy road and the wheels of the carriage skidded a little, she would give a small cry and shrink against him, not so much because she was afraid – very little frightened Molly – but because she knew he would pull her close and whisper in her ear that she was safe, quite safe; he wouldn't allow any harm to come to her.

Not, of course, that he needed any excuse. Before long he was not only holding her, but kissing and fondling her, and a month or so after they first met, they became lovers. That night was etched forever in Molly's memory. The private room above the restaurant where he had taken her for supper and yet more champagne. His lean body and muscled limbs pale in the soft glow of a single lamp burning on an open chest. The desire that throbbed through her own body, making her tremble. The glory of their union, the bliss of lying afterwards with her cheek resting against his shoulder and her legs tangled with his. She wanted nothing more than to stay there all night in his arms under the crisp cotton sheets that smelled of lavender and their spent passion, caring nothing for the fact that Spike would be angry if she didn't return to the lodging house where they had rooms, and would berate her for a fool. She cared for nothing now but Anthony; he was a fever in her blood, a passion that had over-taken all her senses. But at last he had roused himself and said it was time for them to go, and she had dressed herself in the garments that had been scattered all around the room, still trembling a little so that Anthony had to help her fasten the little buttons on her dress and on her boots. He had knelt on the floor whilst she sat on the edge of the bed and kissed each of her stockinged feet before easing them into the boots, his mouth warm on her toes through the silk of her stockings, and it was, she thought, the most sensuous thing anyone had ever done to her.

'Can't we stay a little longer?' she had pleaded, running her hands through his silky corn-coloured hair and sweeping it back from his face.

He looked up at her, those dark eyes – they really were dark, she'd discovered, deep warm brown; it hadn't been a trick of the light that night they'd met – smiling into hers.

'No, my darling one. We must go now. But there will be other nights, and many of them.'

It was that she'd clung to, that promise of more times when they could be alone together, and she had not wondered why he was so insistent that they must go home. It was only later, when the same thing had occurred several times, that she'd questioned him, and even then had been all too ready to accept his excuses. How could she not, when she loved him so? How could she not, when his arms were around her and promises of undying love on his lips?

Through the dark days when the cloud hung low over the River Thames and it seemed winter would never end, into the first warm sunshine when the buds began to burst on the trees along the embankment, Molly and Anthony were together. Her career was blossoming too; it was as if now that it had ceased to be so all-consuming, her only purpose in life, fate had decided to smile on her. She was a regular at the most prestigious theatres, her name appearing ever higher on the bill, and the army of admirers grew ever larger. But of course Molly turned all of them away with a smile and a shrug; she had eyes for no one but Anthony.

It was, however, all destined to end badly. By the time summer came, a blazing June and July when the city sweltered and a heat haze shimmered on the pavements, Molly realised there had been an unwelcome consequence of the nights of passion she had shared with Anthony. She was going to have a child; there was no denying it any longer.

Though she was anxious and a little afraid, she was, in a strange way, also elated. It wasn't the way she'd have chosen for things to work out, but the thought that she was carrying Anthony's baby was undeniably exciting. They'd be married, she thought, and before long, a family.

It wouldn't be all plain sailing, of course. Spike would be angry and upset, she knew; he was already treating her with a cold reserve that hurt after the close friendship they'd shared. And she was a little concerned about how it would affect her promising career. Already her waist was beginning to thicken; she was pulling her stays so tight now that sometimes she found it difficult to draw breath for a high, sustained note, and she knew she couldn't conceal her condition forever. She'd have to take a break from her engagements; she only hoped the opportunities would still be there for her after the baby was born.

But if not, then she would happily settle for being the wife of the Honourable Anthony Thorpe-Bleasedale. Life would be very different – she imagined herself attending grand social events and hosting lavish parties, accompanying Anthony to the ballet and the opera, visiting art galleries and museums. Why these entered her imaginings, since Anthony was a lover of the music hall, she didn't know and didn't stop to wonder. It was just that cultural entertainment seemed fitting for a city gent and his wife.

And then, when she told Anthony of her condition, the dream became a nightmare.

The look of shock that came into his eyes dismayed her; she'd thought – hoped – that he would be as pleased as she was.

'You're not sorry, are you?' she asked anxiously. Though the answer had already been plainly written on his face, she didn't want to believe it.

He laughed, but it was a short laugh, forced and humourless.

'How could I be sorry, darling one?'

'We will be married, won't we?'

'Of course we will.'

'Soon? I can't hide my condition for much longer.'

'Soon. I promise.'

And she believed him. God help her, she still believed him.

The next evening, however, Anthony failed to arrive at the theatre to collect her after the show was over as arranged. Molly was frantic. Was he ill? Had he had an accident of some kind? Been run over by a horse and carriage? Fallen into the River Thames and drowned? Or accidentally shot himself while cleaning his guns – he had told her he was a keen shot with a target pistol. Her imagination running riot, she was forced to call for a carriage and go home alone to the apartment Spike had secured for her when her earnings had warranted the expense. For the first time she regretted that she was no longer living at the boarding house where she and Spike had lodged previously, and found herself longing for the shabby but convivial surroundings, the friends she had made there amongst the other performers, and most of all, for Spike. Though he had been cool with her since the start of her affair with Anthony, he was still a familiar rock to cling to. Worried out of her mind, she simply didn't know which way to turn, but Spike would know what to do.

Spike, however, when she ran to him the next day after a sleepless night full of dreadful imaginings, was less than comforting.

'Of course he hasn't had an accident,' he said scornfully. 'This was bound to happen sooner or later. He's just run off to pastures new.'

'He wouldn't!' Molly protested. 'We're in love!'

'You might be, but not that one. The only person he's in love with is himself.'

'That's not so!' Molly felt the tears gathering, tears born of anxiety and helplessness and lack of sleep.

Spike lit a cigar.

'We'll see. If last night's squeeze didn't fit the bill, then maybe he'll be back tonight. Then again, maybe he won't.'

'But we're going to be married,' Molly burst out. 'We talked about it only the night before.'

At first an expression of surprise crossed Spike's face, then his mouth twisted wryly around the butt of his cigar. He drew in a mouthful of smoke and blew it out in a long stream.

'That explains a lot.'

'What do you mean?' Molly asked, angry now.

'Mention marriage, and you don't see a man like that for dust.'

'But he said—'

'I don't know what he said, sweetheart, but he's taken fright, take my word for it. That's why he didn't turn up last night.'

Molly was white now, what little colour she had had in her cheeks draining away.

'But he has to marry me! He has to!'

Spike's mouth hardened.

'Have you been a silly girl? Is that what this is all about? Are you in the family way?'

Molly couldn't answer. She pressed a hand to her lips, tears gathering in her eyes.

'You have, haven't you?' Spike said, his voice hard. 'I thought as much. I couldn't help but notice you was getting fat, and you haven't been yourself.'

'But we love each other! He's going to marry me!' Molly cried desperately.

'Dream on, sweetheart,' Spike said in the same cold voice.

Molly flew at him, beating at his chest with her fists.

'He is! He is! I hate you for saying such things! I hate you!'

Spike caught her hands in his, holding them against his fancy waistcoat.

'That's as maybe, sweetheart. But I reckon I'm all you've got right now.'

Hot tears flooded Molly's eyes. She tore herself away and ran from the room. Anthony wouldn't abandon her! He wouldn't! But a shard of ice-cold fear was piercing her heart. Deep down she was suddenly very afraid that Spike had only been speaking the truth.

Days passed, days – and nights – of panic and hope and despair. Each morning she woke with a sick feeling in her stomach that had nothing whatever to do with her pregnancy – physically she was remarkably trouble-free – at first not sure of the reason. Then she would remember and begin trembling, her mind racing in crazy dark circles. Surely tonight he would come to the theatre? But he never did. Anthony had disappeared from her life as if he had never been.

She had no idea how to contact him, and realised how little she knew about him beyond that his family were bankers. She didn't even know the name of the bank. There had been no time in their tumultuous affair for talking about such things, and Molly now wondered wretchedly if there had been a reason for that, that Anthony hadn't wanted her to know the first thing about him.

Eventually, driven by desperation, she went to see Seamus O'Connor, the only person she could think of who had claimed Anthony as a friend.

She found him in his office at the theatre, counting the takings from last night's show.

'Miss Dorne, by all that's holy!' He placed a pile of notes on the desk, anchoring it with the flat of his podgy hand. 'An' what are you doing here, may I ask? Haven't I been pressing Spike for you to make another appearance here, and hasn't he been telling me you're fully booked till God knows when?'

'I don't know anything about that,' Molly said. 'Spike handles all my bookings. I'm here on quite a different matter. I'm wondering if I could trouble you to get a message to Anthony – or tell me where I could find him so that I can speak to him myself.'

'Are you not seeing him these days then?' Seamus enquired, looking at her narrowly.

'I haven't seen him in more than a week,' Molly said, trying to keep the desperation out of her voice. 'Is he ill, do you know, or has he had some kind of accident? He was supposed to be meeting me after my show, but he didn't turn up, and I've heard nothing from him since.'

'Ah, I see. Well, mavourneen, sure I'll give him a message for you, but I'd say that' – he pulled a wry face – 'his wife has got wind of his latest shenanigans and put him on a short leash, as like as not.'

All the blood seemed to drain from Molly's head and body, her legs almost gave way beneath her.

'His wife?' she echoed faintly.

'Ah, sure, an' didn't you know?' Seamus deposited the pile of notes in a tin cashbox open on the desk and hooked out an upright chair with his foot. 'You'd better sit down before you fall, so you had.'

Molly sank on to the hard seat.

'A wife?' she whispered again. 'Surely you must be mistaken?'

'No mistake, me darlin'.'

'But you introduced us! Why did you do that if you knew he had a wife?'

'Ah, I'm not his keeper – nor yours neither. An' the poor fellow needs his entertainment. She's a sickly creature, is Frances, rarely leaves her bed. But she keeps a tight hold on the purse strings, for all that. The money is hers, by way of her family. His own family fell into financial ruin, and the title is all poor Anthony has to his name. So if Frances tells him to jump – and she sometimes does – the only question Anthony asks is "How high?" Now, what was the message you wanted me to take to him?'

Molly shook her head, rising from her seat though she could see Seamus only through a haze as dark and thick as any London fog.

'It seems I have been cruelly deceived. There is no message, thank you.'

'No, I thought not. I'm sorry, me darlin'.'

'Not as sorry as I am!' Molly turned for the door and Seamus's voice followed her.

'While you're here, can we talk about you taking a spot on my bill again?'

Molly swung round, her shock turning to anger. 'Oh, I think not.'

'Now don't be like that, mavourneen . . .'

'I never,' Molly flared, 'want to set foot in this place again.'

She kept her shoulders straight and her head high as she marched along the passageway, past a man with a broom, who stared at her curiously, past the wicker costume trunk where she and Spike had sat smoking on the night of her triumph, the night she had met Anthony.

Only when she reached the street did she stop, leaning against the rough stone wall, pressing her hands to her face and feeling tears pricking her eyes, tears she would fight off until she reached the sanctuary of her apartment. And when she allowed them to fall at last, Molly thought they would never stop.

* * *

It was Spike who came to her rescue, Spike who arranged everything, but a very different Spike to the one who had brought her to London. His heart broken and his pride dented, he was colder and more distant than ever, hiding behind a fortress of indifference. Though he was still as much in love with her as he had ever been, it would be years before he and Molly regained the warmth and the easy relationship they had shared before Anthony had bewitched her. He did not, as Molly had half expected, offer to marry her, for he knew there was no way he could accept the child she was carrying and bring it up as his own, though unbeknown to her, he had secretly considered both.

Instead he spirited her away to see out her confinement with relatives of his in Essex, who spread some story of a friend, tragically widowed and unable to face social contact, to satisfy any curiosity about her sudden appearance in their household. He explained her absence from the circuit of London's theatre-land by saying she had contracted some illness or other and that she needed time to convalesce. And he arranged for the adoption of her baby when he was born.

Too bruised, broken and frightened to question, Molly had gone along with all of it. What choice, she had thought, did she have? And what answers?

She had, it was true, dreamed sometimes of keeping her baby, and even stretched the vision to include Anthony, though in her heart she knew she would never so much as set eyes on him again. To pass the endless days when she was mostly shut away from the world, with only Spike's elderly aunt and uncle and her swelling belly to keep her company, she began to crochet a shawl and found comfort in every stitch. She imagined wrapping her baby in it and holding him to her breast, with all a mother's love, and somehow her imaginings bred a hope for a future that, while her thinking mind knew it was impossible, yet offered her a lifeline to cling to. Once, on a rare visit to Chelmsford, she saw a christening gown in a shop and bought it, spending much of her meagre savings on the purchase. But for the most part she sleepwalked, zombie-like, through the weeks and months of her pregnancy.

The baby was born on a blustery day in October.

'He's perfect but for that birthmark on his foot,' the midwife assured her, and pointed it out before wrapping him tightly in his swaddling – a scarlet blotch that spread across one foot like a rising tide. 'No one will ever see it, though, so long as he keeps his boots on.'

Molly was sad to think her child had even this small imperfection, but it soon only made her more protective of him, and when the midwife, all unknowing of the true circumstances, placed him in her arms, she was suffused with love, so strong it took her breath away. Gazing in wonder at the dented head covered in fine downy hair, dark as her own, and the small shell-like ears, gently stroking the tiny curled fist and the peachy soft cheek, she knew she could never bear to let him go. Somehow, somehow she would find a way to keep him and bring him up, no matter what.

But it was not to be. A week later Spike arrived by horse and carriage, and with him a fat, greasy-looking woman he said was a wet nurse. Molly pleaded and wept, almost hysterical, but between them they prised the baby – David, she had named him – from her arms, and Molly was too weak still from the long and difficult birth to prevent it.

Somehow she struggled up from her bed and to the window; her last glimpse of David was in the horrible woman's arms – wrapped not in the shawl she had lovingly crocheted for him, but a rough blue blanket – then they were in the carriage, the door closed after them, and they were gone. She had never seen her son again.

'It's for the best,' Spike said when next he came with the intention of taking Molly back to London. 'He'll be well cared for, and you can get on with the rest of your life.'

'David is my life now!' she wept, but there was no moving Spike. From that moment on he refused to discuss the matter, even to tell her anything about the family to whom her baby had gone.

For that, she thought now, cradling the shawl and the christening gown in her arms and weeping as she had wept so many times over the years, for that she would never forgive him. For a long while she had barely been able to bring herself to speak to him let alone allow him to manage her career. It was that, and the black depression that claimed her, that had driven her to America, still harbouring vain hopes that if she could make her fortune there in vaudeville, she would someday return and find her son.

Things had not worked out as she had hoped, however, and that whole eventful chapter of her life was another story, except that it was inextricably linked to her longing for David. It was that which had driven her to find solace in bad company and comfort in marriage to a most unsuitable man, a confidence trickster who lived by his talent for making folk believe he was a wealthy Italian nobleman, and who would eventually be gunned down by one of his victims. It was that which had eventually drawn her back to England, and to Spike. It was too late by then to resurrect her career, but Spike was her only point of contact with her lost world and her lost son, and he loved her still.

Somehow they had revived their old relationship – with Molly now dependent on him, Spike could no longer harbour resentment – and for her part Molly accepted that what he had done had been what he considered to be for the best. She couldn't have raised David alone in a cold, hard world where to be an unwed mother was a mortal sin; she knew that now. With her good name tarnished, work on the halls would have melted away and there would be no place for them but the streets or the poorhouse. And she couldn't have taken him home to Somerset – the shame of it would have killed her dearly loved parents, to whom respectability was everything. No, Spike had only done what he believed to be the right thing, and she should not blame him for it.

Yet that shard of ice remained in her heart, and no amount of trying to justify his actions to herself could ever quite melt it. Just as the longing for the son she had lost still ached in her, like a sleeping beast that, when roused, could tear her apart, body, soul and spirit, with viciously sharp teeth and claws.

As it had done today when Lucy had unwittingly stumbled upon the neatly wrapped parcel she had hidden away, out of sight but never out of mind.

Molly's tears had stopped now, though her throat ached, her eyes burned, and she had to blow her nose several times so as not to drip over the precious baby garments. Time to pull herself together. Time once again to become the Molly the outside world saw.

What must Lucy be thinking? she asked herself. She owed her niece an explanation. And perhaps it would serve as a warning to her, a much more effective deterrent to foolishness than the mealy-mouthed sentiments Molly had expressed before.

She blew her nose again, then repacked the shawl and the christening gown. But this time she did not hide them away at the bottom of a drawer. She left them beside her pillow.

Then she went downstairs to apologise to Lucy and explain what had lain behind her uncharacteristic outburst.

* * *

As Molly haltingly told her story, Lucy listened quietly, at first in disbelief, and then in growing horror. Though Spike had given her an inkling of what had ailed Molly, he had refused to go into detail, and when Molly eventually came downstairs, saying she wanted to talk to Lucy, he had absented himself.

'Spike likes to bury his head in the sand,' Molly had said drily when he had left the room.

At last the tale was told. A cautionary tale, as Molly would have it.

'So now you know, my dear, why I am so concerned for you,' she said. 'I don't want you to make the same mistakes.'

'Oh Aunt Molly . . .' Lucy was lost for words.

'And you understand now, perhaps, why I became so upset when you said you found the shawl and christening gown. They are all I have left of my baby. A son who is now a grown man, and whom I could pass in the street and not know.' She smiled wanly. 'Unless of course he was barefoot. I'd recognise that birthmark anywhere. But I hope and pray he does not go barefoot. That he is well and happy and prosperous.'

Tears sprang to her eyes as she said it; throughout the telling of her story she had been calm, if sometimes lost for words, and Lucy felt her own eyes filling with tears. She rose from the chair where she had been sitting, transfixed, and ran to her aunt, throwing her arms around her and holding her close.

There they remained, hugging one another, for a very long time.

Chapter Twenty-One

The notice was a slim strip of card pasted across the playbill at the main entrance to the Lyric: *TONIGHT! INTRODUCING LUCY DORNE, SONGSTRESS! JUST SWEET SIXTEEN!*

Joe stood in a thick drizzle that had replaced days of unbroken sunshine, staring at the inch-high words and feeling his stomach tie itself in knots.

He'd been sent to Bath this morning to collect some urgently needed components for medication – their own stock had run out unexpectedly, and Richard Penny had arranged to borrow a supply from one of the big pharmacists in town to tide them over until their new consignment was delivered. He had not had the slightest intention of going anywhere near the Lyric. He was still desperately upset, and bitter too, about the way Lucy had left without so much as a proper goodbye, and the last thing he wanted was to run into her. Yet once he'd collected the bits and bobs that were the object of his errand, he'd been drawn to the theatre as if by a magnet. Just for curiosity's sake, he'd told himself. Just to see what the place looks like.

Joe had never been to a theatre in his life; the town hall and similar local venues marked the extent of his experience of Lucy's new world. He'd been less than impressed when he rounded a corner and saw it. The frontage looked scarcely different to the adjoining buildings; it might have been a factory or a warehouse. But as he drew closer he'd seen the playbills and photographs that flanked the double doors – firmly closed at this time of day – and crossed the road to take a look.

That was when he'd seen the flier. That was when his heart had come into his mouth. He knew at once it was her, though she was billed as being sweet sixteen instead of seventeen, and Lucy Dorne instead of Lucy Day. It didn't surprise him – Molly, after all, used that name – but it did affront him a little. What was wrong with Day as a name? Was she ashamed now of who she really was? But it was a fleeting quibble, nothing more. What mattered was that Lucy was making her debut here tonight. As a professional, not just the star of Stanley Bristow's concert party.

So things were working out for her, going the way she'd planned. She'd be a star, he was sure of it, and he knew he should be glad for her. But with every foothold on the ladder of success she would move further and further out of his reach. Though he had lost her already, the realisation hit Joe all over again, an ache in his gut, a knife in his heart.

His eyes went to the photographs beside the playbills, but none of them were of Lucy. She hadn't yet had one taken, he supposed. But he looked at them all the same, at their studied poses and their provocative smiles – the too-handsome man, dark hair shiny with oil, the pretty girl displaying too much cleavage and garter for his comfort, the grinning dwarves, standing one on the other's shoulders – and felt physically sick. His Lucy didn't belong in this fantasy world, among these glamorous people who somehow seemed to him to be seedy and false. She belonged at home, in High Compton, a beautiful, ordinary girl whom he loved with all his heart.

He sighed and turned away. Pulling his cap low over his eyes

311

against the persistent drizzle and clutching the paper bag containing the medications he'd come to Bath to collect, he began the short walk back to the railway station.

Had Joe but known it, Lucy was only a few yards away, in the darkened theatre, running over her number one last time, and for once nerves were getting the better of her. Twice she missed her intro, and when she did get going, the words she knew so well quite escaped her as she went into the second verse. Somehow she stumbled on, singing the third verse instead, but her mind was still a blank as to what the words she had forgotten were, and she had to repeat the third verse again. As she finished, she clapped her hands over her mouth, mortified.

'I don't believe it! How could I do that?'

'Don't worry, sweetheart. Happens to the best.' Spike joined her on stage, putting an arm about her shoulders.

'But what if I do it tonight? Oh, what are those stupid words? I still can't remember!'

'You're just panicking,' Spike tried to reassure her. 'You'll be fine.'

'But what if I'm not? What do I do?'

'Exactly what you just did. You carry on. But you won't forget again, believe me. Just be sure you come in on the right note, and then keep going.'

'But I don't want to let you down.'

'Don't worry about me.'

'Or make a fool of myself.'

'Lucy, pull yourself together.' Spike's tone was firmer. 'If you've changed your mind and don't want to do this, just say so and I'll take you off the bill.'

The threat was enough to bring her up short. Wasn't this the moment she had yearned for? Her dress – Aunt Molly's, now altered so as to be a perfect fit – was hanging ready for her in the dressing room. The notice advertising her debut was posted outside the theatre. She'd rehearsed yesterday with the full orchestra and been word- and note-perfect. And she'd be wearing the locket Aunt Molly had given her so many years ago for luck.

But she wouldn't need luck. When the audience were there, filling the rows of empty seats, when the chairman announced her turn and she stepped out into the beam of the limes, she'd feel just as good as she'd always felt on stage, and sing as well – better!

'I do want to do it,' she said. 'I've never wanted anything more.'

'Good girl.' Spike squeezed her shoulder. 'You'll be fine, I promise.'

'Of course I will,' was all she said.

It didn't mean her fears could be so easily forgotten, though, and the nerves she was experiencing seemed only to tighten their grip as the day wore on and the moment for her debut came ever closer, tightening and tightening, a spiral inside her, so that she felt quite sick with it. She could manage to swallow only a few mouthfuls of a light lunch, and not a single bite of the little sand- wiches and Madeira cake that Millicent had made that morning.

'Never mind,' Molly said. 'I never could eat before a performance, and it's just as well. The voice is never at its best on a full stomach. But I guarantee that afterwards you'll be hungry enough to eat a horse.'

'I hope not!' The tension was there in Lucy's voice, making it brittle and too bright, and she giggled as she said it.

'Don't worry, darling,' Aunt Molly said. 'It's only natural you're nervous. I always was. Always.'

'Really?' It was hard for Lucy to imagine the poised and

confident Molly feeling this way, but then it was also almost impossible to imagine her upset, as she had been over Lucy's finds in the box room.

'Really. As long as you can harness them, nerves can give you the edge you need,' Molly assured her. 'If a performer tells you he never gets nervous, then either he's lying, or his act is flat as a pancake. Believe me, I know.'

Lucy nodded.

'And you will be there, won't you, in the audience?'

'I'll be there. In a box right beside the stage. But before that I'm going to dress you myself, and help you with your hair and your greasepaint.'

'Oh, thank you!' Lucy had been wondering how she would ever manage the little buttons when her hands were shaking so, and she still hadn't mastered the art of putting on spit-black without getting splodges where it shouldn't be.

'If it's going to be a regular thing, we'll have to see about getting you a dresser,' Molly said. 'But tonight, I want to make sure for myself that you are looking your very, very best.'

Good as her word, Molly accompanied Lucy and Spike to the theatre that evening, and Lucy was grateful for her assistance and her calming presence. She didn't want to talk, though, she just kept running over the words of her song again and again, so afraid was she that she would forget them.

And then, at last, came her call. Lucy jumped up from the chair she had only just sat down on as if it had become red hot.

'That's me! You'd better go quickly, Aunt Molly, or by the time you get to your box you'll have missed my entrance.'

'Never mind the box,' Molly said. 'I think, my darling, I shall watch you from the wings.'

There was nothing now that she could do for Lucy, she knew,

but be there for her. Nothing but will her on – and be ready to help her out if things went awry, though Molly would never have admitted as much to Spike.

As Lucy stood in the wings, waiting to make her entrance, beads of nervous perspiration gathered beneath the thick layer of greasepaint, tickling intolerably, and her heart beat so fast she thought it would disturb the tight-fitting bodice of her newly altered gown. She clenched and unclenched her hands as Aunt Molly had taught her in an effort to release some of the tension that was stretching every nerve in her body, and shifted from foot to foot in her too-tight shoes.

The act on stage – a lady with a dancing dog – was drawing to its close, and the roar of applause from the crowd sounded to her like a living, breathing monster roused from sleep. Then the lady ran past her, the little dog in her arms, and Molly squeezed Lucy's hand.

'Knock 'em dead, my darling,' she whispered, then gave Lucy a little push as her name was announced and the orchestra broke into the first bars of her intro.

Lucy drew one last deep breath and stepped out on to the stage, ducking elegantly beneath the curtain as it rose. The glare of the limes – so much more powerful than the poor makeshift lights she was used to – almost blinded her, and for just a moment the terror leapt in her again as she listened intently for the musical cue she had missed this morning.

And there it was. So obvious – so perfectly *right*. She began to sing, and suddenly she was not nervous any more, but excited, elated, supremely confident.

> *I'm a young girl and have just come over*
> *Over from the country where they do things big*

And amongst the boys I've got a lover
And since I've got a lover I don't give a fig.

The boy I love is up in the gallery
The boy I love is looking down at me
There he is, can't you see, waving his handkerchief
As merry as the robin that sings in the tree.

As she sang the chorus, she swished her skirts and executed the little dance steps Aunt Molly had taught her. This time there was no forgetting the words of the second verse; they came to her as naturally as breathing.

The boy I love, they call him a cobbler
But he's not a cobbler, allow me to state
For Johnny is a tradesman and he works in the Borough
Where they'll sole and heel them while you wait.

By the time she reached the third verse, the one she'd sung twice this morning when she'd been struck by the attack of nerves, she was performing with all the panache of a seasoned artiste, and as she finished, the roar of applause, the whistles, and the cries of 'More!' engulfed her. She had no encore, of course, but as she took her bow, Windy Bray at the piano caught her eye and the orchestra went into one more chorus. Lucy was on to it in a second, and as she sang the final note, the applause was, if anything, even more rapturous than before.

Aunt Molly was waiting in the wings; Lucy grasped her hands, doing a little jig.

'I did it, Aunt Molly! I did it!'

'You certainly did, my darling.' Molly slipped an arm around her waist, leading her back to the dressing room, just as Spike had led her after her first performance so many years ago.

Lucy, floating on a cloud of elation that was marred only by the wish that Joe or Mammy or Kitty could have been here, felt that the whole world lay at her feet.

'The boy I love is up in the gallery . . .' she sang again, and giggled.

And had no idea of the irony in those words, for had she but known it, Joe had been sitting in the very front row to watch her.

He shouldn't have come; he didn't know why he had, except that after seeing the notice this morning announcing Lucy's debut, he simply couldn't keep away. He'd caught a train to Bath, eating a pie and a currant bun he'd bought from the baker's on the way, which earned him some black looks from a starchy-looking woman sitting in the opposite corner of the carriage. He'd retraced his steps to the Lyric, gone in, paid for a seat and made his way up to the gallery, where he'd been early enough to choose a prime position. Then he'd sat, unseeing, unhearing, through the various acts, still cursing himself, still half of a mind to get up and leave. Yet there he remained, as if glued to the rather worn seat. And when the MC announced her – 'For the first time ever on a British stage, I give you our ingénue, the sweetest sixteen you will ever have the fortune to feast your eyes upon, our very own songbird – the delightful Miss Lucy Dorne!' – it was too late.

As Lucy stepped out from beneath the rising curtain, Joe was almost overwhelmed by a cocktail of turbulent emotion. His stomach churned, sadness and regret was a leaden weight in his chest, and the love unleashed by seeing her rolled over him in a dizzying tide. And she looked so amazing! Joe had always thought her beautiful, but tonight, in the glow of the limes, there was something almost ethereal about her. Yet at the same time the energy emanating from her was so vibrant it filled the theatre, magnetising and awesome.

Joe knew the song, of course, it was the one she'd sung on the night he'd fallen in love with her, and the words of the chorus resonated with him. *The boy I love is up in the gallery / The boy I love is looking down at me* . . . But he'd never really listened to the verses, or if he had, they'd never registered with him. Now it was the third verse that was Joe's undoing.

> *Now if I were a duchess and had a lot of money*
> *I'd give it to the boy that's going to marry me*
> *But I haven't got a penny, so we'll live on love and kisses*
> *And be just as happy as the birds on the tree.*

Somehow it summed up the blissful few months they'd shared, their hopes and dreams. Pain washed over Joe in great waves, and the moment she'd finished her number he got up from his seat and stumbled in the semi-darkness back up the aisle to the exit. As he hurried down the stairs and across the foyer, the enthusiastic applause still rang in his ears. They loved her, she was a tremendous success. He should be glad for her, he knew, but to him it meant only one thing. He had lost her forever.

The darkness of the night enveloped him as he left the theatre, and Joe headed for the station and the train that would take him home as if all the hounds of hell were after him.

Chapter Twenty-Two

Following her brilliantly successful debut, things moved so quickly Lucy scarcely had time to draw breath. All unbeknown to her, Spike had invited his manager friend from London to watch her perform, and after the show Lucy met him for the first time at a restaurant just across the road from the Lyric where Spike had reserved a table.

Bernie Haroldson was, she thought, the tallest man she had ever seen, but thin as a beanpole. His jet-black hair was oiled, and a pencil moustache and bushy eyebrows stood out against his pale and narrow face as if a careless artist had painted them unthinkingly on a parchment-white canvas. He was snappily dressed, with highly polished boots, and he carried an ivory-topped cane.

Truth to tell, he frightened her a little, not least because his expression was almost stern, lips pursed around a cigarette in a long holder, and not so much as a hint of a smile in his dark, hooded eyes. Later she would learn that Bernie rarely smiled, the lack of it was no indicator of displeasure, but that first time she met him she found it highly disconcerting. Even when he told her over a bottle of Clicquot that he would like to manage her, take her to London and find engagements for her there, she could scarcely believe he'd been impressed by her performance, so lacking was he in enthusiasm, so meagre with his praise.

'Didn't I tell you, Bernie?' Spike, by contrast, was brimming with pride and pleasure. 'Didn't I say she's the best little singer you'll ever get your hands on?'

'You did indeed, and you were right, dear boy.' Bernie drew in smoke, a slow business, given the length of holder it had to travel, but his expression was still lugubrious.

Spike turned to Lucy.

'Well, Lucy, what do you say?'

Lucy sipped her champagne. She'd never tasted it before, but with the bubbles tickling her tongue and throat she quickly discovered that she liked it, and took another sip, copying the way Aunt Molly held her glass, delicately, by the stem, and trying very hard to make it look as if she was quite used to such luxury.

'That's settled, then,' Bernie said in the low, languid drawl that perfectly matched the rest of him.

And so it was. Lucy presumed that he and Spike must have discussed arrangements at some point, since everything fell into place like the cogs on a well-oiled wheel. But nothing more was said about it in her presence. All she knew was that she was to appear at the Lyric for another two weeks, during which time she was to learn several new numbers and have fittings with Molly's trusted dressmaker for some new costumes. She was then to appear at Spike's Bristol pal's hall for a week, gaining a little experience and finesse, after which, without more ado, Spike would accompany her to London.

Her head whirled, her heart was full of dreams. For the first time since she had left home, she was almost able to forget the horror of Algernon's attack, and the guilt she felt at what she saw as her part in it, as well as at the way she'd turned her back on her old life.

But try as she might, she couldn't forget Joe. Though she had scarcely a moment to stop and think about him, he was always there with her, an ache deep inside, a sweet, sad longing haunting her and casting a shadow over the triumphs she so wished she could share with him. Sometimes she fell asleep with the little locket he had given her so long ago clasped between her hands; often she imagined he was holding her, her face buried in his shoulder, his arms tight around her.

It was over – Algernon had seen to that. She had a new life now, and for all she knew, so did Joe. But in the darkness, away from the bright lights and the adulation, her heart still cried for him and, she thought, it always would.

For all that, London was, she soon discovered, the most exciting place on earth. Streets teeming with people and traffic, motor buses and trams, horse-drawn carriages and carts. The famous sights she'd heard about but never dreamed she'd see – the Tower, Big Ben, the Houses of Parliament, Buckingham Palace, where, of course, Marcus Latcham worked. The underground railway running far beneath those bustling streets – the first time she rode it, she thought it terrifying and wonderful both at the same time, and clung tight to Spike's arm for the entire journey, thinking about the coal mines at home, and Daddy working in the deep seams in the darkness.

As for the theatres, Lucy gazed at them in awe as Spike took her on a guided tour of some of the most famous, and imagined her own name on the bills outside.

He had arranged for her to stay with a cousin of his in Bermondsey rather than the theatrical lodging house Bernie had suggested. He was remaining in the capital for a few days only, and presumably, feeling responsible for her welfare, thought his family would keep her on the straight and narrow.

When he took her there, Lucy was shocked by the squalor of some of the streets, so different to the broad thoroughfares of central London that had enthralled her so. Here the houses were packed tightly together, small and mean, and the people appeared almost destitute, worn and ragged clothing hanging on scrawny frames and with dirty, careworn faces and unkempt hair. Children played in the streets, the girls in pinafores and petticoats a size too large for them, the boys with pudding-basin haircuts and hobnail boots. A railway viaduct and a tall chimney belching smoke dominated the skyline, and a vile smell that Lucy couldn't identify, but later learned emanated from the tannery, hung heavy in the air.

Her heart sank, but things improved when they reached Lynton Road, where Spike's family lived. Here the houses were larger, each with its own tiny front garden, similar in design to the terraces of miners' cottages at home. Some, it was true, were overgrown with weeds, but many boasted shrubs and flowers behind their picket gates. And the door of the Trotters' home was freshly painted, the doorstep scrubbed so clean it was almost white, and the brass door knocker and handle polished to gleaming perfection.

'Here we are then!' Spike said unnecessarily, as he rapped loudly on the knocker. 'Let's hope our Doris has got the kettle on the boil – I could murder a nice cup of Rosie Lee.'

The door was opened by a buxom woman in a vast wrap-around apron and, to Lucy's surprise, a flower-trimmed felt hat. Beneath it her face was full and rosy, with an impressive number of chins, which seemed to ripple all the way down to the collar of her dress. Her smile was wide, if marred by a missing tooth or two, and her eyes, the clearest blue Lucy had ever seen, twinkled warmly.

'Well here we are then,' Spike said again. 'I hope you've got the kettle on, our Doris.'

322

'Course I 'ave! But our Davy's ruined the bleedin' teapot. Scoured it out last week thinkin' 'e was 'elping. Washed out all the bleedin' tannin. Years it's taken me to get that teapot to make a good strong cuppa, and it's all gone down the plughole.'

As she spoke, she was holding the door wide, and Spike, carrying Lucy's suitcase – a new one Molly had bought her to replace her old carpet bag – led the way along a narrow hallway and into a cosy kitchen.

'This is Lucy,' he said, depositing the suitcase in a corner.

'Pleased to meet you, Lucy,' Doris beamed. 'We ain't got much, my cocker, but what we 'ave got we're happy to share. Make yourself at home and we'll get along just fine.'

'You're very kind.' Lucy was feeling shy, despite the warmth of the welcome.

Doris chuckled. 'You get us some good seats at some of your shows and we'll say no more.' She bustled into a tiny scullery beyond the kitchen and opened the back door that led into a small but well-tended garden.

'Davy! Come on in here and meet our guest!' Coming back into the scullery to attend to the promised tea, she paused in the doorway, addressing Lucy. 'You'll get used to Davy. Though it pains me to say it, he's not all there. But he's a good boy. Harmless. Except when he washes out my best teapot!' she added grimly.

Spike had warned Lucy that Doris's son was 'a bit touched', as he put it, and Lucy had found the prospect of living with a boy who was what Annie would more kindly have called simple a little unnerving. She'd never had any real contact with anyone like that, and had always given Toady Griffin, the High Compton village idiot, a wide berth. But the boy who came lolloping in through the open door resembled nothing so much as an overgrown puppy, with a round red face beneath a shock of fair hair and a beaming smile.

'Wotcha.' He extended an eager hand a little jerkily – a very dirty hand, as if he'd been making mud pies in the garden, although with all the recent dry weather there could have been no mud.

Doris, noticing, quickly slapped it away before Lucy could take it.

'What in the world have you been doing?' she demanded. 'Didn't I tell you to keep yourself clean and decent to meet Lucy?'

Davy's face fell. 'Don't be cross with me, Ma.'

'I *am* cross. Wash those hands now, before you get dirt everywhere.'

Doris caught Spike's eye, shaking her head, and Lucy felt a pang of sympathy for Davy. He was, she guessed, a few years older than her, yet his mother treated him like a little boy. It was understandable, but still seemed to her to be dreadfully sad.

According to Spike, there were two other children in the family besides Davy, both girls, who worked as shop assistants in one of the big stores in town. But they weren't at home any more; they were required to live in quarters above the shop. For most of the time it would be only Davy, Doris and her husband Will, who worked as a lighterman at the docks down on the river.

Spike and his cousin chatted amiably while they drank their tea, mostly about family, which of course meant nothing to Lucy as she didn't know any of them, and Davy, his hands now washed to Doris's satisfaction, scooted a toy train about the floor and in and out of a tunnel he had constructed from a cardboard box, all the while making chuffing noises and occasionally imitating a guard's whistle.

'Well, Doris, I'm going to have to love you and leave you,' Spike said at last.

'Aren't you going to stay for your tea?' Doris sounded vaguely offended. 'I've got a nice bit of haslet specially for you.'

'Sorry, me old cock sparrow.' Since being in Doris's company, Spike's cockney dialect had become stronger than Lucy had ever heard it – he was returning to his roots, she guessed. 'Gotta get back, y'know. Me 'all won't run itself. I've already left it for longer than I should, thanks to this little lady. Thought I ought to show her the sights and all that. But now I'm going to leave her in your capable hands. Well, you and Bernie, o' course. I'll just take her case upstairs – it's a bit on the heavy side – and then I'll be on me way.'

'If you must, you must, I s'pose. Will'll be sorry to 'ave missed you, though, and no mistake.'

'Give 'im me best.'

'Will do.'

Good as his word, Spike carried Lucy's suitcase upstairs and floorboards creaked overhead as he deposited it on the landing. When he returned, he put on his hat and made straight for the door. Lucy's heart sank, and she realised she really didn't want him to go.

'You will let Mam know where I am?' she said anxiously. Though she intended to write to Annie and Kitty at the first opportunity, she was always worried that Algernon might intercept her letters.

'Course I will.'

In the doorway he turned, putting a finger under her chin and lifting it.

'Ta-ra, chuck. Next time I see you, you'll be a bleedin' star.'

'I don't know about that,' Lucy said.

'Well I do. You won't want to be bothering with the likes of me and the Lyric then.'

'As if! I'll never forget what you've done for me, Spike.'

'My pleasure, darlin'.' But there was a wistful look in his eyes and Lucy guessed he was seeing not her, but the young Molly.

Then, with a last 'Ta-ra!' he was gone, striding jauntily down the sunlit street to the shadow of the railway arches, and Lucy swallowed at the lump in her throat.

'Pity 'e couldn't stay, but it leaves all the more haslet for us, don't it?' Doris said cheerily. 'Come on then, dearie, an' I'll show you yer room.'

Lucy followed her up the stairs to a small but bright room at the end of the landing, a room not unlike Joe's, she thought, except that Joe's felt as though it was suspended in the tree whose branches brushed the window.

'Just make yourself at home.' Doris smoothed an imaginary crease from the patchwork coverlet on the narrow bed, and straightened a pair of green pottery rabbits that sat on top of the tallboy. 'It ain't much, dearie, but you're very welcome.'

Spike's cousin was a kind, warm-hearted woman. But for all that, Lucy had never felt more alone in her life.

Soon, however, there was no time for loneliness, and indeed little to spend with Doris and her family, much as she was growing to like them. Doris, of course, had been welcoming and friendly from the start, and Davy, though simple, had a loving and gentle nature and was very taken with Lucy, following her around like a puppy dog. She had warmed too to Will, a big, silent man with distant eyes and brawny muscles, who worked as a lighterman.

'What *is* a lighterman?' Lucy had asked – she'd never heard of such an occupation before and imagined it must have something to do with the gas lamps that lit the streets.

'Oh lawdy me, no!' Doris had laughed. 'It's river work – bringing cargo from the big ships up to the docks on a barge.'

'Then why is he called a lighterman?' Lucy was puzzled.

''Cos when the big ships have unloaded some of their cargo they're lighter, of course!' Doris spoke as though it was obvious. 'A very skilled job it is too. Will served an apprenticeship, like his father and grandfather before him. Got his licence when he was just sixteen. Very proud of that he is, and quite rightly.'

As for the girls, Nellie and Mary, they too were as friendly – and as plump – as their mother, but always, on the rare occasions Lucy saw them, smartly, even fashionably dressed. That was what came of working in a big store in the city, she supposed. And though it sounded as if they were worked very hard by their employers, and subjected to very strict rules and regimes, they never complained, simply enjoying their day off and their mother's home cooking.

Sometimes, however, Lucy missed their day off altogether, for Bernie Haroldson seemed to monopolise most of her time. Life was an endless whirl now. There were visits to theatres, smaller and less impressive than the ones Spike had pointed out to her, and in the suburbs rather than the city, but respectable and ambitious none the less. There were rehearsals of new numbers that Bernie thought would suit her, in dusty attics and rooms that had once been stables in mews houses in the rather swanky area where Bernie lived, and there were fittings with dressmakers. Lucy had thought the costumes Molly had had altered for her were perfect, but Bernie had other ideas.

'You gotta stand out, girl,' he told her. 'Gotta have the latest thing. Otherwise you'll be just one of the many, and believe me, there's plenty of girls with good voices all after the best spots.'

Lucy was a little daunted; how could she, a raw newcomer from the country, compete? But within a week or two Bernie had secured her first engagements, and Lucy's star began to rise.

On one occasion Molly and Spike travelled up to town to see her perform, obtaining reservations for the whole family for the best seats in the house, and afterwards they took her, Nellie and Mary for supper and champagne at a grand restaurant. Doris and Will had declined the offer to join them – 'I wouldn't feel comfortable in one o' them places, and neither would Will,' Doris had said, speaking for her husband as usual. 'And our Davy, bless his heart, would only make a show of us.'

Molly was, Lucy could tell, secretly relieved. She'd seen how uncomfortable her aunt was around the boy, eyeing him warily, wincing at his lolloping gait and when drool ran down his chin, as it sometimes did, and generally keeping her distance.

'It must be awful having a boy like that,' Molly whispered to Lucy.

'He's really very sweet.' Lucy had grown very fond of Davy and wanted to stand up for him.

'Maybe. But all the same . . .' Molly shuddered. 'I don't know how Doris copes with him.'

In the beginning, Lucy had wondered much the same, but a late-night conversation with Doris over a shared cup of cocoa had gone some way to enlightening her.

It had come about because one night, still keyed up from performing, Lucy had been unable to sleep. Tired of tossing and turning while adrenalin buzzed in her veins and the words of her song repeated themselves endlessly in her head, she had pulled on a dressing gown and crept downstairs, where, to her surprise, she had found Doris snoring on the sofa.

'Oh – I'm sorry, I didn't mean to disturb you!' she'd

exclaimed, embarrassed, when Doris woke with a start. But as usual, Doris was quite imperturbable.

'Don't worry, dearie. I sat down for a minute when I'd finished clearing up and must have dozed off. I do that sometimes – used to often when Davy was a baby and I couldn't get him to go off. I'd bring him down here so as not to disturb Will, and he'd find the both of us here in the morning.' She yawned. 'Make us a cup of cocoa, there's a good girl. My mouth's like the inside of a parrot's cage.'

Lucy had done as she asked, and it was then, as they sat on opposite sides of the dying fire to drink it, that Doris had become quite ruminative.

'Funny thing, babies,' she'd said, harking back to her memories of nights spent on the sofa with the infant Davy. 'My ma used to say that when they're little they're a weight in your arms, and when they're grown they're a weight on your heart, and never did she speak a truer word. I worry sometimes, you know, what's going to become of him when me and Will are dead and gone. I just hope his sisters will look after him – I shouldn't like to think of him ending up in an asylum or anything like that.'

Lucy really hadn't known what to say, and after a minute Doris had gone on:

'It's sad, really, that he's like he is. But I can tell you, we were over the moon, Will and me, to have him. We thought we'd never have children, you see. Six years we'd been wed, and none came along. We'd more or less given up hope. And then along came Davy, like a little miracle, and blow me down, I was in the club again before you could say Jack Robinson, first with Nellie, and then Mary, one after the other, just like that. It was like Davy opened the door and stuck his great big foot in it. If it hadn't been for him, I don't reckon we'd ever have had children at all.'

'He's her son, and she loves him,' Lucy said now, but she could see that her aunt was unconvinced.

'I still say she's a brick caring for him the way she does,' Molly said. 'I wouldn't have the patience for it, I know that.'

Not even if it was the baby you lost and still cry for? But it was a fleeting thought only. The champagne was flowing, and Lucy forgot all about it as they talked excitedly of the progress of her career.

It was later, much later, the middle of the night really, when she was once again unable to sleep, that the thought popped into Lucy's head. She'd been idly replaying the events of the evening, and the brief conversation about Davy was just one of them, when suddenly she had the most startling idea.

Suppose Davy wasn't really Doris and Will's son at all, but Molly's?

At first she rejected it as impossible, but somehow she couldn't keep from returning to it, and the more she thought about it, the more it seemed to add up.

Spike had arranged the adoption, Molly had said, and who more likely for him to have turned to than his cousin, the very same cousin he'd called upon to give Lucy safe and comfortable lodgings? They were clearly close, and Doris had exactly the sort of kind heart that might persuade her to take in an unwanted baby, especially if she and Will had thought they were unable to have children of their own. What was it Doris had said? *Then along came Davy, like a little miracle.* No mention of unexpectedly becoming pregnant, except that she had, soon afterwards, with one girl after the other. That could happen, Lucy had heard. When a couple stopped worrying about childlessness and trying so hard to conceive, nature took over. Perhaps it had happened to Doris and Will.

What was more, from what she'd been told, Davy would be about the right age and – oh! *Davy!* Hadn't Molly said she'd named her baby David? David – Davy – of course!

Wide awake now, and prickling with suppressed excitement, Lucy was suddenly quite convinced she'd hit on the truth. But it was something she knew she must keep to herself. Clearly Spike, Doris and Will didn't want Molly to know that Davy was in fact her son, and it wasn't Lucy's place to reveal their secret. And besides . . .

All these years Molly had been longing for her lost baby. All these years she'd been praying that he was well and happy, and in her imagination now he was a grown man, out in the world, prospering, married, perhaps with a young family of his own. Finding him would bring her no happy ending, especially in the light of the revulsion she seemed to feel for Davy. Instead of an ecstatic reunion, she would be dreadfully distressed to discover that he was in fact what the world termed an idiot.

Tears started to Lucy's eyes. How cruel life could be! But it had turned out for the best for Davy, she told herself. He was happy in his own little world, and he was much loved. If Molly had managed to keep him, things might have turned out very differently.

Her mind racing, her emotions stirred, it was a very long time before Lucy fell asleep.

Chapter Twenty-Three

Christmas was fast approaching, and with it an exciting new development. Lucy couldn't wait to write her regular letter home so she could tell Annie and Kitty all about it. Bernie had secured her a job in pantomime – she was to play Alice Fitzwarren – principal girl, no less! – in a production of *Dick Whittington*. It wasn't the most lavish panto in town; some boasted transformation scenes that took place behind gossamer gauzes while dancers floated above the stalls by way of harnesses and wires, like so many fairies or angels, and no expense was spared to costume a cast of stars of the music hall, or produce an effect that would have the audience gasping. But it did have the most wonderful representation of a ship, where the decks seemed to sway on a turbulent sea, and fountains that played beneath differently coloured limes as the entire cast made their final entrances and formed an ensemble on stage to rapturous applause.

Lucy was relishing every moment of the new experience, even though she had never acted before and found it difficult to memorise the lines she had been given. She loved the feeling of belonging to a family, all working together to achieve one end, cast and backstage crew alike. She was thrilled with her costumes, tightly laced bodices and skirts that grazed her calf daringly. She enjoyed knowing that she had only to make one performance a night, rather than dashing from hall to hall, and the audiences were appreciative and responsive – no anxieties over awkward punters here. Everyone had come with the intention of enjoying themselves, capturing the Christmas spirit, and behaving like children again.

Most of all, however, much as she missed her family, she was relieved that being in panto had given her the perfect excuse not to go home for Christmas. They were to open for a three-month run on Boxing Day, and the weeks leading up to Christmas itself were swallowed up by endless rehearsals. When they were over, Lucy would return, exhausted, to the little house in Bermondsey, eat the supper Doris had left out for her, and fall into bed too tired to even think.

Deep down she knew she would miss the family celebrations she had grown up with, deep down she knew she would ache with longing for Joe, and be overwhelmed by memories of last year, when they had first discovered the magic of their love. But that part of her life was over and she had to accept it. She could never go home as long as Algernon was there, and she could never admit to Joe the awful thing her stepfather had done to her.

Lucy immersed herself in rehearsals and found consolation in good times with her new-found friends – the panto cast and backstage workers were her family now. From now on, the festive season would be glamour and excitement, and that, she told herself, would more than compensate for missing out on the cosy warmth of Christmases past.

One evening in the second week of the pantomime's run, however, something happened that brought back all the memories of a year ago with unexpected clarity.

When she returned at the interval to the dressing room she shared with Marie Clancy, the slender, long-legged girl who was playing Dick, a message from the stage door keeper was waiting for her, pinned to the mirror above the table where the greasepaints lived during performances.

There was a gentleman in the audience who would very much like to see her after the show. Lucy clucked impatiently – he'd be lucky! – surprised that Billy the doorman had even bothered to write a note for her. Usually he told admirers he'd pass the message on and promptly forgot all about it. About to screw the paper up and toss it in the waste basket, which was overflowing with wads of cotton stained with carmine and dusty with powder, the name of the gentleman suddenly caught her eye.

Marcus Latcham!

'Good Lord!' she exclaimed.

Marie, brushing some dust from the thigh of her brown velvet knee breeches – she must have collided with the edge of one of the scenery flats on her way off stage – glanced at her curiously.

'What?'

'It's the son of our next-door neighbours at home. He's in the audience and wants to see me after the performance. How peculiar is that?'

Marie raised an eyebrow. 'He's come all the way to London to see you?'

'No, no, he lives here. He works at Buckingham Palace.'

Marie looked suitably impressed. 'Sounds as though you could do well for yourself there!'

'Oh no!' Lucy laughed at the very idea. 'He's old enough to be my father.'

'Well? What's that got to do with anything?' Marie asked airily.

'You couldn't be more wrong,' Lucy assured her. 'He is very nice, actually, but I think it's my mother who's sweet on him. She turns pink whenever his name is mentioned . . . or used to . . .' She broke off, realising she hadn't seen her mother, pink or otherwise, for more than six months. 'Anyway, I shall have to give him a few minutes. It would be very rude not to. Do you mind if I invite him back here to the dressing room?'

Marie shrugged. 'Not so long as I'm decent. And even if I'm not, come to think of it. A handsome man who works at Buckingham Palace sounds quite a catch to me.'

Lucy sent word to Billy, and when the second half of the show began and she was on stage in an elaborately distressed frock that was supposed to be all she had to wear after having been shipwrecked on a desert island, she couldn't forget that Marcus was somewhere out there beyond the footlights, watching her. Marcus, who would no doubt report every detail of her performance to Annie and Kitty when he next went to High Compton. Marcus, who had known her since she was a little girl . . .

By the time the show was over and she and Marie had made their triumphal wedding entrance through an archway of glittering gold laced with thousands of pink roses, she had made up her mind. She wouldn't ask Marcus to the dressing room. She didn't want to talk to him with Marie listening avidly to every word, and maybe even trying to flirt with him. She'd meet him at the stage door. Billy, who'd seen it all before, would have no interest in their conversation, and with cast and stage hands coming and going Marcus wouldn't be able to ask her any awkward questions.

She changed hurriedly, passing her white satin and fur-trimmed wedding gown to the dresser and slipping into her own skirt and blouse without waiting for assistance. Then she scrubbed most of the greasepaint from her face and hurried along the corridor at the rear of the theatre.

She wasn't at all sure she wanted to see him, and all the memories of last Christmas that he'd evoke. But at the same time unseen strings were tugging at her heart. She'd tried so hard to leave home, and all that it meant, behind her. Now, it seemed, home had come to her.

Marcus was every bit as nice as she remembered him, and when he suggested buying her supper, Lucy only hesitated for a moment before agreeing. The supper rooms he took her to were not far from the theatre, but quiet and discreet, though almost full to capacity. He complimented her on her performance, though not as effusively as the theatre folk she was now used to, and Lucy felt that he, at least, was being sincere in his praise.

'Pantomime wouldn't be my entertainment of choice,' he said with his twinkling smile. 'But I must say you were very good.'

'How did you know I was appearing as Alice Fitzwarren?' Lucy couldn't imagine the publicity for pantos and music halls would reach Buckingham Palace, or that he would recognise her stage name even if it did.

'Your mother told me. I saw her when I was at home for Christmas.'

Familiar but much-suppressed longing ached in Lucy.

'How was she?'

'She seemed . . . quite well.'

The brief hesitation worried Lucy.

'Really? Is her face healed?'

'Yes. And I should hope it had by now! But from what it looked like in the beginning, I'd say she was lucky not to lose an eye.'

Lucy winced at the very thought. Marcus was right. Annie's injury had looked horrific when she had come to Bath to try to persuade her to come home. 'But she's all right now?' she pressed him. 'Nothing else has happened to her?'

'To my knowledge, no. I've been going home more frequently – my mother and father have reached an age when they need an eye kept on them – so I've seen her several times.' He looked at Lucy, his eyes narrowed and sharp. 'Why would you think something else might have happened to her?'

Lucy twisted the stem of her wine glass between her fingers and chewed the inside of her lip. She'd been brought up never to talk about private family matters, and her suspicions that Algernon abused her mother were just that, suspicions. But she was seriously worried that it might be the case, and all the anxiety she had felt for Annie when she'd seen the state of her face that day came flooding back.

She didn't know Marcus well, but he seemed to be the sort of man you could trust, and she had the impression he thought highly of Annie. If he was going home more frequently, if he knew of her doubts, perhaps he would keep an eye on Annie as well as his own parents. What he could do about it was another matter entirely; certainly he wouldn't interfere between husband and wife. But at least if someone knew what she suspected and reported back to her, she'd know whether things were as bad as she feared, and if they were, she could try to think of a way to deal with it.

'I'm not sure that what happened to her was an accident,' she said at last. 'I may be wrong, of course, but I think Algernon had something to do with it.'

A muscle tightened in Marcus's cheek and frown lines appeared round his eyes, but he didn't look surprised.

'I did wonder myself,' he said, his tone sombre.

'You did?'

'It seemed . . . a little convenient, shall we say? The sort of explanation that covers a multitude of sins.'

For some reason Lucy actually felt a wash of relief. Not that she wanted to think that Algernon was abusing her mother, not that, of course. But not to have had her suspicions dismissed out of hand, to be told he would never do such a thing – that alone felt like a weight lifted from her shoulders.

'I didn't think anyone would believe me,' she said. 'He's so well respected in the town. So . . . pious.'

'That alone doesn't necessarily guarantee anything,' Marcus said grimly. 'Some of the worst offenders are those you'd least expect it of.' He leaned across the table and patted her hand. 'I promise I will call in on your mother when I'm at home, and if there's any cause for concern I'll let you know.'

'Thank you.'

'My pleasure,' Marcus said.

'And you will let me know that Kitty is all right too?' For all that she had convinced herself Kitty was in no danger from Algernon, it still played on her mind. 'Mam writes to me, of course, but I'm not sure she'd tell me anything she thought might worry me, and I know what he's like . . .' The moment the words were out she regretted them.

Marcus's eyes narrowed. 'He hasn't harmed you, has he?'

'No . . . no, of course not!' There was no way on earth she was going to tell anyone, let alone Marcus, about the terrible thing Algernon had done to her. A worm of disgust twisted in her stomach and her cheeks burned hot with shame.

For a long moment he continued to look at her, then he lifted a finger to summon the waitress.

'Shall we order, Lucy? I'm sure you must be ravenous.'

'Oh, I am!' she said, eager to change the subject.

But she couldn't help feeling that however delicious the food, she really was not going to have much appetite.

'Kitty, my dear, I'm ready for you now.'

Algernon appeared in the living room doorway, his copy of John Bunyan's *The Pilgrim's Progress* tucked underneath his arm. They'd been reading it together over the last week – or at least Algernon had been reading it aloud to Kitty, pausing at the end of each passage to explain in detail the deep meaning behind the episode.

Finishing the tome was going to be a lengthy business, but Algernon was in no hurry. He was thoroughly enjoying these sessions, which he pretended were for the purpose of improving Kitty's mind and teaching her the pitfalls and trials that came before a higher understanding of a truly moral life. In fact, it was the sense of self-importance, his posturing, and the sound of his own voice resonating in the quiet of the front room that gave him the most pleasure, not to mention being alone with Kitty, who would sit on the pouffe at his feet, her big soulful eyes fixed on his face, listening intently.

Tonight, however, Kitty made no move to get up from the fireside chair, where she was engrossed in a book of her own that Annie had borrowed for her from the free library that had opened in a room in the town hall.

'Not tonight, Papa,' she said without looking up.

'I beg your pardon?'

'Not tonight, Papa, if you don't mind.'

Algernon's face darkened.

'As it happens, I do! What are you reading anyway?'

'*Lorna Doone*. Mam got it for me.'

Algernon huffed impatiently. 'Romantic twaddle! What in the world were you thinking of, Annie?'

'She's enjoying it, Algernon,' Annie said defensively.

'Books were not meant to be enjoyed. Their whole purpose is to educate and inform. Come along, Kitty. Tonight we ascend the Hill of Difficulty.'

'No thank you, Papa.' Kitty's mouth set in a tight, determined line. She didn't want to go with Algernon, and her reluctance was not only because she was lost in the wilds of Exmoor.

Last night she'd witnessed a scene that had shocked her, and given her pause for thought.

She'd not been feeling well all day, and had gone to bed earlier than usual, taking her new library book with her. But after she'd read for a while and gone to turn out the lamp, she realised the carafe of water on her bedside table was almost empty. Kitty often woke in the night feeling thirsty, and sometimes needed to take one of her pills, so she'd gone down to refill it.

She'd heard Algernon and Annie's voices as she descended the staircase, raised voices. It sounded as if they were arguing. She hesitated and almost turned back; she hated it when they argued. But she really did need to refill her carafe, so she decided to brave it anyway.

As she opened the living room door, however, the scene that met her eyes made her stop short again in horror and disbelief. Algernon and her mother were in the doorway to the kitchen, and Algernon had Annie pinned against the frame, his hand around her throat.

The moment he heard the click of the living room door, he released her, stepping away, his hands clenched to fists at his sides, his face a picture of outraged indignation.

'What do you want, Kitty?'

'Just a drink of water . . .' Kitty hung back.

'It's all right, my love.' Annie's hand was at her throat and she looked very shaken, but she was making a tremendous effort to sound quite normal. 'Come on through. Get your water.'

'You should know better than to creep about in the middle of the night,' Algernon growled.

Kitty was too afraid to point out that she hadn't been creeping about, and it was hardly the middle of the night. She went into the kitchen and refilled her carafe at the kitchen sink. On her way back, she hesitated, looking at her mother anxiously, but again Annie reassured her.

'Everything's all right, darling. Go back to bed. You look awfully tired.'

Kitty went, but for a long time she lay awake, listening for any further sounds of disturbance from downstairs. There were none. She began to wonder if she'd interrupted some game they'd been playing, and her cheeks flamed in the darkness. Then she thought perhaps she'd been half asleep and imagined the whole thing. But next morning, when she looked closely, she could see an ugly red weal round Annie's throat, which she was doing her best to conceal beneath a high-necked blouse. So it hadn't been a dream – of course it hadn't. And that mark looked very angry for something sustained in the course of a game, besides which she thought her mother was rather subdued.

It had set her wondering, and unwelcome thoughts came into her mind. There had been other times when she'd seen bruises, usually on Annie's wrists and arms when she rolled up her sleeves at the sink or the wash tub, and if she'd remarked on it Annie had told her she'd bumped or banged herself somehow and added that she had the sort of skin that bruised easily. And what about the time when she'd had that dreadful black eye and swollen face? Kitty had never questioned her explanation that she had tripped and fallen, but now suddenly she was not so sure. She wished she dared ask her mother if all her injuries were really accidents or whether there was some other unmentionable reason, but she couldn't bring herself to do so. And in any case, she suspected Annie would only tell her the same stories as before.

For the first time Kitty was looking at Algernon through different eyes, and remembering, too, the cryptic warning Lucy had included in her farewell note. She'd always looked up to him as a paragon of virtue, a man whose faith set him above mere mortals. He'd been so kind to her, and his attention had made her feel less of an outcast from the everyday world. She'd thought he could do no wrong. When he chastised Joe and Lucy, it was only because they deserved it; he was trying to stop them from straying into sinful ways. She'd put him on a pedestal, worshipped him almost, but suddenly it seemed to Kitty that her idol had feet of clay. She still found it almost impossible to believe that he could be misusing Annie, and if he was it must be for good reason, but she felt uncomfortable suddenly in his presence.

Now, as he summoned her for the nightly reading of *The Pilgrim's Progress*, something in her rebelled. She really didn't want to be alone with him, didn't want to hear his droning voice (truth to tell, sometimes she found it rather tedious), didn't want him preaching at her about the difference between right and wrong.

'Come along now, Kitty.' He was wheedling now, and somehow that set her teeth more on edge than his bullying.

'No thank you, Papa,' she repeated. And this time she raised her head and looked him directly in the eye. Then she returned to her book.

It was the first time she had ever openly defied him.

Algernon stared at the top of Kitty's head, furious and bewildered. He could scarcely believe that she had refused to join him for what had been, for the last week, their nightly ritual, much less that she would speak to him in that tone, cool and determined. It just wasn't his Kitty.

Defeated, he retired alone to the front room, but *The Pilgrim's Progress* remained unopened. Algernon ran over the brief unsatisfactory conversation again and again, growing more and more angry as a feeling of unease gathered strength.

What had happened to her? Surely what had occurred last night couldn't have anything to do with it? She'd seen nothing – nothing! He had done nothing. Her unexpected appearance had seen to that. But something had changed.

He very much hoped she wasn't beginning to turn rebellious like her sister. He did not want to have to teach her a lesson she wouldn't forget. But if that was the only way to return her to her usual meek and sweet-natured self, then so be it. He would not shrink from what he knew was no more than his duty.

Heat pulsed through his body; he swelled with it. His God had put him on this earth to save sinners from themselves. And if they could not be saved . . .

For a few moments Algernon saw the shadow of the devil from the corner of his eye. But he was too carried away by his own self-righteousness and thoughts of a sweet and submissive Kitty to dwell on that.

Chapter Twenty-Four

The pantomime had been running for a month now, and Lucy had fallen into a comfortable routine. Each evening – or at lunchtime if there was a matinee performance – she took the underground railway from the Elephant and Castle to get to the theatre, and when the show was over she did the same trip in reverse. She now enjoyed the journey through the bowels of the earth that had frightened her so when she had first come to London, and the walk down the Old Kent Road to Lynton Road had become so familiar it no longer held any terrors for her. By day she explored Bermondsey, though she avoided the slum areas, and was often drawn to the leather market, an impressive building with a clock tower where untanned hides were traded, and Southwark Park Road, with its multitude of shops and stalls. The people all seemed to her to be cheerful and friendly despite not having two pennies to rub together, as her mother would have put it. There were sometimes disturbances, it was true, around the many 'boozers' that punctuated her route home, but Lucy had learned that if she crossed the road to avoid the trouble, no one bothered her.

One night in late January, however, all that changed.

The weather had turned bitterly cold, frost painted walls and railings white, though no snow had as yet fallen, and the stars were a myriad of diamond pinpricks in the black velvet of the sky. Lucy walked quickly, partly to get warm, and partly to try to escape the memories that the frosty moonlight was evoking – memories of walking with Joe, not on a city street, but through silver-fronded fields and woodlands.

The Old Kent Road was almost deserted tonight, though lights, music and general merriment spilled out of the doors and windows of the public houses. Most folk were staying close to a fire, Lucy thought, and who could blame them?

A train rattled across the viaduct, sending a cloud of smoke into the clear cold air, somewhere in the distance a dog howled, but otherwise all was quiet.

Lucy walked on, pulling her coat tightly around her, anxious only to get to the warmth of Doris's cosy kitchen.

It was as she passed a dark and forbidding warehouse that it happened. One minute the street ahead of her was deserted, the next two rough-looking figures, one black, one white, had emerged from the shadows, blocking her path.

Alarmed, Lucy tried to sidestep them – to no avail. Before she could even think of running, the ruffians grabbed her, one to each arm, and forced her back against the stone wall of the warehouse. Lucy opened her mouth to scream and a huge rough hand covered it.

'Give us your purse, love,' a hoarse voice hissed so close to her ear that she felt the hot breath and a fine spray of spittle.

Blind panic overtook her. With the man's hand clamped over her mouth she could scarcely breathe, and her arms felt as if they were being wrenched from their sockets. Worse still, she could feel hands mauling her, whether searching her for anything worth stealing or with rape in mind she had no time to wonder. Somehow she managed to wriggle her head a little, and instinctively bit the hand covering her mouth as hard as she could.

'Little bitch!' The hand was jerked away and Lucy took a great gulp of icy-cold air. But the respite was short-lived; her arms were yanked ever tighter behind her and the white man's ugly snarling face was thrust into hers. Fetid breath and fear made her heave. In that moment Lucy thought her end had come.

Exactly what happened next she was never entirely sure. She was totally unaware of running footsteps as another man appeared on the scene; she only knew that quite suddenly her arms were free, one of her attackers was sprawling in the gutter and the other was fleeing down the street. Weak, shaking, and sick to her stomach, she crumpled against the warehouse wall, her knees giving way beneath her so it was all she could do not to sink to the frosty ground. Another hand gripped her arm and she shrank away in terror.

'It's all right. I'm not going to hurt you.'

Lucy raised eyes that were wide with fear. In her traumatised state the man seemed to her like a giant, so tall and broad his bulk appeared to shut out the light of the moon and the gas lamps. Her breath came out in a series of soft sobs and she covered her mouth with her free hand.

'It's all right,' he said again. 'They've gone, the bastards. Come on, love. Buck up now.'

'They wanted my purse,' Lucy managed, her voice faint and trembling.

'And the rest,' the man said grimly. 'You're lucky I was passing and saw what was going on.'

Lucy breathed a little more easily. Clearly this man meant her no harm. He'd come to her rescue. If he hadn't, she dreaded to think what might have happened.

'Thank you,' she said weakly.

'Did they hurt you?' His tone was gruff but concerned.

'I don't think so . . .' She was still shaking like a leaf, her mouth was dry and her knees weak, but otherwise, miraculously, she didn't think she'd suffered any lasting injury.

The man laughed shortly, his breath making clouds of steam in the frosty air.

'They'll be the ones feeling the pain, I reckon. Anyone who tangles with Jake Harper ends up wishing they hadn't.'

The name meant nothing to Lucy but she could see the reason behind the casual statement. Her nerves were beginning to settle a little, and though he no longer looked like a fearsome giant to her, it was no wonder he'd dispatched her two attackers so easily – the hand still supporting her was big as a small ham.

'I'm really grateful,' she said, feeling suddenly shy and rather foolish.

'My pleasure.' His accent was exactly like Spike's – cockney, but not as pronounced as that of Doris and Will. 'But what's a girl like you doing out by yourself this time o' night? Asking for trouble, ain't you?'

'I've always been all right before,' Lucy said, a little defensively.

'Then you've been lucky. Where are you headed? I'll walk you the rest of the way, make sure you get there safe and sound.'

'There's no need, really . . .' Lucy protested.

'Says you. I wouldn't sleep easy in my bed if I left you here all on your o-neo.'

Though she hated the loss of her independence, Lucy didn't feel up to arguing. She was still dreadfully shaken, and the thought of being alone in the dark, apparently empty street was not an appealing one.

'So where have you been all on your own?' her rescuer asked as they set out to walk the remaining distance to Lynton Road.

Lucy stole a glance at him. In the flickering light of the gas lamps his face was all planes and shadows so she couldn't really see what he looked like, and she had no idea who he was. But given the circumstances of their meeting and his kindness in wanting to see her safely home, she could see no harm in telling him the truth.

'I'm appearing in pantomime. I've just finished the evening performance.'

'An actress!' He sounded impressed.

'I'm a singer, really. But yes, I suppose I am an actress now too.'

'And what do they call you?'

'Lucy Dorne – well, Lucy Day is my real name but my aunt was Molly Dorne. You may have heard of her . . . ?'

'Can't say I have. But maybe you'll be famous one day and I'll be able to say I saved your bacon. Mind you, if you don't change your ways, you might be famous for all the wrong reasons.'

Lucy shuddered. She didn't even want to think about it.

A sudden unearthly squawk; a dark shape leaping from behind bushes in one of the gardens they were passing. Lucy squealed, stopping short in her tracks, and felt her knees buckle again.

'Hey! What's up?' The man caught her arm as she stumbled.

'I thought . . . I thought . . .' She didn't know what she'd thought, only that her nerves were in tatters.

'It was only a cat! Strayed on to foreign territory and got chased off, more than likely.'

'I know. Stupid . . . stupid!'

'Not after what you've been through. Come on, hold on to me.'

A little ashamed, but too weak to argue, Lucy did. He was

wearing a coat of some thick rough material; beneath the sleeve his arm felt hard, muscular and reassuring.

Before long they had reached Doris's house.

'This is it,' Lucy said. 'The place I'm lodging.'

'Lodging, eh? No good me hoping you'll invite me in for a cuppa, then?'

He said it lightly, jokingly almost, but it occurred to Lucy that perhaps she should do exactly that. He'd not only rescued her, he'd taken the trouble to go out of his way to see her safely home; the least she could do in return was offer him a hot drink on a cold night.

'I could if you like,' she said. 'My landlady is . . .' She hesitated. Much too complicated to explain the relationship between her and Doris. 'She's a friend,' she said instead. 'And I expect she'd like to thank you too for what you did.'

'Oh . . . there's no need . . . I was only—'

'No. Really. Do come in,' Lucy said.

She led the way along the little hall to the kitchen, her rescuer hanging back as if he was reluctant now to accept her invitation. As she had expected, Doris and Will were sitting with their chairs pulled well up to the fire, Doris knitting, Will dozing.

'I hope you don't mind,' Lucy said. 'But I've had a bit of a scare. This gentleman was kind enough to come to my assistance, and then see me safely home, so I've asked him in for a cup of tea or cocoa.'

'What in the world happened?' Doris asked, incredulous and anxious.

'I was attacked by a couple of thugs down on the Old Kent Road. This gentleman – I'm sorry, I've forgotten your name – scared them off. If he hadn't, I don't know what would have happened.'

She turned to look at her rescuer, seeing him properly for the first time. As she'd thought, he was a good six inches taller than she was, but much of the bulk of him came from the thickness of his coat, and the face she'd been unable to make out properly in the gaslight was angular, with a strong jawline and a nose that looked as if it had been broken at some time. Dark hair was oiled off a broad forehead and his eyes too were dark, with lashes a girl might envy. Her first impression was that he was maybe in his early twenties, and undeniably handsome.

Doris had put down her knitting and was bustling about, wanting to know every detail of what had happened in between offering her unexpected visitor a seat and boiling the kettle for a cup of tea.

Will had woken up properly now, and was looking at the stranger in his home curiously.

'Don't I know you?' he said at last. 'I've seen you somewhere before, I'm sure I have.'

'Course you don't know him, Will,' Doris said scathingly. 'You've been asleep and dreaming.'

Will shook his head and relapsed into silence, but a moment later he piped up again.

'I got it! You're a boxer, ain't you? I've seen you down the Wonderland.'

A few short months ago Lucy would have had no idea what Will was referring to, but now she had no difficulty in recognising the name of the boxing arena on Whitechapel Road that he often visited on a Saturday night. It wasn't something Doris approved of. Will was too fond of betting on the results of the contests – 'throwing your money away', Doris called it – and coming home stinking of jellied eels, which he loved and bought from a man with a tray who made regular rounds of the arena.

She looked again at her rescuer, who was nodding reluctantly, and thought that it was no wonder he had been able to dispatch her attackers so easily.

'So what's yer name?' Will was asking. 'You ain't Tommy Burns, that I do know, nor Curly Watson. Just a minute . . . don't tell me . . .'

'Jake Harper. Peckham Jake.' He said it anyway.

'That's it! Peckham Jake!' Will said, triumphant as if he'd remembered it himself. 'Haven't seen you lately, though. Where you bin 'iding?'

'Oh, here and there . . .' Jake shifted a little uncomfortably.

'Leave yer bloomin' boxin', can't you, Will?' Dolly chided. ''E don't want to be talking shop, do you, my son? An' I want to hear about these varmints that set about our Lucy.' She'd begun to refer to Lucy, rather proudly, as 'ours' since her reputation had started growing. 'I only 'ope you gave them a good hiding like as what they deserved.'

Lucy sat quietly as Doris chattered on, sipping her tea and a 'drop o' me best brandy, to calm yer nerves', as Doris put it when she tipped a healthy shot into a little glass and thrust it into Lucy's hand. Jake had something stronger than tea, too – Will made sure of that – and the atmosphere in the little kitchen seemed almost to resemble a party until Doris suddenly remembered the reason they were all there.

'I don't know, our Lucy. I never thought you'd come to any harm round here, but this 'as got me all worried. You can't be coming 'ome in the dark on yer own again. You'll 'ave to go an' meet her off the underground, Will, there's nothing else for it.'

'Can't our Davy do it?' Will looked less than enthusiastic.

'Course 'e can't, ya great lummox. He'd be neither use nor ornament. I know you're tired of a night, but we can't have Lucy getting set on by beggars and thieves.'

'What if I was to meet her?' Jake offered. 'If you'd trust her to me, that is. Got her home safe tonight, didn't I?'

'Well, yes, but we couldn't put on you like that,' Doris said, well meaning but a little unconvincing. 'And what about your boxing?'

'I couldn't do Saturdays, it's true,' Jake agreed. 'That's when I get most of my fights.'

'I'll take care o' Saturdays,' Will offered, anxious to be let off the hook for the rest of the week.

'Well, if you're sure . . . at least until we can sort something else out. I don't know what we can do to repay you, though,' Doris gushed. Her cheeks were even rosier than usual – she'd poured herself a small brandy along with Lucy's, and it was beginning to have its effect.

'I don't want repaying. The company of a pretty girl like Lucy is more than enough for me.' Jake looked directly at Lucy with a wicked grin.

As their eyes met, Lucy felt her own cheeks growing pink, and she glanced quickly away. But she was beginning to think that, horrible as the incident had been, perhaps her scare hadn't been so bad after all. If those louts hadn't attacked her, she would never have met Jake, let alone have him offering to see her safely home each night. And she had to admit, he was a very attractive young man.

Good as his word, he was waiting for her the following night outside the Elephant and Castle, and each night after that, barring Saturdays and sometimes a Friday too, he came all the way over to the theatre and met her outside the stage door when the performance was over. When they reached Lynton Road he would come in for a hot drink or, more often than not, a glass of beer or a tot of whisky. Doris had discovered he had a liking for steak, ale and oyster pies, one of her specialities, and sometimes she had one fresh out of the oven waiting for him, or a slice of fruit cake, which she served with a chunk of cheese on the side of the plate. Failing that, she would set the table with a platter of cold meat and pickles. 'Got to give 'im something for his trouble,' she would say when Will complained that the lad was eating better than he was.

Davy's nose was put out of joint, of course, at having what he saw as a rival for Lucy's attention, but Jake was very good with him, teasing him out of his sulks, play-fighting with him and always letting him win, so that Davy would roar with delight as he stood over his felled opponent while Will counted him out from the comfort of his armchair.

'Who's your chap?' Marie asked one evening as they wiped the greasepaint from their faces with wads of cotton. 'Pretty keen, isn't he?'

'He's not my chap!' Lucy protested, but as her eyes met Marie's in the mirror she couldn't help smiling, and the pink in her cheeks owed nothing to the vigour with which she was rubbing them.

'You could have fooled me!' Marie tossed her own wad of cotton into the waste bin. 'Well, good for you, I say. I wouldn't say no to a night out with him.'

'No chance!' Lucy teased. 'There's plenty more fish in the sea, but this one's mine!'

It was the first time she had admitted it, but Jake was certainly having an effect on her. Now, instead of pining for Joe, she had begun to look forward to leaving the theatre and seeing him there, leaning against the wall, smoking a cigarette. She looked forward to the journey home, when he would take her arm and make saucy, suggestive remarks. But he never acted on them, and Lucy couldn't help wishing that he would. Something about him was setting her on fire in a way she'd never expected to be set on fire again. Perhaps it was the hint of danger that was so exciting. Whenever she thought of the way he'd dealt with the ruffians who'd attacked her, fierce prickles twisted and spiralled deep inside her, and the lightest touch could set her trembling. It had been that way in the beginning with Joe, but somehow the sensations she was experiencing now were even stronger and more pleasurable. And more than anything in the world, she found herself wanting him to kiss her.

The desire shocked her. She loved Joe, didn't she? But Joe was a hundred miles and more away, she hadn't seen him for more than half a year and he seemed almost unreal to her now, the ghost of a long-gone past. There could be no doubting that Jake was real – real, and intoxicatingly exciting – and somehow the fact that he had made no move on her made him all the more desirable, and something of a challenge.

He really was an enigma. When his eyes met hers they were always full of teasing suggestion, and there was no denying the animal attraction that sparked between them. And yet he hadn't so much as tried to kiss her!

Well we'll see about that! Lucy thought. And began pondering what she could do to encourage Jake to make the move she longed for.

'Oh! I've got something in my eye!'

They were on one of the more deserted stretches of the Old Kent Road. Lucy stopped short, her hand flying to her face, pretending acute discomfort. As strategies went it was hardly original and by no means foolproof, but it was the best she'd been able to come up with, and she thought it worth a try.

Jake stopped too, a step or two further ahead, and turned back, waiting.

'Oooh!' Lucy winced, feigning distress. 'It's really stinging.'

'Perhaps it's a smut from the railway,' Jake offered, but made no move.

'Whatever it is, it hurts!' She waited a moment, rubbing at her eye, then added: 'I can't shift it. Can you take a look?'

'I can . . . but let's get to the next street lamp so I can see better.'

It wasn't quite what Lucy had in mind. She'd hoped he would take the excuse to get close to her where it was darker. But she wasn't going to abandon her plan now.

'Still there?' he asked as they reached the lamp. She nodded. 'Come here then.'

Lucy's heart beat hard against her ribs as she turned to him, holding her eye wide open with finger and thumb. He bent over her, lifting her chin with one of those big hands, tilting her head first this way, then that.

'Can't see anything.'

'Well it's there!'

'Nope . . .'

It was, Lucy thought, now or never. She released her eyelid, twisting slightly so that she was looking directly up at him. And it happened.

Just who made the first move, she was never sure. Perhaps it was simultaneous. She only knew that they were in each other's arms and his mouth was on hers, warm and hard. Her lips parted a little beneath the pressure and time seemed to stand still. It didn't matter that they were there in the circle of lamplight where anyone might see – why should it? Her world had reduced to Jake's searching mouth, his hard, lean body pressed close to hers, the thrills darting in the deepest parts of her.

The kiss lasted for long moments, but not long enough for Lucy. She wanted it to go on forever. Too soon Jake raised his mouth from hers, though his arms were still about her.

'How's your eye now?' he asked wickedly.

'It's better, I think . . .' Lucy was quite breathless.

'Mm. Thought so.' His grin was lopsided, his eyes teasing.

He knows! she thought. He knows I was making it up!

But then he was kissing her again, and it really didn't matter.

Afterwards, of course, everything changed. Jake still met her at the theatre each evening, but instead of going straight home to Bermondsey, they would stop off for a drink or something to eat, and the now inevitable cuddles and kisses, which were becoming ever more intimate. The attraction Lucy felt towards Jake was so strong it was as if she was drawn to him like an iron filing to a magnet, and she was powerless to resist when his hands found their way inside her clothing. And not simply powerless: she wanted it – and more, far more, wanted it so fiercely she trembled with the wanting.

It was as if he had cast a spell over her, she thought, and when she was not with him, drunk on heady desire, and able to think rationally, she could scarcely understand how it was she could feel this way. When Algernon had done that unspeakable thing to her she had recoiled from the thought of a man's hands on her ever again, shrunk from physical contact even with Joe. Yet now it seemed she was craving the very thing that had aroused such disgust in her.

Had it been her own fault that Algernon had attacked her? Had he been right when he had accused her of grievous sin? Was there a devil inside her, tempting her, arousing her, turning her into a shameless harlot? Was that the real reason she had left Joe? The real reason she had felt no longer worthy of him? Joe was a thoroughly decent man, who had been like a brother to her before they had become sweethearts, and he deserved better.

A wife who was as pure as he believed her to be, not some Jezebel.

But Jake . . . Jake was different. He and Joe were like two sides of a flipped coin. There was something about him that was wild and dangerous; with him there was no need to feel ashamed of this sensual side of her nature or of the fact that Algernon had taken her virginity. Jake would be no virgin himself, she felt sure. There would have been other women, and some far worse than she. One of these nights it was going to happen, and none of Doris's warnings nor her own reservations would prevent it. She'd be swept away by her feelings like a bit of driftwood in a stormy ocean, Lucy knew, and somehow she could not care.

Even now, when she was not with him, dark desire twisted inside her. She didn't think she loved him – Joe still held that special place in her heart. But it was as if she'd been a child when she was with Joe, a toddler learning to walk, and now she was a woman, with a woman's passions and desires. Or the passions and desires of a shameless hussy . . . Somehow she couldn't help feeling that Jake wouldn't mind much either way.

There was plenty she didn't know about him, though, and sometimes she wondered about that too. He never talked about a family or his past – if she began to try to probe, he stopped her questions with his kisses. And he was almost as reticent about his present life.

'When are we going to see you down Wonderland again then?' Will asked one night when he brought Lucy home, but again Jake was evasive.

'Sometime soon, I expect.'

'That's the place to be,' Will asserted. 'You know what the purse is when Andrew Jeptha fights Curly Watson at the end of the month? Five hundred and fifty pounds, that's what.'

'It's a title fight, ain't it?'

'An' that's what you should be aiming for, my cocker. I shall be down there that night all right.'

'Losing your shirt as usual,' Doris complained.

'Nah – Jeptha's a dead cert. Big strong black like 'im, he'll knock Curly out cold. Won't go further than five rounds, or I'm a Dutchman.'

'Well don't blame me if there's no proper food on the table for a week,' Doris sniffed, and the questions about where Jake was fighting, and who, were forgotten for the time being.

But when Doris and Will had gone to bed and Lucy and Jake were alone, Lucy's curiosity – along with a daring idea – got the better of her.

'Do you think I could come and see you fight one night when the panto's finished?' she asked tentatively.

'You wouldn't like it at all,' Jake said bluntly.

'I wouldn't like to see you hurt, that's true.' Sometimes there were dreadful marks on Jake's face: black eyes, lips cut so badly that he winced when he kissed her, and his nose looked as if it might have been broken again. But somehow the injuries only added to the glamour – he might have been a gladiator in ancient Rome, she thought – and the danger made him a hero in her eyes.

'You wouldn't like the sort of dives I fight in, neither,' Jake said. 'You're better off staying well clear, Lucy. They ain't no place for a lady.'

'Oh.' She pouted, disappointed, then, as he pulled her close and the familiar desire rose in her, she looked up at him, coquettish and teasing. 'You should know by now I'm no lady, Jake.'

'Enough of a one for me.'

Her disappointment melted like snow on a firedog as his lips covered hers. He kissed her until she was breathless and the longing was a taut wire in the pit of her stomach, twisting and pulling so tightly she almost cried out.

Above their heads a board groaned and she froze, pointing to the ceiling with a warning expression, but a moment later they heard the creak of the bedsprings as Dolly and Will climbed in. Jake winked at her, one of his hands inside her blouse, the other rucking up her skirt.

'Jake . . . !' she protested weakly, but he ignored her, lifting her bodily and lowering her to the floor. And then: 'Oh Jake!'

His body was covering hers, burrowing into her, and the wire inside her shifted again, tightening into a spiral that seemed to tug at the very core of her. This was it, the moment she had longed for and at the same time dreaded, the moment when she would discover if revulsion would overcome sharp desire, or if longing would make her throw caution to the winds and turn her into the sensual creature she had discovered lurked inside her.

The scent of him was in her nostrils, an intoxicating mix of tobacco and something unidentifiable but which was pure male. It in no way reminded her of the smell of her previous, night-marish encounter – chrysanthemums and dank stone – and it only intensified her need. She was ready for him, more than ready.

Then, just as she thought the moment had come, he drew back abruptly, rolling away from her.

'No.' His voice was rough.

Lucy gazed up at him, bereft and bewildered, wanting him only to hold her again as he had held her a moment ago.

'There's something I have to tell you first.'

She'd wanted to know more about him, but it was no longer important. Her whole body, every bit of her, was crying out for him.

'Whatever it is, it doesn't matter,' she said.

For what seemed an eternity his eyes held hers, and she saw the indecision in them, but also the hot desire.

Desire won. He reached for her again, and Lucy forgot his words, forgot everything but the glory of his mouth, his hands, his body, and her own eager and trembling response.

Chapter Twenty-Five

Kitty had been ill again. Dr Blackmore had visited and increased the dosage of her medication and she seemed a little better, but she was still confined to bed. Getting up and dressed exhausted her, and the doctor had advised it was best she didn't even try.

'Complete rest is the only answer, I'm afraid,' he'd counselled.

This latest setback had thrown Kitty into a state of depression worse than any she had experienced before. She'd accepted long ago that she was never going to be able to lead the sort of normal life other girls enjoyed, and tried to find ways to make her solitary existence bearable. For the most part she'd succeeded. She loved to bake when she was well enough, and her painting gave her great satisfaction. But now the days seemed endless. Annie had tried to get hold of a tray table to fit across the bed, but none of the shops in High Compton stocked such a thing, so sketching with a block of paper and soft pencils was the best Kitty could do, and she soon tired of that. It was colour she loved, colour that brought joy into her life. There wasn't much fun to be had in drawing a rose or a bowl of fruit when it was all in black and white and shades of grey.

She sewed a little, but the tapestry she'd been working on entailed the tiniest of cross stitches, which seemed to try her eyes more than usual, and bending over it made her neck ache.

And though she had a few books to read, Algernon had taken to monitoring what Annie borrowed for her from the library, and prohibited anything he deemed unsuitable, so that what was left was either worthy or religious and, Kitty thought, deadly dull.

Day by day she sank deeper and deeper into a dark place and was often close to tears of boredom and despair. She had no appetite, though Annie tried to tempt her with little invalid dishes – tasty broths, coddled eggs and baked custards – and was now thinner than ever and so weak that when she got out of bed to use the commode she became quite dizzy. Sometimes ladies from the chapel came to visit, middle-aged and pious, and their attempts at a bedside manner had quite the opposite effect to what they intended, as did the extra attention Algernon was paying to her.

Every evening after he'd finished his tea he would come to her room and read with her. They'd finished *The Pilgrim's Progress* now, and the religious tracts they'd moved on to were boring and even more obscure, giving Algernon the excuse to explain their meaning at length. But worse, much worse, was what would happen afterwards, when they prayed together. Weak as she was, he insisted she should get out of bed and kneel beside him. God would give her the strength, he said. But that strength seemed only to come with Algernon's assistance. When Kitty swayed on her knees, he would support her, with his hands clasped in supplication around hers, his arms tight about her frail body. When the last Amen had been said, he would lift her bodily back on to the bed and sit upon it himself so that she found herself leaning against him. As he pulled the sheets over her his hand would, more often than not, touch her thigh or her breast through the thin cotton of her nightgown, and Kitty would recoil inwardly, though she made no protest.

How could she, when he was only being kind? Only caring

for her as best he could? He meant no harm by it, and Kitty's face burned as hot with guilt for even thinking such a thing as from the unwanted physical contact. But she couldn't get it out of her head all the same, any more than she could forget her awful suspicion that Algernon might be ill-using Annie. She didn't want to believe it, and she certainly didn't want to believe he was deliberately touching her. He had been a father figure to her for too long, and Kitty was too unworldly to look beyond that. But there was no denying that her feelings towards him had changed. Rather than enjoying the time he devoted to her as she had done in the past, she now dreaded him coming to her room. The sound of his footsteps on the stairs, the heavy, measured tread so instantly distinguishable from Annie's quick, light step, made her heart sink and a sick feeling would start in her stomach.

Tonight had been no different. He had read to her and they had prayed together, Kitty making the most enormous effort to stay upright on her knees without Algernon's assistance. The prayers had seemed to take longer than ever, though she acknowledged that might be because she was anxious for them to be over. Her head was swimming so she did not dare close her eyes but focused instead on the steady flame of the oil lamp on the bedside table, hoping Algernon would not notice.

When at last it was over, she grasped the iron frame of the bed to lever herself up, but before she could do so, Algernon's arm went around her.

'Let me help you, my dear.'

'I can manage,' Kitty protested.

'You'll tire yourself. Lean on me.'

Something in Kitty snapped.

'Leave me! I want to do it on my own.' With all her remaining strength she drove her elbow sharply into Algernon's ribs, wriggling out of his grasp. But as she did so she lost her balance, toppling over to sprawl inelegantly across the rag rug.

For a brief moment fury and outrage distorted Algernon's face before it was replaced with a pained expression, part reproof, part sorrow.

'You foolish girl! What did I tell you? Come now . . .'

He bent over her, lifting her bodily, and Kitty lacked the strength to resist further. Only when he had deposited her against the pillows and plumped down on the bed beside her did she manage to protest.

'Papa . . . please . . . leave me alone.'

'Foolish, foolish girl,' he repeated, and his hand came up to cup her breast. This time there could be no mistaking that it was intentional.

'Papa, don't!' Kitty tried to push his hand away, frightened both by his touch and by the look in his eyes – dark and lustful – but Algernon merely squeezed the harder whilst his other hand went between her legs, bare now, since her nightgown had rucked up in the ungainly struggle. 'Papa . . . please . . .'

'Daughter of Eve.' His voice was low, rough with the primal desire burning in his loins. 'Daughter of Eve, just like your sister.'

'Papa!' She was almost sobbing now.

'Oh my Kitty . . .' He took her hand, pushing it down on to the hard swelling beneath the coarse wool of his trousers.

Kitty recoiled, not just inwardly now, but with every bit of her body, trying to snatch her hand away, trying to escape the suffocating closeness of him. And at that very moment heard her mother calling up the stairs.

'Algernon! Mrs Brown from the church is here to see you! Can you come down?'

Algernon froze, his hands stilled, even his eyes motionless, as if he had become a stone statue.

'Algernon!' Annie called again.

He moved then, rising from the bed, moving towards the door, taking the oil lamp with him. Shocked, dazed and trembling, Kitty wrapped her arms around herself, staring down at her bare legs in the half-light of an almost full moon shining in through the window. Then, slowly, she shifted enough to be able to pull her nightgown down to cover them.

In her innocence she could make no sense of what had happened. She only knew she didn't like it at all. It was wrong . . . wrong! And what had Papa meant by calling her a 'daughter of Eve'? 'Just like your sister', he had said. The words echoed and re-echoed in Kitty's fevered brain. *Just like your sister.* What had he meant by that?

Suddenly Kitty was remembering the veiled warning in the letter Lucy had written her when she left. Was this what she had meant? Had he touched Lucy as he had touched her? Could it be . . . was it possible that it had had something to do with Lucy leaving home?

But Lucy wouldn't be afraid as Kitty was. Lucy was bold and worldly. She might be the younger sister, but she knew more about men and their ways than Kitty would ever know. More than she wanted to know . . .

And then her heart was thundering so hard against her ribs, the weight of it so great in her chest, that she could think about nothing but struggling for the next breath, and the next.

When Annie brought her a hot milky drink some time later, she was still trembling.

'Kitty! Are you all right?' she asked anxiously.

There was no way Kitty could tell her mother what had happened.

'I'm all right.' Her voice was still thready and breathless.

'Have you had another turn? Should I call the doctor?'

'No – no. I'm better now. It's over.'

Until tomorrow night . . . The panic began to tighten in her chest again.

'Mam . . .' she said urgently. 'Will you ask Papa not to read with me again? I don't like it.'

Annie's eyes narrowed. 'It's tiring you? I'll tell him that, of course, but . . .' She broke off, concerned, but uncertain as to how much notice Algernon would take of her.

'If he does, will you be there too? Please, Mam . . .'

'Of course I will, darling, if that's what you want.'

'It is.'

Annie placed the cup of warm milk between Kitty's hands. All her old anxieties had been awakened now, hovering around her like the shadows of a bad dream. She pulled up a chair beside the bed.

'I'll stay with you now, shall I?'

Kitty nodded.

Though there were no confidences that night, it was a long time before a worried Annie went back downstairs.

Her mind was made up. Tossing and turning throughout a long night when her anxiety made sleep impossible, Annie had decided the time had come to act. Somehow she had to find a way to leave Algernon.

She'd thought about doing just that many times, wanting nothing more than to escape his tyranny, his perverse demands on her, and the beatings that had become more frequent and increasingly violent over the past year, but always the necessity of providing a comfortable home for Kitty had been the insurmountable obstacle. She could survive – just – and her frail daughter's well-being was the most important consideration. Despite the restricted life she was forced to lead, Kitty appeared to be quite happy and content, and she and Algernon had always seemed so close. Though that closeness had played a little on Annie's mind, she'd dismissed her misgivings as nothing more than imagination. But there had been nothing imagined about Kitty's distress tonight. Something Algernon had said or done had upset her dreadfully, to the point where she no longer wanted to be alone with him. Annie didn't want to think the thoughts that were assailing her, didn't want to believe that Algernon might have behaved inappropriately towards Kitty, but she couldn't escape them. And for the first time she found herself wondering if something like that might have led to Lucy running away from home.

Surely not! Algernon had no time for Lucy, never had. But Kitty . . .

If her suspicions were correct – and she was becoming increasingly sure that they were – it wasn't just herself suffering at the hands of the monster she had married, but Kitty too. The thought turned her cold. She'd do what she could to make sure they were not left alone together, but she couldn't always be there. She had to get Kitty away to a place of safety. She couldn't procrastinate any longer. And daunting though the prospect was, she had an idea as to how she might achieve it.

Truth to tell, it hadn't been her idea in the first place, but Joe's. Somewhat surprisingly, he was the one person she'd confided in regarding Algernon's treatment of her. Joe had grown up so much in the last year; he was no longer the boy she'd treated as a son, but a young man, perceptive, and with both feet planted firmly on the ground, and it was he who had raised the subject one Sunday a few weeks ago.

He'd arrived early for his weekly roast dinner – the old arrangement was routine again now, though he'd made his excuses several times when Lucy had first left, and Annie knew he was still dreadfully upset about her going – and they'd been alone in the kitchen, Joe leaning against the big stone sink while Annie set pans to boil on the gas rings and checked the progress of the leg of lamb. As she bent over to open the oven door, she winced and half straightened, her hand going instinctively to her ribs. It was over in an instant, but it hadn't escaped Joe's notice.

'What's the matter?' he asked.

'Oh . . . nothing.' But she was still supporting her ribs with her hand, and instead of bending over to look into the oven, she went down on her knees so that the roast was more or less at eye level.

'I just banged myself the other day, that's all,' she said as she basted a little hot fat over the meat, conscious of Joe still regarding her narrowly. 'I seem to be getting clumsy in my old age.'

Joe didn't smile, or tell her she was far from old, as she'd half expected him to.

'You certainly seem to have an awful lot of accidents,' he said. 'Are you sure that's all they are?'

'Whatever do you mean?' Annie closed the oven door, brushing a strand of hair away from her face, which was growing hot, and not only from the heat of the stove.

Joe looked at her, unsmiling. 'It's Algernon, isn't it?'

'Of course not! Why ever should you think such a thing?' But she said it too quickly, and the very force of her denial was unconvincing.

'Well I think he is,' Joe said. 'I know him too well, don't forget – all those thrashings I took when I was a nipper, and it wasn't just because I deserved them. He enjoyed beating me, the bastard. I'm too big for that now, and I reckon he's taking it out on you. I'm right, aren't I?'

368

Annie lowered her head, unable to meet his eyes.

'How many times have I seen you covered in bruises? How many times have you come into the chemist's with cuts and grazes? If they're all the result of accidents, then I'm a Dutchman.'

'I don't want to talk about it, Joe.' Though Algernon had not yet returned from chapel, he might be home at any minute, and the last thing Annie wanted was for him to walk in on this conversation.

Joe was not ready to give up, though.

'You should leave him,' he said. 'He treats you like dirt, always has. You deserve better than that.'

Annie laughed shortly. 'And where would I go? What would I do? It's not just myself I have to consider, remember. I could rough it somewhere, but Kitty . . .'

Joe shook his head, acknowledging the depth of the problem.

'I wish I could say you could come and live with me, but there's hardly space to swing a cat in my rooms. And I'm not sure what Mr Penny would have to say about it either . . .'

'Of course you couldn't take us in, Joe! I wouldn't dream of it. And just think of the scandal it would cause! You're all set for a really good career. I wouldn't want to jeopardise that. No, I'll be all right. You mustn't worry about me.'

'But I do. I've been worried about you for a long time. And I know now I was right to be.'

'I'll be all right,' Annie repeated.

Joe's cyes had narrowed thoughtfully. 'A job as a live-in housekeeper, that's what you want.'

'And what about Kitty?'

'Well . . . maybe she could move in with me. If it was just my homeless sister, Mr Penny might be agreeable. And she'd be right on the premises for her medicine if she was ill . . .'

'It wouldn't work, Joe, though it's kind of you to even think of it. No, I'm afraid things will just have to go on as they are, for the time being at least.'

'You get the local papers, don't you? Keep an eye on the "Situations Vacant". You never know what might come up.'

They'd heard the slam of the front door then: Algernon was home, and the time for confidences was over. But Annie had heeded Joe's suggestion, scouring the columns of both the local weekly newspaper and the *Bath Chronicle*, which Algernon had delivered every evening, and a few days ago she'd seen a situation advertised that had interested her.

A family of gentry with their own estate some miles out of Bath were looking for a housekeeper, and there was the promise of accommodation in 'the gate house' – a cottage on the drive into the grounds, Annie assumed. She'd circled the advertisement and cut it out before throwing the newspaper away, but so far hadn't taken it any further. It seemed such a huge step, and the years had drained Annie of much of her old daring and readiness to break out into the unknown.

Now, however, it seemed to her that finding the advertisement had been a gift from a God she was not at all sure she believed in. As soon as Algernon had left for work, she opened the kitchen drawer where she'd stashed the cutting, took it out, and read it again. Really, it appeared as if it had been meant for her, though she would never have seen it had it not been for the conversation she'd had with Joe. Annie got out writing paper and envelope and sat down at the kitchen table to compose a letter of application. Then, before she could change her mind, she found a stamp, stuck it on, and took the letter to the nearest pillar box, at the end of the road.

As it dropped inside, she felt something she had not experienced in a very long time – something akin to excitement.

If only – if only! – this worked out it could be the answer to all their problems.

The reply, inviting her to attend for interview, dropped through the letter box a few days later with the afternoon delivery. Annie's heart began to race. An interview! How was she going to get there? Brimscombe Hall was a good ten miles away. She'd have to go to Bath and get a taxi from there. She couldn't risk asking Cyril Short to drive her – talk of such a thing would be all over High Compton before she even got home again. The time of the interview was convenient, though – eleven thirty, on a weekday morning. Algernon would be at work; he'd never know she'd gone. But what about Kitty? Should she tell her what she planned? Or simply pretend she was going to town to visit Molly? Knowing Algernon had forbidden her to see her sister-in-law, Kitty wouldn't mention it to him, and though she hated lying to Kitty, there was no point telling her the truth yet in case it came to nothing.

On the morning of the interview, Annie changed into her Sunday best when Algernon had left for work.

'Are you sure you'll be all right, Kitty?' she asked when it was time for her to leave to catch the train to Bath.

'I'll be fine,' Kitty assured her.

'Don't try to get up and do anything. I should be back by early afternoon.'

'Off you go, Mam, and enjoy yourself,' Kitty said. 'You deserve it.'

Butterflies fluttered in Annie's stomach as the train chugged its way to Bath. Once there, a calm determination took hold, and she began to feel optimistic. She found a taxi outside the station and gave the driver the address. He scratched his head for a moment, and got out of the car to confer with another driver waiting in the queue, but when he returned he was looking suitably impressed.

'Right. Brimscombe Hall it is then.'

Town gave way to leafy lanes, and as he negotiated dips and bends the driver talked – trying to discover her reason for going there, Annie thought. She kept her answers short, but through the rather one-sided conversation, she learned more of the man she hoped would be her future employer.

Brimscombe Hall had, apparently, once been the stately home of a minor lord of the realm, but his reckless ways had cost him dear.

'Liked a bet, he did,' the driver told her. 'Horses, dogs, anything that moved. And used to go to Monte Carlo once or twice a year. Anyway, he lost everything. Had to sell up.'

'And the family who live there now?' Annie was reluctant to admit she knew nothing about them, but curiosity got the better of her.

'Made his money through engineering, from what I can make out. An' it's money what talks, even though he might not be gentry.'

The motor car was turning into a driveway flanked on either side by trees. A cottage sat beside the entrance, small and gabled, a little as Annie had always imagined the witch's cottage in 'Hansel and Gretel' might look. That must be the gate house, she thought, and if she was successful in getting this job it would be her home. Well, she could certainly live happily there. The butterflies fluttered again and anticipation brought a lump to her throat.

As they rounded a bend, the big house itself came into view, rambling and impressive, the pale sun turning the Bath stone walls the colour of soft butter.

'You want me to wait?' the driver asked as he pulled up in a broad courtyard.

'If you would, please. I don't expect to be very long.'

'It'll cost, you know.'

Annie bit her lip. She only hoped she would have enough money to pay the driver; she'd brought every penny she'd saved from her housekeeping allowance, meant to buy something nice for Kitty. But really there was no option. She couldn't walk all the way back to Bath.

She got out of the car, straightened her skirts and tucked a stray end of hair behind her ear. Then, with head held high and hope in her heart, she approached the house.

Half an hour later, when she emerged again, Annie was feeling less confident. The woman who had interviewed her – Mrs Trenchard – was, she thought, for all her expensive-looking clothes and rather affected accent, no lady. Big-boned and with a rather coarse face, she nonetheless adopted a superior attitude, and Annie didn't think she'd be the easiest of people to work for. She'd be just the type to pick holes in everything an employee did, and treat them like dirt. Annie would put up with that, though, if only she was offered the position. Anything was preferable to remaining under Algernon's roof, especially since she had become so worried about his unhealthy interest in Kitty. The trouble was, she wasn't at all sure that her interview had been entirely successful.

At first she'd thought it was going quite well. She'd presented herself as a widow, which wasn't exactly a lie, just an omission of the truth of her present marital status, and had provided what she thought were good answers to the questions about her experience, though of course she had had to admit she'd never worked in a house as big as this one. But when it had come out that she had a sickly daughter, Mrs Trenchard's lips had tightened and her eyes narrowed, and the last straw had come when she'd been asked where she was living now.

Annie had heard that many of the advertisements for domestic servants in Bath stipulated that 'girls from Hillsbridge need not apply', and she knew that the twin town had a reputation for rowdy behaviour and a rough element in its population. But there had been no such proviso on the advertisement she had answered, and in any case, she didn't think it would apply to High Compton, which considered itself much better class than Hillsbridge. Not so, it seemed.

'Isn't that at the centre of the coalfield?' Mrs Trenchard had asked, and it was almost an accusation.

Annie had been forced to admit it was indeed, and after that the interview had been terminated quite abruptly.

'We'll let you know.' But from Mrs Trenchard's tone of voice Annie rather thought her mind was already made up.

Deflated and dispirited, she climbed into the waiting taxi, and as they drove back past the little cottage that must be the gate house she could have wept. It would have been perfect! Perfect! But she wouldn't give up hope yet. Perhaps she'd been wrong to think that coming from a mining area had spoiled her chances. Why would it? Surely Mrs Trenchard could see that she was perfectly respectable? Every bit as respectable as Mrs Trenchard herself, maybe more than she had been before she came into money . . .

But Annie was glad, all the same, that she hadn't mentioned anything of her plan to Kitty. All she could do now was go home and wait.

The letter arrived just a few days later. Annie was shaking as she tore open the envelope, but a bad feeling had settled in her stomach, and all the determinedly optimistic thoughts she'd been trying to cling to disappeared as if by magic. Even before she read the carefully worded rejection she knew it was no good.

Mrs Trenchard thanked her for attending for interview but had to inform her that on this occasion she had not been successful.

Annie seldom wept, but she wept now, tears of disappointment and despair. She'd held out such high hopes and they had all been dashed. In that moment she felt that any effort she made to escape from Algernon would end in the same way, not just because she came from what prospective employers looked on as an undesirable area, and had a sick daughter who was dependent on her, but because it felt as though he had somehow cast a spell, like a spider building a web, and she was caught in it, never to be free.

A solitary tear fell on to the sheet of writing paper, blurring the ink so that the words swam in a pool of dark blue. Annie tore it into shreds and threw it on to the fire, watching the corners curl and blacken, then turn to fine grey dust, and that, too, seemed symbolic.

If she wanted to escape, and more importantly, get Kitty away from Algernon, then she was going to have to think of another way. At that moment she had no idea what that might be; she only knew she would stop at nothing to remove her daughter from the clutches of the monster she had married.

Chapter Twenty-Six

'What was it you wanted to tell me last night?' Lucy asked.

They'd made a detour after Jake had met her from the theatre so as to have more opportunity to be alone together. They'd made love again in the shadows of the warehouses, and were now sitting side by side on a rough bench beside a late-opening tea stall down by the docks, each cradling a mug of steaming tea, 'strong enough for the spoon to stand up in the cup', as Annie would have put it. Nearby a brazier glowed in the dark, a halo of warmth in the cold clear night.

Lucy was glowing too, replete and content, her free hand curled into Jake's, her shoulder resting comfortably against his, but she was curious to know what it was that he'd been on the point of saying before it had been forgotten in their mutual passion.

'Oh . . . nothing. It doesn't matter now.' Jake was gazing towards the bulky containers silhouetted against the starlit sky and the stacks of the ships on the river beyond.

'That's not how it seemed.' For all the delicious torpor that was making her drowsy and dreamy, she wasn't ready to let it go. 'Come on, Jake, tell me.'

For a long moment he was silent, then he sighed.

'OK. Since you've asked. There's a lot you don't know about me. For a start, I've done time.'

Lucy was startled. 'You mean you've been in prison?'

'Pentonville.' His tone was flat, emotionless. 'Bloody place. I should never have been sent there, but there was no room in the reformatories for lads my age. But I minded my Ps and Qs and got picked to be sent to Bedford Borstal to learn a trade. "The London Lads", they called us. The trade never worked out, but that was where I got into boxing.'

'Why were you sent to prison?' Lucy's thoughts were reeling.

'Oh, nothing serious. Just a bit of honest thieving.'

His insouciance shocked her. What was honest about thieving?

'But . . . why?' she asked, bewildered.

He shrugged. 'It's what we did. When you ain't got nothing, you can't see the harm in helping yourself to a few bits and pieces from them as has everything they could ever want and more.'

'*We?*' Lucy homed in on the word. 'You mean . . . your family?'

Jake chortled mirthlessly. 'No, the gang I was in with – a bad lot, really. I can see that now. I ain't got no family.'

No family! It was unimaginable. 'No one at all?'

'None that wanted to know me. I got sent to a baby farm when I was just a couple of weeks old.'

'A baby farm?' Lucy had never heard such an expression. 'What's a baby farm?'

He turned to look at her, his expression incredulous. 'Christ, you've led a sheltered life, Luce. A baby farm. A woman who takes in babies nobody wants and gets paid for it. Trouble is, when the money runs out, they get rid of the nippers. Neglect or starve 'em, till they're so weak they kick the bucket. And do

377

worse, sometimes . . . at least I was lucky there. Whoever it was wanted to get rid of me must've kept on paying Mrs Eavy – the woman who took me in – and paying well. Until she dumped one too many of her charges in the Thames and got nicked for it. And hanged. Served her bloody well right.'

Lucy gasped, horrified, and he went on:

'I got sent to an orphanage then, and there I stayed till I ran away, along with a couple of me mates. We lived rough on the streets, getting by with whatever we could lay our hands on. That's how I ended up in Pentonville. I was a bit slow one day, lost my footing, and got me collar felt.' He laughed shortly. 'I'd like to see that bleeding peeler try to catch me now!'

Lucy was left speechless. It was all too much to take in.

'So . . . now you know.' Jake finished his mug of tea and tipped the dregs out on to the ground beside him. 'I don't s'pose you'll be wanting any more to do with me now.'

'Oh Jake!' Not to see him again was the last thing she wanted.

'I should've told you before we . . . well, you know. But I didn't want to lose you, Luce. You're the best thing that's ever happened to me.'

She tightened her grip on his hand, turning her face to his.

'You won't lose me, Jake. You're still the same person you were before. And don't think . . . well . . .' She laughed tremulously. 'You can't get rid of me that easily.'

'You sure?'

'Of course I'm sure! I . . . I think I love you . . .'

She could scarcely believe how easily those words had fallen from her lips. For all the animal magnetism that drew her to him, she hadn't even considered that she might have fallen in love, so sure had she been that her heart would always belong to Joe. But what else could it be – the fierce longing that made her throw caution to the winds, the tenderness filling her now, knowing the terrible start in life he'd had, the hardships he'd endured?

'Oh Luce, thank God for you.' He hadn't said he loved her too, but somehow it didn't matter – the depth of feeling in those words was enough for her. 'Come on, I reckon I'd better get you home.'

'I heard something today I didn't care for,' Will said.

It was Sunday afternoon and he had the day off from his duties as a lighterman. It didn't always work out that way: if a big ship was ready to dock and needed to offload some of its cargo, then he might have to forgo a day of rest, but today all was quiet.

They'd eaten a hearty meal of roast beef with slabs of batter pudding and vegetables that Doris had bought the day before at a market stall – like Annie, she liked to cook what she called 'a proper dinner' on a Sunday – and now they were relaxing over a brew of her strong tea. But Lucy wasn't really listening to the conversation. She was lost in thoughts of Jake – the exciting relationship they were now sharing, as well as all the things she'd learned about his past life.

'You need to hear this, my girl.' Will leaned forward and tapped on the table with his forefinger.

'Sorry . . . what?'

Will waited until he had their full attention. 'You know I keep asking that feller of yours when we're going to see him down the Wonderland again, and he keeps prevaricating—'

'That's a long word for you, Will,' Doris interjected.

'Now I've found out the reason,' Will said, ignoring her interruption. 'He's got himself mixed up with the dodgy side of the business, that's why.'

Lucy stiffened in her chair, but said nothing. Doris, however, was less reticent.

'What you going on about now, Will? What d'you mean, dodgy?'

'There's fights and there's fights, Doris. Nasty stuff. All the bouts down the Wonderland are according to the rules. Very strict about that, they are. Well, they have title fights there, don't they? They can't afford to upset the powers-that-be, and they won't have anybody there that's dodgy. That's why we don't see Jake down there any more. He's gone and got himself blacklisted. That's what I reckon.'

'He wouldn't do something like that!' Lucy was immediately on the defensive with a desire to stand up for Jake.

'Not according to what I heard. Fighting down the Cap and Feather, they say – an' we all knows what goes on down there. Tomorrow night, it's set for. So that'd explain why I've got to come and meet you, wouldn't it?' Will gave Lucy a straight look before burying his nose in his teacup.

Lucy had not the first idea what went on at the Cap and Feather, but certainly Jake had told her he wouldn't be able to see her home on Monday evening. He had to meet his manager, he'd said, and it hadn't even crossed her mind to question it. Why would she? She trusted him implicitly, and even more so since he had told her the truth about his past. Her heart bled for the unwanted baby he had once been, the little lost boy who had endured heaven only knew what hardships at the hands of the people who ran the orphanage he had been taken to, and then the cruel regime of prison.

She could understand now the reason for his reticence about his past. Understandably, it was something he was ashamed of, and wanted to forget. But he'd told her now, had even wanted to confess before making love to her, to give her the chance to walk

380

away. He'd never tried to force himself on her, and even then, when he'd been consumed with desire for her, he'd still held back. She had been the one responsible for what had happened. 'Whatever it is, it doesn't matter,' she had said. And it didn't. What he had done in the past was unimportant. It was who he was now that counted. The man who had rescued her from the ruffians who had attacked her, the man who had seen her safe home every night since. The man who had made the memories of the terrible thing that had happened in her own past more bearable, and filled the empty space in her heart. The man she had fallen in love with.

Algernon would have branded him a sinner beyond redemption, she had no doubt, but she couldn't care less what Algernon would say. He was the evil one; compared to him, Jake was a saint.

But for all that, Lucy suddenly felt horribly uncomfortable. Will might have it wrong, of course, but she didn't honestly believe he had – it fitted too neatly, and she was remembering Jake's reaction when she'd said she'd like to see him fight one day, telling her bluntly that his bouts were no place for a lady. That was probably true, of course – boxing was a man's sport in every sense of the word, and even the respectable venues like the Wonderland would almost certainly be rowdy, and a magnet for the roughest of the working classes, though in her innocence she could imagine nothing worse than a drunken audience at one of the less salubrious halls she'd performed at when she'd first come to London. From what Will said, it seemed the Cap and Feather was not one of the best places to box, but still Lucy couldn't understand why Jake had lied to her. Only a little lie, she supposed, but a lie none the less. She wished she could ask him about it but she wasn't seeing him tonight, and they weren't meeting tomorrow afternoon either, nor on Tuesday, though they'd begun to make a habit of seeing one another in the afternoons. She'd been a bit puzzled when he'd said he'd meet her outside the theatre on Tuesday evening, even had to suppress the awful thought that he might be tiring of her – men did if they thought you were easy, or so Marie had said. But if he had a fight on Monday evening, he probably needed to prepare during the afternoon, and as for the day after, it could be that he'd still be tired, or even afraid he might have some damage to his face that he wouldn't want her to see, damage that would be less obvious by gaslight.

Yes, that must be it. But Lucy felt flat and anxious all the same, and the suspicion that Jake was keeping something from her hung over her, a dark cloud that refused to go away.

Annie was waiting outside the chemist's shop when Joe came down to open up on Monday morning, standing on the step and peering in. He could see at a glance that she was agitated. He slid the bolts and turned the key, anxious to find out what had brought her here so early, and fearing the worst.

'What's wrong, Annie?'

'It's Kitty.' Just as he'd thought. 'I had to call the doctor out to her this morning. He's increasing the dosage of her tablets and she's run right out.'

She thrust a sheet of paper into Joe's hand. 'Here's the prescription. Can you do it right away, Joe?'

Joe frowned. 'Mr Penny's not in yet. I can't do it until he's here.'

'But it's really urgent. She can hardly breathe.'

'It's more than my job's worth,' Joe said, worried. 'You know I'm not qualified yet to make up prescriptions unsupervised. Couldn't Dr Blackmore have given her enough to tide her over?'

'He didn't have any of her tablets with him. He's not the doctor he used to be. I think he's getting old and forgetful. It's high time he retired.'

'You're not the first person to say that,' Joe agreed. 'But how did you come to run out?'

Annie shook her head helplessly. 'I don't know. I thought she had plenty left. Perhaps Dr Blackmore's not the only one losing his grip. She's been managing her own medication, but I should have checked.'

Joe pulled out the upright wooden chair.

'Why don't you sit down, Annie. I'm sure Mr Penny won't be long.'

'I certainly hope not.' Annie checked her watch and sighed, but sat down anyway. She looked tired out and stressed, Joe thought, but that was hardly surprising.

'Have you thought any more about getting a job so you can leave Algernon?' he asked. 'Things would be a lot better if you didn't have to live with that lunatic.'

'That's true enough.' Annie huffed breath over her top lip. 'It's not that easy, though.'

She told him about her high hopes of the position she'd applied for, and the disappointing outcome. 'It would have been perfect,' she finished, 'but it wasn't to be.'

'There'll be other jobs,' Joe said, trying to be optimistic.

'There don't seem to be.' Annie was still scouring the advertisements in the local paper, without success. 'And if there were, I don't suppose the outcome would be any different. Who's going to take on somebody with an invalid daughter? And it seems coming from the coal mining area puts the tin lid on it. Honestly, I'm at my wits' end.'

She was, he could see.

'I just wish there was something I could do to help,' he

said. 'Perhaps I'll be able to when I'm qualified. But until then . . .'

'You're a good boy, Joe. But it's not your problem.'

'I owe everything to you, Annie. It might have been a bad move for you, marrying that beast, but you saved my life.'

Annie smiled wanly, and glanced at her watch. 'Wherever is Mr Penny? How much longer is he going to be?'

'He'll be here soon, I'm sure.' But really Joe couldn't understand what was keeping the pharmacist. It was unlike him to be late. Why did he have to be today of all days, when Annie was desperate for Kitty's tablets?

Another ten minutes ticked by, and Annie was becoming increasingly agitated.

'This is getting beyond a joke,' she said, standing up and peering out of the shop door. 'Kitty's all on her own. If she gets worse and I'm not there . . .' She broke off, and turned imploringly to Joe. 'Surely you could let me have the tablets? It's not as though you've got to mix anything up. It's only a matter of counting them out . . .'

Joe hesitated, torn between the devil and the deep blue sea, as his mother used to say. He shouldn't do it, he knew. He'd be breaking the strictest of regulations. But if Kitty was as poorly as Annie said – and Annie wasn't one to exaggerate – then perhaps the circumstances were exceptional. Her medication could be a matter of life and death to her, and time could be of the essence.

'All right,' he said abruptly. 'I'll do it. But for goodness' sake don't mention it to anybody or I shall be for the high jump.'

'Of course I won't say anything! Thank you, Joe!'

Feeling as guilty as if he were committing a criminal offence, Joe counted out the tablets and gave the bottle to Annie.

She opened her purse to pay for it, but he waved her money away.

'I'll see to it, don't worry.'

Annie thanked him again profusely and left hurriedly. Joe closed the door after her and went back into the dispensary to return the remaining tablets to their proper place. He was still very worried about what he had done, and wondering how he was going to explain himself to Mr Penny. Perhaps, he thought, it would be better not to mention it at all and hope the pharmacist didn't notice that there were fewer tablets left than there should be. Careful as he was with his paperwork, he might well come to the conclusion that a mistake had been made on the last inventory.

It really wasn't in Joe's nature to be dishonest, but desperate situations called for desperate measures. And if anything happened to Kitty because he had stuck by the rules, he would never have forgiven himself.

It really was the only excuse he could make, and if it sounded flimsy, that was just too bad.

Will, bless him, was waiting for Lucy when she left the theatre on Monday evening. 'I see your prince has turned into a frog,' Marie had joked once after they'd left the theatre together and she'd seen Will there instead of Jake. But Lucy felt nothing but gratitude towards Will. She was just a lodger to him and Doris, yet they looked after her as if she was their own daughter.

They took the underground across London as usual and began the long walk down the Old Kent Road, but Lucy was keeping her eyes open for the Cap and Feather. They would pass it, she was sure, though she wasn't quite certain which one of the numerous hostelries that lined the route it was. Though Will usually gave directions by their names, public houses held little interest for her. Tonight, however, was different. She'd thought of little else all day; she'd almost missed a cue during the performance this evening because her mind was wandering, and if Marie hadn't grabbed her by the hand and flashed her a warning look, there might well have been an awkward silence at the point where she should have said: 'Oh Dick, my love, I thought never to see you again!'

If Lucy had been unsure which of the boozers was the Cap and Feather, however, as they approached one hostelry the quiet of the night was broken by a wave of noise – excited shouts and a roar not dissimilar to that of a rowdy music hall crowd – and even before she was close enough to read the sign, Lucy knew this must be the place.

She caught at Will's arm.

'Can we go in? Please?'

Will looked at her aghast.

'You don't want to go in there, my girl.'

'I do! I want to see Jake!'

'No you do not.' Will made to hurry her by, but Lucy was too quick for him. Before he could stop her, she had darted into the alleyway that ran alongside the old stone building, following the sound of the shouts, which grew more deafening with each step she took.

Light was spilling out from an area at the rear of the pub; Lucy turned the corner and stopped short, her way blocked by a wall of jeering, yelling humanity.

She was, she realised, at the edge of a courtyard, bounded by outbuildings and the pub itself. As she tried to worm her way through the crowd, a man turned on her angrily. 'Hey, watch it, love!' His mug of beer bumped against her elbow, spilling some, so that it splashed over her, but Lucy scarcely noticed. Her eyes were drawn like a magnet to a makeshift stage where two men were slugging it out under the hazy light of the gas flares. One of them was Jake, but a Jake she scarcely recognised, bare chest glistening with sweat, every muscle rippling with raw aggression.

Compared to him the other man looked like a giant – no! An ape! A great hairy ape. Even as the horrified thought crossed her mind, his fist, big as a small cabbage, smashed into Jake's face and blood spurted scarlet. She gasped as he staggered backwards, his opponent following threateningly. Then he recovered himself, brushing the blood out of his eyes and lunging forward to catch the other man with a blow beneath the chin, so now it was he who staggered before returning to the attack.

The noise of the crowd was deafening, yet in spite of that it seemed to Lucy that she could hear the thuds of the volley of blows exchanged and her own heart pounding in time. Both men were covered in blood, streaming from cuts to their eyes, their noses, their mouths. So much blood! Why was there so much blood?

And then she realised the dreadful truth – neither man was wearing gloves. A bare-knuckle fight. That was what Will must have meant when he'd talked of the dodgy side of the business.

A man she guessed was the referee sidestepped the fighters as they staggered this way and that, but did nothing to intervene; two more stood hunched at opposite corners of the makeshift arena – the seconds, she presumed, since one hauled the big hairy ape back on to the platform when he lost his balance and toppled down into the crowd of onlookers, and the other took the opportunity to toss a cloth to Jake so that he could wipe the blood from his eyes. There was something vaguely familiar about this man, but Lucy was too shocked and horrified to even wonder what it was.

A hand was gripping her arm; she half turned. It was Will. Without a word he began to drag her roughly through the milling mass of humanity and back along the alley, and Lucy was too dazed with the horror of it all to do anything other than go with him.

'You silly, silly girl.' When they reached the street, he turned on her, more furious than she had ever seen him. 'What in Christ's name were you thinking of?'

'I . . . I wanted . . .' Lucy's teeth were chattering; the words refused to be formed.

'I know what you wanted all right!' Will grunted, propelling her along the street.

For the first time Lucy struggled to free herself from his grip.

'I can't leave him! Will, please . . . he's hurt. We must go back!'

But Will refused to lessen his grasp, or even slow his pace.

'He's got his pals there. They'll look after him.'

'But—'

'But bloody nothing. You don't want to be anywhere near that place. They'll carry on until one of 'em's knocked senseless.'

He stopped walking suddenly, raising a threatening finger that all but touched her nose.

'And not a word to Doris about this! She'd have my guts for garters if she knew where you've just been. And so would Spike.'

'I'm sorry,' she managed.

'Yes, well, I only hope you're satisfied.'

Satisfied! That was hardly the word to describe what she was feeling – shaking from head to foot, frightened, shocked, worried to death about Jake.

'Pull yourself together now, there's a good girl.' They were nearing Lynton Road. 'Just think yourself lucky you didn't get set on again.'

Lucy gulped, struggling to compose herself but still seeing in her mind's eye the raw violence, the brutality, the blood . . .

How could he do it? *They'll carry on until one of 'em's knocked senseless*, Will had said, and his words echoed in her head along with the images of the terrible spectacle she had just witnessed. She'd never forget it, never as long as she lived.

But the only thing that mattered was that Jake wasn't hurt too badly. She couldn't bear it if he was.

Chapter Twenty-Seven

'You've got a visitor!' Doris called up the stairs.

Lucy's heart leapt into her throat. Could it be Jake? She'd not seen him since Will had dragged her away from the bare-knuckle fight and she was going out of her mind with worry, especially since he hadn't turned up last night to collect her from the theatre as promised and after she'd waited for a good half-hour she'd taken a cab home. She'd asked Will if he'd heard anything about the result of the fight, but he couldn't enlighten her.

'Licking his wounds, I shouldn't wonder,' he'd said, tight-lipped and not in the least sympathetic, which was no more nor less than what Lucy had thought herself, but did nothing to allay her fears. She couldn't close her eyes without seeing him, bloodied and battle-stained, and the awful thud of the volley of punches thrown by both men echoed in her ears. He must have been badly hurt; from what she'd seen it was unavoidable. But supposing his injuries were fatal? She'd heard of boxers dying in the ring or shortly afterwards. Though she tried to put such a dreadful thing out of her mind, it still haunted her. Surely if something like that had happened it would have been the talk of the docks today, wouldn't it? But then again, perhaps it had been, and Will just didn't want to tell her.

Now hope leapt. Who would be visiting her but Jake? Unless of course it was Bernie . . . Her heart sank again. Bernie was busy lining up new engagements for her when the panto ended its run next week. Yes, it was probably Bernie wanting to talk to her about some plan of his.

Since she had scarcely slept last night, she had been trying to rest in preparation for tonight's performance, but now she leapt up from the bed and hurried along the narrow landing, eager, but afraid to hope in case she was disappointed.

Let it be Jake! Oh please let it be Jake!

Halfway down the stairs she heard his voice. Oh, thank God! She ran the rest of the way down and into the kitchen. He turned around, and she stopped dead in her tracks, shocked to the core by the state of his face, even though she'd been expecting it. It resembled nothing more than a slab of meat on a butcher's counter.

'Oh Jake!'

'If you two want to talk, why don't you go into the garden? It's quite warm in the sun,' Doris suggested, but her tone was short and a little disapproving, as if she was not best pleased about something.

Lucy glanced at Jake and he nodded.

'I'll bring you out a cup of tea.' Doris set the kettle on the hob with a bang that echoed the shortness of her tone. She must have been shocked at the sight of Jake's injuries too, Lucy thought, and didn't like the way he had come by them. But she had noticed that recently Doris had been less friendly towards him, less ready to spoil him with the hearty suppers she'd had waiting when he'd first begun to see her home, and wondered why.

Once out of the shadow cast by the house, it was, as Doris had said, quite a warm day for March. New growth was

391

beginning to show green shoots on the bushes, and the grass of the tiny square of lawn would soon need cutting for the first time this year. In a corner was a bench, a wooden plank seat supported on a frame of wrought iron. It had once been a chapel pew; when the church had been refurbished, Will had spotted the seats stacked outside ready to be dumped, and brought this one home with him. Lucy didn't really care for it: anything connected with a place of worship brought back too many unpleasant memories. But she was glad of it now.

'Oh Jake!' She reached across to take his hand. He pulled away, wincing, and she saw that his knuckles were as raw as his face, and a river of fresh blood was running down towards his wrist. 'What a state you're in! Just look at you!'

'Not a pretty sight, am I?' He half smiled, and winced again. Every movement opened the cut on his swollen lip. He dabbed at it with his good hand. 'I don't suppose I'll be kissing you for a day or two either.'

But at least he was alive! Lucy was so relieved to see him she'd put up with that.

'I've been so worried about you,' she said. 'When you didn't turn up last night I thought all sorts. I waited and waited, and when you didn't come—'

'Didn't you get my message?' She shook her head, and Jake swore. 'Drat that boy! And I paid him well too. I should have known better than to trust him, but when he got back he swore blind he'd given it to the stage door keeper like I told him.'

'What boy?' Lucy was puzzled.

'He lodges at the same place as me. I help him out when I can – he reminds me of myself at that age. But he's a lazy little beggar, won't do a stroke if he doesn't have to. Just wait till I see him again. I'll tan his hide for him.'

'It might not have been his fault.' Now that Jake was here,

not lying, as she had feared he might be, in the city morgue, Lucy felt inclined to be generous. 'Billy – that's the doorman – might have forgotten to pass the message on. And I came to no harm. I took a cab home when I realised you weren't coming. It's just that I was so worried about you.'

'I suppose you thought I'd abandoned you.'

'Not really. I guessed you were in no fit state after Monday night. It was terrible, Jake!' She shuddered at the memory. 'I thought you were going to be killed.'

His swollen eyes narrowed.

'I saw it,' she admitted. 'Well, a bit, anyway, and that was more than enough. You said I wouldn't like it, and you were right.'

'You were at the fight?' Jake asked, shocked.

Lucy explained how it had come about, and Jake shook his head.

'You shouldn't have been there, Lucy. Anything could have happened to you.'

'Well, it didn't. But I couldn't believe how awful it was! Why do you do it, Jake?'

He shrugged. 'Got to earn a crust somehow. Don't look so shocked. You knew I was a boxer.'

'Not that sort – bare-knuckle. I thought you did it properly, with rules and everything.'

Jake looked affronted. 'We do have rules. Just not the same ones. There's things we're not allowed to do . . .'

'It didn't look like that to me!'

'. . . and we just carry on until one of us gives in.'

'Or gets carried away on a stretcher! It's terrible, Jake! Just look at the state you're in! Will said he'd seen you at the Wonderland, and something like this would never happen there. I just don't understand.'

'Yeah, well, perhaps I couldn't earn enough sticking to the legit. There's good money to be made at fair booths and back-street arenas. You don't even have to win – the spoils get divided up, and believe me, if it's a good fight and goes on long enough, there's a fair bit in the kitty by the time it's over. Though I did win on Monday, thanks for asking.'

'Oh Jake . . . I'm sorry. But I couldn't care less about whether you won or lost. Just as long as you didn't get really badly injured. I mean, I know you're in a bad way, but I was afraid it might be much worse.'

He shrugged again. 'Goes with the territory.'

'How can you treat it so lightly?'

'I've been fending for myself since I was twelve or thirteen, remember. I've learned you have to do what you have to do.' His eyes skittered away, gazing, it seemed, into space. 'Even if you don't like it sometimes,' he added in an undertone.

He was thinking about the thieving that had landed him in prison, Lucy assumed, and horrified as she was at the life he had led – was leading – she couldn't find it in her to blame him. She'd grown to care for him too much for that.

'It must have been terrible for you,' she said softly.

'Yeah, well . . .' He was silent for a moment. 'I've got to wonder, though, if things wouldn't have been a lot different if my mother hadn't put me out to the baby farmers. I might be living in a grand house with servants and the rest, and no need to worry where my next square meal was coming from.'

'I don't suppose it was her fault,' Lucy said, trying to comfort him. 'And for all you know, you'd have been just as badly off. She was a poor girl who couldn't afford to keep you, I expect.'

Jake laughed hollowly.

'Oh, she wasn't poor. Like I told you before, she – or her

family – could afford to pay, and pay well, or I've have ended up in the Thames, in a bag weighted down with stones, like that poor kid Mrs Eavy swung for. No, she was a lady all right. No doubt about it.'

Lucy said nothing. It was only natural, she supposed, for someone in Jake's position to imagine a romantic background.

'You don't believe me, huh?' Jake must have guessed what she was thinking. 'Well take a look at this.' He fumbled in his pocket and pulled out a wallet. 'I've got a picture Mrs Eavy gave me – God alone knows where she got it. It's a bit the worse for wear now; it's been everywhere with me, and I've looked at it so many times . . .'

He opened the wallet of cracked, cheap leather, drew out a piece of paper that was folded in half and half again, and spread it out on his knee, looking at it with a mixture of pride and bitterness before passing it to Lucy.

She took it, and her heart seemed to stop beating.

Looking back at her from the picture, which she instantly recognised as having been cut from a playbill, was a face she knew well. The same face in the photograph in the locket she always wore.

There could be no mistaking it. The picture was of a young Molly.

Her hand flew to her mouth, but she couldn't stop that first startled gasp as she gazed at the familiar face.

'What?' Jake was looking at her narrowly.

Lucy's mind was chasing in crazy circles. If this was a picture of Jake's mother, then it was he who was Molly's lost son, not Davy as she had thought. She could scarcely believe it, but what other explanation could there be?

'I . . .' The words were hovering on her lips; it was all she could do not to blurt them out. But some strong intuitive sense was stopping her. She had to think this through first.

'She's . . . very pretty,' she said lamely.

Jake snorted, but the look on his face might almost have been disappointment.

'I thought for a minute you were going to say you recognised her,' he said.

Lucy could feel hot colour rushing to her cheeks, which had paled a moment ago, and to her intense relief respite appeared in the shape of Davy, approaching them with mugs of tea. He was carrying them carefully and watching his every step, but as he neared them he looked up from his boots, saw Jake's face, and almost stumbled in his surprise.

'Careful!' Lucy took both mugs from him; she didn't want him thrusting one into Jake's injured hand or, worse, spilling scalding tea on the raw wounds.

'You've hurt yourself!' Davy said to Jake in his slow, childlike way. 'How did you hurt yourself?'

'I was in a fight.' Jake took the mug from Lucy with his left hand.

'You shouldn't get in fights,' Davy admonished solemnly.

'No, I shouldn't,' Jake agreed.

'You won't be able to play with me today.'

'Dead right, mate.' Lucy could tell Jake was anxious for Davy to go away and leave them alone, but for once she was hoping for the exact opposite. So long as Davy was with them she would be spared from making a decision as to how much she should say to Jake.

'Why don't you bring out your cigarette cards?' she suggested – Davy was a keen collector. 'I'm sure Jake would like to see the new ones. You've nearly got the full set now, haven't you?'

'Yes, I've nearly got the full set.' Davy's round red face brightened and Lucy wondered how she could ever have thought he was Molly's son. When he beamed like that, he was the image of Doris.

'I'll get them.' He headed for the house, his enthusiastic haste accentuating his lolloping gait.

'What did you say that for?' Jake was clearly annoyed. 'We'll never get rid of him now.'

'I thought you liked him.' Lucy was anxious for anything that would keep the conversation from returning to the photograph.

'I feel sorry for him. That doesn't mean I want him hanging around all the time.'

'He's just a big child, really, who's never grown up and never will. It's sad, and I know Doris worries about what's going to become of him when she and Will are no longer around to care for him.'

'At least they didn't give him away like my mother did me,' Jake said bitterly.

Lucy felt a moment's panic. Whatever she said there seemed to be no way to stop Jake returning to the subject.

But Davy had emerged from the kitchen again, clutching the album containing his latest collection of cigarette cards, and she heaved a sigh of relief.

She wouldn't be able to stay silent forever, but at least she'd gained a little breathing space. That, she knew, was the best she could hope for.

Whereas in the previous twenty-four hours she had thought of nothing but the fight and the injuries Jake had sustained, now it was the shocking revelation that Molly was his mother that occupied her every waking thought and kept her awake at night too.

She'd gained a further respite by insisting Jake was not in a fit state to come to the theatre to meet her that evening at least, promising to take a cab as she had the night before, and Doris had backed her up.

'What you need is to rest up, not go gallivanting around town,' she said in her usual forthright manner, and again Lucy had sensed an impatience with Jake that hadn't been there before.

This was backed up when he had left.

'I'm not sure you ought to be getting so mixed up with him,' she told Lucy. 'I know he's been good to you, but maybe *too* good. It just don't seem natural, somehow. And when I think of the life he's leading . . .'

'You've always known he was a boxer.'

'Yes, but not *that* sort. What do you know about him really?'

A great deal more than is comfortable! Lucy thought, but of course she said nothing. This wasn't something she could share with Doris, or anyone.

After a long and sleepless night, Lucy had reached at least one decision. She really shouldn't tell Jake that she'd recognised the woman he said was his mother until she was more sure of the facts, and certainly not before Molly learned of it. She mustn't find out in some roundabout way, perhaps from Doris, should Jake mention it to her, or, even worse, have him turning up on her doorstep unannounced. But as to how best to approach this delicate matter Lucy really didn't know.

The one person who would be most likely to verify the story was Spike, and under normal circumstances he would be best placed to break the news to her that her lost son had been found. But from what Molly had told her it was he who had supposedly arranged the adoption. If instead he had placed the baby with a baby farmer – Lucy was still finding it hard to get her head round such a terrible arrangement – then he'd hardly be likely to admit to it now. It would be the most awful betrayal of Molly's trust.

Was it possible that Doris and Will knew something? They were Spike's relatives, after all, and it was to his relatives that Molly had gone to have her baby. Could it be that something had raised Doris's suspicions, and that was the reason she had seemingly turned against Jake when in the beginning she had been so welcoming towards him? Lucy decided that the best approach was to pump Doris gently.

Her opportunity came next day; she and Doris were alone in the kitchen washing up the breakfast things.

'Did you know Molly in the old days, before she went off to America?' She tried to make the question sound light and conversational. But right away she drew a blank.

'Not really, no. I did go to see her perform once, at the Pavilion, I think it was – Spike got us tickets. My, what a star she was! But I never got to meet her. Not until she came back and she and Spike got together.' There was nothing guarded in her manner, nothing to suggest she wasn't telling the truth. Disappointed, Lucy knew she'd have to think of another way to approach her problem.

Really, she thought, there was only one way, and that was to tell Molly herself. She could do it gently, to avoid giving her too much of a shock, and then it would be up to Molly to decide what she wanted to do about it.

As soon as the pantomime was over she would take a train to Bath and see her aunt. Until then, somehow, she would keep her secret.

Chapter Twenty-Eight

When older still I daily grew
Time flew.

Though it was less than a year since Lucy had left Somerset, as
the train pulled into Bath Spa station she felt like a stranger. So
much had happened since she had left, and so much had
changed. The girl who had worked in the office of a glove factory
and sung at local concerts had gone forever and her love for Joe
like a sweet sad dream. Her life was in London now, Doris and
Will had become her family and she had fallen in love with a
man who was different to Joe in almost every way.

It pained her all the same that she wouldn't be able to go
home to High Compton to see Annie and Kitty, but there
wouldn't have been time even if Algernon had not forbidden it.
She had to catch an early train back to London tomorrow to be
sure to be ready for an engagement in the evening – a prestigious
hall where Bernie had secured her a booking and she was to be
second from top on the bill. And today – today would be taken
up with the purpose of her visit: talking to Molly. Lucy's
stomach churned at the prospect. What would Molly's reaction
be? Remembering her bitter tears over the loss of her child, her
heartfelt regrets at having allowed herself to be parted from him,
and her longing to see him again, Lucy could only think that

400

what she had to tell her aunt would delight her. But learning what had become of her baby would also be the cause of great distress. She would be bound to blame herself for the dreadful time he'd had as a child, and would be none too pleased at the life he was leading now.

Besides blaming herself, she would surely blame Spike too, and heaven only knew what it would do to their relationship when she discovered that far from finding a good home for David, he had cheerfully abandoned him to a cruel and unscrupulous woman and made payments to keep him there.

Was she doing the right thing in upsetting the apple cart? Lucy wondered for the hundredth time. But there was no way she could simply forget what she had discovered. She owed it to both Molly and Jake to go this far, at least. The rest would be up to Molly.

Outside the station, she took a cab. Strange how quickly she had got used to doing that now that she had money in her pocket. A year ago she would have been nervous of doing such a thing if she even considered it. It was further proof, if proof were needed, that she was a very different girl to the one who had left home desperate yet determined.

She could do this. She had to. But she was not looking forward to it one little bit.

'Aunt Molly, I have to talk to you,' Lucy said.

They'd eaten a light lunch and Spike had gone off on some errand of business, leaving them alone.

Molly's heart sank. She'd been delighted when she'd received Lucy's letter telling of her intention to visit, but from the moment her niece had arrived, she'd had a bad feeling. Lucy was hiding something, Molly was sure; she seemed tight strung and brittle, like a violin string tuned too tight, and there was something odd in the way she was behaving with Spike too. They'd always got along so well together, but today Lucy seemed barely able to look at him, and uncomfortable in his presence.

'Oh my dear, you haven't been a silly girl, have you?' Molly said. 'You aren't in some sort of pickle?'

She saw a quick flush bloom on Lucy's cheeks and feared the worst, but Lucy shook her head.

'It's nothing to do with me, Aunt Molly. Well – it is, but not in the way you're thinking. It's about . . .' She hesitated, clearly unsure how to go on. Then: 'Please forgive me for bringing it up, but you remember telling me about the baby you had when you were a star on the London halls?'

A lump rose in Molly's throat; she swallowed it quickly. Why on earth would Lucy be mentioning that if not to confess that she had managed to land herself in the same boat?

'It's not something I'm likely to forget,' she said. 'Why?'

'What would you say if I told you I think I've found him?' It came out all of a rush, and for a moment Molly could only stare at her niece, flabbergasted.

'I'm sorry, Lucy – what did you just say?'

'He doesn't know it yet. I had to tell you first,' Lucy said. 'I think I've found your baby.'

Molly felt her stomach fall away; the room seemed to tip and swim around her.

'Are you all right, Aunt Molly?' Lucy's voice seemed to be coming from a distance.

Molly reached out for the arm of the sofa and lowered herself on to it.

'Yes . . . yes, I'm all right. But . . . I can't believe it! Are you sure?'

'Almost. You'll have to talk to Spike. But yes, I do think it's him. I wouldn't be here otherwise.'

'Tell me! Tell me! Is he well? Is my David happy?'

A shadow crossed Lucy's face, then she said: 'He's well. But he's not called David any more. His name now is Jake.'

'Jake!' Molly echoed faintly.

'Let me get you a drink,' Lucy said, concerned by her aunt's reaction. 'Just sit quietly and I'll tell you everything.'

'I think I'd like to be on my own for a bit,' Molly said, and Lucy left her as she asked.

There was no way she could have described her tumultuous feelings, which all seemed to blend into one, crowding in on the first disbelief, the rush of pure joy. She trembled with ecstatic excitement and apprehension too at the thought that she might soon meet the son she had given up for lost. Hope and the fear that Lucy might be wrong wrestled within her. Eagerness warred with apprehension. Dismay at his situation reignited all the feelings of guilt that she had given him up so easily. And there was anger too, anger that Spike had deceived her all these years.

If he had deceived her. She had to talk to him. Had to learn the truth once and for all. She'd ask him outright, and she'd know if he was lying. She always did. Except that she hadn't known then, when it had mattered most. She'd believed him when he'd said David was going to a loving home and a life far better than she could hope to provide for him.

Every detail of that terrible day when she'd parted from him came back to her, clear as if it were just yesterday. The last time she'd fed him, bathed and dressed him, held him in her arms. She could see his face so clearly, see his tiny clenched hands with their pearly fingernails and his little foot with the spider birthmark that aroused such tenderness in her.

And then they had taken him from her and there was nothing

but emptiness in her arms and anguish in her heart, an anguish that time had never been able to take away.

She thought about the woman who had been with Spike that day, the woman who had taken David from her. She could still conjure up a clear picture of her, hovering there in her dark cloak like an angel of doom. She'd hated her then and she hated her now. She was a wet nurse, Spike had said, but perhaps in reality she had been the baby farmer.

Molly stood up and walked around the room, arms wrapped about herself, emotions seething and bubbling like a stew left over too high a heat.

Spike would be home any minute, and she was going to ask him without delay exactly what he had arranged for David.

Even as she thought it, she heard the sound of the car outside, the slam of the door, and saw Spike turn in at the gate. Unable to contain herself for a moment longer, Molly went into the hall to meet him.

Spike knew the moment he walked in the door that something had happened. Molly was there to greet him, and he could see at a glance just how agitated she was.

'What's up?' he asked.

'Come in here and I'll tell you.' She pushed open the parlour door, which had closed behind her.

'Let me take off my coat.'

'Now!' Her voice was high, trembling.

He followed her into the big sunny room, unbuttoning his coat as he went.

'Where's the fire?' he asked in his usual breezy way, though he was puzzled and disturbed. She'd been so cheerful when he'd gone out, so pleased to have Lucy visiting.

She turned to face him, her hands making tightly clenched fists at her sides, eyes boring into his.

'That woman who was with you when you took David away from me – who was she?'

Spike was startled; this was the last thing he'd expected.

'The wet nurse?'

'Are you sure that's what she was?' Molly asked harshly. 'She wasn't a baby farmer by any chance, was she?'

Spike's stomach dropped away. She knew. Somehow, after all this time, she knew.

Seeing his dismayed expression, Molly gave a wail of anguish. 'Oh Daniel – how could you?'

'It wasn't like that,' he protested.

She didn't seem to even hear him. 'How could you send my baby to one of those terrible places?'

'Molly, I didn't!'

'Don't lie to me, Daniel! Don't dare to lie to me any more!'

She was becoming more and more distraught. He reached out to her; she drew back sharply.

'Don't! Don't touch me!'

Spike shook his head, helpless in the face of her anger and distress. 'Calm down, Molly, do! You'll give yourself a turn.'

'You sent my David to a baby farm!' She was rocking back and forth, tears streaming down her cheeks now. 'How could you do that?'

'Molly, will you just shut up for a minute and listen!' Exasperated now as well as concerned, he caught her by the arms before she could protest and half pushed her down on to the sofa. 'I arranged for him to go to a good family, just as I told you. A well-to-do childless couple I thought would give him a good life.'

She glowered up at him. 'If that's so, why did you look so

guilty when I asked you about that woman? Answer me that if you can!'

Spike rasped a hand over his chin. 'Because things went wrong, and I knew about it. I didn't know he'd been sent to a baby farm, but I suspected as much. Soon as I heard what had happened I tried my best to find him, and that's God's honest truth. But every which way I turned I drew a blank. I searched high and low, but it was hopeless.'

'You say that now.' Molly's red-rimmed eyes were full of scorn. 'How can you expect me to believe you after the way you've deceived me all these years?'

Spike sat down in the wing chair opposite her, his head in his hands. 'I didn't tell you because it would have done no good, and only caused you great distress. By the time I found out what had happened, it was too late.'

'So what did happen?' Her voice was brittle with sarcasm.

'You going to listen to me now, are you?'

'I'll hear what you've got to say. Then I'll make up my own mind.'

'All right. Just let me finish, though, before you kick off again.' Spike sat upright, his elbows on the arms of the chair. He felt very old suddenly, as if all the cares of the world had suddenly come to rest on his shoulders. He'd kept this to himself for too long, but he'd thought it was for the best. Now he realised he was in very real danger of losing the only woman he'd ever loved.

'Like I said, the couple that took David didn't have any children of their own—'

'Who were they?' Molly interrupted in the same harsh tone.

'I never met them.' He heard Molly's derisive snort and carried on regardless. 'It was all arranged through a third party, but I had no doubt they were well-to-do. They lived in Essex in a grand house, not that far from where you went to have him. The husband was in industry, a self-made man, and, as I found out later, hard as nails. He'd never wanted children, it seems; it was her, his wife, that was desperate for one. So desperate she'd gone into a decline over it, so he gave in and agreed they'd adopt. Hoped it would satisfy her, I suppose, and give him some peace. But it didn't work out that way. She'd gone a bit funny, I think.'

He paused, wiping his mouth with the back of his hand, then went on. 'To begin with she seemed over the moon with David, by all accounts. Spoiled him rotten. Then she turned. Got all depressed because he wasn't really hers. Wouldn't touch him, wouldn't look at him even. It was left to the nurse to do everything for him, and she just got worse and worse. David was seven weeks old when she killed herself. The servants found her, hanging by her husband's dressing gown cord from a beam in the attic.

'Well, that was it for David. The husband wasn't going to keep him. He'd never wanted him in the first place, and he blamed the poor little beggar for pushing her over the edge.'

He glanced at Molly. She was paper-white now, her red-rimmed eyes wide and staring, and she crumpled a handkerchief between her fingers, picking at it compulsively.

'By the time I got to hear of it, he'd long since got rid of David. I went to see him, but the bugger wouldn't tell me anything beyond that he'd been "taken care of". I'd been hoping that some other couple might have taken him on, but when I put that to him he laughed in my face. "That little bastard is costing me a small fortune," he said. Which is how I guessed he'd been farmed out. I knew then I had to try to find him.'

He broke off again, remembering all too clearly how he'd blamed himself – still did. He'd learned the addresses of the so-called baby farms, and visited hovels in the worst slums of the East End. He'd seen things he'd never forget, and would never tell Molly – infants lying three and four to a filthy cot, undernourished, diseased, kept from crying with alcohol and drugs. The baby farmers kept them alive only as long as they were a source of income. Then they were left to die or disposed of, usually in the river. Some were still alive when they were tossed into the murky waters, like so much garbage, in a rough parcel of cloth weighted down with stones. But at none of the places he'd visited had anyone admitted to having David in their care, even though he'd offered good money to take him off their hands.

He'd tried the orphanages then, with no more luck. But he still castigated himself that he hadn't tried hard enough. Molly had gone off to America by then and he'd told himself she'd make a new life for herself and forget about David. She never had, of course, but by the time she came back and he realised she was still pining for her baby son, it was years too late. There was nothing he could do but leave her to think her precious child was happy with the family who had adopted him, safe and loved.

But it had, it seemed, been the wrong decision. Somehow Molly had learned the truth, and she would never forgive him. He wasn't even sure she'd believe his story. He was going to lose her through his own stupid fault, though all he had ever done was try to protect her. He should have known better. He should have known that one day it would all come out, with devastating consequences.

'How did you find out?' he asked. 'After all this time?'

Molly was calmer now, but when her eyes met his he could see they were full of tears.

'Lucy thinks she's found him,' she said.

'Lucy!' How had Lucy succeeded, more than twenty years on, where he had failed?

'Yes, Lucy. It's incredible really. She's met someone. He's called . . . Jake.' She faltered over the unfamiliar name, trying it out on her tongue. 'He was in a baby farm, and then, later, an orphanage, and had no idea who his mother was. But he has a picture of her that was given to him at some time by the woman who was bringing him up. Lucy saw it. It's a picture of me.'

'Good God!'

'But none of his background fitted with what you'd told me, Daniel. Either this Jake wasn't my David, or you hadn't told me the truth of what happened to him. Now . . . well, now it's all beginning to make sense.'

Spike nodded, lost for words.

'I can't bear to think of what he's been through.' Molly pressed the sodden handkerchief to her lips. 'But I think my prayers have been answered, Daniel. I think he's come back to me. My David has come back to me.'

Before Lucy returned to London next day, it was all arranged. She would tell Jake her reason for going home to Bath, and Molly would travel to London to meet him.

'I'm sure he'd come to you,' Lucy said, though she was not really sure of any such thing. Jake had spoken of his birth mother with such bitterness.

But Molly had said no, she'd rather meet him on neutral ground, and Lucy could understand that. She didn't want him coming into her home until she was sure things were going to work out. Besides, Lucy rather thought she would be glad to put some distance between herself and Spike, for a few days at least. There was an air of palpable tension between them, and had been ever since they'd talked.

Talked! Perhaps 'talked' was not quite the right word to describe what had passed between them. Lucy had heard the raised voices, though not what they were saying, and had felt horribly responsible.

But there was no doubting Molly's excitement at the thought of seeing her lost son, and she had asked Lucy to tell him that she would make sure he never wanted for anything again.

Lucy could only hope that in the end everything would work out for the best for all of them. Next day she would take the train back to London and give the news to Jake. Then her part in all this would be over.

Chapter Twenty-Nine

Had Lucy gone home to High Compton, she would have found things there were as bad as ever, if not worse.

It was a visit from Marcus Latcham that had sparked the latest episode. He was coming home to see his parents now every few weeks, and he always made a point of calling on Annie. They would chat over a cup of tea, and the more she came to know him, the more she liked him. It was no longer just a physical attraction, but something much deeper. She looked forward to his visits and was always buoyed up by them for days afterwards. Nothing improper ever occurred, not so much as a word out of place was ever spoken, but she had the distinct impression that he felt much as she did, though she tried to tell herself that was just her imagination playing tricks, and he saw her only as a good neighbour and friend.

Algernon, however, had noticed the glow about her whenever Marcus was in High Compton, and her slightly distracted manner after he'd visited. It was beginning to disturb him, and when he'd come home from chapel on that Sunday to find them laughing together he was incensed. By a supreme effort he kept his rage under control – it wasn't his style to show his true colours to anyone, least of all a man he'd always behaved towards in a sycophantic manner – but the moment Marcus left he turned on Annie.

'What do you think you are playing at, you Jezebel?'

Annie, clearing the cups from the table where they'd been sitting, stopped midway to the sink.

'Whatever do you mean?'

Algernon was red in the face and puffed up with self-righteous fury. 'Don't play the innocent with me, Annie. I know what's going on between you and that accursed man.'

'Nothing is going on!' Annie protested, but a guilty flush rose in her cheeks.

For Algernon it was all the proof he needed.

'Don't take me for a fool, Annie. You're no better than a common whore. And that man – just because he pretends to be a toff, he thinks he can do as he likes. I've seen the way he looks at you and I won't have it. I won't have him in my house. What's more' – he hit out, knocking one of the cups from her hand – 'I won't drink from the same cup as he has used either. No amount of washing could make it clean.'

Annie took a startled step backwards and the second cup wobbled in the saucer and fell, shattering as the first had done on the flagged floor.

'Now look what you've done!' she said before she could stop herself.

'Good!' Algernon was triumphant. 'Your cup is as tainted as his. Now clean up the mess and get my dinner.'

He strode out of the kitchen leaving Annie to pick up the shards of china and mop up the remains of the tea that had spilled across the floor and over her feet.

There it might have ended if Marcus Latcham hadn't returned before leaving for London. He'd heard Algernon bellowing and china smashing as he'd climbed the steps outside the back door and had almost gone back then and there, but thought better of it. Interfering between man and wife was a dangerous thing, and might only make things a thousand times worse. But he didn't feel he could go back to London without making sure Annie was all right. In the light of what Lucy had told him, he was seriously concerned about her, the woman who was coming to mean a good deal more to him than she should.

His mother had been making marmalade the previous week; he begged a pot from her and used it as an excuse to go next door. 'Mother thought you might like . . .' could hardly be interpreted as anything but a neighbourly gesture, he thought.

But after he'd left, satisfied that Annie was unharmed, Algernon exploded again.

This time he waited until Marcus was well out of earshot. Kitty was in her room, resting, and he and Annie were alone.

'How dare you open the door to that man! Didn't I make myself clear?'

'He was just being kind,' Annie said, trying unsuccessfully to placate him.

'Too kind, in my opinion! I will not, I repeat *not*, have him in my house. You will not, I repeat *not*, have any more to do with him.'

Fearing the jar of marmalade might suffer the same fate as the teacups, Annie headed for the pantry, beyond the living room, so that she could store it safely out of harm's way.

'And don't dare to walk away from me when I'm speaking to you!' he bellowed.

Annie turned. 'You're being totally unreasonable, Algernon.'

Before she fully realised what was happening, he had lunged towards her, one hand gripping her arm, the other striking her full in the face. She staggered, the pot of marmalade slipping

413

from her hand and rolling across the rug to disappear under a chair.

'Harlot! Whore!' His fist shot out again, catching her squarely in the ribs so that all the breath left her in an explosive rush and she collapsed in a heap on the floor. 'Will you never learn?'

He kicked her with the toe of his boot, and the last thing Annie saw before she lost consciousness was his powerful figure bending over her, blotting out the fading light.

Kitty, in her bedroom, heard the commotion and crept to the top of the stairs, frightened, wanting to help, but not knowing what to do. Only when she heard Algernon go into the front room and slam the door behind him did she dare to go down, to find her mother, groggy and sick, still lying where she had fallen.

'Mam?' She called her name over and over in a voice that was full of panic; in those first terrible moments she thought Annie was dead – that Algernon had killed her. Annie stirred, trying to raise herself into a sitting position, then groaned and fell back to the floor as the piercing pain in her ribs took her breath away again.

'Oh Mam – whatever has he done to you?' Kitty dropped to her knees beside Annie, her own breath short and hard as it so often was when she was distressed.

'It's all right, Kitty . . . I'm all right,' Annie tried to reassure her, though she patently was not all right at all.

Again she struggled up so that she was leaning against the very chair that was hiding the pot of marmalade, the cause of this latest attack.

'He's really hurt you!'

The imprint of Algernon's fingers burned scarlet across Annie's cheek, but it was the pain she was experiencing at the slightest movement that was really frightening Kitty.

'I'll be all right,' Annie said again, but Kitty could see the tears in her eyes and began to cry herself.

How could she ever have looked up to Algernon as a paragon of all that was good in this cruel world? How could she have admired him so, done his bidding so willingly, loved him as a father? Now that the scales had fallen from her eyes, she detested and feared him. At least he hadn't laid a finger on her since that night when she was ill and confined to her bed; Annie had made sure they were never alone together. Her mother was protecting her, she knew, but she couldn't protect herself. And Kitty knew too that Algernon was infuriated by Annie's constant chaperoning of her; she'd seen it in his eyes along with a dark, obsessive passion that terrified her. He was taking out his frustration on her mother, she thought.

'I'm so sorry, Mam.' Kitty put her arms around Annie, holding her tenderly, so that it seemed their roles were reversed and she was the mother, Annie her child.

'What have you got to be sorry about, Kitty?' Annie asked. 'None of this is your fault.'

Kitty seemed not to hear her.

'I'll make it right, I promise. We'll be free of him soon.'

Annie sighed. Dear, deluded Kitty: the very reason she couldn't leave Algernon. But now was not the time to say so.

'We will, darling. I'll think of something,' she promised. 'Now, do you think you could get a big towel or a bolster case? If I wrap it round my ribs it will help, I think.'

She was beginning to learn how to treat herself after Algernon had inflicted horrible injuries on her. She'd done it before, and she felt sickeningly certain that before she and Kitty could escape his clutches she'd have to do it again.

Chapter Thirty

On the morning after her return from Somerset, Lucy woke early with a feeling of excitement bubbling inside her. At first she thought it was because she was still revelling in the wonderful success of the night before, when she had received a rapturous welcome from the audience at the hall where she had performed and been called back for no fewer than three encores before they would let her go. Then she remembered it wasn't just that. Today was the day she would tell Jake that he would soon be able to meet the mother he had never known.

Thinking of it stirred a little niggle of apprehension too. Supposing he didn't want to meet her? It would be entirely understandable, since he must blame her for the terrible start he'd had in life, but Aunt Molly would be dreadfully upset, and it would be all her fault.

Best to go and see Jake and get it over with, she decided. He might call to see her this afternoon, but then again, he might not – they had made no firm arrangement. She was fairly certain, though, that she'd find him at home this morning. He'd told her he was not an early riser, and in any case he would still be nursing his injuries.

Why oh why did he do it? she wondered as she dressed quickly, shivering a little in the chill of the morning. Though

416

he'd told her it was because he needed to earn a living, she felt sure there must be better ways. But soon he would no longer have to worry about that. Aunt Molly had said she'd ensure he'd never be poor or hungry again.

'My, you're up early!' Doris said as she went into the little living room. 'You were so late in last night I made sure you'd have a lie-in this morning.'

'I want to go and see Jake.' Lucy sat down at the table and reached for the teapot. Her throat was dry from all the bubbly she'd drunk last night. Bernie had taken her out for supper to celebrate her success and talk about other engagements he'd secured for her.

'You've not seen the light yet then?' Doris's lips were clamped in a tight line. 'You can do a lot better than him, you know. A lovely girl like you . . . you could have your pick of any man in London.'

Lucy sipped her tea, wondering why Doris had turned so thoroughly against Jake when once she'd welcomed him into her home. She supposed it must be because she knew now that he was a bare-knuckle boxer and disapproved of it.

What would she say if she knew that he was Molly's long-lost son? But this wasn't the moment to tell her, and it really wasn't her place in any case.

'He saved my life, remember,' she said instead. 'That's good enough for me.'

'There is that, I suppose,' Doris said grudgingly. 'But I reckon it's making you see him through rose-tinted glasses. Now, do you want some cooked breakfast?'

Lucy shook her head. Davy was wolfing down bacon and eggs on the opposite side of the table, and the smell of it, which usually whetted her appetite, was making her feel a little sick.

'Not today, thanks. Just bread and butter will be fine.' She

417

helped herself to a slice from the plate in the centre of the table.

'You going to see Jake?' Davy was mopping up the last of his egg with a chunk of bread; a little river of yellow was running down his chin. 'Can I come too?'

'Not today, Davy.'

His face fell. 'Aw! I got the last cigarette card for my set yesterday, didn't I, Ma? I want to show him!'

'You can show him another time,' Doris said. 'Seems like we haven't seen the last of him. And wipe that egg off your face, do.'

With that she bustled off into the scullery.

'I'll tell him you've completed your set,' Lucy said, trying to pacify the crestfallen Davy.

But it was an empty promise, she knew. What she and Jake had to talk about was a great deal more important than cigarette cards.

Jake lived in an attic room in one of the poorer districts of the East End. Though it was within easy walking distance, Lucy had never gone there without him, and even then once or twice only. After they had become lovers it was nice to have somewhere private where they could be alone, but the place made her uncomfortable. Used as she was to living in the country, with wide-open spaces and fresh air that smelled of nothing worse than the farmyard, she felt hemmed in by the mean houses practically touching one another across the narrow streets, and nauseated by the smells associated with a mass of dirt-poor humanity crammed into a small area – raw sewage, stale cooking, beer, fags, sweat and despair.

And Jake's room was almost as bad. The smells generated by the other tenants wafted up the narrow staircase and even, it seemed to her, through the floorboards, the one little window, high under the overhang of the roof, let in very little light, and the furnishings, such as they were, were dark and depressing – a ring-marked table, a couple of wonky chairs with stained tapestry seats, a bed with a lumpy mattress, a broken spring and blankets that were full of moth holes.

The first time she'd seen it she'd felt utter disgust, and couldn't help comparing it with Joe's little apartment – poky, it was true, and with furniture and fittings that had seen better days, but clean, tidy and bright, with the big sash window letting in plenty of light. But Joe, of course, had grown up in an environment where those things mattered. Jake, on the other hand, had known nothing but squalor at the baby farm and deprivation and enforced regimentation in the orphanage. Her stomach tightened at the thought and she was overwhelmed with sadness for him. But how he would appreciate the change in his circumstances when it came! And how she would enjoy introducing him to the finer things in life!

She rapped on the peeling door and it was opened by a scrawny woman with a baby in her arms and a young child hanging on to her skirts. A stale, fatty smell came with her, as if it had been absorbed into her hair, her clothes, her skin. Bacon, and perhaps sausages and fried potato chips. Lucy was forced to turn her head away a little as the smell turned her stomach. Even Davy's bacon and egg had made her feel sick this morning, and that had been freshly cooked, and only the best cuts. This . . . She thought she would throw up if she didn't take some deep breaths.

The woman – Lucy had never learned her name – recognised her though she had only been to the house a couple of times, and threw the door wide open.

'Aw – it's you. Yeah, he's in, I think.'

Lucy stepped smartly past her, trying to avoid the baby's

hands, filthy and sticky with something – she dared not think what – which were reaching out towards her.

'He's been proper poorly, mind!' the woman called after her.

Lucy didn't bother to reply. Up the three flights of stairs she ran, slowed for the last two steps up to Jake's door, and rapped sharply on it.

For long moments there was only silence. Lucy knocked again, and this time heard movement within, and the creak of the key turning in the lock.

'Lucy!' Jake was bare-chested, bare-footed and bleary-eyed. 'What are you doing here?'

'If you let me come in, I'll tell you.'

He moved aside and she went into the room. The holey blankets on the bed were thrown aside to reveal sheets that looked none too clean to her. One pillow lay on the floor as if tossed aside in restless sleep; the other, rumpled, was blood-stained – he hadn't changed the pillowcase since his injuries had bled on to it, obviously. But she wasn't going to mention that now, though it was clear she was going to have to take him in hand sooner or later.

'Did I wake you up?' she asked.

'Nah – I've been awake for a while now. I just got nothing to get up for.'

'You didn't have,' she corrected him. 'Now you do.'

'So I see.' He grinned.

In the dim light that filtered in through the tiny, high-up window she could see that his face was still bruised and swollen, but at least there was no fresh blood. He was healing, and remarkably quickly.

'So what brings you here so early in the morning?' he asked, but there was an expectancy in his tone, and in his eyes too, that

Lucy found puzzling. At his next remark, she thought she understood.

'I'd better make myself decent then – unless you've got other ideas.'

'Not today, Jake. I want to talk to you.' But still the thought of being with him in that special way was sending little thrills through her.

'How are you?' she asked.

'I'll live.'

'That's good. Because there's somebody I think would be very unhappy if you didn't.'

His eyes, still a little swollen, narrowed.

'Who's that, then?' But the expectancy was there again, almost as if he knew what she was about to say.

She'd been wondering how best to break the news to him, but the way the conversation had progressed made it easy for her.

'Your mother,' she said. 'I have a confession to make. I recognised her the moment you showed me her picture, but I couldn't say anything then. I had to speak to her first, make sure there was no mistake. Well now I have. And she wants to meet you.'

She hadn't meant it to all come out in such a rush, and she was dismayed, though not altogether surprised, when he turned away, reaching for his shirt, which lay on the tumbled bed, not putting it on, but holding it bunched up between his hands as if it were a missile he would like to hurl at someone or something.

'Well I'm not sure I want to meet her.'

'Oh Jake . . . I can understand how you must feel . . .'

'Can you? Can you really? She abandoned me, Luce. Left me in a bloody baby farm! She's never given a tinker's cuss about me. Why should I want to meet her? She's nothing to me.'

His voice was full of bitterness and the long, strong muscles in his bare back and arms were taut and rippling.

Lucy went to him, slipping her arms about his waist and leaning her cheek against his shoulder.

'You don't mean that, Jake. If you did, you wouldn't have kept her picture all these years. And she didn't abandon you – well, not in the way you mean. She thought you'd gone to a loving home, been adopted by people who could give you far more than she ever could.'

'She had money,' he said in the same bitter tone. 'She could have kept me if she'd wanted. I suppose I'd have spoiled her chances. Nobody wants a bastard.'

'She did want you.' Lucy was desperate to make him understand. 'And she's never forgotten you. I've seen her cry for you, cry as if her heart would break.'

'Oh yes?' Those taut muscles flexed again, then he turned abruptly, still holding his balled-up shirt so tightly that his grazed knuckles were white between the blotches of angry red. 'How do you know all this anyway?'

Lucy swallowed hard at the ache in her throat.

'Because she's my aunt, Jake. My father's sister. She was a singer on the halls twenty and more years ago. That picture you have is from one of her playbills. Her name was—'

'Belle Dorne,' he said.

'How do you know that?' she asked, startled.

For a moment he looked blank. Then: 'Well, you told me. You told me you took your stage name from your aunt.'

'That's right, I did.' Lucy took his hands. 'She wasn't in a position to keep you. She didn't have money then, and she truly did believe you'd gone to a loving family who wanted you very much.'

'Then how did I come to end up in a baby farm?'

'It's a long story. Why don't we sit down and I'll tell you.'

'All right. Go on then.' At last Jake pulled the crumpled shirt over his head, then sat down on the bed. Lucy sat beside him and began to explain.

As she came to the end, he was still stony-faced, but some of the tension seemed to have left him.

'She's truly sorry for what happened, and she wants nothing more than to make it up to you,' she said urgently. 'She asked me to be sure and tell you that you'll never want for anything again.'

He laughed shortly. 'Oh yes?'

'Yes! She's well-off now, and she wants to ensure you share in that.'

'Why would I want her money?' He said it savagely, with a flash of the same aggression he'd shown to her attackers on the night he'd come to her rescue, the same aggression she'd seen him exhibit in the boxing ring. Even when he was quite calm and normal it was there, just below the surface, and it was one of the things about him that she found so irresistibly attractive.

'I think you could use a little,' she said gently. 'This place, Jake . . . it's not very nice. And the things you have to do to earn a living . . .'

'I get by.'

'All right. If you feel like that about it . . .' She wouldn't pursue that line. It was clear he had his pride. 'But won't you at least meet her, for her sake if not for your own? She's a good person, Jake, kind and generous and great fun. And it would mean so much to her.'

He sighed, threw back his head, staring up at the ceiling where a large damp patch stained like a shadow, dark against the now yellowed whitewash.

'All right.' He looked at Lucy, grinned. 'But not for her. For you.'

Lucy felt as if she were melting inside.

'You won't regret it, Jake. And it means you have a family now – I'd be part of your family.'

'I s'pose you're right.' He reached for her. 'As long that doesn't stop me doing what I've wanted to do ever since you walked in here.'

Lucy smiled and went happily into his arms.

It was some time later when she pulled herself up from the grubby sheets, rearranging her clothes. Though Jake's lovemaking could make her forget everything else in the heat of the moment, when it was over she was all too aware of her sordid surroundings.

'I have to go. And we haven't yet talked about when and where you are going to meet Molly. She wants to come to London to meet you.'

'What, all the way from America?'

'No, silly. She lives in Somerset now. I'll let her know you're agreeable and I expect you'll be able to meet at her hotel.'

'Hotel, eh?'

'You can hardly entertain her here, can you?' Lucy got up. 'I really have to go, Jake. Doris will have my dinner ready.' She headed for the door.

'You want me to walk you home?'

'Not looking like that! You haven't even had a shave today.' She rubbed ruefully at her cheek, sore where his chin had rasped it.

'And you love every minute of it.' He went with her to the top of the stairs. 'You don't mind if I don't come down?'

'Not a bit. Just as long as you don't change your mind about meeting Molly.'

Lucy headed down the stairs feeling pleased with herself. As she reached the front door, it opened and a man came in. A big, burly man, roughly dressed. He glanced at her narrowly then pushed past her and started up the stairs. It was the man who had been Jake's second in the bare-knuckle contest, she felt sure, and her heart sank. Did that mean Jake had another fight arranged? She hoped not. But once again she was struck by a feeling of familiarity, just as when she'd seen him in the courtyard of the Cap and Feather that night; as though she'd seen him somewhere before and in quite a different context. It niggled at her, making her unaccountably uneasy, but for the life of her she could not think why, except that he wasn't the sort of man she liked to think of Jake being mixed up with.

But she wasn't going to let that spoil her sense of achievement. She'd managed to persuade Jake to meet Molly, and for the moment that was all that really mattered. If she'd failed, she didn't think she would have been able to face her aunt

She was not the only one feeling pleased with themselves. Jake, too, was jubilant.

He'd played things just right, he thought, smiling to himself. Not too eager, but making her think he was doing her a favour. Apart from one or two silly slips, such as going straight into pretended reluctance to meet his mother without asking how Lucy had found her, and then coming out with her name like that, it had gone perfectly, and he didn't think she'd noticed those. Really, she wasn't difficult to fool. Or perhaps it was that he'd missed his calling. Perhaps he should have gone on the stage, as an actor.

Never mind, it no longer mattered. Things were looking set fair for him now. Everything was working out exactly as he'd planned.

* * *

Molly could scarcely wait to meet her long-lost son. The moment the letter from Lucy arrived telling her Jake was willing to see her, she booked a room at the Savoy, her favourite hotel in London, and less than a week later was on the train heading for the capital.

Things had been a little strained between her and Daniel, but she was too happy to hold it against him now. Besides, she actually believed him when he told her he'd never intended for things to work out the way they had. He was, essentially, a good man. She was still angry that he had deceived her, but when she thought about it rationally, she knew that he had done it because he truly believed it was in her best interests.

He'd offered to accompany her to London – in case things should go wrong, she knew. He hadn't said as much, but she'd seen the anxiety in his eyes. He knew how much this meant to her, and was worried for her. But it was something she had to do alone. She wanted to be able to spend time with David – Jake! – getting to know him, catching up on the lost years, without any distraction. She was nervous, of course; she could feel the flutter of her heart and the tightening of her throat as she thought about how that first meeting would be, and her nerves seemed stretched and taut, prickling just beneath her skin. But the nervousness only added a sharp pitch of excitement to her anticipation. Her head buzzed with a million questions. What did he look like now? Was there anything of Anthony about him? Anything of her? Lucy had described him, but no words could paint the elusive picture. She had to see him with her own eyes, talk to him, hold him . . . oh, how she longed to hold him!

She had wondered, too, about the wisdom of booking in at the Savoy and asking that he meet her there. She'd stayed there once or twice when she was in London, though Daniel always chided her for her extravagance. She loved the serene atmosphere and the luxury, the stateliness of the vaulted public rooms, the comfort of the private ones, the beds made up with pristine fresh linen. She even loved the doorman in his topper and tails who greeted her with courtly respect. It would, she thought, make the perfect setting for the reunion, with no nosy manager or porter getting an eyeful as they might in some lesser establishment. David wouldn't be used to any of that and she hoped he wouldn't be intimidated by it, but she'd just have to make him feel comfortable – and it wouldn't be too long before he came to feel as much at ease there as she did. Heavens, she herself had once felt strange and way out of her league, a miner's daughter from a humble home in the country. Now she took it all for granted and could scarcely remember a time when she hadn't felt that the grand life wasn't her due. Perhaps David would be the same.

And if not, then how she would enjoy teaching him! How she would enjoy spoiling him, spending money and time on him, making up for lost time. There was nothing whatever to be nervous about. He was her flesh and blood. What could possibly go wrong?

It had been arranged that they would meet at eleven o'clock in the grand public area; the doorman had been briefed and Molly was there and waiting by a quarter to, just in case David should be early. She couldn't have remained in her room a moment longer in any case. The nervousness had really kicked in now, the excitement mounting, so that her skin prickled with it and her stomach had tied itself in knots. Despite the luxurious comfort of the bed, she had slept little, and had been quite unable to eat the delicious breakfast that was delivered to her room. She had soaked in a warm bath – the Savoy boasted hot and cold running water in the marble bathrooms, as well as electric lighting throughout the hotel – then dressed her hair with fingers that trembled, and powdered the dark circles underneath her eyes, wishing for the greasepaint that could cover a multitude of sins. But the effect would be grotesque nowadays, she knew, rather than flattering. She was no longer young. She had to accept that. But it didn't stop her regretting that David would never see her as she had once been, the beautiful young woman in the picture he had kept all these years.

In the grand scheme of things it didn't matter, though. The only thing of any importance was that after all these years of longing for him, she had found him.

Somehow Molly forced herself to sit still in the brocaded chair she had chosen because it gave a clear view of the hotel entrance. Each time the door opened her heart thudded with expectation; each time when it turned out to be some fine gentleman she felt sick with disappointment. Perhaps he'd changed his mind and wasn't coming after all. She told herself she was being foolish; it wasn't yet time. But still the anxiety gnawed at her. If he didn't come, she couldn't bear it.

An ornate French clock chimed the hour, sharp and clear as cut glass. Molly smoothed down her skirts and folded her hands in her lap to keep them from trembling, but not for one second did her eyes leave the door.

And then suddenly, almost unexpectedly, there he was.

She knew instantly that it was him. Even if he hadn't been younger and more powerfully built than most of the hotel's clientele, even if the cut of his coat hadn't marked him out as not of the class that normally frequented the Savoy, she felt sure she would still have known. He stood for a moment, looking a little awkward, a little out of place, and Molly could wait no longer. She covered the distance between them, came to a stop in front of him. She half registered his face: crooked nose, bruises faintly visible around the square jaw, eyes dark as jet, with lashes long as a girl's.

'David,' she said. He was still David to her and always would be.

Then she threw her arms around him, hugging him as she had ached to do through all the long years.

Chapter Thirty-One

'Well I suppose that's that, then,' Doris said.

Lucy had just told her what was going on: that she had discovered Jake was Molly's long-lost son, that Molly had come to London and was in fact meeting him this very morning at the Savoy. There was no longer any need to keep it a secret – Molly had given her permission to share it with Spike's family. She'd been to see Lucy perform last night, and taken her out to supper afterwards. Lucy had never seen her aunt so happy and excited.

'Of course you must tell Doris and Will,' she'd said. 'The whole world will know soon. I haven't the slightest intention of keeping my son a secret a moment longer.'

'Are you sure that's wise?' Lucy had asked. She'd imagined that Molly would invent some story to explain the sudden appearance of Jake in her life; an illegitimate child was a stigma few would admit to, and though show-business folk would probably be open-minded and forgiving, much of the rest of society would look upon it as a scandal.

'If I had been brave enough then to refuse to care what people thought I'd never have lost him,' Molly said. 'Now I'm lucky enough to have found him again I'll show the world I'm proud of him, and not in the least ashamed of myself. And in any case,' she added, 'it will come as no surprise to Doris and Will. Daniel tells me he stayed with them when he was scouring London to try and find David. The only part they don't yet know is that he's one and the same as the young man who rescued you from being robbed, or worse.' The smile she could scarcely keep from her lips for two minutes on end escaped once more, lighting up her face with joy and incredulity. 'It's like a miracle!'

'It is,' Lucy said. 'But . . .'

She hesitated, not knowing quite how to put into words the one thing that was bothering her – that when she finally met Jake, Molly might be disappointed. He was, after all, something of a rough diamond. There were things about him even she found disturbing and shocking, and she was in love with him – the bare-knuckle fighting, the sordid attic that was his home, the untamed element of raw savagery just beneath the surface that she also found so exciting.

'I know he's had a terrible upbringing.' Molly seemed to have read her mind. 'I know it's bound to have left its mark. I'm prepared for that. But he's mine and I'll love him whatever. All I want now is to be able to try to make it up to him.'

Lucy had nodded, satisfied. Aunt Molly was a realist; she knew the young man she was going to meet was not the same one he would have been if she had raised him herself, and was simply happy to have found him.

Doris, on the other hand, seemed less ready to accept him, which Lucy found strange, given how welcoming she'd been in the beginning.

'You don't seem very pleased about it,' she said now.

Doris, who had been cleaning the living room when Lucy had begun her story, retrieved her duster and tin of polish and began rubbing the table in sweeping circles.

'To be truthful, Lucy, I can't say as I am.'

431

'But why?' Lucy asked. 'Until recently you seemed to like him.'

Doris said nothing, just polished ever more vigorously. Her mouth was set in a tight line.

'It's made Molly really happy,' Lucy said a little defiantly.

'Perhaps she doesn't know yet what he's like.'

'What is it you have against him, Doris?' Lucy asked, exasperated. 'If it's the bare-knuckle fighting, then Molly knows about that. I've told her. Is that what it is?'

'And the rest.'

'But *what*?'

'All right, if you really want to know.' Doris set the tin of polish down on the table with a bang. 'He's a thief.'

'He *was* a thief, I know,' Lucy said. 'But that was when he was young and desperate. He served his time for it and it's all in the past now.'

Doris snorted. 'You think so. Well, once a tea leaf, always a tea leaf. He's still at it, Lucy.'

'I don't believe you.'

'I didn't want to believe it myself, let me tell you.' Doris pulled out one of the dining chairs and sat down heavily. 'But more than once after he'd been here there was money missing out of my purse. The first time it happened I told myself I must've made a mistake, spent it meself and forgotten. But when it happened again I knew I wasn't mistaken. Will gave me my housekeeping out of his wage packet only the night before, and I hadn't been anywhere to spend it. Oh, he was crafty, I'll give him that. A ten-shilling note and some loose silver, that's what was gone. He did it random like, hoping I wouldn't notice.'

'He wouldn't! He couldn't . . .'

'Wouldn't have taken him more than a minute. Slippery hands, rogues like him have got. You can't tell me he was never out of your sight. You'd only have to go out to the lav, or into the scullery to fill the kettle for a cup of tea, and he'd have my purse open and back again where I left it before you could say Jack Robinson.'

Lucy was shaking her head, disbelieving, and dismayed that Doris could think such a thing of Jake.

'It couldn't have been Davy, I suppose?'

High spots of colour rose in Doris's cheeks.

'No it could not! He'd never do such a thing! And what would he want money for anyway? Whatever he wants I gets for him.'

Lucy was unconvinced. Magpies didn't need the shiny objects they stole, but they took them anyway.

'And that's another thing – Davy.' Doris really had the bit between her teeth now. 'What would you say if I told you I saw Jake kick our Davy when he thought there was nobody looking?'

'They play-fight! You know that.'

'I know this wasn't no play,' Doris said grimly. 'A proper kick it were – and sly. Made our Davy yelp, it did. But o' course, he wouldn't say nothing. Idolises Jake. Though he did keep his distance for a bit.'

'Then it must have been an accident.'

'I know what I saw,' Doris maintained stoutly. 'He's a bad lot. He's taken advantage of you, thought he could take advantage of me. And he'll do the same to Molly. She'll give him anything he wants, and he'll take it. An' he'll finish up breaking her heart. That's what I'm afraid of.'

'He doesn't want anything from her,' Lucy protested. 'He said so.'

'Words are cheap, ain't they?' Doris rubbed viciously with her duster at an imaginary spot on the table. 'I'm sorry to say it, Lucy, but I wouldn't trust that one any further than I could throw him. He had me taken in for a bit, I admit it, and there ain't no flies on me. It'll be child's play taking in Molly, with her so over the moon at finding him again. And he's pulled the wool over your eyes good and proper. Wormed his way in with you and wound you round his little finger so he got what he wanted.'

Lucy's immediate assumption was that Doris had guessed they were lovers, and she felt her cheeks growing hot. The smell of bacon frying for Davy's breakfast had made her feel sick again this morning, and so had the sharp, acrid smell of the clinker when Doris had been lighting the living room fire, and the awful thought had popped into her mind that perhaps that lovemaking might have precipitated unwelcome results, and like Aunt Molly before her she was going to end up in a pickle. The shadow of anxiety hung over her now, making her all the more keen to defend Jake.

'He's never treated me anything but well,' she said defiantly. 'And he came to my rescue, didn't he? For that alone I trust him.'

Doris's mouth twisted into an expression of disgust.

'An' don't you think that was a bit convenient?'

'What do you mean?' Lucy demanded.

'Well, that he of all people just happens to be passing by when you gets attacked? Don't that seem like a bit too much of a coincidence to you? 'Cos it does to me.'

'This is getting ridiculous!' Lucy was beginning to be really upset by Doris's litany of accusations. 'How could he possibly have known that I was his mother's niece?'

Doris snorted. 'With your name plastered on billboards all over London, it wouldn't take a genius to work out you were related, would it? If he knew his mother was Belle Dorne, what better way to get to meet her than through you? Having you sing his praises as a hero and your saviour would certainly smooth his path, I'd say.'

'He'd never heard of her – he told me!' But even as the words passed her lips, they triggered a jolt of unease. She could clearly remember him displaying ignorance that first night, yet on the day she'd told him she knew who his mother was, he had seemed to know all about her.

'I reckon he had it planned out nicely,' Doris went on. 'I'm not saying she ain't his mother, just that I'd bet my bottom dollar it was all a set-up so he could use you to get to her. An' I don't like it. I wonder if he'd have been half so keen to meet her if she was some poor woman without a penny to her name. No, what I'm afraid of is that he's going to end up breaking her heart – and yours too. It's a darned shame, but there's rogues like him everywhere. You can't be too careful.' She leaned over and patted Lucy's arm. 'I'm sorry if I've upset you, but I think the time's come to speak my mind. Now.' She put down the duster and stood up. 'Why don't I make us a nice cup of tea?'

'I don't want a cup of tea.' Lucy was feeling sick again, so sick she could suddenly think of nothing else.

As the bitter taste of bile rose in her mouth, she leapt up, brushing past Doris and rushing for the back door. But the need to vomit was too great; there was no time to get out to the privy at the bottom of the garden. Instead, Lucy was forced to run to the big stone sink in the scullery, where she was violently sick.

Though she didn't believe a word of what Doris had said, all the joy had gone out of the day, leaving her scared and anxious. How could it be that she felt suddenly as if everything was tumbling about her ears? As if everything good had unexpectedly turned sour?

For a long while after the heaving stopped, Lucy remained leaning against the sink, weak and wretched.

* * *

Algernon was ill – poorly enough to call for Dr Blackmore. Since he had been blessed with an iron constitution, such a thing was almost unheard of. Apart from the occasional cough or sniffle, the only malady he could recall was a bout of gastric influenza, not so long after he'd married Annie. He'd blamed her cooking for it until it had been pointed out to him that half the town, including many of the chapel congregation, had been struck down by the same bug. In all the years he'd been working at the glove factory, the number of days he'd taken off for sickness could be counted on the fingers of one hand, and when he'd begun feeling unwell the unfamiliarity of it had alarmed him.

'I'm sure it's nothing serious,' Annie had said, showing little sympathy, but the symptoms had worsened dramatically. Algernon's vision was so blurred he could scarcely read the page before his eyes when he opened his Bible, his ankles and legs swelled so that it was impossible to get his feet into his boots, and his heart raced and thumped against his ribs, beating so hard and fast it made him dizzy.

'It looks as if your heart is playing up,' Dr Blackmore said when he had examined him.

'I've never had a bad heart. That's Kitty's problem,' Algernon protested, though trying to talk was making him breathless.

'It seems to be yours too now.' Dr Blackmore regarded him seriously over the rim of his spectacles. 'If you overdo things at your age it can happen.'

'I'm fit as a fiddle!' Algernon was outraged at what he considered to be a slur. 'And I haven't done anything more than usual.'

'Getting worked up won't help either,' the doctor counselled. 'I'll prescribe you some medication that should help, but more than anything you need to take things quietly. Bed rest, light, nourishing meals, and no stressful upsets.'

'He hasn't been eating either,' Annie put in. 'He usually loves his food. But yesterday Kitty made a lovely mutton pie – one of his favourites – and he hardly touched it.'

'How is Kitty?' the doctor asked.

'Oh, you know, up and down, but she seems a lot better since you increased her prescription.'

'Good. Well if he's not eating, make sure he has plenty of milky drinks, and I would say a glass or two of home-brewed, but I suppose that's against his principles. Can you pick up the medication from the chemist's, Mrs Pierce?'

Annie nodded.

'Good. Get him started on it straight away, and I'll look in in a day or two and see how he's faring.'

'Can I not go to chapel?' Algernon asked – a question that hardly needed answering, given the state of him.

'I won't be responsible for the consequences if you do.' Dr Blackmore was writing out the prescription. 'Complete rest is what you need. If that and the medication do the trick then we'll review the situation and find out exactly how much you can do without becoming ill again. In the meantime I suggest you go to bed and stay there.'

'You heard the doctor,' Annie said when he'd packed up his medical bag and left. 'Let's get you upstairs, and then I'll run down to the chemist's.'

She was eager to pack him off to bed; having him sitting here in the living room was oppressive, and the thought of him being there all day for the foreseeable future, watching and criticising her every move, was not a pleasant one. But at least in his present state he wouldn't be beating her, or making his other disgusting demands. She rather hoped Dr Blackmore's medication didn't

437

work too quickly, for she had the feeling that a recovering Algernon might well be even more ill-tempered than usual.

If only it didn't work at all! If only his heart would give out completely! she thought, and was instantly ashamed of herself. Wishing anyone dead, even a monster like Algernon, was wicked.

But who could blame her? If Algernon were dead, she and Kitty would be free. It would be the answer to all their prayers.

Lucy was in turmoil. Try as she might, she simply couldn't forget what Doris had said. For one thing, Doris wasn't the sort of person to have irrational notions. She was one of the most easy-going and level-headed people Lucy knew. For her to have said the things she did, she must be convinced in her own mind that Jake was not quite what he seemed. Lucy found it hard to believe he'd stolen from Doris, or kicked the big gormless Davy when he thought no one was looking, but was it possible that was because she didn't want to believe it? As for him having somehow engineered their first meeting . . . well that was utterly ridiculous, though it was, as Doris had said, a huge coincidence.

It had been fate working in mysterious ways, Lucy told herself. And yet still the doubts niggled away at her.

As if all that was not bad enough, she was beginning to be very afraid she was indeed pregnant. She still felt horribly sick in the mornings and she rather thought she was late for her time of the month. She wasn't awfully good at keeping a note of dates, so she couldn't be absolutely sure, but her last period did seem to have been quite a while ago.

The thought that she might be going to have a baby turned Lucy cold. Though she'd love to have children one day, this was not the right time, nor the right circumstances. Her career, which was just taking off, would come to an abrupt halt, and she wasn't at all sure how Jake would react to the news that he was to become a father. It could be history repeating itself, Lucy thought anxiously. She could find herself in exactly the same position as Molly had. Except that she could never contemplate giving her child away to strangers, especially now she had seen at first hand what the result of such an arrangement could be.

And the worst of it was she couldn't even share any of this with Jake. Molly had invited him to spend a few days in Bath, so that they could get to know one another better and Jake could meet Spike and some of their close friends. She seemingly couldn't wait to show him off, her secret son, and with Doris's dire predictions hanging over her, Lucy couldn't help but be anxious for her too. She loved Molly dearly and couldn't bear the thought of her being hurt after all she'd gone through. Supposing Doris was right, and Jake was really only interested in Molly's money? But no, that couldn't be right. She'd had to practically beg him to meet her. She was worrying quite unnecessarily.

Yet still all the pros and cons went on running ceaseless circles in her head, tormenting her, in tandem with her fears that she might be pregnant.

Since she'd left High Compton and come to London she'd seemed to lead a charmed life, and she'd begun to take it for granted that good fortune would continue to smile on her forever. Now, however, she'd been jolted back to grim reality. Being a success on the halls didn't mean she'd never have to worry about anything ever again. It didn't make her any less vulnerable to all the things that could suddenly go wrong.

She wished she could talk to Doris again, try to persuade her she was wrong about Jake. Since Doris had got her concerns off her chest, she'd been much more her old self, open and warm-hearted, as if by acquainting Lucy with her doubts she'd salved her conscience. Lucy knew that what she really wanted by trying to convince Doris she was wrong was to convince herself. But it wouldn't be wise to open that particular can of worms again; she didn't want to argue with Doris, who was the cornerstone of her life here. And she certainly couldn't tell her of her fears about her condition, though if there was any foundation to them, Doris would have to know soon enough.

In an effort to put all this out of her mind, Lucy tried to concentrate on her career. If there was any chance she might soon have to give it up for a while, at least, she needed to build up her reputation so she would not be readily forgotten. She pressed Bernie to book her even more engagements, even if it meant a return to running between halls to fulfil them, and Bernie was happy to oblige.

The telegram was delivered to Doris's door midway through the morning. Doris and Lucy were enjoying a cup of tea and a slice of freshly made fruit cake – elevenses, Doris called it, and Lucy found that the nausea that kept her from eating breakfast had passed by then, leaving her ravenously hungry. It was Davy who answered the door; he'd been scooting his toy trucks along the hall since it was raining and he couldn't be outside. But Doris got up anyway and went to the doorway, not trusting him with whoever it was calling.

'Who is it, Davy?'

'Telegram!' Davy said, repeating what the delivery boy had said. 'Telegram!'

He held out the square buff envelope to her, beaming with pride, as if it was all his own work. Doris took it, thanked the boy, who was still at the door, and tipped him a silver threepenny bit, then went back into the living room.

'It's for you, Lucy.' Her face was grave. A telegram usually meant bad news of some kind.

'For me?' Lucy was suddenly feeling sick again, the fruit cake heavy in her gullet. Like Doris she knew the implications of a telegram, and her initial panicky thought was that something had happened to Kitty. In those first feverish moments she was already blaming herself for not having somehow made the effort to meet up with Kitty when she was in Somerset. It was now getting on for a year since she had seen her – too long when her sister was in such a delicate state of health. If Kitty had died with Lucy having never seen her again, she didn't think she could bear it.

Holding her lip tight between her teeth and hardly daring to breathe, she tore open the envelope and unfolded the sheet of paper. Then her breath came out on a long sigh of relief.

The telegram was indeed telling her of a death in the family. But it was not Kitty who had passed away. It was Algernon.

Chapter Thirty-Two

Lucy took the train home the very next day.

'I have to go. There's been a death in the family,' she had told a fuming Bernie. But there was no way she could fail to fulfil that same evening's engagement. She couldn't let the theatre management and her audience down at such short notice. And it wasn't as though it had been Kitty who had died, as she had feared. But Annie would need her, all the same. There would be so much to be taken care of, and Kitty was bound to be upset, considering how much Algernon had seemed to mean to her; she would be of very little help even if she was having one of her spells of better health.

Besides all this, Lucy was suddenly desperately anxious to see her mother and sister again. She had missed them so much, wept silent tears over their letters to her and hers to them, worried about them. Now all those moments of regret and the uncertainty in her own life at present seemed to merge together into one great snowball of longing. Lucy wanted her mother as she had not wanted her since she was a little girl, and was filled with a sense of urgency in regard to Kitty. And of course, if she went to Somerset she would be able to meet up with Jake. But surprisingly she didn't feel as eager to see him as she once had. Something had changed subtly in her feelings towards him. All

442

the worrying and wondering of the last days had made her wary; she no longer totally trusted him, she realised, and in fact she wondered if she knew him at all.

As for Joe . . . The thought of seeing Joe again made her cringe inwardly. How was she ever going to face him after what she had done to him? It was going to be horribly awkward, to say the least of it.

From Bath she took a cab to High Compton, staring almost unseeing as the familiar landscape unfolded. Her heart leapt into her throat as it drew up outside the house that had once been her home. All the curtains were drawn at the windows, a mark of respect that also informed passers-by of a death in the house.

Carrying her overnight bag, Lucy went up the path and tried the front door. It opened; someone had gone in or out this morning or it would still have been locked.

'Mam?' she called as she went into the hall. 'It's me!'

Annie emerged from the living room; the door to the front room was shut, Lucy noticed, a feeling of dread prickling over her skin. It was there that Algernon would have been laid out. Even now, when he could no longer hurt her, his very proximity sickened her. Besides, she had never seen a dead body, and her stomach curled in on itself at the thought of one lying just the other side of that closed door.

'Lucy – darling!'

Annie hugged her, and putting down her overnight bag, Lucy hugged her back. Her mother had lost weight, she thought.

'Let me look at you!' Annie held her at arm's length. 'Oh Lucy, it's so good to see you!'

Lucy studied her mother's face. She looked tired, but delight was shining out of her eyes, and at least there were no visible signs of her having suffered abuse.

'It's good to be here,' she said. 'But Mam . . . what on earth happened? Algernon always seemed so fit!'

'Come on in and I'll tell you.'

Lucy followed her mother into the sitting room. Kitty was lying on the sofa; Lucy perched on the edge beside her, kissing her, then taking her hands.

'Oh Kitty, how are you? I've missed you so much!'

Kitty was very pale; her hair, braided into two plaits, fell over her thin shoulders.

'I'm fine,' she said, and smiled at Lucy, but it was a wan smile.

'This must have been an awful shock for you.'

'Mm. But what about you, Lucy? You're quite the star these days. I didn't think you'd have the time to come home.'

'Of course I came!' Lucy turned to Annie. 'So what happened?' she asked again. 'Was it a heart attack?'

Annie sat down on one of the upright dining chairs.

'It was his heart. At least, that's what Dr Blackmore seemed to think when he visited a couple of days ago. He prescribed something that he thought would help, but he just got worse. He couldn't breathe, and his legs swelled up like balloons. He was in a terrible state really. And then . . . well, he just seemed to pass out. I tried to get the doctor to him again . . .' She faltered, guilt-stricken that in truth she hadn't tried very hard; that she'd left it too late for her own selfish ends. A part of her of which she was ashamed had been hoping that without proper medical attention he would die.

'When I went for Dr Blackmore, I found out he was away, gone to visit his daughter down in Devon. Dr Mackay from Hillsbridge is covering for him. I came home thinking I'd go next door and telephone for him – Marcus has had one put in for his mother and father so they can get in touch with him if they need to.' There was awe in her voice: a telephone in an ordinary private house was practically unheard of. 'But it was getting late, and I didn't like to bother them. Then Algernon took a turn for the worse, and before I knew it, he was gone. Just like that! It was awful, wasn't it, Kitty?'

'Awful,' Kitty agreed faintly.

'I wish I'd been here for you, Mam,' Lucy said, genuinely regretful.

'Well.' Annie pulled herself together with an effort. 'There didn't seem much point in calling out Dr Mackay then. So I just ran down the road for Mrs Barker to come and see to him.' Lay him out, she meant, Lucy knew. 'She said it would be all right to leave calling the doctor until the morning, so that's what I did. But would you believe – he still hasn't been.'

'You mean nobody has certified the death yet?' Lucy asked. She wasn't sure what the procedures were, but that sounded about right.

'Not yet, no. I'm expecting him any time. He's busy, having to look after Dr Blackmore's patients as well as his own, I expect. Oh!' She broke off expectantly as a knock came at the front door. 'Perhaps that's him now.'

She got up hastily, but the knock was followed by the sound of the door opening and a man's voice called out: 'It's all right – it's only me.'

Lucy's heart leapt into her throat. Joe! She hadn't expected to have to face him so soon.

He came into the room, and his serious expression turned to one of surprise when he saw Lucy.

'Lucy!'

'Hello, Joe.' Her heart was thumping uncomfortably fast.

'What are you doing here?' He sounded almost accusing.

'She's come to do what she can to help, of course.' Annie

445

spoke for her. 'All the way from London.'

'Right,' Joe said shortly, then turned to Annie, ignoring Lucy as if she hadn't been there. 'What's happening then, Annie? Has the doctor been yet?'

'No, I thought it might be him when you knocked. You're early, Joe. Shouldn't you still be at work?'

'Mr Penny let me go. It was quiet – it's always quiet on Wednesdays.' Wednesday was early closing, when all the shops in town shut at one o'clock. 'So you haven't been able to do anything about the undertaker yet?'

'I've let him know, but he won't touch Algernon until the death certificate's been signed. Oh, I do wish that doctor would come!'

'He'll be here. He's a good chap, and quite young.' Joe was still studiously avoiding looking at Lucy. She stayed where she was, on the sofa beside Kitty, wishing the ground would open up and swallow her.

But she was glad, all the same, that he was here. It would take some of the load off her shoulders. She had no idea what needed to be done at a time like this, but Joe would know.

She felt a sudden pang of longing that took her by surprise. She'd forgotten how safe she'd always felt with him. Forgotten, too, how good-looking he was. Not ruggedly handsome, as Jake was, but good-looking in an open, honest way, as if his inner goodness was shining through and lending beauty and depth to features that might otherwise have been quite ordinary. Strange, she'd never really looked at him like that before, even when she'd fallen in love with him. Now she was seeing him through fresh eyes.

'What do you think caused it, Joe?' Annie was asking, calling on his opinion as a professional – he was, after all, if not a doctor, a pharmacist, and to her that was the next best thing.

Joe, however, shook his head. 'I really don't know, Annie. It certainly seems like heart failure, but it's strange he never had any symptoms before.'

'People do drop dead of heart attacks without warning,' Annie said.

'Well, yes. But he didn't just drop dead, did he? There was the swelling and the blurred vision and all that. And the medication Dr Blackmore prescribed should have helped if it was just his heart. I made it up myself, and it's good stuff – not unlike what you take, Kitty.'

'Dr Blackmore did say that if it did no good he'd have to think again. But he's off visiting his daughter, so of course he never had the chance.'

Another knock at the front door. Annie got up again, brushing down her skirt.

'Perhaps that's the doctor now.'

It was. Dr Mackay was a Scot, and the pleasant burr of his voice carried in from the hall, along with the click of the front room door opening and closing again. Lucy shuddered, imagining Algernon lying there.

'Well – Lucy.' At last Joe turned to her, acknowledging her presence. 'I'm surprised you found the time in your busy life to come home.'

Colour burned in Lucy's cheeks.

'I'd have come long ago if it hadn't been for *him*.' She jerked her head in the direction of the front room, just the other side of the wall. 'He forbade me, and to be honest, I couldn't be in the same house as him even if he hadn't. He was a wicked man, Joe, and I'm glad he's dead.' She squeezed Kitty's hand. 'I'm sorry, Kitty. I know you were very fond of him, but—'

'No, I'm glad he's dead too,' Kitty said quietly.

Lucy looked at her sister in surprise. 'But I thought . . .'

447

'I used to be blind, but I've seen another side to him this last year. And yes, I'm as glad as you are that he's gone.'

Lucy experienced a sharp pang of fear. What had happened for her sister to have had such a change of heart? Had he done something unspeakable to her too?

Though she'd tried to warn Kitty to be careful of him, she'd never really believed her sister was in any danger – it had been Lucy's rebellion that had sparked the attack, and the fact that she was behaving in what he might have seen as a provocative manner. Kitty was far from being either rebellious or provocative and Algernon had always treated her differently. Now, however, Lucy wondered anxiously if she had been wrong.

'He's been ill-treating Mam,' Kitty went on. 'Did you know that?'

'Oh no!' Lucy groaned. Though she had suspected as much, she'd hoped desperately that she was wrong about that too. How could she have deceived herself so? But equally, what could she have done about it? If she'd tried to interfere it would probably only have made things ten times worse. 'Oh Mam, why ever didn't you leave him?'

'How could I? We had nowhere to go, and Kitty . . .' Annie broke off, shrugging helplessly.

'She did try, but it didn't work out.' Joe spoke with the authority of one who had been the recipient of Annie's confidences, though he had shared them with Kitty. 'She was trapped.'

'Well, she's free now.' Kitty spoke with grim satisfaction. 'And so am I. He won't be hurting either of us any more.'

'Amen to that.' Joe turned to Lucy. 'How long are you here for? Will you stay for the funeral?'

'I'll be here as long as Mam needs me.'

'Good. But it's a bit late in the day for that, I'd say.'

'I had my reasons,' Lucy said, guilt making her voice sharp.

'Oh yes, we know all about your reasons.' His lip curled as he spoke, and Lucy could have wept. She hated this distance between them when once they had been so close, hated the antagonism where once there had been love. It hurt even more than she'd anticipated. Explaining why she'd left as she had was the only way to breach the wall of ice that Joe had erected, but she couldn't do that, and even if she could, there was no guarantee it would make much difference. She had hurt him too deeply. Things between them could never be the same again.

The sound of the front room door being opened and closed again stopped the conversation in its tracks. Annie and Dr Mackay came back into the living room, Annie looking anxious and the doctor thoughtful and serious. Instead of getting out the relevant forms and completing them as Lucy had expected, he sat down on one of the upright dining chairs, set his medical bag down beside him, and addressed Annie.

'I'm sorry about this, Mrs Pierce, but I really don't feel I am in a position to sign a death certificate.'

'What do you mean?'

'Why not?'

Annie and Joe spoke simultaneously, breaking the stunned silence.

Dr Mackay shifted uncomfortably. He was kind and caring, both as a man and a doctor, and it gave him no pleasure at all to cause further upset to a bereaved family. But he was also professional through and through, and his conscience simply would not allow him to issue the necessary paperwork when he had serious doubts as to the cause of death.

'I didn't attend Mr Pierce in the days or weeks preceding his death,' he said tentatively.

'No, but Dr Blackmore did,' Annie cut in.

'And from his own observations he might well be happy to sign a certificate. But I'm afraid I'm not prepared to do that.'

'It was his heart!' Annie protested. 'Dr Blackmore said so!'

'Quite possibly it was. I don't want to question the judgement of a colleague. All I'm saying is that I'm not conversant enough with the origins or progress of Mr Pierce's condition to make a judgement as to whether his death was due to natural causes.' He ran a finger round the inside of his shirt collar, which suddenly felt uncomfortably tight.

'But I can't arrange the funeral until I've got a death certificate,' Annie said, distressed.

'I realise that, and I'm sorry. But that is the whole point of the law as it stands. A funeral shouldn't take place until the cause of death has been established.'

'That's ridiculous!' Annie burst out. 'We know the cause of death!'

'You think you do, Mrs Pierce, and you may well be right. On the other hand, I'm less sure that it's as straightforward as you believe.' The doctor stood up. 'By rights I should be reporting my doubts without delay to the coroner. Out of deference to my colleague, I'll speak to him first. He's due back tomorrow, and I'll discuss it with him then. But for the moment I'm afraid there's no more I can do.'

With that he picked up his bag, and although Annie followed him into the hall, arguing and pleading, he refused to change his mind and do as she asked.

'What a pompous idiot!' Lucy exclaimed, but surprisingly Joe took his part.

'He's got to do what he thinks right, Lucy. If he didn't diagnose Algernon's condition himself, then he's quite within his rights to be cautious.'

'Algernon's dead, isn't he? Surely that's good enough?' Annie had come back into the room and Lucy turned to her, eyes bright with passion. 'Whatever is that doctor thinking of, Mam? Oh, I could kill him for putting you through this! And here's Joe defending him!'

'I'm only saying—'

'Oh, I know what you're saying!' Lucy flashed. 'I suppose as a pharmacist you've got to suck up to doctors, but I think it's a disgrace. What did he mean – he should be reporting it to the coroner? Anyone would think Algernon had been murdered!'

A small strangled gasp made them all turn and look at Kitty. She was white as a ghost, hand pressed to her mouth, eyes closed.

'Kitty?' Annie was alarmed. 'Are you all right?'

Kitty sobbed again. Her breathing was uneven and laboured. All this had been too much for her, Lucy thought, while Annie, having so recently witnessed Algernon's sudden decline and death, was cold with the fear that her daughter might suddenly go the same way.

Putting her distress at the doctor's refusal to issue a death certificate to one side, she went to Kitty.

'It's all right, my love. Don't upset yourself. Everything is going to be all right.'

'No it's not!' Kitty gulped. 'It's not all right at all! He's still cursing us! He'll never leave us alone, never!'

'Don't talk so silly,' Annie said, but Lucy had the most dreadful feeling that Kitty was right. Even from beyond the grave Algernon was exerting his evil power.

'You're just upset, Kitty,' she said nevertheless.

Kitty sank back deeper against the cushions.

'I'm tired,' she whispered. 'So tired.'

'I think you'd be best in bed,' Annie said. 'Joe . . . ?'

451

'I'll take her up.' Joe crossed to the sofa, preparing to scoop Kitty up into his arms, but her next words stopped him in his tracks.

'It's all going to come out, isn't it?'

'What, my love?' Annie's tone was gentle but puzzled. 'The way he treated me, you mean? I don't care about that now. I don't care about anything except that we're free, and together.'

'But we won't be . . .' Kitty had begun to cry, weak tears gathering in her eyes and running down her pale cheeks. 'They'll send me to prison . . . or worse . . .'

'Why on earth would they do that?' Annie expressed the bewilderment they were all feeling. Kitty was delirious, she must be. 'This is nothing to do with you. Nothing at all.'

Joe, however, was looking at Kitty narrowly. An awful suspicion had crept into his head when Dr Mackay had refused to sign the death certificate – a suspicion borne out by his own, admittedly less than comprehensive, medical knowledge.

'What are you saying, Kitty?'

Kitty sobbed, and when she spoke, her voice was so soft the words were almost inaudible.

'It is to do with me. It is! Because . . . because I killed him.'

Lucy, like Annie, was gazing at Kitty in disbelief, thinking that the shock of all this had unhinged her fragile sister. Only Joe gave credence to her words.

'It was your medication, wasn't it? You gave him your medication.'

Kitty nodded, wiping the tears from her cheeks with her fingertips.

'You did what?' Annie asked, stunned. 'But how?'

Kitty swallowed hard. 'I stirred it into his food and drinks.'

'Oh dear God!' Annie gasped. She'd wondered why Kitty had taken it upon herself to wait on him after he became ill, making him little treats and sitting with him until he'd finished them. Now she knew. But . . .

'But he took bad before that,' she said, unwilling even now to believe that Kitty had deliberately poisoned her stepfather.

'You'd already begun giving it to him, hadn't you?' Joe asked gently. 'That's why you became ill yourself, because you weren't having what you needed, you were feeding it to Algernon. It's why you ran short. And when Dr Blackmore upped your dosage, you were able to take a little yourself and still keep giving it to Algernon as well.'

'Oh Kitty!' It was all coming horribly clear to Annie now; she hadn't been able to understand how Kitty had come to run out of her medication the day she'd had to hurry to the chemist's to replenish her supply. 'But how did you know . . . ?' She broke off, unable to finish the sentence: *How did you know it would kill him?*

'I didn't really, not for sure,' Kitty said tremulously. 'But Dr Blackmore did warn me once to be careful, because too much could poison me. I started saving some of my dosage, and then I put it in his tea. I was afraid he'd taste it, but with all the sugar he took he didn't seem to notice. You know how strong and sweet he liked his tea, Mam?'

Annie nodded. It was true: she'd always been horrified at the amount of sugar Algernon stirred into each cup.

'I could see it was working when he got ill,' Kitty went on, her head bent so that her words were almost lost in the blanket of crocheted squares Annie had covered her with. 'After that it was easy. All I had to do was keep on giving him as much as I could without him noticing.'

'But it really looked as if his heart was giving out.' Annie was still struggling with what she was hearing.

'Some of the symptoms would be similar,' Joe said. 'The

very thing that strengthens a weak heart would make a healthy one work too hard. What Algernon was really suffering from was digitalis poisoning. And when Dr Blackmore prescribed him quinidine – that's what it was, I know, I made it up myself – then that would have just made him much worse. Some drugs react badly with one another, and those are two of them.'

'But why, Kitty?' Lucy asked, the first words she had spoken since her sister's shocking confession. 'Whatever made you take a chance like that?'

'I had to do something! You weren't here – you don't know what it was like, how he was treating Mam. And we couldn't get away from him. Joe told me Mam had tried, but it didn't work out, and she couldn't leave because of me. So I knew it was all my fault, and I had to do something.'

'Of course it wasn't your fault, you silly girl! You should never have done something like that for my sake,' Annie said.

'Not just for you, Mam.' Kitty's teeth, small and pearly, chewed at her bloodless lips. 'He was doing things to me too, things I didn't like. And whatever happens, I'm not sorry I did it. I'm just glad he's dead and can't hurt us any more.'

Lucy's stomach clenched, her hatred of her stepfather growing and swelling till she thought it would choke her. So she had been right: in the end, the monster had turned to Kitty.

'If I'd been here, Kitty, I'd have helped you do it,' she said, her voice low and vicious.

'I'm glad you weren't, then.' Kitty reached out a hand to her sister. 'If they send me to prison – hang me, even – It doesn't matter much. What sort of a life do I have anyway? But you . . .'

'Oh Kitty!' Tears were welling in Lucy's eyes. She couldn't bear it that her sister should have come to this. 'Look, you mustn't tell anyone what you've told us. You've got to keep quiet about it, and with luck no one will ever know,' she said urgently.

'But if there's a post-mortem it's bound to come out, isn't it?' Annie looked as if she too was on the verge of collapse as this nightmare unfolded, and seeing it, Joe spoke up.

'It might not come to that,' he said, trying to sound a good deal more positive than he was feeling. 'Dr Blackmore might well sign a death certificate and that will be the end of it.'

'And if he doesn't?'

'We'll cross that bridge when we come to it,' Joe said steadfastly. 'Now, I think we could all do with a cup of tea – or something stronger.'

From his pocket he extracted a quarter-bottle of good brandy. 'I had a feeling this might be needed, and at least there's no one now to tell us no, is there?'

Despite the pragmatic front he was putting on, Joe was seriously worried. If he'd been able to recognise the signs of digitalis poisoning with his far from comprehensive medical knowledge, it was small wonder Dr Mackay had done so. When he talked to Dr Blackmore, they were bound to come to the same conclusion: that either Algernon had for some reason helped himself to Kitty's medication, or someone – Annie or Kitty herself – had given it to him deliberately with the intention of doing him harm. Either way they'd refuse to issue a death certificate without a post-mortem, and from then on the law would take its course.

The very thought of it turned Joe cold. He could well understand that Kitty had been driven to doing what she did out of sheer desperation, but would a jury understand? Would a judge be lenient? He couldn't see it somehow. A man of standing in the community had been murdered, and the prosecution would no doubt try to paint Annie and Kitty as grasping women who, not content with living comfortable lives at Algernon's expense, were greedy for more. The house and whatever savings Algernon had would all go to Annie. To the uninitiated it would appear the perfect motive.

And whatever the verdict, he felt sure the trial would result in a death sentence for Kitty. With her fragile health she would never survive the stress of an appearance at the assize court, let alone prison.

Well, he wouldn't let it happen. If the two doctors called for a post-mortem and the result was as he feared, then he would take the blame. He'd tell the truth about Algernon and say that he had taken matters into his own hands. There was even the incident of the pills he'd dispensed at Annie's request on the day she'd come to the chemist's desperately worried as to what would happen to Kitty if she didn't have them right away. He shouldn't have done it, and he'd kept quiet about it, but if the stock records were checked, the missing pills would back up his story. If he was believed, he'd hang for it, of course, but so be it. Kitty had said her life was hardly worth living, and at this moment Joe felt the same.

Loving her as he did, to see Lucy again had been sheer torture. Over the last year he'd made a huge effort to accept that he'd lost her, even if he couldn't forget her, and he'd begun to think he was succeeding. What a joke! The moment he'd walked in and seen her, he'd known nothing had changed. He wanted her as desperately as he ever had, loved her with the sort of blind, unthinking adoration that took him over, body and soul.

But she didn't want him. She'd made that clear. Well, now she had the life she'd longed for, and a new love, in all likelihood. Any vague hope he'd clung to that one day she would tire of London and come home to him had gone now, and a black despair had taken its place. No, if the worst happened and Algernon's death was investigated, he'd be only too glad to take the blame for it. He loved Annie and owed her more than he could ever repay. If he was able to save Kitty, perhaps it would go some way to settling the debt.

Chapter Thirty-Three

Molly was searching in vain for her favourite ring. Spike had given it to her last Christmas – an enormous emerald in a setting of tiny sparkling diamonds – and it had scarcely been off her finger since. But now it seemed to have vanished into thin air. It wasn't in her jewellery box – she'd emptied that out on to the bed to make sure it hadn't fallen into the wrong compartment – and it wasn't on the shelf in the kitchen where she thought she'd left it. She'd taken it off the previous evening to wash up the supper things, not a chore she often undertook, but with Jake in the house there were more used plates and glasses than usual, and she'd decided to do them herself rather than leaving them for Millicent to clear up in the morning. Whether she'd put it back on again or not she couldn't remember; since Jake's arrival she'd been too distracted to think straight. But if she had, she'd certainly have taken it off when she undressed for bed, in which case it should be either in the jewellery box or possibly on her dressing table, and it wasn't.

She went back downstairs to search again. Perhaps it had been knocked down and rolled into a corner, or under one of the kitchen cupboards, but there was no sign of the missing ring.

Beginning to be seriously worried, she went into the lounge, where Spike was sprawled in an easy chair reading the morning paper.

'You haven't seen my ring anywhere, have you?' she asked.

'No. Why? You haven't lost it, I hope.'

'So do I!' Molly said with feeling. 'I can't find it, though. I was sure I left it in the kitchen, but it's not there now.'

'It's in with your other jewellery, I expect. You had a fair bit to drink last night. You put it away and forgot you'd done it.'

'It's not with my other jewellery. I've looked. The last thing I remember is taking it off to wash up the supper things. I just don't know where it is, Daniel.'

She went to the chair she'd been sitting in last night, running her hand down between the cushion and the frame, but without much hope. She couldn't imagine the ring had simply fallen off – it fitted her finger perfectly.

'I don't suppose that son of yours knows anything about it?' Spike said.

'David? Why ever would he?'

The newspaper crackled as Spike laid it in his lap.

'I don't know. I'm just saying. And his name's Jake now, not David.'

Molly bristled. 'Are you implying what I think you are?'

Spike huffed breath over his top lip. 'I don't know what to think about him, Molly. I know you're over the moon at finding him again, and I was pleased too. After feeling so darned guilty all these years, of course I was. But there's something about him that's not quite right.'

Molly straightened, one hand still down the side of the chair.

'That's an awful thing to say! And do keep your voice down – he might hear you.'

'He won't. He's upstairs.'

Jake had indeed gone to his room to change his shirt; he was going to go into town to take a look around, see some of the sights of Bath. Molly had offered to go with him, but he'd said he quite fancied pootling round on his own, and she hadn't pressed him. The last thing she wanted was for him to feel stifled by her.

'But he might be down at any minute,' she warned.

'I might be wrong – I hope for your sake I am.' Spike folded his newspaper and laid it down beside his chair. 'Come on, I'll help you look. It would be a great relief to me to find the darned thing – and not just because it cost me a small fortune. I shouldn't like to think we had a thief under our roof.'

No amount of searching turned up the missing ring, and Jake, when he came down, dressed for town, said he hadn't seen it either.

'It's a mystery,' Molly said, giving up the hunt at last. 'I expect it will turn up in the last place you'd expect.'

Spike said nothing – he didn't need to. His face was saying it all. And little as she wanted to think that Jake was capable of stealing from her, Molly was beginning to harbour unpleasant doubts herself, and acknowledging that in her heart of hearts she agreed with Daniel, at least in part. There was something about Jake she didn't like either.

In her first delight at being reunited with her long-lost son, she'd tried to push her misgivings aside. But still they hovered on the edges of her consciousness, an insidious discomfort with him that she couldn't quite identify. What was it? She didn't know, and she didn't like that she was experiencing these negative feelings. He was her son. The lost baby she'd longed for. She'd known the circumstances of his dreadful upbringing would have left their mark on him, and had been prepared to accept that and try to make amends. But still she couldn't quite escape a feeling of dismay, no matter how hard she tried.

There was something about him that she found almost repulsive, though she couldn't quite bring herself to admit as much, and neither could she quite dispel a pervasive unease that might almost have been disappointment. In some almost unidentifiable way she didn't feel what she'd expected to feel, and he wasn't as she'd hoped he'd be, though she didn't want to admit it, even to herself.

He wouldn't steal from her, though, would he? Of course not! It was unthinkable!

But the unpleasant suspicion, once aroused, refused to completely go away.

Molly was not the only one entertaining negative emotions towards Jake.

'Why don't you go to Bath and see him and Molly, forget all this for a bit,' Annie suggested. 'There's nothing you can do here, and I'll be perfectly all right.'

But she looked far from all right: there were great dark circles under her eyes as if she had not slept, her hands were trembling and she kept listening for the knock at the door that would announce the arrival of Dr Blackmore.

'I'm not leaving you and Kitty with all this hanging over you,' Lucy said decisively. 'I want to be here when the doctor comes.'

But somehow, important as she felt it was to be there to support her mother at this terribly anxious time, it was not the only thing stopping her from going to Bath. For some reason she couldn't quite explain, Lucy didn't want to see Jake.

Or perhaps she could explain it. Since coming home, the subtle change in her feelings for Jake had intensified. In some strange way he seemed almost unreal to her, as unreal as her glamorous London life seemed now that she was back in the old

461

familiar surroundings. Neither could she quite forget the things Doris had said. She had enormous respect for Doris, who'd had nothing to gain from pointing out to Lucy what she saw as the flaws in Jake's character and the enormous coincidence of him having come to the rescue of his long-lost mother's niece. The shadow of doubt made her uncomfortable, and where once the element of danger just below the surface had intoxicated her, now it only seemed to contribute to her misgivings. Had that intoxication taken over her senses, blinded her to the person Jake really was?

No, perversely, it was Joe she wanted to see. If she thought about it logically, she knew there was nothing he, or any-one, could do about the terrible situation Kitty had landed herself in, but she still yearned for his calming presence, his pragmatic words. And she wished too that she could make things right with him; she hated the gulf that yawned between them, especially now when she needed him more than she ever had.

'I think what I will do is go and see Joe,' she said.

Annie looked surprised.

'He'll be at work.'

'The shop shuts at one. I could catch him then. I just want to know if he's had any more thoughts about . . .' She broke off, unable to put into words the terrible dread that was hanging over her that Kitty might be tried for murder. 'And the doctor won't come then, will he? He'll be having his own dinner.'

'I hope he'll be here before that,' Annie said. 'Not knowing what's going to happen – that's the worst part.'

Lucy was not sure she agreed with her. If Dr Blackmore too refused to issue a death certificate and called for a post-mortem, things would get much, much worse. But it was true, the waiting was horrible.

By a quarter to one the doctor had still not arrived, and Lucy got her coat.

'I'm going then, Mam. I'll make sure to be back by two.'

'What about your dinner?'

'I'm not hungry,' Lucy said. She hadn't been able to manage any breakfast, and she was sure it would be the same now. Her stomach revolted at the very thought of food.

'I'm not either,' Annie admitted. 'I must take something up for Kitty, though, even if it's only a bowl of soup or a milky drink.'

Kitty had remained in bed this morning, weak and exhausted by all the upset of the previous day.

Lucy set out at a smart trot and managed to reach the chemist's shop just as Joe was turning the sign to 'Closed'. As he saw her through the glass, his expression became one of alarm and he quickly opened the door.

'Has something happened?'

'No. The doctor still hasn't been. I just wanted to talk to you.'

'Oh, right.' His tone was wary, but at least he didn't shut the door in her face. 'You'd better come in.'

She followed him through the shop and up the stairs to his apartment. He'd made some changes, she noticed – a new armchair had replaced the old and shabby one, and there was a clean chenille cloth on the table covering the scorch marks. She couldn't help comparing the bright and cosy space with the squalor of Jake's attic room. What was more, she was suddenly remembering the times they'd spent here together, the closeness and the kisses, and her heart ached for the precious, innocent love they had shared.

'I'm sorry if I'm disturbing your dinner hour.' She felt shy and awkward now that she was here. 'Please go on and eat.'

'I'm not sure I want anything.' But he got a loaf from the bread bin anyway and began sawing off a slice. 'What about you?'

Lucy shook her head. 'No thank you.'

'You've got to eat.' He fetched the cheese in its covered china dish from the cupboard.

'I can't. I'm too worried. What's going to happen, Joe? Do you think Kitty is going to be tried for murder?'

He cut a chunk of cheese with a savage thrust.

'I'll see to it that she's not.'

'How can you do that? There's nothing you or anyone else can do, is there? If there's a post-mortem and an inquest, it's bound to all come out.'

Joe speared the chunk of cheese on the prong of the cheese knife.

'I'm going to say it was me.'

He hadn't meant to tell her, or anyone, what he planned, but the words were out before he could stop them.

'You *what*?' Lucy was gazing at him, startled and incredulous.

'I'm going to tell them I was the one who gave Algernon an overdose of arrhythmic medication.' Joe looked almost embarrassed now, as if he'd been caught doing something he shouldn't.

'Joe, you can't!' Lucy exclaimed, horrified.

'Well that's what I'm going to do. I've made up my mind,' he said, still a little sheepish, but also stubborn.

'But why? You'd be putting a noose round your own neck!'

'I owe your mam everything,' Joe said with feeling. 'Kitty would never stand up to a trial – the stress of it would kill her. I'm not going to let it happen.'

'She'd never let you take the blame. And neither would Mam, come to that. She'd say it was her that did it before she'd let you hang for something you didn't do.'

Joe shrugged. 'We'll just have to wait and see who they believe, won't we? I'm the one with access to drugs, after all.'

'And Kitty and Mam are the ones with motive. Algernon has been ill-treating Mam for years, and I think that recently he's been abusing Kitty. You heard what she said. That would count as a defence, wouldn't it? Especially if I were to tell them what he did to me . . .'

She broke off, realising what she'd said, but somehow it no longer mattered. In the past she'd been too ashamed to tell another living soul what Algernon had done to her; now the only thing of any importance was to show the world what an animal he had been so that Kitty and Annie would be believed and, hopefully, shown leniency.

Joe was looking at her narrowly, gripping the cheese knife so hard that his knuckles turned white.

'What did he do to you?'

Lucy swallowed hard. She didn't want to remember, let alone talk about it. But she'd gone this far, she couldn't stop now. And if the worst happened, it wouldn't be just Joe to whom she had to tell her awful story. It would be a courtroom full of people, and a whole world outside.

'He raped me.' She felt the hard rim of the seat of one of the dining chairs behind her knees and sat down, twisting her hands together in her lap. 'I hope to goodness things didn't go that far with Kitty, but I'm certain he was molesting her.'

'He raped you!' Joe repeated. For the moment he was more dazed than angry; that would come later.

'Yes.' Haltingly, Lucy told him everything, and saw his face grow darker with every word she spoke.

'It's the reason I left in such a hurry,' she finished. 'I couldn't be under the same roof as him for a moment longer. Besides, I needed something to aim for, something to help me forget what had happened. And it has, really, until now . . .'

'Why didn't you tell someone?' Joe demanded. 'Why didn't you tell *me*?'

'I couldn't. I just couldn't. I was too ashamed.'

'You had nothing to be ashamed about. That bloody bastard . . . If I'd known, I'd have wrung his bloody neck!'

'You see? That's another reason I couldn't tell you. I didn't want to cause trouble. I never thought then that he'd do anything like that to Kitty – when he did it to me he seemed more . . . angry than anything. As if he hated he, wanted to punish me. But he was always so fond of Kitty. He was different with her, wasn't he?'

'He was, yes. But God alone knows what goes on inside the head of a man like that.'

'I know. I should have known . . . I feel as though this is all my fault. If I'd been here . . .'

Joe was shaking his head. 'You're not to blame, Lucy. For any of it. I just wish you'd told me.'

'I couldn't. I just couldn't. I can't believe I've told you now.'

'I'm very glad you have. At least now I know the reason why you went off like you did. I thought . . .'

'I know, and I'm sorry. But it wasn't just that I couldn't tell you, Joe. I couldn't be with you either. Not after what happened. All I wanted was a fresh start, somewhere I knew nobody and nobody knew me.'

'Well, you got what you wanted.' The bitterness was back in Joe's voice. He flicked the chunk of cheese off the point of the knife with a savage movement and cut another, though he hadn't eaten the first. It was as though he was imagining he was sticking the knife into Algernon, Lucy thought – or even, perhaps, her.

'I ought to be going,' she said. 'I want to be back in good time in case the doctor comes. When he does, Mam will need me.'

'OK.' He had turned cold again, off-hand, almost. Though he now understood the reason for her hasty departure, the hurt remained, made worse, perhaps, by knowing that she'd shut him out, been unable to confide in him.

Lucy hesitated, reluctant to leave him like this and wishing with all her heart that she could turn the clock back and do things differently. Though a year ago she'd thought her only option was to make a new life for herself, she could see now that in reality all she had been doing was running away when she should have stayed and been brave enough to tell the truth.

What a fool she'd been! She'd hurt the people she loved the most – and maybe the truth would have saved her mother from another year of Algernon's cruelty and her sister from his evil perversions. At least she would have been here for them, not hiding away in an unreal world. As for Joe . . .

Joe was the strongest, kindest, most honourable man she had ever known. She could scarcely believe he was willing to risk his reputation, even his life, for Kitty's sake, and yet at the same time she knew it was Joe all over. They'd never allow him to do it, of course, but that didn't alter the fact that he was willing to take responsibility for their sake. And this was the man she'd tried to forget by deluding herself that she was falling in love with Jake.

Jake! Why, he wasn't fit to lick the dirt off Joe's boots! The crazy fever he'd aroused in her was cold and clammy on her heart now, as cooling sweat lies on the skin when the crisis is past. How could she ever have believed she loved him? But that had been her way of excusing to herself her wanton behaviour, she supposed.

She'd been wrong, so wrong, but now the scales had fallen from her eyes. It was Joe she loved, had always loved. It was Joe, and the closeness they had once shared, that she wanted, more than anything else in the world. But she had thrown it all away and now it was too late.

Even if he could ever forgive her for the way she'd treated him, which seemed doubtful, she was beginning to be horribly certain she was pregnant, and she couldn't, wouldn't, saddle him with another man's baby.

Feeling empty, wrung dry, frightened for her own future and even more frightened for Kitty, she set out to walk home.

Dr Horace Blackmore drove his pony and trap up High Compton's main street and made the right turn into the road where the Pierce home was situated. The pony moved at a slow pace – like him, she was old and tired, he thought – but he was in no mood to hurry. This was, in fact, a call he was dreading. He'd delayed making it as long as he could, but now he could put it off no longer. One of his patients was lying dead and he owed it to him and his family, if not to the law, to do something about it without further delay. But even now he had not entirely made up his mind what that something should be.

He'd been in turmoil ever since Dr Mackay had come to see him. He'd come home after visiting his daughter in a mellow mood – the few days' rest had left him feeling refreshed, and he had more or less decided he would retire very soon and move to be near her. And then Mackay had come knocking on his door and given him more cause for worry than he'd faced in years. Bad enough that Algernon Pierce's heart should have given out when he was not on hand to attend him; far, far worse than he could ever have imagined was the interpretation Mackay was putting on it.

At first he'd been scornful almost. Though Mackay seemed a decent enough chap, he was young, keen and full of modern ideas, which, after more than thirty years in general practice, Horace Blackmore had little time for. They always wanted to make their mark, these young doctors, were always on the lookout for something out of the ordinary that they could try out their new-fangled treatments on. And, no doubt, eager to show the old brigade that they had had their day.

'It was his heart, not a doubt of it,' he'd said, hoping that would be an end to the matter. But Mackay hadn't given up so easily, and as he went into detail, Horace had begun to feel uneasy.

When he'd examined Algernon a few days before his death, it had never crossed his mind for one moment that there might be a sinister explanation for his sudden decline. But now, little as he wanted to believe it, he had to admit there was reason in Mackay's argument. The symptoms could indeed have been due to digitalis poisoning; in fact, given that Algernon had never previously shown any signs of suffering from heart trouble, it was all too plausible. And there had been ample medication in the house to constitute a fatal overdose – he knew, he'd prescribed it himself in ever larger quantities to the ailing Kitty.

He suspected, too, that there was a dark side to Algernon. He'd seen Annie with too many bruises and other injuries, and thought that either she was more accident-prone than any woman he knew or the injuries were not due to accident at all. Perhaps Annie had finally had enough of his beatings and decided to do something about it, and in his heart of hearts he could not find it in him to blame her. But the fact remained – he'd been negligent. If Algernon had indeed died of digitalis poisoning, then he'd failed to spot it when he'd visited, and indeed had only exacerbated matters by prescribing another heart medicine. The two would have reacted together and hastened Algernon's death. Put at its most blunt, by making out that prescription, it was in fact he, Horace Blackmore, who had killed Algernon Pierce.

With a heavy heart, Horace pulled on the reins and brought the pony to a stop outside the Pierces' gate. The law was the law and by rights he should do as Mackay had suggested and refer the matter to the coroner. On the other hand, he didn't want to end his distinguished career with a blot like this on his copybook. He wanted to be remembered as a good doctor, a doctor who could always be relied upon, and he thought he had been. But this . . . People would quickly forget all the times they'd had cause to be grateful to him for his diagnostic skills and his care. He would be forever the doctor who had contributed to the death of one of his patients because he hadn't spotted what was going on. 'He was past it,' folk would say. 'Should have retired years ago.' And so, perhaps, he should. Would a younger version of his self have failed in this way? He didn't think so. And Mackay, damn him, had seen what he had missed.

And been so magnanimous about it!

'You must do whatever you think fit,' he had said. 'I'm not going to call your judgement into question – you know the family better than I do, and everything I've said will remain between the two of us. I just thought I should explain why I, personally, didn't feel able to issue a death certificate.'

It was open to him, then, to draw a cloak over the whole unfortunate episode, and no one would ever know he'd failed in his duty. Except for Dr Mackay. And himself. Whether he answered for it or not, Horace Blackmore didn't think he would ever forgive himself, for what he had failed in and for what he was about to do. Certainly he would never forget.

Chapter Thirty-Four

'Thank God! Oh, thank God!'

Annie took the piece of paper from Lucy, clutching it to her breast as if it were a promissory note for a fortune, and to her, of course, it was worth far more than that. No money on earth would be enough to compensate for the torment this death certificate was saving her, or for the almost certain loss of her beloved daughter.

'Thank God!' she said again, all other words failing her.

She'd been upstairs, asleep, when the doctor had finally come. Lucy had insisted she should try to get some rest, for she'd scarcely slept the last couple of nights, and said she'd call her if she was needed. She'd intended to just close her eyes so she would hear the knock at the door when it came, but exhaustion must have overtaken her. She'd heard nothing, been aware of nothing, until she'd come to see Lucy standing at the end of the bed with that all-important piece of paper in her hands.

'Thank God!'

'It's all right, Mam, I think he's heard you.' Lucy, too, was sufficiently relieved to be able to joke a little, though in her heart she was echoing her mother and the stress of the last half-hour was making her tense and shaky.

She'd been so terrified that Dr Blackmore was going to refuse the death certificate; knowing what she did, it had seemed inevitable that he would agree with Dr Mackay that the condition that had caused Algernon's death had not been natural.

And as if that had not been bad enough, she'd been forced to accompany the doctor into the front room, where Algernon had been laid out on the floor, covered by a clean white sheet and with a penny holding each eye closed.

She should, she supposed, have been glad that he could no longer hurt her, and seeing him lying there dead should have been a blessed relief. Instead she had felt nothing but fear and revulsion. In death Algernon still terrified her: the waxy face looked to her like an evil gargoyle; the hands, gnarled and white as marble, folded across his chest as if in prayer, were the same hands that had invaded her body; even his feet, sticking straight up under the covering sheet, were grotesque. She'd shivered, drawing the curtains to let in enough light for the doctor to see by, and closed her eyes as she turned around to shut out the horrible sight. Then, steeling herself, she'd opened them again. She would never, she hoped, have to see him again. This was her chance to make sure that the monster her mother had married was really dead. But still, even from beyond the grave, he seemed to be mocking her, and the smell in the room, faintly sweet, but mostly the scent of a vase of chrysanthemums Annie had placed on the desk, reminded her horribly of the smell of the chapel the night he had attacked her. She pressed her hands to her mouth as nausea rose in her throat and felt Dr Blackmore touch her arm.

'It's all right, my dear. He's gone. There's nothing to be afraid of.'

'He was a wicked, wicked man,' Lucy said before she could stop herself. 'He pretended to be so pious, but he was evil through and through. You'd never believe the things he was capable of. The things he did.'

A strange expression had come over Dr Blackmore's face then. Had she not known better, she might have thought it was relief. His brow, which had been deeply furrowed, seemed to clear, then he nodded, and patted her arm.

'I've seen enough. You can draw the curtains again and we'll leave him in peace.'

Lucy looked at him sharply, then did as he asked, hardly daring to hope that this nightmare was over. They'd returned to the living room, and even as he wrote out the death certificate, she was terrified he might change his mind. But he had not. She saw him to the door and stood taking in deep breaths of the cool, clear air as she listened to the gentle clip-clop of his pony's hooves going away, back in the direction of High Compton. Then and only then did she go upstairs to wake her mother and tell her and Kitty the good news.

Dr Blackmore was not the only visitor that afternoon. An hour or so later, Lucy answered the door yet again to find a young man she had never seen before standing on the doorstep. He was slightly built, with dark hair springing from a high forehead, and his jacket was open at the neck revealing a white clerical collar.

He looked a little taken aback to see Lucy.

'I'm sorry . . . I think I must have the wrong house.'

'No, I don't think so. You're looking for Mrs Pierce, I expect?'

'I am, yes. But . . .'

'I'm her daughter. Lucy. I live in London now, but I've come home to do what I can.'

'Ah, yes. I've only been here a short time – weeks, in fact.

I should introduce myself. I'm the Reverend Callow. I've taken over from Reverend Boody, who's moved on to a new ministry. How is your mother bearing up at this sad time?'

Lucy didn't quite know how to answer him. She could scarcely tell him her mother felt nothing but relief at Algernon's death, albeit the manner of it had caused her a great deal of anguish over the last twenty-four hours.

'She's in the living room,' she said instead, ushering him in. 'And Kitty is there too. You know Kitty, I expect.'

'I do.' Was it her imagination, or did the back of his neck turn slightly pink as he said it?

She leaned past him, pushing open the door.

'You've got a visitor, Mam.'

'Oh – Reverend! How good of you to come.' She didn't look overly pleased, though; Lucy suspected she had a healthy dislike of anyone connected with the chapel that Algernon had devoted his life to.

Kitty, on the other hand, couldn't have looked more delighted. She sat up straight against the couch pillows, smiling more widely than Lucy had ever seen her.

There were condolences, there were questions, there were prayers, and there was discussion about the funeral. The Reverend Callow seemed surprised that the undertaker had not yet begun making arrangements, but Annie explained that Dr Blackmore had been away, and that it was only an hour or so earlier that he had issued the death certificate. At that the reverend offered to go and speak to the undertaker himself; he could kill two birds with one stone since they could decide on a day for the funeral while he was there – unless Annie had any objection. Annie said that no, she would just like it to be as soon as possible. And all the while Lucy could not help but notice that Kitty never took her eyes off the young minister, while he made a point of including her in the discussion, and was definitely turning a little pink when he spoke to her. Kitty, of course, was looking suitably solemn, as befitted a bereaved daughter, but Lucy could see there was a smile hiding behind her eyes just waiting to burst forth.

How wonderful it would be if Kitty actually found someone to love! she thought. And who better than a man of the church – just as long as he didn't have the same disgusting proclivities as Algernon. But just because Algernon had used his religious fervour as a cloak for his dark and twisted desires didn't mean that everyone who was a devout chapel-goer was the same. And certainly this young man could scarcely have looked more wholesome, the last person to entertain evil thoughts.

'You like him, don't you, Kitty?' she couldn't resist remarking when he had gone at last, and Kitty had blushed.

'Does it show?'

'Well I could tell, certainly, but I am your sister,' Lucy said. 'And judging by the way he was looking at you, I should think he'd be nothing if not pleased if he did notice.'

Kitty giggled – actually giggled – and Lucy turned away, smiling. But the thought struck her that it seemed their roles were about to be reversed. Kitty might well have a sweetheart before the year was out, while she . . .

She couldn't go back to Jake, she knew that now, even if she was pregnant with his baby. But Joe was lost to her. The future stretched ahead, bleak and daunting. She wouldn't think of that for the moment, Lucy decided. She would simply revel in the fact that Algernon was dead and thankfully no one, not Kitty, nor Annie, nor Joe, was going to be blamed for it.

She no longer went to chapel, and it had never meant very much to her, but at that moment Lucy echoed the words her mother had repeated over and over like a mantra. 'Thank God!'

If he existed at all, he had, it seemed, been looking after all those she loved the best. And for that she was truly grateful.

Night-time. The second night in her old bed, in her old room. The first night Lucy had slept well, tired out from the long journey from London, comforted by the familiar surroundings. All her things were still there, just as she had left them, even Victoria in her bed in the drawer of the tallboy.

'You've been very neglected these last years, haven't you, Victoria?' she had said, smoothing down the satin skirts, now yellowed a little with age, and she'd taken her out and propped her on the windowsill where she could see her.

Daddy had seemed to be there too, stroking her forehead until she fell asleep. But tonight . . . tonight, thoughts of all that had happened that day, and of her own predicament, chased one another round inside her head, and sleep refused to come.

And then she was drifting, not quite asleep and not quite awake. Algernon was there, waxy and cold as an effigy carved out of marble. She felt his hands on her body, thrust them away, and the scene mutated so she was no longer in the chapel, with its suffocating smell of damp and dust and chrysanthemums, but in the open air, a Bermondsey street, and the hands were the hands of the man who had attacked her. Greedy hands, forcing her back against the rough stone of the warehouse. Panic engulfed her and she struggled, trying to push the man away. His face was close to hers, and at first he looked like a crazed and sneering Algernon, but then that too mutated into the face of her unknown attacker, and she could see it clearly, more clearly than she had done since that night.

She screamed, and the sound of it brought her abruptly back to full consciousness. For a moment she lay as if paralysed, tears rolling down her cheeks, her body bathed in perspiration. Her attacker's face was still there before her eyes, ugly, feral almost, but also oddly familiar. And suddenly Lucy realised why.

She'd seen that face on two occasions since the attack and yet not realised it was one and the same man, though she had been puzzled as she had felt she recognised him. The first time had been at the bare-knuckle contest – the man who had been in Jake's corner. The second time was when she passed him on the stairs leading to Jake's attic room. How could she not have realised it before? But as the implications became clear, Lucy turned cold beneath the sheets.

Jake had not only known her attacker, it would seem they were friends. And that could mean only one thing – Doris had been right when she'd said it was all too much of a coincidence. Lucy had been singled out deliberately, and Jake had been on hand to rescue her and worm his way into her confidence. Unless she had taken leave of her senses, there was only one explanation.

Jake had planned the whole thing.

If sleep had been elusive before, Lucy knew that now it would be impossible. She pushed back the covers and got out of bed. The chill night air made her shiver, and her nightgown, wet with sweat, felt clammy on her shoulders and back. But she didn't want to get back into bed; she was too afraid of the images that lurked there, terrifying and all too real. Her head was buzzing with the realisation that Jake must have set up the attack on her as a way of getting to Molly. As Doris had suggested, he'd seen her name on a billboard and realised she must be related to Belle Dorne, his mother. Perhaps he'd even thought she was Belle's daughter – his sister. She shivered again, this time with revulsion. How could he have made love to her if he'd thought that? But no, of course he'd known that wasn't so before things had gone that far between them, and in any case, he'd been reluctant in the beginning to so much as kiss her – or had that been just another ploy to gain her trust?

Lucy pulled the blanket of knitted squares from the bed and wrapped it around herself. Then, quietly, so as not to disturb the rest of the house, she went downstairs, hurrying past the door to the front room even though it was firmly closed, and into the kitchen. It was warmer here; though the fire had gone out in the living room grate, some of the heat lingered. Lucy fetched a jug of milk from the pantry and set some to heat on the hob, all the while thinking about Jake and how they had met. He must have followed her from the theatre, she supposed. How many times had he done that without her knowing it before he'd been confident of her routine? That thought, too, was chilling, that she could have been so blissfully unaware of someone dogging her footsteps. Then he'd persuaded a couple of his shady pals to pretend to attack her so that he could play the knight in shining armour and gain her gratitude and her confidence.

Not that she imagined they would have taken much persuading. They seemed to have taken perverse pleasure in terrifying her. How could Jake have been a party to that? How could he have allowed her to be frightened half to death for his own ends? And really, why had it been necessary? Why hadn't he simply approached her outside the theatre, told her who he was and asked where he might find Molly? Instead he'd played her for a fool, inveigling her into smoothing his path for him.

If he could be so sly and conniving, Doris's other accusations seemed all the more believable too. A man like that might well not be above stealing anything he could get his hands on, or kicking a backward boy who idolised him when he thought no one was looking.

And this was the same man she'd thought she'd fallen in love with – and who was the father of the baby she was now almost sure she was carrying. What despicable traits might her child inherit from him? It didn't bear thinking about.

Lucy sipped her hot drink and shuddered, wondering suddenly where Jake's evil ways had come from. Not from Molly, certainly, and although he'd had a terrible start in life, that didn't altogether excuse or explain his lying, stealing and casual cruelty now that he was a grown man. More likely he'd inherited them from his father, along with his swarthy dark looks that were so unlike Molly's and the rest of the fair-skinned Day family. Certainly from what Molly had told her, his father had been a cheat and a liar too, deceiving his wife and leading Molly on before abandoning her.

But Lucy had imagined Molly's lover as a weak-chinned aristocrat, pale and foppish, not a man with almost Mediterranean looks, and certainly in no way the dangerous, ruthless character that was Jake. Unless . . .

The thought struck her like a lightning bolt from a heavy dark sky. Suppose Jake was not really Molly's lost son at all? Suppose he was a chancer who had somehow happened upon her tragic story? It was certainly true that David had been abandoned by his adoptive parents and sent to a baby farm; Spike had confirmed that. It was also quite likely that he'd ended up in an orphanage. Could it be that Jake had met him there, learned of his illustrious mother, and then, when he had seen the name 'Dorne' on the theatre billboard, decided to pretend to be him in order to gain all the advantages that would come from being Molly's son? Was it possible that all unknowing Lucy had introduced a cuckoo into the nest?

Around and around went the confusing thoughts until Lucy's head ached with them. Nothing made any sense. But on one thing she was determined. Somehow she had to discover once and for all whether Jake really was Molly's son, or whether Molly too was being duped. It would break her heart if she was, but Lucy couldn't see that she could possibly go on letting Jake take advantage of her if he was an imposter. Yet how could she confirm his identity one way or the other? And how would she ever be able to right the terrible wrong she had been party to?

Chapter Thirty-Five

Good as his word, the Reverend Callow had visited the local undertaker, told him that a death certificate had now been issued, and asked him to call as soon as possible.

Seward Moody worked out of a poky office in the yard of a local building firm and his coffins were made in their carpenters' shop. He was a man who looked to have been born to the part, tall, thin, with a cadaverous face and a permanently mournful expression. No one in the town had ever seen him wearing anything other than his funereal black, the trousers and jacket sleeves both a little too short for his long legs and arms, exposing bony ankles and wrists, though the top hat that completed the outfit came out only when he walked at a suitably respectful pace in front of the horse-drawn hearse on the day of the burial. But for all that he was both a figure of fun and a man to be avoided, Seward was efficient and reliable. The following morning at around ten he arrived at the house to take measurements and begin making arrangements.

'It would be advisable to proceed without delay, given the length of time since the deceased departed,' he opined, sitting at the dining room table with a notepad to hand and a cup of tea at his elbow. 'It's fortunate the weather is still chilly for the time of year, but it could suddenly turn warmer. I suggested to the minister that we should be looking at two or three days, and he didn't seem to think there would be any problem with that. Do you concur?'

Annie nodded her agreement; it couldn't come soon enough for her, and she felt sure that the powers-that-be at the chapel would be accommodating given Algernon's devotion.

'Now – the coffin. You'd like that to be of the finest dark oak, I expect.'

Annie nodded again. She'd checked Algernon's finances and discovered he had a goodly sum in savings, far more than she had expected, but then he always had been parsimonious. Now, although it seemed a terrible waste of money, she thought it only right that some of it should be spent on giving him a funeral in keeping with his standing in the community. But she couldn't help a pang of resentment remembering the cheap coffin, identical to the other eleven, that had been John's last resting place.

Seward made a note.

'And the horse-drawn hearse?'

'Yes.'

'I presume I can leave it with you to talk to the Reverend Callow with regard to the finer points of the service?'

'Yes.' Annie glanced at Kitty and saw that faint flush rising in her cheeks as it always did at any mention of the new minister.

After settling the remaining details, Seward tucked his notepad into his small black attaché case, finished his tea, which must have gone cold by now, and rose.

'Once again, may I say how sorry I am for your loss. And rest assured, I shall set things in motion right away.'

The following afternoon he was back with the coffin, a handsome affair that the carpenters had worked late to finish. He had brought Cissie Barker with him, and the two of them went into the front room to 'attend to the deceased', as he put it. He must also have spoken to the Reverend Callow, for shortly afterwards the clergyman arrived to discuss the details of the funeral service. When Seward and Cissie had left, he offered to pray over Algernon with the family.

Lucy shrank inwardly, but couldn't see how she could avoid it. She was feeling horribly sick, and a pain that she hoped desperately might mean that her period was about to start was niggling in the pit of her stomach. Steeling herself, she followed the others into the front room.

The coffin of dark oak was supported by a trestle that Seward had brought with him. It was lined with ivory silk, and Algernon, dressed by Cissie in a gown also made from ivory silk, lay with his head resting on a matching pillow, his arms folded across his chest as if in prayer. His fingernails had grown, she noticed; they looked like claws against those marble hands.

She folded her own hands over her aching stomach, and as the Reverend Callow's solemn tones fell into the unnatural stillness of the room, she silently uttered a prayer of her own.

Dear God, help me to do the right thing.

Then simply: *Dear God, please help me!*

But in her heart of hearts she could not believe her prayer would be answered.

Spike sat in the lounge bar of his favourite hostelry, frowning into a large whisky and fretting over the decision he had to make.

It was just as he'd feared – Jake had been responsible for the disappearance of Molly's ring.

Just why he'd been so sure of it he couldn't explain, beyond that almost from the first he'd taken against Jake. He'd done his best to like him, for Molly's sake, had even let him drive his precious motor car, but the antipathy remained, growing stronger with each day that passed. Perhaps it was a sixth sense he'd developed growing up in the East End of London; perhaps it was the way Jake fawned over Molly but could be caught with a scowl and a calculating expression on his handsome face when he thought no one was observing him. But whatever it was, Spike distrusted him, and when the ring had gone missing, he'd decided to go into town and trawl the pawn shops. He'd thought it was strange that Jake should have wanted to explore Bath alone the very day after the ring had disappeared – he didn't strike Spike as the sort who'd want to take a tour of the Roman Baths or the Pump Room. And his suspicions had proved to be correct. He'd seen the ring in the window of the second shop he went to, and had gone in and purchased it – severely undervalued given the not inconsiderable sum he'd paid for it in the first place. Then he'd questioned the pawnbroker, who had been cagey at first but had eventually supplied a description of the man he'd bought it from. It fitted Jake to a T.

The discovery that he'd been right gave Spike no pleasure, and he'd gone into the bar to have a drink and think things over before going home.

The prospect of telling Molly was not one he relished. She'd fly to Jake's defence without a doubt, and come up with all kinds of excuses for what he'd done. But for all that she'd surely know in her heart of hearts that her son was not the man she'd thought him to be and be dreadfully upset. If he could spare her that, he would, perhaps by pretending he'd found the ring somewhere in the house. But if he went down that route, he would have to confront Jake, tell him in no uncertain terms that his behaviour was totally unacceptable and threaten to call the police should anything of the kind happen again.

The trouble was that Spike was not a confrontational man.

He liked peace and harmony – 'anything for a quiet life', as Molly sometimes teased him – and he shrank from the thought of the encounter. Jake, he suspected, had a nasty temper if roused, and an accusation of theft was sure to cut to the quick. What was more, Spike had no real proof that the ring had been stolen from the house and not lost somewhere else entirely, nor that Jake had been the one who had taken it to the pawnshop. Short of dragging him back there – which wasn't going to happen – and getting the uncle to identify him, everything was conjecture.

By the time he'd downed his second large drink, Spike had talked himself into doing nothing for the moment. He'd keep an eye on Jake, make sure he wasn't left alone in the house, and perhaps Molly would come to see the light without any interference from him. Jake couldn't stay forever. He'd have to go back to London and his life there, whatever that was, and with any luck this would all fizzle out like a damp squib on a wet Guy Fawkes Night.

Spike went to the bar and called for another drink, just for good measure. There wasn't much that a nip or two of good Scotch whisky couldn't settle, he thought.

When Spike arrived home, in a fairly mellow mood now, Molly had some news. Annie had telephoned, calling from the Latchams', to let them know that Algernon's funeral had been arranged for the day after tomorrow.

'I'd like to go to show some support for Annie,' she said. 'You'll drive me, won't you?'

'Course I will.' But all his misgivings were surfacing through the rosy haze of alcohol. He didn't like the thought of Jake being left alone in the house whilst they were gone.

'You'd better come too, my son,' he told him.

485

Jake grimaced. 'I didn't even know the man.'

'That was your good fortune,' Molly said. 'But we won't be going for him, we'll be there for the family. And I'm sure Lucy would like to see you. Her mother and sister know all about you now – Lucy's told them – and I expect they will be anxious to meet you.'

Jake still looked reluctant, but the mention of Lucy had given Spike an idea.

'She's got to get back to work sometime. Bernie's champing at the bit with her gone so long. I'll get hold of him, tell him to sort out her bookings. She can ride back with us, and catch a train to London. You could go with her, Jake. Make sure she gets back safely.'

'I'm in no hurry,' Jake said.

Spike swallowed the desire to tell him he was no longer welcome in his home.

'You don't seem in any hurry to see Lucy either,' he said instead. 'She's got to get back to London if you haven't. The funeral might be your last chance to see her for a while.'

'In any case, she could do with your support,' Molly said. 'This isn't going to be easy for her.'

Jake shrugged. 'All right, I'll come if you think I should. It's just that I don't care much for funerals.'

'I don't think any of us do,' Molly said. 'But that's neither here nor there.'

'I've got to go – why shouldn't you?' Spike added maliciously.

Molly's son had gone down another rung in his estimation. He didn't seem in the least caring towards Lucy. She deserved better – and so did Molly. But a sweetheart would be a great deal easier to get rid of than a son, and he had a nasty feeling that in that regard Jake was going to prove something of a limpet.

* * *

The funeral was scheduled for two in the afternoon. At one thirty precisely, the hearse drew up outside the gate.

Lucy, who had been watching for it from the bedroom window, felt her stomach contract. Some people thought the gleaming carriage and the horses with their black feathered plumes the most wonderful sight, but she was only turned cold by it.

'They're here,' she called, hurrying downstairs.

Annie, already wearing her Sunday-best black coat and hat, opened the front door and Lucy went into the living room – she didn't want to see the coffin carried out of the house. Joe and Kitty were there, Kitty in dark brown velvet, the closest thing she had to the obligatory black, and Joe wearing a black tie and armband. His eyes met hers and narrowed slightly, a signal of solidarity that warmed her heart. He'd been behaving almost normally ever since he'd arrived earlier this morning, as if he knew how much she was dreading this and had put his hurt feelings to one side so as to give her what support and comfort he could.

When the coffin had been loaded on to the hearse, they filed out to stand awkwardly behind it, Lucy and Kitty on either side of Annie, Joe beside Lucy, and as it moved away, he took her hand. A few people had come to their gates to watch the cortège pass by, and as it turned into the high street, women with shopping baskets stopped and bowed their heads respectfully and men doffed their caps. But Lucy scarcely noticed them. Her world had shrunk so that she was aware only of Algernon's coffin, glimpsed between the black velvet curtains at the rear of the hearse, the steady clip-clop of the horses' hooves, and Joe's hand squeezing hers. Most of all Joe's hand. It might have been her heart he was squeezing.

A small knot of onlookers had gathered on the pavement opposite the chapel. Lucy recognised a few faces, but as the hearse came to a halt, she glanced to her right, and her heart came into her mouth. Waiting beside the chapel porch were Molly, Spike – and Jake. What was he doing here? She hadn't expected to have to face him until this evening. It had been arranged that she would go back to Bath with Molly and Spike after the funeral so as to catch a late train back to London.

Joe must have seen him too – he released Lucy's hand abruptly, and tears gathered in her eyes. How could she ever have thought that Jake could take Joe's place? She must have been mad – and what had that madness cost her? There was no way now she could hope to rekindle the love she and Joe had shared. He seemed to have begun to forgive her for leaving as she had, even if he still found it hard to accept that she'd been unable to confide her real reason for going. But he'd never be able to forgive her for becoming pregnant by another man. Even now, just seeing Jake standing there as one of the family, he'd turned cold again. The distance yawned between them like an Arctic desert. And just when she needed him most . . .

The smells that had so revolted her on the night Algernon had raped her wafted out through the open door, where the Reverend Callow waited, and as they followed the coffin inside they grew so strong they seemed to choke her – dust and damp and cold, and the sickly scent of chrysanthemums. Lucy covered her nose and mouth with her hand, trying to blot it out, feeling so sick she was terrified she might throw up right there in the aisle. But miraculously the first wave of nausea passed, though it left her weak and shaky, and that niggle had begun again in the pit of her stomach.

The chapel was full, and the service seemed to go on forever – the prayers and the hymns and the tributes, long-winded and sanctimonious. Lucy shifted uncomfortably on the hard seat, very aware of Joe beside her and Jake in the pew behind, but at last, just when she thought it would never end, the last prayers were said, the six bearers came forward to hoist the coffin on to their shoulders, and Annie led the way out of the pew, motioning the others to follow.

Another wait whilst the coffin was reloaded on to the hearse, another walk at a suitably funereal pace, and they were in the cemetery, on the other side of the road from the churchyard where Lucy's father and the others who had died alongside him in the terrible accident had been laid to rest. Rooks cawed in the trees, and the Reverend Callow's voice seemed to be blown away on the chilly wind that had sprung up.

Lucy glanced across the newly dug grave, where wooden planks now supported the coffin above the abyss below, to where Molly, Spike and Jake stood, Spike a little apart, Jake with his hand beneath Molly's elbow. There was something creepy about the intimate gesture; Lucy had never heard the word 'syco-phantic', let alone used it, yet if she had, it would have exactly summed up Jake's attitude, and once again she felt nauseous.

The bearers were moving forward now, taking hold of the broad canvas bands threaded beneath the coffin and slowly lowering it. Of the three on her side of the grave, one was a hunchback, another a short but swarthy man whose jacket strained over bulging muscles. For some reason Lucy focused her eyes on him, watching, fascinated, as the too-small coat rode slowly up his back, then pulled away from his bull-like neck to reveal the wine-coloured stain of an enormous birthmark.

Quite suddenly the breath caught in her throat. The birthmark! Why hadn't she thought of it before? She had spent the last day wondering how it could be proved once and for all whether Jake was an imposter; now, in a blinding flash, she had the answer. Molly had said her David had a large birthmark on his foot, and joked that she could pass him in the street and not know him unless he was barefoot. Birthmarks of that kind didn't usually disappear without trace. Even if it hadn't grown with him, and she suspected it would have, or if it had faded a little, it should surely have left a mark. But she had no recollection of seeing such a mark on Jake's foot. True, the light had been quite dim on most occasions when she had been alone with him in his attic room, but on the morning she had gone there to tell him Molly wanted to meet him it had been broad daylight and Jake had not been wearing boots or even socks. The funeral scene was nothing but a blur to her now; all she could see were Jake's bare feet padding across the bare boards, and jutting up from the grubby sheets as he lay, hands behind his head, after they had made love.

There was no birthmark, she was sure of it. Jake was an imposter just as she had feared, and it was she who had introduced him into Molly's life. The full horror of the situation sent ice-cold waves through her veins. She couldn't let this charade go on any longer. But what should she do about it?

They were back at the house – the family, Jake, the Reverend Callow and Marcus Latcham, who, unbelievably, had come all the way from London to attend the funeral. Annie and Kitty, who was showing signs of exhaustion, had ridden home with Molly and Spike; the others had walked. The antagonism between Joe and Jake was very marked, and Lucy was glad Marcus and the reverend were with them. They'd drunk cup after cup of tea and nibbled at the sandwiches and slab cake Annie had prepared before they left, all but Jake, who ate as heartily as if he had not had a good meal for a week. And all the while Lucy's head was buzzing with the awful certainty that

Jake was not really Molly's son. Seeing him sucking up to her was turning Lucy's stomach, and she trembled with dread at the thought of shattering her aunt's happiness, though she knew it would have to be done. There was just one shard of hope to cling to – Jake could never have come up with this plan if he hadn't known that Molly had lost a secret child, and how could he have known that if he hadn't met the real David, perhaps in the children's home, in prison, or in the shady world he inhabited. That must mean that the chances were he knew where David was now. If she could somehow elicit that information, it would soften the blow for Molly. Unless . . .

Another awful thought occurred to Lucy. Jake must have been very sure that David had no intention of seeking out his mother – did that mean that David was dead?

The atmosphere in the crowded house was too much for her; she felt she would stifle if she didn't get some fresh air. She let herself out of the back door, climbed the steps and walked up the sloping garden path, putting as much distance between herself and the house as possible. As she reached the rhubarb clump, she stopped, looking at the pale pink shoots that were beginning to poke through the earth. There were a few rotted stumps and some of last year's umbrella-sized leaves, brown now around the edges, lying on the bare earth beside the plant, and she remembered that long-ago day when she had hid herself there to cry over her broken doll and Joe had come to her rescue. It had seemed like the end of the world to her then; now, in comparison to the problems she faced, it was just a tiny white-flecked wave on a seething ocean. If only all her troubles could be solved so easily!

'Lucy.' She hadn't noticed Joe approaching up the path. 'Molly and Spike are ready to leave. They said you've got a train to catch.'

'Yes. Not for ages yet, though.' Lucy was shrinking inwardly, wanting to put off for as long as possible the moment when she would be alone with Molly, who she had unwittingly betrayed, and Jake, who had used her for his own crooked purposes.

'I'm just passing on the message.' His eyes narrowed. 'You don't look very pleased about it.'

'Oh, it's just . . .' Lucy felt as if she had the weight of the world on her shoulders. 'You will look after Mam and Kitty, won't you?'

'You know I will.' Joe hesitated, kicked at a loose stone, which went scudding down the path, then made up his mind. 'You don't have to go, you know. You could stay here with us.'

A lump rose in Lucy's throat. If only! If only she could turn back the clock and have everything as it used to be, except without Algernon. But it was too late for that.

'I can't, Joe,' she said softly.

'Because of that son of Molly's?'

'No!'

'Why not, then?'

Because I have engagements to fulfil. Because I have to try to sort out a mess of my own making. Because I think I'm going to have a baby . . .

'I just can't.' Her voice was thick with unshed tears.

At her words, Joe's face shut down, hiding his hurt in a pretence at indifference, as he always did.

'You'd better go then, hadn't you?'

He turned, walking away from her, and suddenly Lucy wanted desperately to tell him everything, have him make things right, as he had by mending Victoria all those years ago. He couldn't, of course, no one could, but all the same . . .

'Joe!' she called, her voice tentative but urgent. 'Joe – wait!'

He stopped, looking over his shoulder at her. 'What?'

'It's all so awful . . . I don't know where to start . . .'

At that very moment Spike appeared at the top of the steps, calling to her. 'Come on, Lucy! We're waiting for you!'

'I'm coming.' She gave Joe one last agonised look. He responded with a small impatient shake of his head. It was too late. The moment had passed. There was nothing for it now but to leave with Molly, Spike and Jake and try to sort things out for herself.

They were indeed waiting for her. Molly had put her coat on and was kissing Annie and promising to visit again soon, Jake had draped the black muffler Spike had loaned him over the collar of his jacket. Lucy went up to her room to collect her bag, which was packed and ready to go, and when she came down again they were in the hall with the front door open. She went into the living room to hug Kitty, who was resting on the sofa, and say goodbye to Marcus Latcham and the Reverend Callow. Annie and Joe came with them to the gate, where Annie kissed and hugged her, and for a long moment Lucy buried her face in her mother's shoulder, desperately trying to control the tears that were aching in her throat. But Joe stood stiffly to one side, his face taut and guarded, avoiding any contact.

Into the rear seat of Spike's motor car, beside Molly – Jake, having cranked the engine to life, was sitting up front with Spike. Heart feeling like a lump of lead in her breast. Pain niggling again deep in her stomach. As Spike pulled away from the kerb, she looked back – Annie was waving, Joe standing, hands in pockets, head down, as if he was trying to avoid seeing them go. Lucy's heart lurched. *Oh Joe! Why, oh why, have I been such a fool?* The suppressed tears sprang to her eyes. She gazed determinedly out of the window until she had managed to control them. And by then they had turned the corner and Mammy and Joe were out of sight.

Chapter Thirty-Six

'Why don't I drop you at the station?' Spike said as they drove down the Wells Road into Bath.

'Her train's not for another half an hour and more yet,' Molly objected.

'No, but it's hardly worth going home and back again, is it? Jake will wait with her, won't you, Jake? The walk will do him good.' There was a note of sarcasm in Spike's tone, and Jake picked up on it.

'Trying to get rid of me, eh?'

'Of course he's not!' Molly said hastily. 'But Lucy can't wait all that time on her own. It's getting dark.'

This much was certainly true. With the heavy cloud cover that not even a stiff breeze earlier had blown away, the light was fading fast and already Spike had turned on the headlights, which cast a pale narrow beam in the gathering gloom.

When he pulled up on the station concourse, Jake climbed down and opened the rear door for Lucy.

'Just make sure you do good tomorrow,' Spike said to her over his shoulder. 'That's a gem of a booking Bernie's got you.'

Molly tutted. 'Of course she will! Have you ever known Lucy do anything less?' She reached over and squeezed Lucy's hand. 'It's been lovely to see you, my darling.'

The car pulled away, Molly waving from the rear window, and Lucy and Jake were alone.

There was a tea stall on the concourse, around which a few people were gathered.

'D'you want a cuppa?' Jake asked.

'No thank you. I've drunk enough tea today to sink a battleship.'

Besides . . . this was her chance, Lucy thought, to talk to Jake and find out what she could about what she was certain now was his wicked deception.

'Let's just get my ticket and go up to the waiting room.'

She bought her ticket and they climbed the stairs leading up to the platform, but the door to the waiting room was closed and locked. Jake swore, but Lucy was secretly pleased. There would almost certainly have been other passengers in the waiting room had it been open; several were hunched on the wooden benches that were scattered along the wall of the offending waiting room and the stationmaster's office, and more would join them as the time for the train's arrival approached. Lucy didn't want to say what she had to say in the hearing of others, even if she didn't know them from Adam.

'Let's walk down to the end,' she suggested.

Jake grinned. 'Sounds like a plan.'

Reading his mind, Lucy's lips tightened. If Jake thought she wanted to go to the quiet dark spot to find privacy for some lovemaking, he was going to be seriously disappointed. And it was clear that was exactly what he thought. As they walked, he draped an arm about her shoulders, and the minute they were past the station buildings and beyond the light of the gas lamps, he pulled her towards him, trying to kiss her.

'No, Jake.' Lucy twisted away. 'I want to talk to you.'

'Sounds serious.'

'It is.' She waited until they had reached the point where the platform broadened out, bordered only by iron railings, and drew him towards them, well out of sight and hearing of anyone who might also decide to take a walk to keep warm.

'What's this all about?' Jake asked. Though he said it lightly, she could hear the undertone. He'd guessed she might be pregnant, she thought, and was none too pleased about it. But she wasn't going to mention that; it was something she intended to keep to herself for as long as she could.

'I know,' she said. The railings were cold and hard behind her back; she leaned against them for support.

'Know what?' He sounded puzzled now.

'You're not Molly's son at all, are you?'

'What are you talking about?'

'You are not Molly's David.'

'What makes you say that?' There was aggression now in his tone, but he was clearly rattled.

'All sorts of things. But mainly the birthmark.'

'What?'

'The birthmark. You don't have a birthmark, do you?'

'Bloody birthmark? Course I have.'

'All right. Where is it? You don't know, do you? Tell me where your birthmark is and I'll believe you really are David. But I don't think you can.'

'This is bloody ridiculous!' Jake blustered.

'You see? I know I'm right. You've played me for a fool from the start. What I want to know is how you came to know so much about Molly.'

Jake was not giving up so easily. 'She was famous in her day. Everybody knew Belle Dorne.'

'But not that she had a secret son. It was news to me, and I'm her niece. My guess is that *he* knew, though – David. You met him somehow, he told you who his mother was, and you decided to impersonate him. I'm right, aren't I?'

Jake was silent now. In the dim light cast by the gas lamps on the street below, Lucy could see that his face was dark with fury.

'And what if you are? What are you going to do about it?' he growled, his voice low and threatening.

Lucy swallowed hard. She was afraid now. She'd always known Jake had a dangerous streak; it was one of the things about him that had excited her. There was nothing exciting about it now, but Lucy was determined not to be deterred. It was her fault that Jake was in Molly's life; she had to do what she could to make things right.

She lifted her chin, looking him straight in the eye. 'Aunt Molly will have to be told, of course. But first I want to know where the real David is now, and how you could be so sure he wouldn't look for her himself. Is he dead, Jake? Did you kill him?'

Jake's thoughts were racing. Thinking on his feet had always been his forte; it had got him out of trouble more times than he cared to remember, singling him out from most of the other ruffians and criminals who inhabited his world. He prided himself on being not only bigger and stronger than most of them, but also a great deal cleverer. The stunt he'd pulled by pretending to be Molly's long-lost son was something none of them would think of in a million years and it had worked like a dream, all his meticulous planning and scheming paying off. Now he couldn't quite understand how things had gone so wrong. A birthmark . . . a bloody birthmark he couldn't possibly have known about . . . but Lucy had implied there had been other things too, other slips, and she'd come pretty close to working out the truth.

Well, one thing he knew for certain. He couldn't let her go

497

telling Molly and ruining everything, not now, when everything he'd always wanted was within his grasp: easy money, the good life. He'd have to make sure she didn't do that. His fingers tightened on the black muffler Spike had loaned him. He'd thought the thing was foppish and had only accepted the offer to curry favour with Molly. Now he was very glad he had. Lucy was only a little bit of a thing, it wouldn't be difficult to slip it around her unsuspecting neck and tighten it. And with a train coming soon, he would have the perfect way of covering up what he had done. Nobody would notice a red weal around the neck of a girl who had been run over by a steam engine and carriages.

Jake was beginning to feel pleased with himself again, congratulating himself on his own cleverness. Lucy wanted to know how all this had come about; well, Lucy should know, and much good would it do her. And he would have the satisfaction of knowing that at least one person would be able to appreciate what a coup he'd pulled off.

'David Fulham's not dead,' he said with a sneer, 'but he might as well be. He went off to America, and as far as I know he's still there.'

'Fulham,' Lucy repeated. 'Is that his name?'

'That's what they called him at the orphanage. Boys that didn't have no name were called after places in London. Me – I was Peckham. Peckham Jake.'

'So you did meet him in the orphanage?' Lucy was still asking questions, not realising that with every one he answered she was as good as tightening Spike's scarf around her neck.

'Yeah. I always knew he was something a bit out of the ordinary. There was this woman used to come and see him, bring him a few treats, you know? An apple, a piece of fruit cake or bread pudding – we were always glad when she came. We knew we'd have a feast after she'd gone – taking it off David was easy as pie. He wasn't what you'd call a tough, far from it. Proper weakling.' His lip curled scornfully. 'To start with we thought she was his mother and we teased him about that. She didn't have much to recommend her in the looks department. Fat and greasy, that was her. But she made a decent fruit cake.'

'Who was she?' Lucy asked.

'Turned out she'd been his nurse, looked after him before he got sent to the orphanage. She told him his father was gentry, he said, and his mother was a star on the music halls. Well, we took that with a pinch of salt – nearly laughed him out of town, I can tell you. But he had this picture of her what the old nurse had given him. I pinched it one day, just to rile him really, and didn't think no more of it. But when we was older I came across it where I'd put it in me wallet, and damn me, I found out he'd only been telling the truth.'

'How do you know he went to America?' Lucy was still probing, still trying to find out anything that might be useful to her. As if!

'I bumped into him one day – just luck, you might say. Our paths hadn't crossed for years. I'd been to prison and I was making a living fighting – legit at first, till I got blacklisted for doing a bit of the bare-knuckle stuff on the side – and what I could pick up here and there by my wits. He – well, he seemed to be doing well for himself: served an apprenticeship with a printer, and had what he thought was a decent job, though it wouldn't have been my cup of tea. We had a drink together and he told me he was off to America, to try and find his real mother. He'd heard she was over there. Well, that got me thinking. There's some as always come up smelling of roses. And I reckoned that just wasn't fair. It was when I saw your name on the playbill that I got the idea. Thought it might be worth doing

499

a bit of fishing. And what do you know, I struck lucky.'

'But for all you knew David could have given up searching in America and come back to this country. He could have seen the playbill too, and followed it up.'

Jake shrugged. 'There's times when you've got to take a chance. And times when you make your own luck.'

He was talking now with one ear and eye for the signals that would herald the approaching train. He had to time this just right. Too soon and he'd be left holding up a lifeless body. Too late and he wouldn't get her to the edge of the platform in time. He heard it now – a dull clank. Just a few more minutes and the London train would be drawing in. He was chancing his luck that it had enough carriages to pull well into and beyond the platform, but even if it didn't, if he'd already strangled the life out of her, she'd lie unseen on the track until it pulled away again. His hands tightened on the muffler, sliding it round his neck.

'Well, now you know it all, Lucy. Or as much as you need to. Now, how about we kiss and make up?'

'Kiss? You?' The scorn in her voice was unmistakable. But he had to get her close enough for his purpose.

'Come on, darlin'. We've had some good times, haven't we?' he sneered.

Lucy put out both hands, pressing them against his chest.

'You disgust me!'

The train was coming. He could hear it chugging out of the darkness, still some way back up the line, but there could be only moments before it pulled into the station. Mercifully none of the other passengers had ventured this far up the platform. In the half-light no one would see him and Lucy, and if they did they'd think they were a pair of lovers. And no one would hear her if she screamed. But she wouldn't scream. He'd make sure of that.

He lunged for her, pulling her close and winding the scarf round her neck before she realised what was happening, beginning to tighten it. She let out a cry – he hadn't bargained for that – struggling frantically, her hands at her throat. But she hadn't a hope in hell. A few more moments and it would be over. A few more moments and she would no longer be a threat to the lifestyle he'd dreamed of ever since he was a small boy with nothing except his fists and his wits.

With a vicious move he jerked the muffler tighter, pushing her back against the railings.

The darkness was closing in around her, everything going black. Her thumbs were jammed beneath the black silk that was strangling the life out of her, but she was no match for Jake. She was going to die.

And suddenly Daddy was there with her. She couldn't see him, but she felt his presence, more strongly than she had ever felt it in the long years since she had lost him. *Daddy!* It was a silent, desperate scream. And he seemed to be speaking inside her head. *Go back, Lucy. It's too soon.*

With the last of her strength, Lucy jerked her hands free and clawed blindly at Jake's face. The roaring in her ears drowned out his cry of pain as one of her fingers plunged into his eye, but the noose around her neck loosened momentarily. She gasped, taking in a gulp of air, sharp and cold, razoring her throat and burning in her lungs. Then, in a quick movement born more of instinct than conscious thought, she brought her knee sharply up between Jake's legs and was startled by the immediacy of his reaction. The muffler was no longer tight around her neck and Jake was staggering backwards, doubled up. This was her chance. But her legs were heavy and weak; she thought they were about to give way beneath her. Somehow she gained control of them, attempting to stagger past Jake, and flee down the platform towards the lights and the people. As she did so, he lunged at her, grabbing a handful of the fabric of the hem of her coat, and stopping her in her tracks. Lucy screamed again, but it rasped on her throat, nothing more than a whimper. And the train was coming. She could hear it chuntering down the track, slowing. The clatter and the hiss of steam would drown out any sound she might make. She would be unable to attract anyone's attention.

But, miracle of miracles, the figure of a man was heading up the platform. A man who looked for all the world like Joe. Again Lucy opened her mouth to try and call out, again her tortured throat muffled the sound. The man must have seen her; he had broken into a run. Joe! It was Joe! She could scarcely believe it, but now a new dart of fear knifed through her, not for herself, but for Joe. She'd seen Jake fight. Joe wouldn't stand a chance against him.

Instead of struggling now, she turned towards Jake, kicking out again, and this time the toe of her boot connected with the soft tissue of his face.

'Bitch!'

And then everything was happening at once. Afterwards she had no clear recollection of it, just a series of impressions – the train pulling into the station, the thuds and grunts of a struggle, other people surrounding them, running footsteps, and someone screaming. For a moment Lucy thought it was her, that her voice had miraculously been restored. It wasn't – it was one of the female passengers, who had just witnessed an awful sight.

Somehow in the melee Jake had decided the odds were stacked against him and decided to make a run for it. But he had tripped and fallen on to the track in the path of the oncoming train. Fate, it seemed, had played a hand. But for ever after Lucy was sure that she had been looked after that horrible night by a guardian angel. A guardian angel she had recognised for a brief moment as her darling dead daddy.

'What are you doing here, Joe?'

Teeth chattering, still barely able to make out what had happened, Lucy sat on a chair in the stationmaster's office, Joe crouched down beside her. A gas fire had been turned on; the heat from it was burning her hands as she hugged a rough grey blanket someone had put around her shoulders.

'I wasn't going to let you go like that,' Joe said. 'I caught a train into Bath – I was dead lucky there was one that got me to Green Park with just about enough time, though I had to run all the way between the stations. And thank God I did!' His face was grim, his teeth gritted. 'What the hell was going on, Lucy?'

'He was trying to kill me.' Her throat still rasped; talking was painful. 'I knew the truth about him. But what am I going to do? How am I going to tell Molly?'

'What – that he's dead? I should think the police will do that.' Joe, in shock himself, hadn't quite taken on board what Lucy had said. Now he saw all the remaining colour drain from her face.

'He's dead?' she whispered.

'I should think so. I didn't wait to find out. You're the only one that matters.' He chafed her cold hands between his own, trying to warm them. 'Thank the Lord I followed you, that's all I can say. I didn't know what good it would do, but I couldn't let you go. Not just like that. You mean everything to me, Lucy.'

'Oh Joe!' Weak tears filled Lucy's eyes. He meant everything to her too. But even if Jake was dead, nothing had changed.

'I expect the police will be wanting to ask you questions, and you're not up to it yet. I'm taking you home, Lucy, as soon as we can slip away. We'll get a cab.'

503

'No . . . not home. I have to go to Molly.' She struggled to her feet.

The thought of telling her aunt everything was a dreadful one, but it had to be done, and it had to come from her. A wave of nausea overcame Lucy, and suddenly the pain was back in the pit of her stomach, sharp and insistent. She gasped, pressing her hands against her belly.

'Lucy?' Joe said urgently. 'Are you all right? Should I call a doctor?'

'No . . . no . . .'

As she took a step towards the door, she felt a sudden rush of wet warmth between her legs.

The room was swimming around her, going further and further away, and once again her knees felt rubbery and insubstantial. She took one more faltering step forwards and felt them give way beneath her. Then the darkness was closing in like the slow-moving shutter of a camera, and Lucy collapsed, quite gracefully, into Joe's arms.

'Molly, sit down, love, there's something I have to tell you.'

Spike stood nervously in the centre of the drawing room, one hand, moist with perspiration, thrust into his trouser pocket, the other squashing an unlit cigar between his fingers.

Joe had found him at the Lyric and broken the news to him that Jake had been killed in an accident and Lucy was in hospital. His initial concern had been for Lucy, of whom he was very fond, his first thought that he would have to contact Bernie and let him know that she would be unable to fulfil her engagements on the following evening. He didn't give a jot for Jake. But Molly was going to be another kettle of fish entirely. She was going to be devastated at losing her son so soon after finding him again, and he really didn't know how he was going to tell her what had happened.

Not that he knew much. Simply that the blighter had fallen under a train. It was all a bit of a puzzle really. If he'd been drunk, Spike could have understood it. But as far as Spike knew, he hadn't had a drink all day. Certainly there had been no beer or liquor at the funeral – Annie had banned it out of deference to Algernon's principles. As to why Lucy had collapsed, he didn't know that either. Joe had said little beyond that she was being kept in hospital overnight. It must have been shock that did it, he supposed. He only hoped Molly wasn't the next casualty.

'What is it, Spike?' Molly could tell from his demeanour that something serious had happened. Her voice shook but her face was set into firm lines and her hands grasped the arms of the chair. She was ready for whatever was to come.

'It's Jake,' he said. 'There's been an accident. I'm sorry, my love, but there was nothing anyone could do. You know what I'm saying?'

Molly closed her eyes momentarily, head bowed, lip tightly clamped between her teeth. It seemed an age to Spike before she raised her eyes to his, eyes that were brimming with tears, and asked in a voice that was deathly calm:

'What happened?'

He told her all he knew, and she listened with that same unnatural calm. And then she spoke, words that he had never expected to hear from her.

'Perhaps it's for the best. He wasn't a very nice person, Daniel. I'm ashamed to say it, he was after all my son, but . . .' Her voice cracked now, and the tears began to run down her cheeks. 'He wasn't what I hoped he'd be. And certainly not what I'd want for Lucy.'

Spike nodded, heartily relieved that she was taking it like this.

'I'll get you a drink, love. A large one.'

Molly took it, sipped it gratefully. She felt hollowed out, desperately sad. The son she had longed for all these years was dead, but for the moment she was too numb to mourn him properly. Yet the sadness she was feeling was not just for his loss. It was for the disappointment that had overtaken the first ecstatic joy. The doubts that had niggled. The guilt that she did not feel at all as she had thought she would feel towards her child. Where was the bond? Where was the maternal love that should have excused him everything? It hadn't been there. Truth to tell, she hadn't liked him very much.

For a long while Molly sat quietly, pondering, trying to analyse her feelings and summon up the grief she knew she should be experiencing. But however she tried, she could not quite dispel the undertow of relief. She hadn't liked Jake, she hadn't liked the things he did and said, but she hadn't been able to help feeling that she was responsible. She'd given birth to him, she'd given him away. If he was less than perfect, it was her fault, and she'd needed to somehow make it up to him. But her responsibility didn't end there. If he'd done anything to hurt Lucy, and she was horribly certain that he would have, Molly knew she would have blamed herself.

Now he was dead, and it was as if a weight had been lifted from her shoulders. It wasn't the way a mother should feel, and she wasn't proud of it. But that was how it was and nothing could change it.

Lucy lay in the hospital bed, physically drained and still shaky from her ordeal, which seemed oddly unreal, more like a nightmare from which she hadn't fully wakened. The details of it were hazy, slipping away from her, whilst the aura of it remained. How could she have been so stupid, she wondered, as to think Jake would not try to stop her from telling Molly what she had discovered? Why had she put herself in such a position? It simply hadn't occurred to her that he would try to do her harm in such a public place, with other people just yards away. But of course he'd been desperate. Especially since he'd told her so much about the real David . . .

A faint smile lifted her lips. He wasn't dead. He was in America. He'd served an apprenticeship as a printer. His name was David Fulham. It wasn't much to go on, given that she'd always understood that America was a vast country, but it was a start. Molly could begin searching, and if he could be found then he would almost certainly want to meet her. He'd gone there, after all, to try to find her, Jake had said, and he had no reason to lie about that.

But she didn't want to think about Jake. Didn't want to think how he'd tricked and used her, wanted even less to think about how gullible and foolish she had been. How could she ever have thought she loved him? How could she have been taken in by him and led astray by his roguish charm?

She shuddered and pressed her hands to her stomach, flat as it had ever been. She wasn't even sure there had ever been a baby growing there. Perhaps she had just been so stressed that she had imagined it. But whatever, it was over now. She need have no more fears that she might give birth to the spawn of a man who, like Algernon, had been a monster in his own way.

Once she got out of hospital she would be free to get on with her life. Free to go back to the London halls and pursue her career. But the thought no longer excited her. What was the point of fame and fortune if it meant it attracted people like Jake, who wanted only to take advantage of her success? What was the point of anything if it took you away from all those you loved most? She didn't want to leave Kitty, who was so frail that every day she spent with her might be her last; she didn't want to leave Mam. And most of all she didn't want to leave Joe.

Had he forgiven her? It seemed so, for he had swallowed his pride and followed her to Bath to try and stop her from going back to London. Would he forgive her if he knew just how she had betrayed him with Jake? She hoped with all her heart that he would. She and Joe were always meant to be together, she thought, her eyes closing.

She reached out a hand to him, felt the touch of his fingers on hers. The horrors seemed far away now. Contented, peaceful at last, Lucy drifted off to sleep.

The house felt different. Annie had gone through it, ruthlessly disposing of all Algernon's things, and Kitty had been strong enough to help her. All the ornaments she had hated had gone. The space they had occupied might have looked bare, but now the few bits and pieces Annie had brought with her from Fairley Terrace were displayed to their best advantage, not crowded in beside the china figurines and other clutter, or packed away out of sight. The rooms had been aired, the curtains pulled well back to let in the spring sunshine, and Annie had removed the dark antimacassars from every chair. 'A clean sweep', she'd called it, and felt not the slightest guilt at removing every trace of Algernon from their lives.

Lucy and Joe sat close together on the sofa in the front room, hands entwined. They had so much to talk about, so many plans to make.

'I don't think you should give up your career just yet,' Joe said. 'I don't want you ever to feel I was responsible for you not achieving your ambitions.'

'I don't care about them any more,' Lucy said, and she meant it. 'All I want is for us to be together. It's all I've ever wanted, really.'

'You say that now, but you might well come to feel differently.' Now that he felt sure of her, Joe had gone back to his old, pragmatic self. 'When I've finished my apprenticeship, I shall be able to get a job anywhere. In London, if that's where you need to be. Then later, when we decide to start a family, we could move back to Somerset if we want to. Nothing has to be set in stone.'

'As long as we're together,' Lucy repeated. 'I'll never again do anything that might come between us. I'll never be so stupid again, I promise.'

'I hope not.' It still hurt, that there had been someone else for Lucy, but Joe was trying very hard to put that out of his mind.

'I won't be,' she said fervently, and then a thought struck her. 'Why don't we get married right away? I know if I go back to London we won't be able to make a proper home together just yet, but . . .'

Joe was bemused; such an arrangement was unheard of. But Lucy's eager face was warming his heart.

'Please, Joe! I don't want a big wedding, and in any case it wouldn't be right. People still think we're in mourning.' She touched the black band he was wearing over the sleeve of his jacket. 'We could do it in London, where nobody knows us. With just Mam and Kitty and Aunt Molly and Spike as witnesses. And Doris and Will and Davy would be able to come too . . . and Marcus Latcham,' she added as an afterthought.

She and Annie had had a heart-to-heart only a few evenings ago, and to her surprise Annie had confessed to having feelings for Marcus – and that she rather thought he felt the same way.

Lucy had been surprised – she'd never thought of her mother in that way – but also glad. If anyone deserved some happiness it was Annie, and Lucy had thought her beloved father would approve, too, if he knew about it.

They'd talked too about all that had happened since Lucy had left High Compton.

'I can't believe I could have been so stupid,' Lucy had said, feeling small and hot with shame. 'And I can't believe I could have put you and Kitty and Joe through all that worry either. I am so sorry, Mam. Can you ever forgive me?'

Annie had taken her hand.

'There's nothing to forgive, Lucy. You're here now. That's all that matters.'

'But—'

'Shh! I don't want to hear another word. You're my daughter, and I love you. One day you'll have a child of your own, and you'll understand that. You've been through a terrible time all on your own, but that's over now. Everything is going to be all right, and I am just so glad you and Joe have found one another again. Hold on to him, Lucy, and never let him go.'

Lucy thought now of her mother's words.

'I refuse to go back to London unless we can be married,' she said, pressing her lips together and looking at him with a challenge in her eyes.

'I suppose I shall have to go along with that,' Joe said.

And then she was in his arms, and it was a long time before either of them said anything more.

Postscript

Soon I shall find in passing on
Time gone.

Another year, another wedding. The bride, her gown of filmy silk muslin skimming her slender body, her veil held in place by a coronet of orange blossom, carried a bouquet of wild flowers she had gathered early that morning in one hand, the other tucked into the crooked arm of the young man who was giving her away.

Kitty had never looked more beautiful, nor Joe more handsome, Lucy thought as she followed them to the door of the chapel where the Reverend Boody, returned especially for the occasion, stood waiting.

For a moment, as she approached the heavy oak doors, her stomach clenched. She could never step inside this chapel without a feeling of dread. But she wouldn't think about it today. Since Kitty was marrying the Reverend Callow, there could never have been any question as to where the wedding would take place, and Lucy was determined not to let the dreadful memories of the past mar what was for them all a joyous occasion. Instead she concentrated on being the perfect matron of honour to Kitty, and remembering her own wedding, quiet, just as they had planned, but the happiest of days.

511

The chapel was full. Though the guest list had been small, just family and close friends, every member of the congregation seemed to have turned out to see their young minister wed. As the little procession made its way up the aisle, there were admiring glances and whispers and many a lace-edged handkerchief pressed to lips that smiled through emotional tears.

Annie, of course, was in the front pew, and standing beside her was Marcus Latcham. Their relationship, too, had blossomed – Lucy felt sure there would be another wedding when a decent time of mourning had elapsed. Perhaps she would move to London with him; Lucy would like that. It would be so good to have her mother nearby when she was working, and with a good and loving husband at her side, Kitty would be well taken care of, she knew.

As she saw him standing at the altar rail, turning to smile at his bride as she walked slowly up the aisle on Joe's arm, Lucy's heart lifted. She was happy, so happy for Kitty that she had found love after such hard and lonely years, and the Reverend Callow – Philip, as she now knew he was called – clearly adored her.

In the pew behind Annie and Marcus, Molly was smiling proudly.

'Beautiful!' she whispered to Spike.

'Ain't she just?' Spike whispered back, and though Molly was uncertain whether he was referring to the bride or to his protégée, Lucy, shining like the star she had become in her gown of rose pink with a large picture hat trimmed with roses, it really didn't matter. This was Kitty's day, and for every other member of the congregation no one could eclipse her. Daniel – well, Daniel was Daniel and always would be, and she loved him for it. She had quite forgiven him now for keeping from her the fate of her beloved David. For the whole of her life he had been her rock, her safe harbour, and Molly knew just how lucky she was. Her happiness and well-being had always been paramount for him; now he was doing everything in his power to trace her long-lost son. She knew how fearful he had been of telling her of Jake's trickery, but if she was honest, what she really felt when she learned the truth was relief at knowing that her lack of maternal feelings for him were natural.

Would Daniel be successful? Might she one day be seated on the other side of the aisle at a wedding such as this as mother of the groom? How wonderful that would be! She had missed so much of David's life, but if they could be reunited at last, Molly knew that her happiness would be complete.

The service began, the vows holding somehow even more meaning for Lucy on hearing them again so soon after she and Joe had spoken the same sacred words. 'In sickness and in health' had an added poignancy too, and Philip Callow looked deep into Kitty's eyes as he said it.

Joe's part in the service was done now; as he took his seat in the pew beside Annie, he caught Lucy's eye and smiled, a small secret smile, and she knew he too was thinking of their wedding day.

The sun slanted in through the small high-up windows, casting patches of light on the bare flagged floor, the air was sweet with the scent not of chrysanthemums, but of roses, and Lucy's heart lifted.

The past was over and done with; from now on she would think of the chapel not as an oppressive place, the very air laden with horror and fear, but as a place of joy.

The future spread out before her and all of them, and now it was full of promise.